Blue

Persuasion

ALSO BY BLAKELY BENNETT

Bound by Your Love Series

Stuck in Between

Bittersweet Deceit

My Body Trilogy

My Body-His

My Body-His (Marcello)

My Body-Mine

Co-Authored

The Demarcation of Jack

Blue
Persuasion

Blakely Bennett

TandemWriters

BLUE PERSUASION

TandemWriters

Copyright © 2015 by Blakely Bennett

This is a work of fiction. Names, character, places, brands, media, and incidents are either the product of the author's imagination or are used fictitiously.

Cover design by Clarissa Yeo
Logo design by Olivia E. Bennett
Edited by Harper Jewel aka Suze

ISBN: 978-0-69236-702-5 (Trade Paperback)
ISBN: 978-1-94274-841-0 (eBook)

Blue Persuasion is as much about friendship as it is about love. "Blue" is dedicated to the girls that helped me survive and thrive in junior high school. Thank you Lauren S., Kim S., Lainie S., Karen S., and Helen H.

AUTHOR'S NOTE

This is the third installment in the Bound by Your Love series that centers on the romantic lives of a close-knit group of friends. It's not necessary to read the stories in order, but *Stuck in Between* is the first.

As you will see, each chapter is headed with a song title. The melody, title, and/or lyrics inspired me to choose each song for its corresponding chapters. If you're into music like I am, I hope you enjoy the accompaniment.

Warning: This novel contains light bondage and discipline, with graphic sex scenes.

ACKNOWLEDGMENTS

Thank you to all my readers and fans who keep me motivated to write. Without you, there would be no point. As with each novel, it takes a team to get the book ready for you.

Harper Jewel aka Suze is my wonderful new editor and has made *Blue Persuasion* sing. Clarissa continues to blow me away with her ability to get just what I want for my covers.

I could go on and on for days about my husband. His are the first eyes to read my work, and his suggestions and encouragement keep me grounded, just as his undying support and belief in my craft allows me to soar.

My test readers are my second helpers in making the book the best it can be. Warmest hugs to Tami C, Serena K., Ann P., Sara S., Kim L., Brenda L., Debbie R., and Danni.

A special thanks to my family, friends, and street team that provides me with the moral support necessary to continue chasing the dream. Love you all!

CHAPTER ONE

Bitter Sweet Symphony

by The Verve

The Chart House restaurant in Fort Lauderdale, Florida, had a filled lobby and a line of waiting patrons out the door, which was typical for a Friday night. The ambience of the water and palm trees, along with a reputation for delicious seafood, brought a steady stream of customers, especially on the weekends.

As I walked through the crowd, I adjusted the collar of my long-sleeved, dark gray shirt, and noticed a guy in line staring at my covered cleavage as if he could unearth a view. Thankfully, I wasn't in the red short-shorts and tight white T-shirt I had to wear at my previous job.

Please don't let any sleazy men be seated at my tables tonight.

Although my tips weren't as good at The Chart House, I felt far more comfortable looking like a professional and being modestly covered.

That night, I wore my dark auburn hair pulled back in a tight ponytail, with my bangs hanging just past my eyebrows. As always, I hoped the conservative clothes and hairstyle would discourage the steady stream of men from first leering, and then attempting to accost me as they had at my last job.

"Judy, can you pick up table eight?" Stan shouted over to me. He joined me at the side station as I changed out the coffee filter. "They're friends of mine." He dropped a creepy wink at the same time my stomach dropped, but I shook it off. He was my manager, after all, and I simply didn't have the time or energy for an argument.

"Sure, Stan." I peered around the partition through the crowd, and then filled up two water glasses. Outside on the patio, a warm, salty breeze greeted me as I approached the seating area.

Two big, burly men—my least favorite kind—occupied the brown, woven-back chairs around the circular, glass table that could seat four.

My five-foot, five-inch small stature left me feeling intimidated by most men. I had often wished I stood as statuesque as Lainie, a member of my group of friends. At least I was taller than Jacqs. Recently, they both had hooked up with members within our group, but that's another long story, two actually, and for another time.

Steeling myself for the inevitable, I curved my shoulders inward in an effort to diminish the abundant size of my breasts. Boobs seemed a better term for them as they were much larger than necessary, which left me with no understanding or empathy for those who actually paid for boobs my size. My narrow waist didn't help matters, as it accentuated my top-heavy frame.

My mother went on and on about how I should be grateful for my good fortune. According to her, I had inherited my large bosom and wide hips from my father's side of the family, and from her side, a narrow waist and high-rounded butt. To her, this was a gift straight from the gods. If you ask me, it was hell-derived. What sixth grade girl would be happy with breasts already busting out of a DD-cup bra? None, I assure you. By thirty-one years of age, my voluminous mammaries hadn't become any easier to deal with, and I would never share my current bra size with a soul, having cut all the tags out of mine.

As I slowly approached my boss' friends, the man at the table with the thick, coarse, graying beard eyed me from head to toe.

"Well then! What do we have here?" he said, grinning to his friend.

Ignoring him, I placed the water glasses in front of them. "What can I get for you?"

"You, for starters," the younger, clean-shaven man said as he reached out to touch the nametag situated above my left boob, "...Judy."

I abruptly shifted to the side. "What would you like to drink?" Even though I knew alcohol would *not* help my current dilemma, I had to ask. *Damn, I need a new line of work!*

"My name is Dick, and I'll take a Bloody Bull," the bearded man said to my chest. "Do they make you button up your shirt all the way like that?"

Brushing off the question, I turned toward the other man and held my pen at the ready.

"A dry Manhattan ... and it's Keith." He shook his head at Dick, appearing almost apologetic.

I had learned the hard way that the ones who seemed the nicest could be your worst nightmare. Walking away, I contemplated going back to college, for the umpteenth time, to finish my degree in creative writing. Maybe it was time to give up waiting tables and stick with just bartending. At least when I doled out drinks, I had a counter between the men I had to serve and me. Even in a nice establishment like The Chart House, I still felt vulnerable.

My phone vibrated in the pocket of my apron, prompting me to check on all my tables before placing the drink order. I scurried to the bathroom unseen and entered a stall to check my text.

> **Bond:** I'm staying at the apartment tonight. Can you come by?

I typed back quickly.

> **Me:** I have to be at Babes in Tattooland early tomorrow to meet Cat.
> **Bond:** Finally biting the bullet, huh?
> **Me:** Yes.
> **Bond:** Bring the tattoo design to show me and spend the night.
> **Me:** Time?
> **Bond:** Come by after you get off from work. I'll take a break and meet you upstairs.
> **Me:** Okay. I have to run.

I didn't take the time to wait on his response. After washing my hands, I rushed out to serve a few meals and deliver the drinks to Dick and Keith.

"How long have you been working here?" Dick asked.

I held back what really shot through my mind, *One day too many*. Instead, I put on my server-smile and said, "A few months."

"You'd make a lot more money doing something else." The implication was crystal clear, but he elaborated anyway. "I could hook you up with a few clubs. You'd have to show more skin though," he accentuated with an impish grin.

"No thank you. What would you like to order for dinner?" I asked, bristling and struggling to maintain a smile.

"A woman as beautiful as you, with your stunning

proportions…" Keith interjected. "You could make a fortune."

"The Applejack Sea Bass is very good," I announced, fighting to keep it together. You'd think I'd be used to it by now, but as the saying goes, *It Never Gets Old* for men like these. In my case, it never got any easier, either. I tilted my head to either side and stretched my neck. "If you'd rather have steak, then I recommend the prime rib."

"Why are you so uptight?" Dick demanded.

Somehow, his parents knew what they were doing when they named him.

"If I told you the truth, I'd get fired. How about you place your orders and let me get back to my other tables?"

"How about not? I won't say anything to Stan." He reached out to grab my arm.

I swiftly sidestepped his attempt. "Right, well…" I contemplated for a brief second whether losing another job was worth being honest, and I decided, yes. Getting hired had never been a problem, the only perk my body granted me. I let it all spill out, "If men would stop assuming that my appearance means I want sex 24/7, life would be a heck of a lot easier for me. I have no desire to strip or to show off my body for anyone's enjoyment other than my boyfriend's or husband's, that is if I can ever locate a decent man in South Florida. And those odds are looking more dismal every day."

"You're neglecting the gifts god gave you, young lady," Dick declared.

"You and my mother would get along well, *Dick*," I said, making sure to enunciate his name. "It seems you need more time to order. I'll check on my other tables and be back in a few." I stalked away before they had the chance to respond.

By the end of the night, I desperately needed a shower

to wash away the grime and the never-ceasing emotional toll extracted for looking like a walking blue-eyed, dark-haired, voluptuous blowup doll.

My shotgun one-bedroom apartment had a narrow design plan with a tiny kitchen. The hardwood floors gave it some character and since moving in, I had slowly been making it my own by collecting art pieces and paintings when I could scrape up the money. Having a female roommate hadn't worked out well for me, and living with a male seemed like an even worse option. I didn't much care for living alone—particularly in this neighborhood—but it definitely beat the alternative. I fanatically kept my doors and windows locked at night.

The one mirror in my tiny apartment hung over the sink in the pink bathroom surrounded by yellow Post-It notes with positive affirmations. *Smile, it's a new day. I love and approve of myself. I trust myself. I am beautiful and smart and that's how everyone sees me. I am safe and sound. I have given up criticizing myself. I trust my inner wisdom.*

Ignoring the rest of the yellow stickies and wiping the moisture off the mirror from the steamy shower, I applied blue eyeliner as I got ready to go over to Bond's place. My long, thick eyelashes didn't need any mascara. I threw on jeans, a bra that held me in tightly, and a blue tank. After slipping into a pair of sandals, I grabbed my overnight bag, wallet, and keys, and then headed out the door.

On my way over, I thought about Bond. Only his family called him by his real name, Mitchell. Maybe because he detested his given name, he had taken to doling out nicknames to all the people in our friendship circle. He had dubbed me "Sweet Judy Blue Eyes," shortly after we met. He said it was because of my striking blue eyes. After a while, I became "Blue" to our group.

The guys in our friendship circle, Bond, Red, Stay, Kev, and Dawg didn't intimidate me at all. They had taken the time to get to know me outside of my looks. Most men made horrible assumptions about me, even before learning my name.

Bond and I had been having sex on and off for years without the group's knowledge, which had to be a feat of magic worthy of a Houdini illusion, as not much was held sacred within our group of friends. Our fuck-buddy status started shortly after Red and I briefly dated. I never could get past Red's huge size, and he never could get past my dark needs and insecurities. With Bond and me, we had an understanding. We didn't poke at each other's vulnerabilities.

I can't say I was happy when Jacqs began to date Red and continued seeing Bond, but recently, Bond and I had resumed our steamy, dark sex, so it was hard to care. Plus, unlike Red, he understood my insecurities and used them to his advantage.

After pulling into the parking lot of the CroBar Club, where Bond deejayed, I texted him, letting him know I had arrived.

I exited my aged, brown Corolla hatchback, making sure the driver's side door closed all the way by knocking it with my hip. Bond lived in an apartment above the club, so I waited by the steps that led up to it.

"Hey," he said as he approached.

"Hey yourself, handsome."

He wore dark jeans, a fitted black dress shirt, and shiny black boots. The top of his long, brown hair was pulled back, highlighting his light brown eyes and making them as stunning as ever. He took my hand and led me up the steps.

My body responded, knowing what was to come as the thumping bass from CroBar's vast stereo system followed us up the stairs.

"Don't have much time now, but I'll make up for it later." He unlocked the door to his apartment.

"I'm sure you will, dude." I smiled his way, and his face lit up in return.

Bond kept his place relatively neat, which always impressed me, considering the 'bachelor-pad' atmosphere. He led us over to the black leather couch sitting atop an oriental rug.

Although the space wasn't much bigger than mine, the furnishings spoke of money that I certainly didn't have. He received an income from a trust his grandparents had set up for him and his father controlled. Rumored amongst our group, Bond would be coming into a substantial inheritance in a few years. I never asked him about it directly, and it really didn't matter to me. Unlike my mother who liked to use her attractive looks to garner perks from her latest conquest, I vowed to make my own way in life. Bond and I had never been in love, however, I did love him like family but with an outlandish, wild chemistry thrown in. To me, he was the most misunderstood of all of our friends. He would cut off his left arm for anyone in our circle and in some ways, he was as tenderhearted as I was, only he hid his softer side behind macho bravado.

Bond's thumb stroked my palm, causing my body to vibrate. "How was work?" he asked.

"Oh, you know, the same old bullshit, but I did okay in tips." I had to raise my voice so he could hear me over the music pounding through the floor. "Stan stuck me with friends of his who wanted to set me up as a stripper."

"Sorry, Blue, that's gotta suck. Did it remind you of

the situation your father put you in?"

"Yeah, for a second, but let's not go there. I'm not a fifteen-year-old girl anymore. Plus, your text came at the perfect time and cheered me up." I scooted closer to him. If anyone could help distract me from my plight in life, it was Bond.

Sweeping me into his aura, he pulled me in close and kissed me deeply. After he sufficiently stole my breath, he clutched my hair in his fist and yanked my head back, then he bit his way down my neck.

The delicious pain made me gasp and squirm. "Oh yeah!"

He nipped up the other side of my neck, causing me to yelp. "Strip," he ordered.

While I quickly shed my clothes, Bond went to the bathroom and returned with a towel, which he draped over the left armrest of the couch. He turned me to face him as I stood there with my arms wrapped over my breasts.

"Cut that out," he growled at me, taking my small wrists in his hands and bringing my arms to my sides. He scanned me from head to toe. "I'll make those tits of yours suffer when I get back."

He knew exactly what I needed. Just his words made my thick, dime-sized nipples strain for his crop. He clasped my tight buds and pulled me around to the end of the couch. Setting my bottom on the edge, he roughly pushed me over. My back arched when it hit the seat cushion, situating my butt higher on the armrest with my calves dangling over the side.

Watching Bond, I spread my knees wide, dipped my fingers into my wet entrance, and coated my clit with my juices. Like my huge breasts, I felt embarrassed by my protuberant nub.

"I've got it," Bond said, swatting my hand out of the

way. "This is why you need to be tied up. After all this time, you still doubt I can make you cum? Repeat after me, 'You're in control.'"

"I'm in control," I said and laughed.

"You will pay for that," he said with a wicked grin. "Arms above your head. Now!"

"Yes, sir," I responded with plenty of cheek as I saluted.

"You must be itching for a really hard session later. Now shut up and let me take care of business." He unbuttoned his jeans and slid them down. Never one to wear underwear, his long cock jutted out in rapt attention. After rolling the condom over his hard erection, he pierced my wet labia in one fast stroke.

"Oh, hell yes ... take me hard," I growled thickly.

His thrust kept rapid time with the hammering bass that rose up through the floor as he used his thumb to manipulate my bulgy clit.

I clasped onto the edge of the cushion over my shoulders and pulsed into him, helping him to stab deeper. I needed it hard and fast, and he didn't disappoint.

As my clit swelled, Bond used more pressure, rubbing back and forth across my raised bud. He savagely forced his pelvis against mine, bringing me right to the brink of relief as the sweet friction started to overwhelm me.

"Do it," he yelled.

"Ohhh god ... harder!" I cried.

As soon as my orgasm began, he increased his propulsion and pinched my nipples, sending me even higher over the bewitching edge into senselessness.

"Oh, sweet Jesus!" I screamed, gushing over Bond's cock as my electrified contractions fired between my boobs and my swollen clit.

He paused and smiled at me.

I prayed that someday "my Bond" would manifest, but as each year flew by, I became less and less hopeful. Silently, I thanked "this Bond" for making the wait less arduous.

He held his hands out to me and tugged me to my feet. He pulled me away from my musings when he shouted, "Flip over!"

As I bent over the side of the couch, face first, he split my long hair in either fist and yanked me back onto his shaft. His extreme drive knocked my pussy against the edge of the couch. That, coupled with the yanking of my hair, caused the pure sense of pleasure and pain that allowed me to lose myself and thoroughly enjoy sex with him.

Not long after, his deep roar rumbled in his chest. He jackhammered throughout his climax, adding his call to the chorus of music surrounding us. His body blanketed mine, and I could feel his pounding heart against my back. Once his breathing slowed, he stood and spanked my ass.

"Make yourself comfortable, and I'll wake you when I'm back later." He slipped off the condom and using the side of the towel lying under me, he wiped off his cock and thighs, and then buttoned up his jeans. He tossed the condom in the trash and left.

As soon as the door shut, I stood and cleaned all the wetness between my legs.

I loved being in Bond's apartment alone. Somehow, it made our friendship even more intimate. I dug my short, satin robe out from the very back of his wall of closets. The mirrored doors cast my reflection back to me, and I quickly turned away. I vowed to hold onto the vision of how Bond saw me, not how I saw myself.

I bounced up onto his king-size bed, where his *007 Octopussy* poster hung above the headboard, and I scanned the rack of paddles, whips, restraints, and other bondage paraphernalia that hung on the left wall. I wondered what he might use on me later.

Restless and not tired, I wandered back to the living room and looked through the photo album of Polaroid pictures of women that sat on the coffee table. Naked from the waist up, I marveled at how he had gotten so many women to expose their breasts for his camera. I was very happy to see none of the gals from our group had posed.

I grabbed a quick snack, and then got ready for bed. The day had worn me out, so it took me all of five minutes to doze off to the pounding bass vibrating the small apartment.

"Blue, wake up." I felt someone shaking me. I scurried up to the top of the bed, making myself as small as possible and tucked my legs in against me. My heart raged inside of my chest.

"It's just me," Bond said gently into the silence.

"Sorry," I responded, trying to brush off my reaction. "Have you been drinking?"

"Just a few beers. I stopped drinking the hard stuff altogether."

"Okay, no missionary."

His shoulders lowered, and he shook his head. "You don't have to keep reminding me, Blue. I won't forget."

"Yeah, sorry. I'm just waking up." I lowered my legs and sighed.

"Do you want to pass until tomorrow?"

"No, definitely not. Just give me a minute in the bathroom, and I'll be ready." I swung my legs over the side of the bed.

"Great. I'll set everything up."

"Great." I hopped down off the mattress.

He spanked my naked ass on my way to the bathroom.

"Hey!" I yelled, giggling. "We haven't started yet!"

"Just getting you warmed up."

"Stop it and we'll get to it sooner," I fake whined with my hands on my naked hips.

"Who's in charge here?"

"Is that a trick question?"

He placed his hands on my shoulders and turned me to face the bathroom.

I bent over in submission, presenting my ass to him, but before he had a chance to spank me again, I ran off.

"Now, you're really going to get it!" he called after me.

"Sure, uh huh." I laughed and closed the bathroom door behind me.

When I exited after freshening up, I saw a black crop, a brown strap paddle, and a full-headed black flogger lying on the side of the bed. Looking up, a coarse, beige rope hung from an eyebolt in the ceiling with leather cuffs attached. However, what really garnered my attention was Bond, standing naked in front of me, his five-foot, ten-inch, slender frame suiting me well.

I loved that he had let his long, brown hair loose. I'd always had a thing for men with long hair.

His full shaft and bulbous head let me know he was just as excited as my pounding heart indicated. Between his defined, smooth chest, hard cock, and the tools he'd set out, my pussy blushed appreciatively and my clit poked out.

"Are these nipples ready for my abuse?" he asked, squeezing them tightly between his fingers. He led me under the eyebolt near the side of the bed. "Do you want a gag? I'm not going to be gentle."

I shook my head rapidly. "No." I hated anything that

could potentially restrict my breathing.

"Don't disappoint me," he warned. He attached the padded leather cuffs to my wrists and tugged the rope until my arms stretched above my head, my feet still resting firmly on the ground. He brought over a thick piece of bamboo and used the long side of the rope to tie my ankles to the wood, keeping my feet fixed far apart.

Completely exposed, I no longer had control over the outcome. My body vibrated and my breathing became low and shallow.

"Your expression is such a turn on. Did you know that submission makes your eyes glow? I want the rest of your body to feel it too." He ran his hands all over me as he devoured my mouth. Our intense chemistry sparked, increasing the sexual tension as he squeezed my breasts, plucking at my nipples.

I twisted and turned from the flare of his fingers digging into my flesh, causing my juices to run onto my thighs.

He slapped my boobs, and I wallowed in the sensation. Deriving pain from my body allowed me to enjoy the pleasure. Bond knew how to find the outer edges of my resistance. I could already tell he planned to push them.

As if hearing me, he chose the strap and began working on my back, striping me with force as I squealed out with each strike. He had awakened every nerve ending, sending chills up and down my spine.

I trembled with arousal.

After throwing the strap down, he glanced up at me and twitched his eyebrows. He teased between picking up the crop, which I had experienced numerous times with him, and the flogger, which he seldomly used on me. With crop in hand, he started on the pulp of my large breasts, slapping closer and closer toward my nipples. Right and left, he alternated, until he landed directly on target.

"Ahhh," I cried, so high on the endorphins being released, the acute sensation had me gasping.

He then found a rhythm, back and forth, landing squarely on my peaks.

"Ohhh … ohhh … ohhh!" I cried with each snap of the crop.

When the treatment ceased, he knelt down and reached between my thighs, caressing my clit with one hand while rubbing my G-spot with the other. He stopped and said, "I'll be right back." He quickly returned with a towel that he spread on the carpet under my soaking wet pussy.

My cum had migrated past my thighs onto my lower legs.

"Are you ready for more?"

"Yesss," I hissed through gritted teeth.

"Just remember, you asked for it." He picked up the flogger and started swiping my back with the many leather lashes, sending tremors over the surface of my skin. Once he struck the front of my body, I knew he had been taking it easy on me. He used the whip and swashed over my breasts harder than before. I screamed over the ferocity, twisting in my restraints and loving every second of it.

Then he took me completely by surprise. He used the flogger on my thighs, until it landed right on my protruding clit.

"Uhhh … Uhhh … oh, holy hell!" I yelled, instinctively attempting to close my legs.

"Spread those knees wide and expose your pussy to me," he ordered as he slapped the leather hard against my thigh.

He used his fingers to fondle my nub while with his other hand, he yanked on my urgent nipples. Right at the brink of an explosive climax, he stopped and resumed flogging the front of my body.

Off and on, the sweet torture continued, until I couldn't

take it anymore. "Please!" I cried out.

"If you insist." He seared me with his kiss just before he sucked my right nipple into his mouth and continued to manhandle my clit.

The hard detonation racked my body, shaking me to the core, making my knees weak as I struggled to stay balanced on my legs. My squirt shot out, firing repeatedly, and covered his hand. Once my orgasm trailed off, I collapsed onto Bond as he captured my weight.

He held me until I could stand on my own, then he untied my ankles and decreased the tension in the rope above my arms. Lifting my body, he perched my knees on the edge of the mattress with my face down, my arms arching back behind me. Under me, he replaced the towel, and then donned a condom. He groped the front of my body and played with my clit before seeking penetration. He knew if he kept me right at the brink, his stiff cock would cause my titillation to fire off again.

The thick head of his shaft shoved against my labia while he wrapped his arms around my torso. He pulsed into me, using his control over my body to sluice out and slam back in. "You may touch yourself," he whispered seductively.

I rubbed the very tip of my clit and began to gush even before my second climax struck. My body erupted as he continued to seek his own liberation.

He rode me hard throughout my potent orgasm. His girth widened just as he slowed down his unrestrained pace. He shifted his hips from left to right, rubbing every spot in my canal. His arms held me captive as he used me to find his own release. He whispered, "I'm right there." The roar I had come to love sounded, and I could feel the heat of his release. We stayed locked together, still flying high from our copulation.

"That was incredible, Blue," he sighed. "Let's clean up and get into bed. Then you can show me the tat you're getting."

We snuggled in bed for a while, and I felt completely satiated and content. I reached down into my overnight bag and showed Bond the tattoo that would be permanent in just a few hours.

"Where?" he asked. He lay on his back holding the drawing above us.

"At first I was thinking the top of my foot, but Cat said that's a no-go because it's very painful for a first tattoo. Plus, this particular design needs to be larger so you can see the cherry blossoms in the wings of the dragonfly, don't you think? She says she plans to give it lots of dimension with shading and make it appear to be flying. It's going to go on my right shoulder blade."

"Not sure I agree with her. You like pain," he said with a wide grin. "That, and Cat's a light touch with the tattoo machine." He scanned my body as if to find the perfect spot. "I'm sure you could handle a tattoo on your foot … man, you were so fucking hot tonight. I'm getting hard again just thinking about it." He chuckled and looked back at the design. "Yeah, I think this design should be larger."

"Is Cat the one who fixed your previous tattoo?"

"Yep, and she also did Red's tat."

I reached across him and touched his right deltoid, tracing the Celtic knot surrounded by the flames of the sun. The whole group now knew the significance of that tattoo. He had lost his fiancée in a car crash many years ago.

"Are you nervous about tomorrow?" Bond asked.

"Cat's an amazing artist, so no. If it were anyone else, I probably wouldn't do it in the first place."

"Gotcha." He leaned across me and turned off the lamp.

I lay the art rendering of the tattoo on my bag and

cuddled up close to Bond. Taking in a deep breath and letting it out slowly, I sank into the bed and his arms, smiling and thinking that tomorrow should be an interesting day.

CHAPTER TWO

Down the Line

by Jose Gonzalez

In the morning, I did my best to be quiet so Bond could continue to sleep. After getting dressed, I gathered my belongings from the side of the bed and tiptoed toward the bedroom door.

"Make sure to switch out the toothbrushes in the bathroom before you go and come say goodbye," Bond rumbled in his rough morning voice.

His comment twisted in my gut, but I did as he asked. Jacqs had spent the night, not long ago, and found my toothbrush in place of her own. She didn't know it was mine, but it caused friction in their relationship. They seemed to move past it quickly. Even though I totally accepted the need to do so, being second place, as much as I understood and expected it, still hurt.

Climbing into the bed, I forced my feelings of inadequacy aside and snuggled up next to Bond, breathing in his masculine scent of sandalwood and warm, musky skin.

He kissed my head and held me close. "Don't be mad at me, Blue. I just want to avoid the drama and all the questions."

"I know. I get it." I did understand. It just made the distance between me and my one and only crystal clear, and I didn't care for the reminder. I sighed heavily. "Get some rest and call me when you're free, or I'll see you on Wednesday at Red's."

"I'll find time before then. I can't wait to see how your tat comes out and have your body under my control again. My palm is already twitching." He smacked my ass through my jeans, and I squirmed against his growing erection.

"Sorry, dude, I don't have the time." I laughed and pushed away from his chest. "I'll text you later."

Babes in Tattooland stood out against the shop fronts around it. The lighted marquee done in fancy tattoo writing had two large red roses on either side of the "in" on the sign and an artistic swirl across the bottom of the lettering. The flamboyant sign hinted at what the customers might find inside the establishment.

The red and black checkerboard tile, red walls covered with tattoo pictures, black furniture and fixtures, along with the hard music, defined the ambience. *Killin' It* by Krewella blared through the shop speakers, and the waft of antiseptic filled my nose.

"Blue!" Cat shouted and waved once I entered.

I walked past two black couches and a counter full of piercing options to Cat's station toward the front of the open-floor area. The fact that the establishment was mostly empty left me more at ease.

Catherine, Cat to our group, had been involved with Kevin, Kev, since I knew them. They had an interesting dance I had yet to figure out. It seemed like many in our gang were pairing off, which left me feeling even more alone.

Shaking away the feeling, I handed Cat the stencil she had previously created and we hugged each other.

Her striking appearance fit with the tattoo shop. She

wore tight red jeans and a black cut-and-tied T-shirt she had altered herself. The butterfly ribbing on the back showed the straps of her red bra. Her blue-black long, angled bob reflected the light and just like her name, she applied her smoky eye makeup so it came to a cat-like point.

"Where is everyone?" I asked.

"It's still early. The place will start filling up in another hour or so. Saturdays are busy for us, and I'm booked for the rest of the day."

Looking around, I said, "Kind of odd that the decor is so masculine for a place where there are only female tattoo artists."

"Most of our customers are men so I guess that was the owner's thinking."

"Makes sense. So should we get started?" I asked, my voice wavering.

"It's normal to be nervous your first time. Take off your shirt and lie face down. I'm going to enlarge the stencil, and I'll be right back."

I yanked off my top and lay down, struggling to find a comfortable position for my ample boobs. Finally settled, I rested my cheek on my folded arms.

When Cat came back, she said, "You wore a sports bra? Smart thinking. I'm pulling down the right strap and will cleanse the area."

After she applied the stencil, she held up a mirror so I could see the placement over my shoulder.

"Looks good to me." My voice wavered.

"Relax."

The next sound I heard was a sharp buzzing as she began to tattoo. The pain immediately fired off my endorphins and after breathing through the first several pokes, I adjusted. Zoned out, I didn't stir until I felt a wind-like sensation sending ripples and chills across my skin. *It's not windy out*, I thought. I gently turned my head and watched the door close behind a broad, towering man with long, rich brown, shoulder-length hair.

The eminent Native American pierced me with dark mahogany eyes and paused.

My nipples pinched tightly in response to his gaze. *Not for us girls*, I said silently to my breasts. I turned away from the door.

The magnetic pull drew closer, and my body tensed in response. His scent—completely male—overpowered my senses. The mix of the ocean, light soap, and pheromones made my head spin.

"Are you hanging in there, Blue?" Cat whispered into my ear.

I tilted my head up. "Yeah, I'm fine."

"You're shaking."

"I am? Ummm ... okay. I'll be still."

"Very nice work," a deep, bass voice rumbled above me.

"Hey Tate," Cat said. "I'll just be another fifteen minutes or so."

"I'm good on time. Great design. It's interesting that you coupled cherry blossoms within a dragonfly. Do you mind if I sit here?" Tate asked, pointing to the chair situated above the head of the table.

Yes, I mind! I screamed inside my head. Apparently, they didn't hear me.

"No," Cat replied. "Blue, this is Tate, Tate, Blue."

"Nice to meet you," he said. Although he gave the correct greeting, his creased forehead and turned-down lips said anything but.

I nodded my head in response, scared to speak aloud. The shaking Cat mentioned had morphed into agitation.

Warning, warning, warning, my mind shouted. The rest of me felt a very different message. My body's ambiguity roused me, and I had to get up.

"Do you know the symbolism?" Tate asked. The timbre of his voice sounded almost angry.

"Sorry, I need to ... go ... use the restroom," I forced out, pushing to a sitting position. I kept my eyes downcast and stood. "I'll be right back." I shuffled off to the bathroom.

After using the toilet and calming my racing heart, I walked back to the table with my arms crossed over my chest in an effort to hide my boobs.

"What do you think?" Cat asked expectantly.

In my vexed state, I hadn't checked out the tattoo. "I decided to wait until you're done."

"Cool. Tate says that the cherry blossoms symbolize beauty and the fragility of life, and the dragonfly totem carries the wisdom of transformation and adaptability."

"Huh, I didn't realize," I said, taking a chance to look directly at him as I perched on the edge of the table.

Close up, I noticed he wore baggy jeans and a fitted T. He had a light five o'clock shadow and high cheekbones. The sharp edges of his face strongly contrasted his soft, full lips. His stern expression rattled me.

"Maybe unconsciously, you did," he said, penetrating me with his stare.

"I..." I couldn't think of a response, so I blurted out, "Are you Native American?"

He tilted his head as if to say, "What do you think?"

Entangled in his gaze, he seemed to see straight through me. I turned around to see if anyone stood behind me.

"No, you," he said.

"No," I responded.

"Right. I'll be in the reception area," he said to Cat as he continued to stare at me. His gravelly voice seemed lower than before. He took a deep breath and stood. "Nice to meet you." Again, the words were polite, but the tone and stern expression were anything but.

"Yeah," I said, averting my eyes and lying back down.

After he walked away, Cat scolded, "Why are you such a weirdo with men? He was totally attracted to you."

"He's not my type. He's huge, stoic, and all-confident, and those men are the worst trouble."

"You're wrong about this one, Blue. I've been working on him for years. He's one of the good guys."

"Really? He seems full of issues to me. Does he ever smile?" I lowered my head and found a comfortable position.

Cat rested her hand on my back and said, "I'm sure he smiles."

"Okay, I believe you. He's just not my type."

"But I don't believe *you*. Ready?"

"Whatever. I'm ready. Let's talk about something else."

"Okay. Have you heard from your mother lately?" she asked as she resumed tattooing.

"Unfortunately. She wants me to come over on Sunday to meet her latest conquest."

"Will you?"

"Probably. I haven't seen her in a while, and at least I'll get that out of the way. I mean, I love her, but I'm dreading it. Not so much seeing her but meeting her latest beau. She has the worst possible taste in men. The minute she leaves the room, they're all over me. I've stopped telling her about it, because she just thinks I'm jealous. Telling her what I really felt, which was disgusted, didn't help. Plus, they never seem to hang around for long. Maybe she's finally found a decent man. I doubt it, but I can hope. How's yours?"

Cat shifted the tattoo machine. "Pretty much the same, but I'm a bit worried. She hasn't been as mean lately as she usually is."

"And that's a bad thing?"

"Well, it's certainly not normal for her. I asked if she was feeling okay, and she just brushed me off."

"Do you think we're all such good friends because we have horrible mothers?"

Cat stopped tattooing when she erupted in laughter. Good thing, because I cracked up as well.

"Jacqs's mom is great and so is Kev's, so I think that theory is shot."

I chuckled once more and said, "Right. I love Jacqs's mother. I've never met Kev's, though."

"That's because she lives in Connecticut with his dad, who's also great."

"Ahhh. That makes a lot of sense to me. Kev is great and very loving. You're very lucky, Cat."

"Yeah, yeah, that's what everyone tells me."

I shook my head at her and rested my cheek back on my arms.

Once Cat completed the final touches, she cleansed the tattoo. She led me to a large mirror and had me turn my back to it, handing me a smaller one to look into. "What do you think?"

"Holy moly! That's ... that's way more than I thought it would be. I don't mean in size, but wow! How did you get so much dimension in it? Oh, and I love the iridescent blue. It looks 3D. How did you do that?"

"She's the best," Tate commented, startling me. "I won't let anyone else work on me." He had invaded our space yet again.

"I'm going to apply ointment and cover it," Cat said as

I handed her back the small mirror. "You need to wash it with antibacterial soap, which I will give to you, and use A+D Ointment twice a day for three days. Then I recommend coconut oil, but whatever kind of lotion you have will work. Once you get home, take off the bandage. Try to keep it uncovered as much as possible."

"I have to work tonight," I said, leaving my sports bra strap down and pulling my T-shirt over my head.

"Either go without a bra on—"

"That's not possible," I interjected.

"Then use a strapless one."

"I'll figure something out. You're incredible, Cat." I hugged her tightly. "I just love it."

She smiled to me and then said, "Tate, I'll go check her out and be right back. I'd like to see how your back healed first before we continue onto your thigh."

He peeled off his shirt and watched me over his shoulder. He seemed to want me to see, and I don't think he was showing off Cat's work either.

I think he wanted me to see him. "Holy Toledo!" I exclaimed.

A flying golden eagle, on the diagonal, spread from his right shoulder down across his coppery, wide back to his left hip where his jeans cut off the rest of the design. I could imagine that the bird's left wing crossed the top of his butt cheek and covered the side of his left thigh. It was an amazing work of art.

Another tattoo covered his left deltoid. Cat had tattooed it in such a way that it looked like a colored drawing. The bust of a Native American woman with a feather headdress and long braids abutted a Viking facing in the other direction with a metal helmet, face guard, and a long, full beard.

I forced myself to walk away and dragged Cat with me. "Damn, Cat. I had no idea how talented you are. That's some amazing art."

"It's what I love."

"Thank you is the appropriate response. I thought I was the one who had issues with compliments."

"I've never gotten used to receiving them. A foreign concept in my house growing up."

I touched her arm and said, "I understand."

She stepped behind the counter and put the cleanser, instructions, and some of her business cards in a bag.

"So what's the damage?" I asked. When I paid for the tattoo, I added a healthy tip and turned over the slip so she wouldn't see it until after I left. Waving, I took the bag and walked out of the shop without looking back.

Once inside my apartment, I pulled off the cloth tape surrounding the saran wrap Cat had laid over the tattoo. I removed my sports bra and other clothes and collapsed on my bed with my cell phone in hand, careful not to lie on my right side. I texted Bond.

> **Me:** I'm home and about to take a nap. The tat is incredible and can't wait for you to see it.

I figured he was still sleeping and after setting my alarm, I fell out, too.

As soon as I awoke, I felt the throb on my shoulder. I downed two over-the-counter pain meds and showered. I couldn't let the flow of the water hit my back, so I had to lean forward to rinse my hair. After drying off, I read some of my positive affirmations as I applied blue eyeliner. *When I believe in myself, so do others. I attract only healthy relationships. Happiness is my choice.* I didn't know if it helped, but my women's group counselor seemed to think so.

In my drawer full of bras, I found one that allowed the straps to crisscross in the back. It didn't pull me in tight enough or offer the support I preferred, however, it would have to do.

As always, I dressed in jeans and a black Tap 42 T-shirt for my bartending job. Fortunately, they let me choose the work shirt I liked best. Most of the women working in Tap 42 favored the shirt with a plunging neckline. Instead, I wore the women's less revealing shirt or the men's short-sleeved button-up. I went with the baggier of the two so it wouldn't press against my sore shoulder.

I much preferred bartending to waiting tables, but unless I wanted to show off my assets at other types of establishments, I had to work my way up to full-time at Tap 42. Gratefully, I had two night shifts a week, which allowed me to work less at The Chart House.

The bar/restaurant had a long, wide bar down the main space. Wood strips of various colors and lengths covered the far wall. It gave the surface an interesting look and texture. The forty-two beers, each with its own tap, hung centered on the back wall of the bar. The busy Saturday nights left no place for dwelling on life issues. However, I started my shift at five o'clock while the place sat mostly empty.

Rick, my Saturday evening regular, sat at the far end stool. I had heard he'd been recently divorced. The forty-something man didn't speak much and never hit on me, making him one of my favorite customers.

After stocking the bar for the busy night to come and

checking all the taps, I proceeded to wipe down the expansive, shiny brown countertop. A charged jolt stopped me, and I bucked my head around, trying to locate the cause. Rick still sat at the end of the bar, and the couple at the two-top table ate as if nothing torrid had taken place. I pushed the sensation aside, grabbed the big plastic container, and headed to the back to fill it with ice.

As I hauled the heavy bin back toward the mixing station, I saw the cause of my excitement: Tate along with Cat. I lowered the ice, glared at Cat, and texted her.

Me: What the fuck!
Catherine: Be nice!

I wanted to smack her for playing matchmaker when I told her I wasn't interested. Lifting the plastic bin again, I walked forward and set it on the edge of the sink. Keeping my head down, I dumped the ice into the receptacle near the hard liquor. "Get it over with," I whispered to myself. I approached and tossed a coaster in front of them both. "What'll it be?"

"One of the IPAs on draft," Tate said, leaning on the bar instead of taking a seat on one of the white, backless stools. Maybe his ass hurt from the tattoo, and I can't say I was feeling sorry for him.

"You?" I asked Cat.

"Just water. I need to get back to the shop."

After retrieving a frosted mug from the cooler, I poured the beer into the glass, giving it the perfect foam head. Placing the water and beer down on the coasters, I said, "So was it the boobs or the small waist?"

His eyes blinked a few times, but otherwise his sour expression didn't change. "Excuse me?"

"Sorry, never mind. I'm sure you're a great guy, but you aren't even slightly my type."

"Blue, cut it out!"

Repeating Cat's cadence, I said, "Cat, stop meddling!"

Tate slowly lowered his beer to the counter. "How can you decide that without talking to a person or getting to know anything about them? Isn't that like me judging you solely on your..." He waved his hand up and down, his eyes following the movement and finished, "...your assets?"

"Well I... Yes, I guess it is exactly like that. Men your size ... they intimidate me, and I've had a few rather unpleasant—I'll be right back." I hurried away to ostensibly help Rick at the other end of the bar.

Tate's stare scorched my back and elicited a desire I couldn't contend with. Not that I thought he was slightly interested in me, if the permanent scowl on his face meant anything. I prided myself on learning from my mistakes. No big, angry men with swagger, and he had both in abundance. Plus, his ability to stir me when not in my immediate proximity set off all my alarms.

I made Rick another dry martini and swapped out his old drink for the new. Silently, I prayed for the bar to fill up and fast.

With my eyes downcast, I walked back to Tate, who had finished his beer, Cat nowhere in sight. "Another?"

"Sure. Cat took off," he said, his white teeth flashing for a millisecond before his jaw clinched again.

Do I cause him pain? Maybe his ass is burning.

"Cat seems to think we could be friends."

I tilted my eyes up, trying to make sense of the man in front of me. "Does she often push you on people?"

"Nah, this is a first."

I saw the very first hint of a smile that quickly

vanished. "I'm not open for anything more than that," I said, but immediately wished I had kept my mouth shut.

"Neither am I."

"Oh?" I was completely offended. Now I was the one with the scowl on my face. "You can do just friends?"

"Yes, Blue, I'm quite capable of that." His deep brown eyes unnerved me as if they could penetrate my self-protection while he gave nothing of himself away. And yet, his gaze permeated me and filled me in a way no one ever had.

My pussy sure as hell liked him as it pulsed in response to his stare. "Only my friends call me Blue." I didn't like how he said my name at all. It carried way too much familiarity or something I couldn't quite place.

With a serious expression he said, "Okay, Judy."

"Why?" I took the rag from the sink and used it to wipe the bar between us.

He stopped my hand, and held it in place under his. "Why did I let her drag me here? Or why should we be friends?"

"Either ... both," I said, looking away. My heart raced at his touch and caused my face to blush. Wetness gathered between my thighs and when I glanced up at him, I knew he could tell. I crossed my free arm across my errant nipples.

His expression remained unchanged. "You know why." He lifted his hand off mine.

Only I didn't, but I remained silent. Maybe he could feel me, like I felt him. But if that were the case, he sure hid it well. "And if I say no?" I threw the rag down in the sink underneath.

He shrugged and shook his head as if it mattered not a bit to him either way.

"Well if it matters so little to you," I flung at him, waving him off. I rang up his two beers and placed the receipt down in front of him.

"That's not what I said. You're tough."

"Life has a way of doing that." So many thoughts raced through my mind: my brother's friend, my father's client, my mother's boyfriends, my floor mate in college and others. Too many fucked up scenarios to process.

As if Tate could read my thoughts, his voice filled with compassion. "Yes, it does."

"So..." I said, waiting for him to pay and leave.

"We could go out with Cat and Kevin." He took his wallet out of his back pocket and left it on the bar, unopened.

"Sounds too much like a double date." I watched a server I didn't know leave a check for the couple across the way.

"We can hang out in a group?"

I looked back toward him. "I don't know anything about you, Tate. How about we start there?" My phone vibrated and I said, "I'll be right back." I pushed through the swinging kitchen door, pulled out my cellphone, and saw messages from Cat and Bond.

> **Bond:** Let's shoot for Monday night. Can't wait to see it and you. ;)
> **Catherine:** Give him a shot. You won't regret it.

To Bond I typed:

> **Me:** Perfect. I'm off Monday.

And to Cat I texted:

> **Me:** I already do.

Back out front, before I could say anything, Tate started, "I'm forty-three, I teach English and writing classes at FAU, and I'm healthy."

I scanned him up and down, taking in his shoulder-length, shiny, rich brown hair and imagined the tattoos that lay underneath his tight red T-shirt and relaxed-fit, black jeans. I scrunched my nose and upper lip. "A college professor? Really?"

"Don't sound so surprised." His expression remained neutral, but I got the feeling he was impressed with himself, or maybe he just liked surprising me.

"Well ... you look more like a Rough Rider than a teacher. Do you like it?"

"I love my work and I used to be a biker, but I don't think you mean the Rough Riders who were the first United States volunteer cavalry."

I burst out laughing over my faux pas. "Holy moly," I mumbled and laughed some more.

He seemed to be struggling not to laugh with me. He continued, "Outlaws, Warlocks, or another motorcycle gang is probably what you were going for. I was part of a group of bikers, but we had no crest or creed other than drinking too much and fighting too often."

"Were they all Native Americans?"

"No, but we were all young and dumb shits at the time."

I laughed again, and this time he joined in.

His laughter transformed his face, causing his dark eyes to sparkle. The moment passed too quickly.

"Do you still ride?" I asked.

"Yes, but not as often anymore. I make sure to do the charity runs like Toys for Tots and love to take a long ride on a cool winter's day. Did you know you crinkle your nose when you're thinking?" He didn't wait for me to respond. "Cat tells me you're working on a novel. What do you write about?"

"That's personal."

"Oh. I was under the impression that you'd like to publish your work someday."

I sighed heavily. "Yeah, that's true, but I don't really know if what I'm writing is any good."

"You haven't let anyone read it?"

"No. It's my escape and my dream, and I'm not ready to find out I'm wasting my time."

"I can understand that. Dreams and reality are rarely in alignment." A flash of regret played across his features, quickly replaced by the stern set of his lips. "However, if you ever want some feedback, I've got a lot of experience with storyline help and editing."

"Yeah, thanks, I don't know." I was so caught up in the conversation I hadn't realized two new people had sat at the bar.

"Judy, can you take their order?" Stuart asked, tilting his head toward the end of the bar. The bar manager had come up behind me without my being aware.

"Oh, yeah. Going," I responded, looking at Tate in question and then breaking eye contact.

More patrons filed over to the bar, and I mixed and pulled their drinks. I could feel Tate's stare like the red laser light at the end of a sharp shooter's rifle. The heat of his attention followed me everywhere. Before I could change my mind, I stalked back over to him. "I'm probably going to regret this, but are you free Wednesday night?"

"Yes," he muttered in what sounded like a breath of relief.

"Let me talk to a few people, and I'll let you know. This isn't a date. I want to make that clear."

"Agreed. Think about letting me look over some of your work."

"Please don't take this the wrong way, but would you mind taking off?"

He held my stare, and I didn't immediately back down. He seemed to know that his presence was an intense distraction, and I didn't much care for his astute cognizance. Without breaking the connection, he fished money out of his wallet and lay it down in front of him.

I gave in and reached for the bills.

"I'll take off, but first let me give you my number."

I punched a few buttons on my phone and brought up the address book. "Here." I offered him my phone.

His fingers brushed mine, and I gasped in response. He seemed to have zero reaction to the contact.

I felt my nipples responding again. They were like rebellious teenagers. I wrapped my arms around my chest and waited for Tate to give me back my phone.

When he replaced it in my hand, he said, "See you soon."

As soon as he left, I could feel my pulse settle and my shoulders relax. Seeing him again seemed stupid and problematic. And yet, he seemed to have a sad story of his own that I was now curious about. Curiosity killed the cat, as they say, and part of me wanted to track down one particular Cat.

Tap 42 steadily picked up and even with four of us behind the bar, we mixed drinks non-stop, pulled beers, filled the ice bucket, ran the register, and cleaned glasses. When it got that busy, even the pushy guys didn't expect to get my attention for more than a second or two.

Since I opened that night, I didn't have to stay until closing. Once the crowd at the bar began to die down, I was able to leave for the night.

CHAPTER THREE

You Could Be Happy

by Snow Patrol

F or most people, Sunday morning was either a day for rest or religion. My Sunday, however, included the women's group and meeting my mother's latest "wallet." Neither prospect felt the least bit appealing as I sat eating oatmeal at the kitchen table by the window.

I usually felt better after attending the women's group, that is, if Charmaine didn't show. She had a major bug up her butt about me and usually gave me a hard time. Without her there, it felt more like a supportive group of women listening to each other. For Charmaine, group therapy was more like an action sport. Serve, volley, lob!

I slipped into a pair of black shorts and a tank and then remembered I'd be heading straight over to my mother's after the meeting. Even though the heat index was pushing up the mercury, I changed into jeans and a baggy T.

Once at the Hollywood Bread building, I took the elevator to room 312. Only Ann, the group facilitator, had arrived so far.

"Hey, Judy, did you have a good week?"

"Ups and downs. The usual. Yourself?"

"I'm close to finishing my supervised hours and hopefully, I'll be able to set up my own counseling practice soon."

"That's very exciting. Are you planning to stay in the area?" I wondered aloud.

"My husband and I haven't decided yet. We're

considering staying put or moving closer to my parents."

"That could be good or bad, depending on your parents," I said, laughing.

"So true." She laughed with me.

Two other women strolled in and took seats in the circle of chairs. The non-descript room, with grey walls and carpet, did nothing to inspire joy, but we managed anyway. I checked email on my phone to fill the time before the group started.

I looked over at Ann, who glanced at the clock on the wall.

"Okay, let's get started," she said, smoothing her skirt over her thighs.

Seven of us awkwardly glinted at each other. No one seemed to want to start. I never planned to speak at these gatherings, but Ann usually coaxed me to do so. When the silence became too acute, I blurted out, "I sort of met someone."

"How do you *sort of* meet someone?" Charmaine demanded as she breezed into the room.

Did she time that on purpose?

Her name didn't suit her at all. For me, Charmaine elicited images of a sophisticated, petite, French woman. The real Charmaine reminded me of my junior high school gym coach. She wasn't unattractive, but the hard planes of her face and body reminded me more of a body builder. However, her appearance definitely reflected her personality. Hard as steel.

After she sat down, she crossed her legs and leaned in toward me. "Well?"

"He's not at all my type, and assures me he's only interested in friendship."

"What a crock of shit!" Charmaine exclaimed empathically. She looked around the group for support.

Ann spoke up, "What part are you referring to, Charmaine? I'd also like to see you sit back in your seat and consider your words."

"Right," she acquiesced, sitting up straight. To me she said, "Men never want to be *just* friends. Even if you're gay. They think they can convert you."

She's gay? I raised my eyebrows in curiosity.

"Not that I'm gay," she continued and shifted in her seat. "Also, I doubt Miss Prissy's feigned disinterest is real. If that were the case, she wouldn't have mentioned him."

Ann turned her body toward Charmaine's seat. "I think this is a clear example of you assuming too much without listening to what she has to say. Asking questions is a much better way to get at the truth rather than jumping to conclusions."

"Yeah, yeah," she clucked, waving her off. "That's what you keep telling me. She just gets under my skin. Miss Perfect who hates men giving her attention, when all the rest of us wish we were so lucky."

"Empathy is a very necessary skill to be an effective manager," Ann explained to Charmaine. "We can discuss that during your time. Judy, would you please continue?"

"His name is Tate and I met him ... through a friend of mine, Cat. They showed up unexpectedly at my work, and Cat thinks we should be friends. He is hard to read, though. But something he said has stayed with me."

Suzie, sitting just to my right, asked, "Is he hot? Do you have his number?"

I glanced at her and then spoke to Ann, "I told him he wasn't at all my type, and he said that I was judging him like people judge me all the time without getting to know me, which you know I abhor."

"Was he right?" Suzie asked.

"Yeah, I guess. I mean, I'm not sure where you draw the line between learning from the past and being prejudiced in the future."

"Nicely put," Ann said. "So did you agree to see him again?"

"I'm toying with the idea of inviting him to the weekly gathering of my friends. That way, it'll be clear it's not a date."

"But you're hesitating?"

"Invite me and I'll distract him for you," Suzie said, twitching her eyebrows.

"Yes, I'm hesitating. My friends are my world, and I have a real safety and comfort with them. Really, they're my family, other than my aunt. What if they like him and I don't? I know I'm judging him based on his size and his scowl—"

"Which is just like men judging you based on your rack," Charmaine shot back.

"Or women, as in your case," I countered, staring back at her.

"Touché," she capitulated.

"There's also this unnerving feeling when he's around. Part of me wants to run toward it, but mostly I just want to hide from it."

"What is the feeling?" Ann asked.

I closed my eyes to allow myself to feel the sensation. "Vulnerable. Like my normal defenses aren't there to protect me."

"I can see why you would be hesitant," Ann said. "My gut tells me this might be a growth opportunity for you: balancing openness while taking care of yourself."

"I guess we'll see."

I half listened to the rest of the shares and discussion. The other half of me dissected every moment of my interaction with Tate, as if I could discern something that would put me at ease instead of feeling like a young, scared girl. Nothing became clear and if anything, I felt even more confused. Not having control over my body's desires around him put me on edge. The fact that he had zero response to me in that way just pissed me off.

On my way to my mother's house, I stopped by Publix and picked up some dessert. My angst had shifted from Tate to meeting my mother's boyfriend. Of boyfriends past, Trey had been the worst. I still lived at home at the time and at every chance, he cornered and groped me. His dirty smirk still visits my dreams on the odd occasion. I told my mother about him, and she insisted I was jealous of her and was trying to sabotage "the best thing that ever happened to her." I stayed away from the house as much as possible, bathroom and bedroom doors always locked when home. Fortunately, for us both, she kicked him out a few months later.

Knocking on my mom's front door, my heart pounded.

A man, I guessed to be in his mid-fifties, answered the door. "You must be Jude, I'm Daniel," he said, extending his hand right out to me and taking the dessert in the other.

Clasping it in return, I took in the man before me. He looked nothing like my mother's usual fare. He wore khakis and a short-sleeved, collared polo, shirt. His salt-and-pepper hair was short and neat. His pale blue eyes stayed focused on my face.

"Nice to meet you," I said. Glancing over his shoulder, I took in the house where I had spent my childhood. Unchanged as ever, I recognized the pale blue walls and the southern knickknacks my mother so loved, lining all available surfaces. Time travel might not exist, but it sure felt like it did when I came back home.

Peeking up, I saw my mother waiting for me. I approached her with my arms open, and she embraced me in a tight hug. "He's different," I whispered. She, too, seemed different. Gone were the tight jeans and low-cut blouse. The flowery dress gave her an understated sexiness. "You look wonderful, Mom."

"You? What's with the baggy clothes, Jude?" She tugged on my shirt.

Ignoring her I asked, "So Daniel, what do you do?"

"Whatever the hell I want," he responded, a huge smile breaking over his face. I liked him instantly. "I'm retired and love to travel, read, dance, and do anything on the water."

"Sounds like a good life." I followed my mother into the kitchen, Daniel trailing behind us.

Bagels and all the fixings covered the table. I made myself a plate, spreading cream cheese over an onion bagel, topping it with smoked salmon and tomato. "Mom, how's Helena? I haven't heard from her in a while."

Helena was my mother's sister and the only adult in my parent's circle for whom I ever held any respect. My father's parents were hideous people, and my mother's mother died young from breast cancer. Their father, always angry, had more reasons to be after she died. Years ago, Helena had battled breast cancer and won. Recently, the tumors had returned, and it wasn't looking good for her.

My mother's face dropped and Daniel rubbed her back. "She's been in and out of the hospital."

"She hasn't returned my calls."

"Honey, she's doing chemo again and doesn't want to see anyone. Send her an email. You have a better chance of hearing back that way. Just send your love, Sugar."

"Okay." I knew death was part of life, but I couldn't allow myself to acknowledge the possibility.

We ate in silence until Daniel asked, "So what do you do?"

"I wait tables and bartend. I aspire to write novels and I dabble."

"That's interesting. The market is really changing in that arena with all the eBooks out now. I love my Kindle. I don't travel without it."

I swallowed a bite of food and said, "Yeah, I'm still fond of paperback books, but I'm sure I'll succumb eventually."

"Cicely and I were just talking, and she tells me you aren't in touch with your father—"

Odd question. "Or brother," I said, taking another bite.

"You have a brother?" he asked, looking from my mom to me.

I guess they don't know each other that well.

"Thanks, Jude," my mother muttered. "When Hatch and I divorced, he took Matt and I kept Jude." She paused and caught my eye.

I shook my head no.

"Jude stopped visiting Hatch and for reas— Matt stopped coming here as well."

"It's complicated," I said, bristling in my seat.

"Sounds like it, and it's clearly an uncomfortable subject for you both. I would've treaded lighter had I'd known."

My mother touched his shoulder and smiled.

We continued to eat, the silence filling the room like a helium balloon about to burst. Once we finished the meal, I stood to remove the dishes to the sink.

"Jude, I'll take care of that. Sit and let's chat," my mother said, patting my vacated chair.

"I need to get going. Laundry, house chores, etcetera."

"What about dessert? I didn't mean to run you off," Daniel said.

"Not at all, and I'm totally full. Thanks for making my mother so clearly happy." I gave my mom a hug goodbye and said, "See you soon."

"Love you, Sugar," she called to my back.

"Love you too," I said over my shoulder from the foyer.

Back at my apartment, I washed my tattoo and applied the A+D Ointment. I left my T-shirt off and sat in front of my computer. Ignoring the dust and laundry, I sorted through my writing. Could I be brave enough to share something with Tate?

I had a couple of novels I had started and never finished: the story of my life—way too personal to share—and my current novel, *Soul Adjacent*:

Like any other Saturday night, we close the front section of Beverly Hills Cafe, topping the ketchup, salt, and pepper, and wiping down the tables. I closed out my receipts earlier with the shift manager. After finishing my chores, I go to find Jacy.

"Meet at Crush?" I ask. Crush is our favorite alternative dance club.

"Yeah, I need to run home, tuck in Cheri, and shower. My mom's going to watch her."

"Great! I'll see you there. Is Tee coming tonight?"

"Yeah, but Katness—"

"I know, a forever waste of my time."

On the way to the townhouse, which I share with my

younger sister, I chastise myself for chasing the unattainable. I even understand what motivates me. What good is psychology if it changes nothing? Knowing the cause without a way to fix it is its own torture. I crave a deep connection but constantly choose to obsess over men who either lack the ability or have zero interest in me beyond friendship. My latest obsession, Tee, he and I are great friends. However, he loves the drama and younger, stick-figure blondes who couldn't be more my opposite.

My father and I never connected on a real level, and he has little interest in me other than to lecture that I should go into a career like physical or occupational therapy so I can make more money. He will expound about politics or healthcare but other than knowing his opinions, I know nothing about him. He knows even less about me. I never feel comfortable or safe to be myself around him. I spent my childhood trying to morph myself into someone else so he might notice me. Old habits die hard, as they say.

At my place, I run up the stairs, pull off my work clothes, and step into the steaming hot shower. I wash the smell of work off my body and hair and then dry off quickly. The faster I get to Crush, the sooner I can dance. I slip on a fitted pair of jeans and sleeveless black top with enough spandex to hold in my chest. It crisscrosses in the back and barely reaches the edge of my jeans. Once in strappy sandals, I take my license and some cash out of my wallet and shove them into my jean's pocket. Back in the bathroom, I shake out my brown, curly hair and part it on the side.

Unlike most people, I go dancing to dance. I don't wear makeup or drink. I'm usually lost in my own world or that of my friends when we dance together.

Once in my sporty CRX, I head out to the club.

After paying and flashing my ID, I enter Crush as the hard alternative music immediately beckons me. The large front room holds tables and chairs on the left and a long bar on the right.

Passing the first room, I enter the space with the dance floor on the right and a bar down the center, people filling in on all sides. At the back of the place and on the edge of the dance floor sits another bar. Everything in the place is black except for the raised wood dance floor.

I pass all the loitering patrons and step up to dance near the stage, which they use on the odd occasion that they have a live band. The big black speakers pound out Jane's Addiction's "Been Caught Stealing," and I immediately get lost in the rhythm, grinding to the beat, eyes closed.

I'm not sure how much time passes but soon, I'm surrounded by my workmates. Jacy has her hair up in a thick braid starting at the top of her head and she's swinging it around, keeping people out of her immediate vicinity. Tee is dancing between and around us, no girlfriend in sight. Jill, Monica, and Brad are there too.

When the music switches over to a Red Hot Chili Peppers' song, I walk out to the front bar and reach over the side to grab a clear Solo cup. The bartender nods to me. At the water dispenser next to the bar, I fill the cup and drink. I think about going outside to cool off but decide to dance more first.

Walking back, I see my group has migrated to the other end of the dance floor. I go around to the far steps and look up. A guy across the way is staring at me. My soul riveted, I no longer hear the music or the sounds coming from the bar. I amble toward him as he does the same. Neither of us speaks at first.

"Corey," he finally says.

"Katness, but most people just call me Kat."

He holds out his hand and enfolds mine in his. A pulse of energy takes hold and affects every cell of my body. I shake slightly.

"Let's dance," he says, tugging me out to the center of the floor.

Our bodies synchronize as he easily guides me to the beat of "Never There" by Cake. We sway back and forth, Corey lowering us to a squat and dancing up again. He stares at me while we dance. I'm so caught up in the moment, it's almost like dancing with my eyes closed but with someone else. Intense and pure.

Several songs pass in a blur until he says, "I'm here with some friends and should probably—"

"Oh right, sure. Thanks for the dance," I say, pulling away.

"Wait," he says.

"Fucking crap! I can't share that! He'll think I'm an idiot for even trying." On a whim, I Google the meaning of the name Tate, thinking there might be some Native American significance.

English meaning: Cheerful. *Not!*

Native American meaning: A man who talks too much. *Double no!*

Did his parents have any idea what they were doing when they named him? One obscure website listed Tate as meaning wind. Somehow, that one fit. *Wind it is.*

I clicked out of Google and combed through a few other files of my writing.

Thankfully, my phone rang, saving me from torturing myself with more of my bad writing.

"Yep," I said.

"So?" Cat said.

"Shouldn't you be tattooing someone's ass?"

"Did you cut off his balls, or did you actually talk to him?"

I plopped down onto my unmade bed and lay back gently. "My tattoo is healing great. Thanks for asking."

"Bluuuuue," she whined.

"If I tell you, you will just push me, and I haven't decided."

"I promise to behave. Go for it."

I rolled onto my left side and confessed, "He gave me his number. I might invite him to come on Wednesday to Red's. *Might* being the operative word. He says he wants to be friends, but I think it's merely because you pushed him into it."

"A friend that plays with your clity?"

"Shut up, Cat. I was clear that I'm not interested in dating him, and he's not looking for that either."

"We could use some fresh blood in our group. Ask him to tag along."

"Squeezing another alpha male into that group?" I laughed. "I'll see what Bond says about it."

"Who cares what Bond thinks? Just invite him. Maybe Samantha and Tate will hit it off."

"I think it's time to lay your matchmaking skills to rest."

"Kevin says that all the time. I can't help myself. So, chica, how was your visit with your mom?"

"Good, bad, and indifferent." I sat up and scooted to the head of the bed.

"Care to be more specific?"

"She seems happy but failed to mention that she has a son. Daniel, her latest boyfriend, seemed surprised, although he handled the news well. My mom had on a dress, which was a nice change. I just hope she isn't morphing herself into what she thinks Daniel wants. He's retired and seems to have money. I never know with my mom. I love her, but she's always seemed more like a sister than a mom."

"Maybe she's finally growing up."

"One can hope. Have you heard from your mom?"

"Yeah, she said she was fine and to back the fuck off. She must be feeling better."

"It's a bit screwed up when you hope your mother reverts to a bitch. Ha!"

"It sure is. So what did you really think of Tate?"

"He's a bit serious, don't you think? Too much man for me and very hard to read. Interesting enough. He wants to read some of my work."

"We all do."

"I'm not sure I'm ready."

"Bite the bullet, bitch. You can't get better in a vacuum."

"I'm the bitch? Mirror much?"

"Kisses on your ornery ass, my friend."

I harrumphed and dissolved in giggles. "You're too funny. Hey, did you suggest that we double date, 'cause if you did—"

"Yes, I know, you'll bury me under your ginormous breasts."

"Boobs to you, lady."

"Don't call me lady! Bitch I can take, lady, never."

We both cracked up.

"Is that a yes? You did suggest it or not?"

"Nope, it must have been his bright idea. Let's!"

"Pass. Maybe Wednesday though."

I spent the rest of the day editing my story repeatedly in an attempt to get it up to par. The dinner shift at The Chart House went relatively smoothly and after a shower, I crashed for the night.

CHAPTER FOUR

Do I Wanna Know?

by Arctic Monkeys

U nlike most people who dreaded the first official day of the workweek, I loved Mondays. I typically had the whole day off from work and took in a step aerobics class or two. I, unfortunately, had to pass because I usually wore two sports bras to hold me in tightly, one on top of the other. My new tattoo made that impossible. It was starting to itch, which I took as a good sign.

I printed out the first chapter from my book, *Soul Adjacent*, and left it on the table, still undecided if I could summon the courage to share it.

A text buzzed my phone, and I woke up the screen.

> **Bond:** They called me to come in to the club tonight. I don't have to stay late. Can you meet me there?
> **Me:** What time?
> **Bond:** 9:30?
> **Me:** k. See you then.
> **Bond:** Blue?
> **Me:** Yes?
> **Bond:** I'm looking forward to it.
> **Me:** Me, not so much. :P
> **Bond:** Your ass will pay for that.
> **Me:** Promises, promises.
> **Bond:** Itchy palm = a painful, red ass.

Me: See you soon. :*

Later that night, after showering and applying light makeup, I slipped into a blue printed handkerchief dress. The front didn't dip too low and the back crisscrossed, leaving my tattoo uncovered. I loved the drape on the bias, and it matched perfectly with my strappy navy heels.

Once at the CroBar, the loud music assaulted my ears as I pulled on the heavy black door. A few patrons sat, tossing back their drinks. I found a stool at the corner of the bar closest to the deejay booth and lay my small handbag on the counter. I ordered an iced margarita and then strolled over to Bond.

"Look at you," he said, trailing his finger down the V in my dress. "I thought you don't like to wear anything that shows cleavage."

"Too much cleavage, and look," I said, spinning around so he could see my tattoo.

Bond whistled. "It's awesome. Hang on a sec." He leaned over, blended the next song in, and stood back up. Arctic Monkeys' *Do I Wanna Know?* began thumping out of the huge black speakers. "The tat's better than I imagined."

"Yeah, me too."

"I shouldn't be surprised. Cat's the best. Damn, you look sexy tonight." He pulled me in close and kissed me.

His behavior took me by surprise and once he let me go, I scanned the place behind me to see if anyone was watching.

"Jacqs isn't here," he whispered into my ear, causing me to shiver.

I let out a slow breath and lowered my shoulders.

He kissed me again, passionately, pulling me tightly against him. His hands migrated to my ass and he grunted.

My thong underwear left my globes uncovered for grabbing and he noticed. "Clint better get his ass here soon and let me out of this booth," he grumbled.

I laughed and floated back over to the bar. Bond and I were like puzzle pieces that almost fit together but not quite. With him, my self-esteem floated high one minute and then plummeted the next. When I had to witness him with Jacqs, the way he looked at her, my heart crumpled a bit. I took a sip of my margarita, trying to focus on the positive, when a woman sat down next to me.

"Now I know," she huffed.

Shifting to face her, I took in the gorgeous blonde-haired woman next to me. Long, flowing, wavy hair, bright green eyes assessing me, straight white teeth biting her lower lip.

"Were you talking to me?"

"Rory," she said, holding out her hand.

Are we on an interview?

She straightened her shoulders as I had seen Jacqs do on a number of occasions when she became nervous. "And yes," Rory continued. "I was talking to you. You're Bond's girlfriend, and I've been wondering why I haven't been able to get him to ... notice..." She cleared her throat. "Ask me out, and now I know."

"Contrary to appearances, I'm not the obstacle." I removed the thin red straw from my cocktail and took a drink, tasting the salty rim.

"Come again?" She held her palm out to stop me from responding and leaned forward. "Hey Frank, can we get two more margaritas over here when you get the chance?" Frank waved from across the bar and Rory settled back into her seat. "So..."

Somehow, I knew she was asking for my name. "Judy."

"So, Judy, did I not just see Bond aggressively necking with you?"

Necking? "Yes, well, it's complicated. And as I said, I'm not the competition. I'm the filler."

"Oh? I think I see. It's the little one then? That's a relief."

"Excuse me?"

"Don't get yourself in a huff," she said, patting my thigh. "It was a compliment. You are ... well ... every man's dream. I'm not into women, but for you, I might even change my mind. I don't mind sharing." She winked.

I rolled my eyes and shook my head. *Is she coming on to me?* "Compliment or not, you're up against love and it doesn't matter, in that case, what she looks like. Besides, Jacqs is a beauty inside and out."

"I wouldn't expect anything less from Bond. Why not just become a threesome?"

I burst out laughing, wishing Cat or Lainie were there with me. They would completely appreciate the crazy conversation, not that they knew about Bond and me. I wasn't about to tell this new woman Bond's personal business or mention that a threesome already existed, only I wasn't part of it.

Red, Jacqs, and Bond seemed to be making it work. How much longer it would last, was anyone's guess, and we were all wondering.

"Sorry," I snorted, struggling to get my outburst under control.

Frank kindly distracted us when he placed our drinks in front of us.

"Okay, so the threesome is out," Rory said. "Why be second best?"

Ouch! Just take a sword and plunge right in, woman whom I don't know at all. "A better question would be why are you stalking a man who clearly has his hands full?"

"If I told you, you'd just laugh." Her bravado failed momentarily, and I saw behind the mask of confidence. I recognized a kindred spirit. We, all of us, are desperate to be loved and to find our own safe place to land. As my life sped by, that eventuality seemed less likely and sometimes it pulled me so far down, like the gravity keeping us glued to this planet. I felt sorry for her. "I won't laugh," I promised.

"He's my soulmate. He's just too distracted to recognize me."

"What makes you think that?"

"It's not a thinking, it's a knowing. I felt it the day I started working here."

"You work here? I didn't realize."

"It's a part-time gig and I'm off tonight. I'm a kindergarten teacher during the day and I love it, but it doesn't pay much. Thanks for not laughing. My older sister thinks I'm a silly girl that needs to grow up and is constantly trying to set me up with stiffs from her law firm. I couldn't be further from their type. I'm not motivated by money and I have tattoos."

"I just got one," I said, turning my shoulder to show her.

"Wow. I mean, that's incredible. The colors are so bright and it feels like the dragonfly is in flight. You must give me his card."

I opened my small purse and found one. "Her. Here you go."

"Awesome! I now know who I'm using for my next tattoo." After she drank some of her margarita, she asked, "Any advice for me?"

"You're asking me to help you get Bond?"

"Well ... I ... I don't know what more I can do. I don't want to make a nuisance of myself, but I can't give up."

"You're clearly asking the wrong person. As I've been told on numerous occasions, timing is everything. Seems to me you need to be patient."

"I'm not a patient person."

"Well then, I've got nothing." I waved to Frank.

"What can I do for you, beautiful?" Frank asked.

"Dos Equis for Bond and the tab, thanks."

"Don't let me run you off," Rory said with her shoulders down and her bottom lip in a pout.

"It's not that I lack empathy for your situation, it's just that I can't help you and honestly, if I could, I probably wouldn't."

"Yeah, I get that." She sighed heavily and finished off her drink. "Don't leave. I'm taking off anyway."

"Hey girls," Bond said, coming up behind us and startling us both.

I tilted my head up and Bond kissed my temple. "I ordered you a beer."

"Let's take it to go. Frank?"

Frank held up the bottle.

"Don't open it."

"Gotcha," he said as he approached with the beer and the bill.

"Put that on my tab," Bond said. "Rory's too." He gave her a wink.

I saw her face brighten, and I wanted to smack Bond. Men could be so dumb!

"Later," he said to her and pulled me along with him. I looked back at Rory and shrugged.

Once upstairs, I stomped. "What the hell?"

"What the hell what?" he said calmly, walking into the kitchen and opening his beer.

"You've never been openly affectionate to me at the

club and dude, you're fucking blind."

"Not my best choice but Blue, have you looked at yourself in the mirror? I couldn't help myself. And blind?"

"Rory. Leave that girl alone," I shouted over the music pounding through the floor of the apartment.

"She's a sweet kid and works hard." He shook his head. "I don't see the issue."

"Blind and dumb."

"The point?"

"Never mind. You'll sort it out eventually. So you like the tattoo?"

"Almost as much as I like seeing you in this dress." He placed the beer down on the kitchen counter and pulled me toward him. Against my neck he said, "Very naughty to wear a thong under it." He cupped my ass in his hands, gathering the material up in his palms, until I felt the heat from his fingers.

I groaned from his touch and the warmth of his breath against my neck.

Bond kissed his way up to my mouth, swallowing the sound. His hands and his lips worked to make my panties damp. "How's your shoulder feeling?"

"My shoulder?" I said, leaning flush against him.

"The tattoo?"

I laughed. "Tight and itchy."

"No bondage tonight then," he decided as he pulled down my thong. "But I do owe you a spanking for teasing me so mercilessly. My cock has been rock hard since you walked into the club."

I reached between us and rubbed over his zipper. The head of his cock poked out the top of his jeans. "He's very hard," I concurred. "Shall we free him?"

"Soon." He spun me around and pushed my upper

body over the kitchen counter, my ass exposed to the cool, air-conditioned room, the skirt of the dress draped at my waist. His warm palm caressed over my ample bottom, starting at my hips, and kneading his way to the crevice between my globes. His fingers spread my buttocks wide and then massaged them back together. "You've been a very bad girl," he grunted as his hand spanked my ass for the first time that night.

The heat from his strike spread out from my ass, migrating to my nipples and pussy. He didn't allow me to wallow in the sensation too long before the next spank landed on the other side. Bond didn't dick around with a light punishment. No, he used plenty of force, allowing me to get lost in the pain and titillation. After thoroughly reddening my ass, at the edge of my tolerance, he lifted me up onto the kitchen counter and spread my thighs wide.

"Sopping wet and sticking out," he said as he rolled my bulbous clit between his fingers. "Pull down the top of your dress and take off your bra. I'll be right back."

I did as directed, wondering what he went off to get. When he returned, he held a chain with loops on either end. He twisted and pulled on my right nipple and then lassoed it, pulling the loop very tight. My left nipple received the same treatment. The chain hung between my breasts. "My alligator clips are too small for your big nipples, but this works great. You would look so good in my album."

"Never happening," I said, raising an eyebrow and laughing.

"So sexy, I had to try." He tugged the chain, causing me to groan. As he nipped his way up my right thigh, I yelped over the duel sensations. The tip of his tongue finally flicked across my clit, while his left hand wrapped around the back of my upper leg, and his right held the chain taut, forcing my nipples down.

My body shook as he took my swollen nub into his mouth and sucked as his tongue danced around my entrance. He paused and I moaned from the loss of the heat of his mouth.

"Lean back against the cabinets and bring your pussy right to the edge, legs spread wide."

I shifted my hips forward and placed my feet on either side of me, spreading my legs as wide as possible.

"So fucking sexy, Blue." He spread my wetness from my pussy onto my ass and spit to add more lubrication. Just before dipping his head back down, he said, "Take care of those nipples for me." His mouth lowered as his finger penetrated my ass.

"It's going to get wet," I cried, rolling my blood-filled peaks between my fingers.

His mouth and hands knew what to do to prolong the climb and intensify the release. He swirled his tongue around the folds of my pussy, finally centering on my clit. He licked it soft and slow as he worked a second finger into my ass. Then he increased the pressure of his tongue and the propulsion of his fingers.

"Oh, holy hell, Bond, I can't hold it..." A geyser erupted out of me as my orgasm rapidly fired. My heart pounded as light shot from behind my eyes. I struggled to stay on the counter, my legs dropping over the side.

Bond scooped me up and easily carried me into his bedroom. He stripped and lay on his back on the center of the bed, beckoning me with his hand. As I pulled the dress over my head and stumbled on weak knees, he rolled a condom onto his shaft. I climbed on top, straddling his firm cock. He guided me down, and set the pace with his hands, fingers digging into my hips.

I played with the chain between my nipples, staring

straight down at his grinning mouth. He took my right hand and placed it over my pussy. He tugged the chain as I leaned back on my left hand, circling my hips in time with my fingers on my clit.

"So damn sexy, Blue. Give it to me. I want you to cum again for me."

The closer I came to the tipoff, my eyes lost focus and rolled up into my head. I could still see Bond's sexy smile and his ultimate acceptance, even with my lids shut tight. Just as the orgasm swam over me, I opened my eyes and hooked Bond's gaze. "For you, now!"

"Give it to me," he said, taking control of the pace again, roaring his release, just chasing after mine.

I collapsed over his chest, both of us breathing heavily.

Bond then shifted to the side, removed the condom and tossed it in the trash. He situated me back on top of him, running his fingers down my spine. "Damn, that was good. You seemed more open tonight."

"Did I?" I said, snuggling in close, my head on his chest. "I wanted to ask you something."

"Okay." He wrapped his arms around me.

I inclined my head to watch his reaction. "Are you okay with me inviting someone to our get-together on Wednesday?"

"Male or female?"

I shoved his shoulder. Then I crossed my hands over his chest and rested my chin. "It's a man that Cat tattoos. He's a big, hulking Native American, large like Red. Bigger I think. Cat thinks he and I should be friends."

"What do you think?"

"He seems very ... I don't know ... closed off. Maybe that's just with me."

"You like him," Bond stated, sitting up and situating

me on his lap.

"I don't know him at all. He fires off all my warning alarms. Big, confident, distant. The more I talk about it, the less I understand why I'm even considering it."

"Invite him."

"Did you not hear what I just said?" I asked, crawling off his lap and crossing my legs.

"Blue, I want you to be happy."

"You aren't listening, Bond. Besides, he isn't open to anything more than friendship anyway. This guy isn't potential."

"I am listening, beyond your words. You can't use this, us, to keep you back."

I slapped my thighs with my palms. "Back from what? Never mind. Why are men so fucking frustrating? I think he is only doing it because Cat put him up to it."

"Invite him. I want to meet him."

"I'm going to go," I chuffed, moving to get off the bed.

"Don't be mad at me," he pleaded, grabbing my arm.

"Do you know how often you say that to me? Would it be so much to ask that you be a little jealous instead of pushing me on someone who doesn't even want me?"

"He wants you. He might not want to want you, but make no mistake, he ... wants ... *you*."

"You don't know what the fuck you're talking about." I threw his hand off me but didn't move to leave.

"I know our situation isn't easy on you. I live it daily with Red and Jacqs. I get it."

"You don't have to hide it."

"That's true." He stroked my cheek. "I love you, Blue. You know that and ... you also know we're temporary. You help me survive my crazy threesome situation, and I keep you from being sexually starved and lonely. Maybe I'll be jealous when I meet him."

"Yeah, right. I know you're right but... Forget it."

"What are you going to do?"

"Invite him on the very off chance that it pisses you off!"

"Very funny. Come here." He scooped me back up in his arms and rocked me back and forth, his warm breath against my cheek.

We gently kissed for a while and then I got up to leave.

"I'm going to head home. I want to do some writing before work tomorrow, which is a double shift. See you on Wednesday."

Bond walked me out and hugged me by the door. "See you Wednesday."

Melancholy followed me to my car. I didn't think it would be the last time Bond and I would spend intimate time together but for some reason, the end felt much closer. Tears struggled for their release as I fought with the driver's side door to get in.

CHAPTER FIVE

Waves

by Mr. Probz

No writing happened before work. I did get one thing off my list though: texting Tate. I rewrote the text several times before settling on:

> **Me:** We're all gathering at Red's at 7 p.m. tomorrow night. I'll send the exact address soon (don't know it off the top of my head).
> **Tate:** What should I bring?
> **Me:** They usually have beer and hard lemonade or cider to drink. If you like a particular kind of beer, you can bring that or a snack.
> **Tate:** Okay. See you then.

Then I texted Cat.

> **Me:** I invited him. Would you mind sending him Red's street address? I don't know it off hand.
> **Catherine:** Consider it done. Lainie will be so excited.

When I texted back, I pulled Lainie into the conversation.

> **Me:** You told Lainie?
> **Lainie:** I'm assuming you mean about Tate. Yes, everyone knows.

Me: Jesus Christ, people. Do not embarrass me. This is not a date!

Lainie: Of course, I won't.

Catherine: But I might.

Me: Death by boobs, coming your way, Cat.

Catherine: Good thing I have nine lives.

Lainie: Lucky for you. Don't worry, Blue, I'll make her behave.

Me: Is Stay coming?

Lainie: All the usual suspects plan to be there.

Me: Great...

Lainie: It'll be fine.

Me: Especially if I don't show.

Catherine: Don't even think about it.

Me: I'm off to work. See you bitches later.

Catherine: Later.

Lainie: Later.

On Tuesday, The Chart House wasn't its usually bustling self for lunch. The stormy weather seemed to keep the regular customers away. Fortunately, the skies cleared by dinnertime and I did okay overall. A coworker asked me to cover her dinner shift for Wednesday night, and I almost said yes. However, something, or more like someone, kept me from taking her shift.

By the end of lunch on Wednesday, a firm knot had formed in my gut. I decided to strap my breasts down as well as I could manage and take a late afternoon step aerobics class.

My elevated heart rate, along with the good sweat, helped me garner some control over my emotions. *He's just a man. One I don't particularly know or like. My friends will be around, and who cares what he thinks. I don't have to share my writing if I don't want to. He's nobody to me.*

Once home and showered, I couldn't decide what I wanted to wear. No makeup for sure. Back and forth I shifted hangers, hoping something would jump out at me. We would probably sit outside part of the time, and it was warm as hell. I decided to dress as I normally would. I threw on a pair of short black shorts, a tight, white sports bra with a loose-fitting, pink tank top that mostly covered the shorts.

I debated whether it would be better to get there early, before him or after. After won out. At about 7:15 p.m., I slipped into my black flip-flops, grabbed my cell phone, the chapter from my novel, a bag of Kettle chips, and my driver's license.

When I arrived at Red's, I spotted a red Harley parked on the side of the road, the chrome engine sparkling clean. I parked away from the bike and left my driver's license and the pages in the car.

Red's cream-colored home with multiple arching windows and a red, barrel tile roof had a long circular drive and tall palms out front.

Just before entering, I berated myself for making the occasion more important than it should be. I struggled to shrug off my judgment of myself. *I trust myself. I'm safe and sound. I trust myself. I'm safe and sound.* "Okay, let's get this over with," I said aloud to myself and then turned the door handle.

I opened Red's door and passed through the front sitting room. The hardwood floors shined as I strolled through the wide doors, under the high ceilings, and made my way to the kitchen. *Why didn't I bring a bottle of tequila?* I thought. I really could've used a shot.

The large, open space had a counter that ran from the opening to the back wall, cabinets above and below. The sink faced an outside window, the refrigerator situated between the dishwasher and the stove. Next to the swinging door that led to the dining room was a walk-in pantry with an extra freezer.

I rummaged in an underneath cabinet for a bowl. Finding one, I poured the chips into it and set it on the counter. When I looked up, I saw that most of the gang sat outside around the pool. Samantha and Tate chatted on the inside couch, facing the back of the house.

See, he can smile, just apparently not with me.

Samantha and I physically had nothing in common. She had a slight frame, long legs, flowy, white-blonde hair, and blue-green eyes like her sister, Jacqs, all which made her look younger than her twenty-five years.

I observed Tate laughing at something Sam said and then he caught me watching him. I quickly turned away and made a beeline to the fridge, my back facing them.

"I wondered if you'd show," he mused, standing way too close.

My adrenaline fired as I spun around, still holding onto the refrigerator door. He appeared to have made more of an effort in dressing. His loose-fit, dark-blue jeans looked new and his pale-green dress shirt looked pressed. He checked me out as I scanned his appearance.

"Are there shorts under there?" he asked, lifting the hem of my tank, grazing my thigh with his fingertip. His touch singed my skin, and my wayward nipples jumped to attention.

Our eyes locked, and I could have sworn a brief smile flirted on his lips. Was he playing with me? "What do you want?" I asked.

"What do you mean?" His eyebrows drew together in a look of confusion.

Finally! I had knocked him off his game. "A drink?"

"I'm good," he said, holding up his beer.

I grabbed a hard apple cider and popped the top off with the church key hanging from a magnet on the fridge. "Have you met everyone?"

Our eyes connected once again.

"Yes. Cat did the introductions." His stare bore into me. This man didn't just look at me, he infiltrated me and I didn't like it, but neither would I back down.

"Great," I said as I glowered back at him.

"Who is Bond to you?" he asked, leaning against the counter near the sink.

"How do you mean?" I mirrored his posture.

"He seemed to grill me the most."

I did my damnedest to suppress a smile. "Does that mean you've been grilled by everyone?"

"You didn't answer my question. Everyone but Sam."

"Bond is the one who brought most of us together. He thinks it's his job to look after the group." I took a sip from my cider and slowly set it on the counter, all the while maintaining our eye lock.

"Again, no answer. Clearly, more than you want to let on." He stood up straight and took a swallow of his beer.

"What makes you think Bond's grilling has anything at all to do with me? We're all friends and have been for a long time."

"He asked about my intentions." He dipped his head, his long hair falling forward, and yet his eyes remained glued to mine.

"I'll kill him." I shook my head. "I told him there was

no potential between us."

He raised his right eyebrow. "You and Bond?"

"Oh my god, no. You and me."

"I see."

"Is it always going to be this way?" I blurted out.

"What way?"

"Difficult. What is it about me? I saw you with Sam. You smiled and actually laughed. With me, you just have this pinched, gruff expression, like I stepped on your insole."

Then he laughed and I knew he was laughing at me.

Great!

He continued his relentless stare. Just as soon as his laughter subsided, the groove right above his nose returned, as did the downturn of his lips.

"What!"

"Later." He finally looked away and for a moment, I felt vindicated until I realized that Bond and Red stood next to me.

"Coming outside?" Bond asked as he retrieved two beers and a cider from the fridge. He placed the drinks on the counter and swept me up in a hug. "Not sure about him," he whispered into my ear as he placed me back down.

Glancing up, I saw a new expression on Tate's face, this one more confusing than the rest. At a loss, I turned to Red who hugged me as well. "Jacqs is dying to talk to you."

Taking my cue, I grabbed my bottle of cider and headed toward the French doors, having to pass closely by Tate to get out. He touched my waist and in that moment, I knew he felt it too. Enough space existed between us. He did it on purpose. Before the night was out, I planned to confront his bullshit.

Out back, I took a deep breath, allowing the warm wind to flow through my hair. Finally relaxed again, it wasn't hard to see that Tate turned me into a stress ball, the exact opposite of what I was looking for. It was time for Tate to find another place to land. Fortunately, Bond seemed to be on the same page.

Before I had a chance to greet everyone, Jacqs grabbed my hand and pulled me over to the swinging loveseat. "Tell me everything!" she said, rubbing her hands together.

"There isn't anything to tell. This was all Cat's doing. He isn't looking for a relationship, and he isn't even remotely my type."

"What?" she practically yelled, throwing her hands up. "That man is undeniably hot and intelligent. What the hell is wrong with him?"

"I seem to put him on edge, and not in a good way. Don't you find him standoffish and aloof?"

"No, not at all. He seemed really friendly up until the time Bond drilled him with questions."

"Well, he is with me. Don't get attached, I have no plans of inviting him again."

Jacqs lowered her shoulders. "I had such high hopes. Oh well. Sorry, Blue."

"No worries at all. Men and me, we've got issues."

Jacqs laughed. "Nah, you just need to find the right one ... or two."

"You're a right comedian, you are. One would be nice, but at some point I just have to be realistic." I leaned back, watching Tate join our friends by the pool as the swing rocked.

"That's a load of crap. You're still plenty young. It's not like the 1800s where you would be considered a spinster."

"If you're trying to make me feel better—" I kicked the ground so we continued to sway.

"Me, I'd be considered a whore or a courtesan."

Tate glanced back at me just as Lainie crossed between us, heading our way.

"I think it's time to give your historical romances a rest," I said to Jacqs.

"Maybe, but I'm not giving up hope for you!"

"Carry on, if you must, but keep it quiet." I stood up and gave Lainie a hug.

As statuesque as ever, Lainie towered over us both. She had taken to wearing her sandy-brown hair wavy. Finding love with Stayman had certainly softened her demeanor. She seemed happy. It was hard for me not to be envious.

Jacqs headed back to the group.

"It's nothing," I said to Lainie.

"The way he watches you? I'd say it's something."

"It might be something, but nothing that would lean toward a good outcome."

"I'll take your word for it. Stayman invited him over to our place. I assumed you would be coming too."

"You know what they say about assumptions..."

"Gotcha." She took the empty bottle from my hand and asked, "Another?"

"Yes, thanks." I took a deep breath and strolled over to the pool.

Before I had a chance to sit, Cat said, "Tate would like to see Adjustable Bend, and I told him you'd take him out to the dock."

"You mean down that very well-lit path?" I asked, pointing. "Only if you promise to cut it out."

She flashed me the three-finger Girl Scout salute.

"Come." I waved Tate after me. At least I might get some answers. After a few steps away from the group, I said, "All her, right?"

"No, I asked to see the yacht, but I assumed Red would show me."

I stopped walking. "Let me go get him then. He knows

all the specs and stuff."

Tate didn't say anything and neither did he move. He just stared.

"Fine!" I uttered, walking on without him.

He quickly caught up.

"Why are you here?" I asked, stopping on the dock in front of Adjustable Bend.

"You invited me."

"Why are you different with me?"

"I don't want to want you."

"Then don't. It seems simple enough." I talked as if unaffected but was really shaking and hoped he couldn't tell in the dim light. I felt stupidly desperate for his touch.

He stepped closer to me, and I didn't move. With his fingers, he brushed my auburn hair off my shoulder so it lay down my back. For once, he didn't look at me and yet, I stared at his face. His lips parted slightly and his eyes darted around, finally alighting on my face. "Your upper lip is much smaller than your lower," he whispered, tracing my lips with his finger.

I wanted him to let me in, but the idea scared the shit out of me too. Just this little bit of attention was too much. Too acute, too angst-filled with regret and yet, nothing had happened so far.

The sexual tension reached a fever pitch, leaving me barely able to breathe and then he stole my breath with a kiss. His hands clutched my upper arms, pulling me tightly against him, while his tongue breached my lips. His taste liquefied me, my body pooling against his, melting to the hard planes of his torso. Then he stopped, holding me away from him, his heat vanishing as quickly as it had arrived.

"Shit," he muttered.

"You're good at wooing the ladies, I can tell. A real charmer." I shook out of his grip and climbed aboard the yacht, going down the steps to the belly of the ship. At the table, I sat down, watching Tate maneuver down the steps. Before he had a chance to say anything, I said, "I don't do well with ambiguity and you're clearly confused."

He paced the few steps away from me and then back again. "I don't do love or romance or relationships."

"Again, why are you here and don't give me the bullshit that I invited you."

"I want you," he confessed and for a second, I got a glimpse behind the veil.

"You mean you want to fuck me and yet, it's not about my small waist or my gargantuan boobs?"

The door on his emotions quickly shut. Stoically he said, "They aren't a deterrent but no, it's not— I felt you the moment I stepped into Babes in Tattooland, before I ever laid eyes on you."

"And?"

"I don't want emotional entanglement."

"Are you married?"

"No."

"Divorced?"

"Yes, but that's not open for discussion."

"Kids?"

"Also, not up for discussion."

"Got it. It's time for you to leave. You've invaded my sacred space with my friends, and I can't let you have it. They're all I've got."

"You're already involved anyway. How do the rest of them not know?"

"How do you know?"

"Bond didn't act like a friend but a protective lover. I was here long enough to get the gist of the dynamics. Jacqs is with Red and Bond. Maybe more Red than Bond. Kevin and Cat are like an old married couple. He's far more in love with her than she is with him, and Stay and Lainie are still in the honeymoon phase. Other than Sam, you are the only one not exactly coupled, if I'm correct. Bond's the only one who didn't take to me. Why do you think that is?"

"Not the only one."

"Fair enough."

"Maybe he can tell that you'll eat me up and spit me out. If you think it's jealousy, you're wrong. We love each other, but not like that. At least, he doesn't. If strictly sex is what you're after, I'm a master at it. However, I highly doubt we'd be compatible in that arena."

"Based on what?" He looked flabbergasted for three beats until he garnered control of his emotions again, like a steel door lowering over his features.

"Let's just say my needs aren't run of the mill."

He grunted and adjusted himself in his pants. "Neither are mine."

I caught a glimpse of why he might wear his pants baggy and it ran down his thigh. *Holy fuck! Maybe just once?* When I looked up, he had resumed his implacable stare.

"Walk me out?"

"Okay."

He went up first and held his hand out to help me back onto the dock.

I waited while he said his goodbyes. I told Jacqs I would be taking off as well. Red welcomed him back anytime, and Stay said he would be in touch.

Once outside, I said, "I thought you told me you don't ride much."

"I was in the mood. Did you bring me some of your writing?"

"I did, but I don't see how that matters now."

"It matters. I'll walk you to your car."

I shrugged my shoulders and led the way. Of course, the driver's side door gave me fits.

"Move," he said and jerked the door open. "I have friends that can fix that for you."

"It costs money, which I'd rather not spend."

"So what do you do? Climb in through the passenger side?"

"Sometimes."

"Do you know how exasperating you are?" He didn't let me answer. Before I knew what happened, he'd sandwiched me between him and the side of my car. He pressed his cock against my mound, grinding it as he captured my mouth. Tasting him again, I lost all common sense. His tongue dipped into my mouth, exploring and tangling with mine. I wanted him in the worst possible way, willing to sacrifice my sense of self-preservation and self-worth.

"Follow me home," I breathed against his lips.

"I can't promise—"

"No promises. Wait, what are you doing?" I asked as he climbed into my car and set the pages and my license on the dashboard.

He took my hand and lay it against his thigh. "I can't ride like this. Give me a few minutes."

"Holy hell. Okay." I took a couple of deep breaths and stared straight ahead, moving my hand to the steering wheel.

"Okay," he said as he got out of my car. He leaned back in. "Do you have condoms?"

I shook my head, no.

"Drug store on the way? I'll follow you." He grabbed the chapter off the dash, tossed my license back on the seat, and closed the passenger door.

CHAPTER SIX

Broken

by Lauren Hoffman

"**W**hat the fuck are you doing?" I said to myself in the rearview mirror. "Only the dumbest thing possible, I'm sure," I responded. Never one for a one-night stand, it seemed I was heading toward my very first.

Odd that he didn't have a condom.

The loud engine of his motorcycle, revving beside me, garnered my attention. Damn, he looked hot as hell on his bike, even with a helmet on.

I drove down the road with Tate following behind, my body and mind arguing the entire time.

It's just a fuck. We can do this.

It's hard enough on you with Bond. Don't be an idiot.

I'm not being an idiot. If anything, I'm being a horny woman.

At least Bond cares about you. This guy is emotionally constipated with some real issues. You're being reckless.

It's one night.

Your place is a mess. You're letting his big cock scramble your head.

Shut up!

I slammed my palm against the steering wheel as I turned into Walgreens, determined to go through with it. Consequences be damned. It wasn't like I liked the guy or my emotions were even in the mix. His cock seemed impressive, and I did want to see if he was a show-er or a grow-er, but that wasn't why I was willing to risk my self-esteem in the balance.

His touch, his mere presence, sent all my wiring into a fit. No man had ever affected me in that way. Not even Bond. I wanted him in the worst possible way, and it seemed mutual.

Tate strolled out of the drug store with a brown paper bag and a six-pack of something. Placing both in his leather saddlebag, he then swung his leg over his bike and replaced his helmet. He nodded in my direction, his expression as serious as ever. Was he going to the dentist or to a fuck?

Don't, I said to myself. Instead of analyzing every moment leading up to the present, I turned up my stereo to drown out my thoughts. I belted out *Spectrum* with Florence, keeping time on the steering wheel. Flipping on the right turn signal, I turned into my apartment complex and parked in my designated spot as Tate settled his Harley by the side of the cinderblock building.

He followed me up the stairs to the third floor and invaded my apartment the moment he stepped through the threshold. "You live alone?"

"Yes," I said, kicking off my flip-flops.

He scanned the small space, settling the bag and six-pack on the kitchen table.

My nerves flared out of control. I couldn't figure out what to do with my hands, and all I could see was the dust lining the framed artwork and the small statues on the shelf. "Cayman Jack? You like margaritas?" I asked, noticing what he bought.

"Cat said it was your favorite drink."

I narrowed my eyes and scrunched my nose. *He bothered to find that out?* In the kitchen, I found the church key and opened two bottles. After handing him one, we clinked the glass, and took a drink.

His penetrating stare lassoed mine, and I held my own. At least my hands now had something to do. I rolled the bottle between my palms and then laughed. He looked so damn serious.

"Is this painful for you?" I asked.

"No questions." He took the bottle from my hands and placed it on the table. Behind me, he moved my hair away from my neck, causing chills to cascade down my spine. Just his touch mixed pleasure with pain as if his stern nature scratched at my soul as he awakened the rest of my body. His masculine scent filled my senses. He bit down where my neck met my shoulder, causing me to groan. He wove his hand into my hair, spiraling it around his forearm, gathering it into his fist. He exposed the front of my throat for his mouth, devouring each spot with his lips and teeth, marking me.

Trembling, I struggled to steady my pulse and remain standing. My knees turned into weak little ninnies.

Grabbing the hem, he pulled my pink tank top over my head and reached behind me to unhook the industrial sports bra I wore.

"Leave it," I said, covering my chest, more especially my hard, straining nipples.

He glared down at me with his dark mahogany eyes.

"They're too much." I shook my head.

"Let me be the judge."

Giving in, I lifted my arms so he could pull off my bra. "Be careful of my tattoo."

Gently, he slipped off the garment as his eyes left mine to take in my mammoth boobs. "Stunning," he whispered, the crevice in the middle of his forehead as deep as ever.

Then his hands explored my naked back and pendulum breasts, and I let him. Everywhere he touched, the heat of his caress lingered. His gaze held me captive, dissolving my will and restraint. With my nipples clasped between his fingers, he pinched and tugged. "I want to hurt you," he grunted.

"Ohhh. You will soon enough ... I imagine." Maybe his comment should have scared me, but it didn't. Instead, my hands managed to find a use. First, they became lost in his rich, brown hair, then progressed to his broad shoulders, and finally lit on the buttons of his pale-green shirt. His smooth, coppery skin and ripped stomach made me moan. After freeing the last button, my hands ran down his chest, brushing his nipples along the way. They followed the trail of hair and sexy V disappearing into his jeans. My fingers traced the bulge down his thigh.

He grabbed my wrist and groaned. "Not yet." He scooped me up and kicked open the bedroom door, settling me at the end of the bed.

"I don't do missionary."

"Why?"

"No questions."

He nodded. "Let's see the rest of this playground," he said, contending with the button on my shorts. I lifted my hips so he could remove them, and off came my panties as well. He pulled me to my feet, his hands invading every bit of my skin with the warmth of his big palms and soft lips. He nibbled up my neck until he mauled my mouth with his fierce kiss, pushing me back onto the bed.

His body came down on top of me, and I immediately struggled to get out from under him, punching his chest with my fists. He got the message and flipped me on top of him.

Beyond my control, my eyes filled with tears and I gasped. I buried my face against his shoulder so he wouldn't see. Between my naked thighs, I unbuttoned his jeans, determined to get his cock inside me as fast as possible. He grabbed both wrists to stop me.

"What?" I called out.

"You're crying."

"Reflex reaction. I told you, no missionary."

"I can do gentle."

"Jesus, Tate, if I wanted gentle, you wouldn't be here."

"Do you do missionary with Bond?"

"What happened to no questions?"

"Just answer this one."

"Okay, but then you'll owe me one."

I could see him thinking, searching for a way out of it. Maybe he decided it wouldn't matter, since we never planned to see each other again. "Okay," he finally said.

"No, not with Bond, not with anyone."

"Just to be clear, is it any position where I'm over the top of you?"

"No. Just full body weight on the front of me."

He flipped me over onto my back and dragged me to the bottom of the bed, grinding his jean-clad cock against my already sopping pussy. "So I can lean over you like this, my body weight on my arms?"

"Yes, but I'm certain it will feel much better once you take those jeans off." I began unzipping them, but he stopped me again.

"How about like this?" He flipped me onto my stomach, raised my hips and covered my body fully with his. He swung his hips against me.

I reached back behind me and tugged at his pants.

As he bit my shoulder and chuckled, he moved his hips out of reach.

"Are you planning on hurting me in the form of

abstinence?" I groaned and turned back over, taking in his expression.

Then he really laughed and a fissure split open, allowing a quick blast of sunshine to escape the dark clouds. Just as quickly, the sun hid back out of sight. "It's been awhile."

Apparently, a bit of information escaped through the crack. "Laughing?"

"No. I don't think I'll be able to hold out very long."

I shrugged. "We'll just have to do it a few times then."

"Good thing I got the big box."

"Go get them and let me see your tattoo," I said with a chuckle of my own.

When he came back into the bedroom, I gaped. Sans jeans, his cock was more formidable than I imagined.

"Now I see how you will hurt me. I'm up for the challenge, or that is anyway."

He threw the twelve-pack of magnum condoms on the bed. Apparently, he also had high hopes for the night.

Mesmerized by his appendage, I stepped forward and touched him. It flinched and grew at the contact. Stepping around him, I took in the finished tattoo of the golden eagle across his back and down his left butt cheek and thigh. "Wow, it's remarkable. Does it hurt?"

"No, I'm a fast healer."

Walking back around, I noticed another tattoo under his right arm, but I couldn't make it out. "What's that?"

He just shook his head.

"Okay." In that moment, I assumed it had something to do with his ex. I glanced up at Tate while he looked down at me. "I know my question."

He appeared pained, but he nodded.

"How long has it been?"

He shrugged. "Over three years."

Over three years?

Over three years?

Over three years. Wow! I held out my arms to him.

He scooped me onto his lap as he sat on the edge of the bed. Holding either side of my face, he kissed me deeply, searching my mouth with his tongue. He swallowed my sigh, as I dissolved against him, his taste muddling my mind. His hands possessed me, touching my neck, shoulders, and then my back. Grasping my ass, he pulled my wetness against him, rubbing it along his shaft.

"Does this actually fit into anyone?" I whispered against his neck and pointed down.

The corners of his lips rose just slightly. "Yes, Blue." He had used my nickname, but I didn't correct him. From behind him, he retrieved a condom as I scooted down his legs so he could roll it on. Lifting me by my hips, he helped lower me down onto him as his eyes locked onto mine. "Take your time," he sighed.

"Good thing I'm wet."

"Very wet."

"Very wet, oh yeah," I groaned as I tried to force more of him into me.

"Wait."

I held off, our eyes remaining connected. He bit his lower lip in his struggle. "Okay," he muttered after a few moments. When I forced myself down on him, he thrust up to meet me, filling me more than I'd yet experienced. We rocked back and forth, the pain and pleasure of his size weaving a delicious concoction.

"Holy shit! Oh yeah, take me. Don't stop."

"I need a minute." He held me tightly against him, but I still tried to wiggle my hips. He lifted me off his cock and laid me on my back, my legs hanging off the end of the bed.

I covered my mound, knowing my clit must be sticking out.

On his knees, between my legs, he asked, "What are you doing?"

"My clit pokes out too much."

He pulled my hands away and held them at my sides, breathing across my clit. "Who gave you that idea? Bond?" he asked, the anger in his voice very evident.

"No. He would never."

Breaking eye contact, his mouth lapped at my wetness, exploring the valleys between my folds until he found my bulbous peak. "It's perfect," he murmured against my clit. "You're perfect."

I decided to store that compliment for later.

I'm perfect.

"Oh, that feels amazing," I cried.

"Tastes so good." He let go of my wrists and let his hands wander again, branding every surface of my skin: my breasts, nipples, stomach and finally, my pussy. He played with my labia, tugging my lips as his tongue danced against my arousal.

My back arched when he plunged two fingers into my entrance and increased the pressure on my clit. "Oh Tate, I'm close, please don't stop."

"No way," he mumbled.

With his free hand, he smoothed over my hip, pulling me tighter against his mouth. His large fingers plunged deep inside me while his warm, wet mouth flicked me over the edge.

"Unholy god, please, oh yesss. Now!" Unable to hold back, I gushed against his mouth. I could hear him gulping and laughing until my orgasm fired again, and all sensation ceased except for the rocket that tore through my body and set flight. I hovered outside of myself until his warm hands brought me back to my body.

"That was incredible. I've never been with a squirter before."

"I should have warned you. When I'm really turned on, I lose control over the waterworks."

"No apology necessary. Nor will I apologize for what I'm about to do." He turned me over and raised my ass into the air. I cried out when he plunged in deep, his chest hovering over my back. My right cheek lay against the mattress, my arms at my side, until he lifted them behind me and used them for leverage.

His fingers found my clit and applied pressure in time with his forceful incursion.

Sounds I didn't recognize spilled out of me as he grunted in time with his thrusts. I never wanted it to end. I could've stayed right there for millennia, shrouded in the energy and warmth of his body filling me to completion.

However, the thousand years abruptly ended once my orgasm took over, constricting around his large cock, firing pain and pleasure alternatively. My pulsing contractions brought off Tate, who grunted my name in my ear, his warm release trapped in the condom between us.

Neither of us moved right away, both of us breathing heavily. Eventually, he pulled out of me and left the room. When he returned, he had on his jeans and carried two margaritas.

"Thanks." I took a sip, wondering if he planned to leave already.

"I'm not done with you yet," he announced, his jaw firmly set.

"Did I say that out loud?"

"No. Your face is like a movie screen."

"That seems wholly unfair given nothing much plays on yours."

Deflecting my comment, he said, "Interesting Post-It notes on your mirror."

Fuck! I buried my head in my hands in mortification. How had I forgotten about that? "I don't have people over here often."

He tilted up my chin. "Other than Bond."

"Why do you care?"

"Call it curiosity. Why is it that everyone is privy to the fact that Bond and Red are both fucking Jacqs and yet no one knows about you and Bond? It makes no sense to me. Why would you put up with it?"

"For someone who doesn't want to share anything about his past, you sure are nosy."

"It's not the same."

"It's only not the same because it's about me instead of you."

He pushed me over and bit my butt.

"Ouch!" I giggled, covering my ass with my hand.

He bit the other side and then he took me completely by surprise. He poured some of the cold margarita on my lower back and the crevice of my ass and licked it off. "Your ass is incredible. I can't decide whether I like your breasts with your big nipples or your ass the best."

"Thank you," I said, rolling onto my back. I usually hated compliments about my body but coming from him, I ate them up like the best supper in the world.

"I have another question."

I rolled my eyes.

"Are you rolling your eyes at me?" He leaned over me and tickled my sides.

"Cut it out," I cried, laughing.

"Not a chance."

I kicked at him to get him to stop.

"Okay, okay," he said, raising his hands. "It's good to know you're ticklish." He winked at me.

He winked at me? I'm perfect, and he winked at me and he loves my ass. *Kill me with kindness, why don't you!*

"Your mind is doing cartwheels. Don't hurt yourself."

I sat up and stared him down, playing his own game. "A question for a question."

"Okay. Why not hook up with Red? Seems like a foursome would make the most sense."

"You're not going to let it rest. Fine! Red and I dated briefly years ago. We weren't compatible."

"Why?"

"That's two questions."

"Not really. I want to understand why you aren't involved with Red too."

"He didn't have patience for my insecurities and wasn't into inflicting pain other than a mild spanking." My face blushed. "I mean ... I'm not into any serious stuff but—"

"And Bond?"

"No, your turn. The tattoo. Let me see it. And tell me what it means."

He reluctantly raised his right arm and underneath, on his side, I saw a tattoo of a sailor passionately kissing a blonde 1950s woman.

Looking back into his eyes, I said, "It's beautiful. What does it mean?"

A dark cloud enshrouded his features, and I almost didn't want him to answer. He lifted his drink from the side of the bed and drained it. "My ex-wife and I wore those costumes to a Halloween party where I proposed."

Wow, how romantic! I thought, but kept it to myself.

My stomach clinched in response to the energy emanating from him. I needed to shift the mood. "Yes, to your question about Bond."

"I see. Well, no, I don't. Why are you selling yourself so short?"

"You don't know anything about it."

"It's plain to see. You're willing to subjugate your self-worth to be with Bond. Why would he even ask that of you?"

"You don't understand anything. Bond's the first man who took the time to know me beyond how I look. Our whole group is that way. They don't see a body, they see me. You have no idea what it's like. Is the situation ideal? No. When is it ever? Certainly not with your wife or you wouldn't be a judgmental, shut down, shell of a man. A hot man but—"

Fuck!

"I'm sorry. I shouldn't have said any of that."

His expression was unfathomable. I couldn't tell if he planned to throttle me, fuck me, or leave.

He sat on the end of the bed next to me, shifting me to straddle him again. He brushed my hair away from my face and then pillaged my mouth. It hurt, but I didn't want him to stop. I pushed myself against him, fighting with the button on his jeans. This time, he helped me remove them. He sheathed his hard cock with a condom, and I slid home once again.

We both groaned and smiled, our eye contact absolute. He held me so tightly, completely controlling the pace. "Can you cum this way?" he asked, pausing.

I shook my head. "It feels amazing, but I need my clit to be in play."

He stood, carrying me with him, my legs wrapped around his waist. He set me on the edge of the kitchen table. "Lie back." After I did, he maneuvered my legs against his shoulders and pushed in farther.

"Oh god, that's deeper," I moaned.

The fingers of his left hand found my clit and rolled around the protruding bud. His right held me at the edge of the table so he could continue his invasive penetration.

"You clearly ... haven't forgotten ... what to do," I mumbled.

He bestowed upon me a rare, full smile. "I feel inspired."

He's inspired!

The way he rocked his hips and slammed into me, all the while manipulating my clit, had me grunting animalistic utterances.

"Tate?"

"Yeah, baby?"

"Oh ... I'm going to cum again, hard. Ohhh, so hard. Holy fuck, I'm cumming!" I struggled to keep my eyes open, wanting to see him see me. "Ahhh," I yelled, once the last and strongest contraction pulled at my core. My eyes closed of their own accord.

Tate paused in his onslaught on my pussy, allowing me to catch my breath, his hands floating over my breasts, stomach, and thighs. Then he started again and plunged in so hard and deep, I slid back on the table.

My eyes flew open.

He gripped my shoulders and pounded into me without mercy. My gush splashed between us, not slowing him down one bit.

I knew my insides would be sore tomorrow, but I didn't care one lick.

He continued, and I coaxed him on.

"Give it to me, Tate. I can take it. Oh fuck yes, fuck me. You're going to cum so hard!"

He called out my name, "Bluuue," his eye contact drilling me like his cock. Then everything came to an abrupt stop. He closed his eyes, pulled out of me, tossed the condom in the trash, fetched his jeans and shirt, and left.

What the fuck!

I sat on the table, looking around, trying to make sense of what had just happened.

Mother fucker!

Forcing myself to get up, I grabbed a towel from the bathroom and wiped up the table and the floor underneath. I dried myself off and dumped the towel on the pile of laundry.

My head swam in a pool of confusion. I thought we were having a great time. I checked the time on my phone: 10:45 p.m.

> **Me:** I did something very stupid.
> **Catherine:** Male or female cavalry needed?
> **Me:** Female, definitely female.
> **Catherine:** Should I see if the girls can do an early breakfast? I mean I won't be there. Me and mornings? A foul combination. Or do we need immediate intervention?
> **Me:** Video chat?
> **Catherine:** Two minutes.

In the bathroom, I applied coconut oil to my tattoo. It was sore from the table fuck. Then I wrapped my robe around me and sat at my desk. I woke up my computer to see who was on.

> **Catherine Mangiacotti**
> Everyone's up.
> **Judy Radford**
> Okay.

Cat initiated the video chat.

Sam in sweats and a white T, Jacqs in pink pajamas, Lainie in her robe, and Cat still dressed the same as earlier in the night popped up on my screen.

"Give us the dirt," Lainie said.

"Yeah," the rest chimed in.

"Did you go home with Tate?" Sam asked.

"He came home with me."

"Woohoo!" Jacqs called out.

"I thought there might be something between you two," Lainie said.

"It was a disaster," I said.

They groaned.

"Well not at first. Once we got back to my place, it seemed fine, good even, but then he just took off and didn't even say goodbye. What kind of dick does that?"

"Wait," Cat ordered. "Back track. Did you meet the anaconda?"

I broke out in hysterical laughter while Lainie, Jacqs, and Sam seemed utterly confused. Then I watched as a light bulb flipped on in Jacqs' mind.

"Bigger than Bond's or Red's?" she asked.

"No comparison," I confessed. Jacqs knew I had slept with Bond once at one of our get-togethers, when he showed up shitfaced. She wasn't at all pleased. Frankly, neither was I at the time. Bond had called out "Jacqs" while he was busy fucking me. Not my best day.

"Get the fuck out of town," Jacqs said.

"Seriously. It looks perfectly natural on his tall, wide frame, but it feels ungodly inside."

"Oh my god," Sam said and laughed.

"Are we going to talk about his huge cock all night? Get to it woman! Stay is impatiently waiting for me in bed, if you know what I mean."

"Sorry, Lainie. The dude's a mess. I mean worse than Bond ever was. I just feel like a stupid idiot now. I have no idea what I did to make him run off."

"Maybe it has nothing to do with you," Sam said.

"How often does a guy pull out of you and then just take off?"

"Lately, not at all, but that's not the point. You said he was a mess, so I'm sure it had to do with him and his baggage and not you."

"Thanks Sam. I convinced myself I could do a one-night stand, I mean, I never have before, but I have to assume running out the door isn't a standard part of it."

"They will usually give you a few minutes of cuddling before they dress and leave," Sam said.

"Sorry, Blue," Cat interjected. "He seems like a great person. I know he went through a rough divorce, but that's all I know. Frankly, I want to hear more about his cock!"

"I'm curious to know how you knew, Cat," Jacqs said.

"Care to enlighten them?" Cat asked me.

"You go for it," I said.

"It's big enough that it runs down his thigh. I could see its outline through his jeans."

"We need to invite him back over to Red's and go skinny dipping again," Sam said, giggling.

"Right, so you all can gawk at him? I think you're missing the point. I'm not going to see him again, you all won't see him again, and your job is to help me not obsess about it or him!"

"Blue, don't do what you're about to do," Lainie warned.

"Yeah, Blue, don't," Cat said.

They were referring to my horrible habit of dissecting and obsessing about a situation to the point of driving myself crazy with it. "That's why we're video chatting. You're my stopgap to texting him a long rant."

"Put the phone down!" Jacqs demanded. "I highly recommend you turn it off and go to sleep."

"Sleep? That's highly doubtful."

"Do you want to see him again?" Sam asked. "Something tells me you will."

"If it hadn't ended the way it did, maybe. He tugs on all of my crazy, though."

"Sometimes you have to move through it with someone to get past it," Lainie said.

I could only imagine she was referring to her affair with Mason before she ended up with Stayman.

Just then, Stay's image filled her box. "I'm taking Lainie to bed. Blue, I hope everything's okay. Whatever the dude did, I'll punch him out the next time I see him."

I chuckled. "Thanks, Stay, but that won't be necessary. Night Lane."

"Call me tomorrow. Laters." Her video box disappeared.

"No sense in keeping you all up," I said to the rest of the gang.

"Hang tough. Don't text him," Sam said.

"I won't," I agreed. "Love you guys."

We all disconnected and then my phone vibrated. My heart raced and lodged in my throat. I woke up my phone.

Catherine: You going to be okay?
Me: I thought you were Tate. Yes, I'll be fine.
Catherine: If you have to obsess, at least choose to obsess over the good parts. The big parts.
Me: Very funny.
Catherine: Later.
Me: Later.

After brushing my teeth, I climbed into bed and stared at the ceiling. *Anaconda, now that's funny.* I tried to focus on all the positives: perfect, best ass, stunning, breaking his three-year sex fast with me. But, I couldn't help wonder what I did to practically shove him out my apartment door.

My phone vibrated again and my heart jumped out of my mouth and pulsed on the mattress next to me. At least it felt like that.

Bond: You fucked him????

And here I thought I wanted a jealous Bond. Be careful what you wish for, as they say.

Me: News travels at lightning speed.
Bond: Jesus, Blue.
Me: It was a one-time thing. Why are you upset?
Bond: Something's not right about him. I don't want you to get hurt.
Me: I get hurt all the time. It's become my life.
Bond: I don't mean to hurt you.
Me: He made an interesting point.
Bond: What?
Me: He wanted to know why you and Red sleeping with Jacqs was out in the open and yet, our fucking is a secret.
Bond: You told him?
Me: No. You did.
Bond: Bullshit.
Me: Your behavior did. He said you grilled him like a protective lover and not a friend.
Bond: You know why we keep it a secret. To avoid the drama.

Me: Why does Jacqs get the respect of the openness, but not me?
Bond: I thought you wanted it that way, too.
Me: I don't know what I want anymore.
Bond: Because of Tate?
Me: No Bond. Because of me. I'm going to go. I'll talk to you tomorrow.
Bond: Okay. You know I love you, Blue.
Me: Yeah. I love you, too.

I wished Tate had kept his opinions to himself. Now all I could see was how fucked up my life was. Instead of appreciating my time with Bond and looking forward to being in his arms again, I was left to question what I was doing to myself. *Nothing like fucking, taking off, and leaving a maelstrom of havoc in your wake.*

What pissed me off the most was how my body responded to Tate. I loved my sex with Bond but with Tate, just his hands on my body or his breath on my neck drove me crazy. He didn't need to whip my nipples to get me soaking wet, his penetrating stare took care of that.

He would get a piece of my mind the next time I saw him. It seemed inevitable. Even with all the insecurity plaguing me, the connection we forged, even in the short time we spent together, wasn't something he could just walk away from. He would be back.

CHAPTER SEVEN

Lost in My Mind

by The Head and the Heart

B y Saturday evening, I had sufficiently mind-fucked myself over my night with Tate. I had convinced myself I would hear from him after a day or so. As the seconds, minutes, hours passed me by, sadness and anger filled my heart. I barely made it through the days of work with my mind constantly churning over the details. In bed at night, the memory of his touch haunted me to distraction. I had to masturbate just to get some peace and sleep.

While at work, I found a few hours of respite as Tap 42 cranked up. Too busy to think about Tate, I actually enjoyed myself. I even put my flirt on a bit, and my tips reflected it. At the end of the night, I could feel a bit of angst creeping back in, so I helped Stuart close up.

"Want to get a drink?" he asked as we were putting the mugs away in the cooler.

"Oh?" I said, looking up.

He was a decent looking man: curly blond hair, green eyes, medium height with lots of energy. "You know, an alcoholic beverage at another establishment?" he asked, sweeping his hand in front of all the liquor bottles like a model on a game show.

"I've found that work and play don't mix well together."

"It's just a drink," he insisted with a cheeky smile.

"Thanks, but I'm going to pass."

"It's that big guy with the long hair, right?"

"Huh?" I handed over the last of the mugs.

"When I saw him, I figured I missed my chance."

I threw the towel I held into the laundry bin. "He's nobody. Listen, is it okay if I take off?"

"Yeah, see you next week."

"Thanks."

Rain poured down around me as I struggled with the driver's side door. "Crap. What the fu…" I became exasperated and climbed in through the passenger door.

When I arrived at my apartment, I rummaged in my bag for the key and slid it home. A large manila envelope fell in when I pushed the door open. I picked it up, examined it, and dropped it on the kitchen table. My cold, wet clothes needed to come off and then straight to the shower with me.

A fret began to roil in my stomach. I assumed, with some trepidation, that the envelope had come from Tate and it held my chapter. I took the fastest shower of my life, wrapped myself in a towel, and ran back to the kitchen table. I raised the metal clasps and shook out the contents. The first chapter of *Soul Adjacent*, creased in the middle, fell out along with several Post-Its covering the title page, a business card for auto repair, and a folded note.

Before I had a chance to read anything, my phone vibrated.

> **Bond:** Are you coming tonight?
> **Me:** No, I don't think so.
> **Bond:** Come on, Blue. We don't have to have sex. We can talk.
> **Me:** About?
> **Bond:** What we're going to do. I don't want you to think I'm taking you for granted or I'm ashamed of

you. That's totally wrong.

Me: I just got home from work. Let me eat something and then I'll let you know.

Bond: Okay.

I decided to make a turkey sandwich as a way of procrastinating before reading the envelope contents. Sitting back down with the plate, I opened his note, taking in his left-handed slant.

Blue,

I'm sorry for my departure. It became too much, and I just had to get out of there. There's no excuse for leaving you like that. I've never done anything so flawed.

I'd like to see you again, but I feel like I need to lay it all out there. Not the past, I'm not willing to share that, but what I'm capable of and not. I will say that nothing and no one has ever felt like it does with you. Nothing even remotely close. And we've barely scratched the surface of our mutual sexuality. That's what I can offer, but I'd prefer to discuss it in person.

"I'm sure you would," I said aloud and continued reading.

Either way, I hope we can stay in touch.

I read your chapter and enjoyed the start of the story. I think it reads a bit clunky in present tense and in my notes, I make suggestions about changing over to first-person past tense. You should definitely keep at it.

Tate

Underneath, in pencil it read:

94

I waited here for two hours hoping to see you. The rain chased me away.

I pulled the chapter in front of me and laughed. The Post-Its had nothing to do with the story. Six yellow ones covered the page. They read: *Avoid half-breed American Indians with bad attitudes. Blue is everyone's favorite color. My clit is perfect. I'm a sex goddess. I am a breath of fresh air. I am a talented writer who should share her work.* I could not stop smiling.

I went into the bathroom and placed five yellow squares around the edge of the mirror, covering others to make room. The one with *Avoid half-breed American Indians with bad attitudes* I posted smack in the center of the mirror and laughed.

Back in the kitchen, I finished my sandwich and looked over the chapter. On the last page it read: Are you Katness? There were a lot of red lines throughout, but I could easily see how his suggestions would make the story better.

I felt excited.

Now a normal person would be happy enough with that, but I was far from normal. Was I happy because I heard from Tate? Or because Bond sounded like he was ready to come out to the group? I wasn't sure I really wanted that. Was my mood uplifted because Tate liked my story? Or maybe because we would see each other again? Blah, blah, blah, and around it went.

And then, I didn't feel so excited anymore. Did I want what either of them offered? Why did men only want halfway with me? Could I stand another relationship that had no chance of progressing? Should I go see Bond? Text Tate? Decide to be a lesbian? I sometimes wished I could just turn a switch like that.

I tapped the screen on my phone and sent a text.

Me: I found your envelope.

Tate: Sorry I missed you.

Me: Loved the Post-It notes.

Tate: Thought you might. What are you up to tonight?

Me: Undecided.

Tate: Maybe I can help you decide.

Me: Okay, should I go see Bond? He wants to talk about letting the group know about us.

Tate: That's an easy one, not tonight.

Me: Why?

Tate: Because you're coming to see me?

Me: You ended that with a question mark, but it didn't seem like a question.

Tate: Blue, I'd like to see you.

Me: I don't know. Seems to me you're offering me the very same thing you said I shouldn't settle for.

Tate: I am.

Me: Great.

Tate: It's all I have, but you're right, you deserve more. However, I can't stop thinking about you and our time together on Wednesday night or I'd leave you alone.

Me: Neither can I. Your hands.

Tate: My hands?

Me: Yes, and your departure.

Tate: I'll come to you.

Me: Definitely not. Well maybe. My first thought was that you wouldn't be able to take off if I came to you, but you could still kick me out of your place. How about neutral territory?

Tate: Where?
Me: The Beach. Hollywood.

I loved the beach at night. I rarely had the opportunity to go because it wasn't safe for a woman in South Florida to go there alone.

Tate: Okay, I'll meet you by the bandshell in 20.
Me: Perfect.

Once dressed in shorts and a T-shirt, I texted Bond.

Me: What time are you getting off?
Bond: 3 a.m. or so.

I checked the time on the stove: 12:45 a.m.

Me: I'll text you when I'm coming over. It'll be awhile.
Bond: Good! Anytime.

I filled a glass with water and drained it. Phone and keys in hand and driver's license in my pocket, I hopped down the steps to my car. I fought with the car door, but this time I won. The door creaked and popped as it shut. Once settled, I turned up the music and sang *Rude* along with MAGIC! I loved the reggae beat.

During the day, it was impossible to park on Johnson Street in front of the bandshell. At night, I had my choice of spots and pulled in next to Tate's Harley. I didn't even have to feed the meter because it was after hours.

"Hi." No smile on the jean-clad man.

"Hi, cheer up, it's a beautiful night, and the rain has

already passed through."

"I'm happy to see you."

"That's usually followed by a smile." I pushed up the corners of his mouth.

He cracked a small smile.

"Let's walk down past the shops where it's dark."

"Good idea," he said, smiling.

I playfully punched his shoulder. "It's so we can see the stars."

"Uh huh."

I shot him a dirty look.

He pulled out a blanket from the side pack on the bike.

"Good idea." I kicked off my flip-flops and walked onto the sand, making a beeline to the shore. The ocean wind blew my auburn hair back off my shoulders. I loved the feel of the warmth hitting my face. The beach alone made me ecstatically happy. "Thanks for meeting me here."

"My pleasure."

"So?"

"So?"

"You wanted to do this in person and now's your chance."

He threw the blanket over his shoulder and took my hand, looking directly at me in the dim light. "I'm sorry for running off Wednesday night and thank you for meeting me here tonight."

"You're welcome."

"I want you. I can hardly think of anything else."

His words sent a frisson through me and my pussy tingled. Ignoring my body's outlandish response, I asked, "But?"

"I will never marry again or love again or share my life with another person."

"Wait a sec. So what are you suggesting?"

"Sex and friendship."

"I'm not sure you and I have the same definition of friendship. Maybe you mean acquaintances?" I yanked my hand free.

"No, I mean friendship."

I took a couple steps forward along the water's edge and looked back at him. "How can we be friends if you have no intention of sharing yourself with me? In my world, you share something, I share something, and that's how we get to know each other."

"My past isn't all of me."

"By definition, it is. We have this moment and everything else is in the past."

"I want to know about you, just no questions about me."

"Even your childhood?"

"I may share now and again, but no questions."

I continued strolling, contemplating his words. Did I want to be naked with him again? *Hell, yes.* Did I want to sign up for another Bond scenario? *Hell, no.* Could I keep myself, my heart separate? *Doubtful.*

We had walked far enough that we were behind the houses on Hollywood Beach. Tate unfolded the blanket and spread it over the sand.

I sat down, crossed my legs, and leaned back on my palms.

He moved in behind me and drew my back against his chest.

I felt his warm breath against my neck. "What am I going to do with you?"

"I have several ideas."

"Tell me how this would work. Do we date?" I snuggled in tightly against him, his unique smell enveloping me. I had to force myself to focus on the conversation.

"You mean other people?" he asked.

"No, but let's address that later. I meant you and me. Go to dinner, the movies? Hang with mutual friends, etcetera. Or do we just meet up when we want to fuck?"

"How do you want it?"

"That, sir, is a trick question." I swiveled around until I faced him, my legs folded in front of me. Even in the dark, his penetrating stare affected me.

"Are you always this open?" he asked

"No, definitely not, but if you mean honest, usually."

"Fair enough."

"At least in our case I know you want me for my body. The very thing I've strived to stay away from. And yes, Katness is based on me, on my insecurities and my desire for deep connections. My friends are everything to me, even when I get jealous or feel slighted. Now that Bond seems open to the idea of telling the group about us, I'm not sure I want it."

He leaned forward and took my hand into his cozy palms. "Why?"

"Because it will shift the dynamic, and I'm not sure I want it to. Now, it's more cut and dry and that's so much better for me than ambiguity. If the group knows, then whom does Bond give his attention to? I'm plenty used to it not being me when the gang's together. Part of me thinks it might be a relief to Jacqs, and the other part thinks it might sever our friendship. I don't know. Maybe it would be worth it if we had potential for the long-term, but we don't."

"Why not?" he said, circling his finger around my palm.

"That's very distracting."

"It's meant to be." He leaned forward and kissed the side of my head.

I waited until his eyes returned to mine. "I don't love Bond like that, and he definitely doesn't love me like he loves Jacqs."

"Have you ever been in love?"

"Once, at least I thought I was, but I was young. Not as an adult."

"Who was it?"

I shook my head. I wasn't about to bare my soul to a man who had no intentions of doing the same. My brother's best friend broke my heart irrevocably. But unlike Tate, I hadn't entirely given up on love. "You're only forty-three, right?"

"Yes."

"You could easily live another forty or fifty years."

"So?"

"That seems like a long time to go without sharing your life with someone. I'm not asking, I'm just saying. I don't have the greatest outlook on love, especially since men seem to only want me at a distance."

Tate cringed at my comment. "That has nothing to do with you, Blue. I haven't wanted anyone at all in over three years."

"Okay."

"Okay?"

"I'm saying yes. For as long as I can take it or until I meet Mr. I-want-all-of-you."

"And dating other people?" he asked.

"I can and you can't."

He pulled me onto his lap and tickled my sides. "And you think that's fair?"

"Completely fair. You don't want more, and I do."

"Okay. Now kiss me."

And I did, over and over until his hands began to roam. "Oh," I moaned. "Your hands swallow me up."

"Take off your bra," he said, kissing his way down my neck.

"Just my bra?"

"Yes."

I reached back, unhooked the four clasps, and pulled the straps off through the armholes of my black tank. Then I smoothed the shirt back down.

Over the top, he traced the outline of my breast with his fingers, circling my nipples, but not touching them. "Beautiful. I mean, truly." Then his hands each held one as if weighing them. "I want you for more than just your body."

"Says the man holding my boobs. Uh huh."

He shoved me onto my back, one hand lifting my shirt, the other snaking into my shorts. "I also want you for what I can do to your body." His warm hand massaged my breast while his potent fingers adroitly circled my clit.

I groaned against his mouth as his full, soft lips collided with mine. "Holy smokes!"

Then his blessed mouth lowered over my right nipple, and my back arched over the extreme suction. His teeth grazed back and forth over the tip.

My pussy flushed in excitement.

"You like that," he grunted. He moved his mouth to my other nipple, giving it equal attention all the while his fingers tapped against my clit.

"Harder," I moaned.

He bit down hard, and I cried out into the night.

"Shhh, you can be so loud."

I started giggling and shaking. "Me? You should hear yourself."

"Do I need to tickle you again?"

"If you mean tickle my clit, then yes. You're doing a fine job. Do you have the condoms with you?"

"No, I left them in your right end table."

"I'm on the pill."

"I won't have sex without them."

"I get it. So are we done?" I sat up, his hand still lodged in my shorts.

"Not even close." He pulled off his shirt and situated me between his legs with my back against his chest.

I yanked my shirt over my head and sighed back into the heat of his body.

"Take off your shorts."

I quickly kicked them and my panties away and resettled myself against him.

His large hands sculpted my body, caressing every inch of my skin. One hand scooped up my breast, twisting my nipple with his fingers and the other spread my thighs wide and played in my wetness. The warmth of his mouth settled on the back of my neck, teasing with his tongue and teeth.

I tilted my head back and gasped over all the competing titillation. "Please," I called out.

"Kiss me." He shifted me slightly so he could dip his head over my shoulder and ensnare my lips.

I groaned into his mouth, tasting him, feasting on his flavor and scent.

He held me tightly against him as my orgasm began to quake.

I broke off the kiss and stared out at the ocean as the contractions shook me. My soul road the waves, up and down, until it flew back to me. "Holy whoa."

He chuckled against my neck. "You have a fondness for the word, 'holy,' I've come to discover."

"Holy shit that was good." Smiling, I pivoted sideways as he wrapped me up in his arms. I sighed against his chest. "Someone needs some attention," I whispered, touching the hard heat against his thigh.

"Not tonight."

"What do you mean? Why?" I looked up into his dark eyes.

"I want you to come to my house, soon."

"Will you let me play with it? I haven't gotten to taste you yet."

Smoothing my hair against my head and down my back, he said, "We have plenty of time for all of it."

"Do we?" Truthfully, I had no idea how long I could keep my heart out of it, but I felt determined to try. "What time is it?" I searched my discarded shorts for my phone.

He got to his first. "Two-thirty-seven. Time for a swim?"

"No. I've got to go soon."

"Early day tomorrow?"

"No ... I—"

"I see."

"I'm not going to—"

"It's none of my business." He pulled his encompassing body heat away from me and began to dress.

"Don't be like that," I said, staring up at him.

My warm lover had morphed back into his cold, hard self, his lips turned down, the crease on his forehead pronounced. "It's going to take some adjusting," he said.

"On both our parts." I pulled on my panties and shorts.

"Yes, I suppose that's true. Can we at least agree in the future not to double book?"

"Of course. I had plans with him first, and he wants to talk." I fastened the clasps of my bra in front of me, shifted the closure around to my back, slipped the straps over my arms, and rearranged my breasts inside the cups.

"Understood." He yanked his shirt over his head, his erection still pronounced through his jeans.

"You, my friend, have your work cut out for you, and I thought it was just me."

"How do you mean?" he asked, lifting the edge of the blanket.

I stepped off and grabbed my stuff. "Me? I have to keep from falling in love with you, and you? You have to pick a side. You can't be possessive and at the same time not want me fully in your life."

He shook out the blanket and seemed to be contemplating my words. "You're right."

"Say that again. It has a nice ring to it."

He dropped the blanket and lifted me into his arms, my feet rising off the ground. With his left hand, fingers buried in my hair, he forced our mouths tightly together. His kiss reinforced our connection, placing more rivets affixing us together. For someone who didn't want a commitment, he sure seemed determined to possess me with his mouth. Once he placed me back down on the sand, we stared at each other, silence hanging between us.

I looked away at the ocean and sighed heavily. To deflect what I was really feeling, I said, "I'll be fine, I think. You're not that loveable." I laughed and ran away along the edge of the water.

He quickly chased after me, catching me in a few strides. We both slowed as he captured my hand in his. We strolled through the sand until we reached the bandshell and crossed over to where we parked.

"Thanks for coming to talk to me," he said as we stood in front of the door of my car.

"Thanks for the incredible O. I can definitely get used to that."

"Good." He tugged on the door to my car and finally got it to budge. "Listen, call that number. The guy owes me a favor."

"Okay." I climbed inside my car.

"Do you work tomorrow?"

"Yes, the dinner shift."

"And Monday?"

"I'm off all day. Although, I definitely want to get in a step class or two."

"Come over tomorrow night. I'll text you the address. You can shower at my place." He leaned over and kissed me.

"Right, okay. See you tomorrow night then."

"You're crinkling your nose again," he said as he walked away.

"And you're smiling, even if only on the inside."

His back shook slightly.

I backed up my car, pulled out, and drove down Johnson Street to A1A. Turning onto Hollywood Boulevard, I made my way to the parking lot outside of the CroBar Club, facing the railroad tracks.

Me: I'm just pulling in.

The car console read 3:15 a.m. I walked past the door to the club and found Bond sitting on the steps leading to his apartment.

"Do I want to know where you've been?" he asked, brushing sand off my calf.

"I guess that depends."

He took my hand and led me up the stairs. I could hear music coming from the club, but the volume was low. He sat on his black leather couch and ran his fingers through his long hair. I waited.

"Is it Tate?"

"Yes," I answered, running my tongue along my swollen lips.

106

"Do you plan to keep seeing him?"

"I do." I shrugged.

Bond shook his head and took a deep breath. "He can't possibly give you what you need."

"I know."

"You know?" He shifted to face me. "Then why are you seeing him?"

"Why am I seeing you?"

"Come on, Blue. We're friends, we have history. You and me, we help each other get through life."

"That's true, but you aren't offering me anything more than he is."

"You deserve better. You, of all people, deserve more. Why do you settle for men like us?"

"Knowing why doesn't change it at all. Either I live like a hermit, or I take the good with the bad. Love has always come at a price. *Always*. Besides, my good friend, you are doing *exactly* the same thing."

"Rory says hi, by the way."

Now it was my turn to shake my head. "Dude, really?"

"I'm not doing anything with her. I'm practically monogamous for the first time in a really long time."

"Oh my god that is so funny. I guess for you, two people is the closest you'll ever come to monogamy."

"I'm not sure anymore. I'm thinking more and more about wanting a family."

My eyes opened wide.

"Don't be so shocked."

"Uh, sorry. So what do you want to do about us? I'm not sure I want to tell the gang. I mean, if we were in love or something... And with me dating Tate, it makes it even more awkward."

"Whatever you want, Blue. I just can't stand hurting

you. You're one of my best friends, and that's the last thing I want."

"I know and it's nice to hear it too. Can we go snuggle in bed? I'm exhausted."

"Let me shower and I'll join you."

Once we were both in bed, facing each other, Bond said, "Please be careful with Tate."

"How do you mean?"

"Something's not right about him. Not that he's dangerous or anything, but when he wasn't talking to someone and was just staring off, he seemed... I'm not sure of the right words. Damaged. Maybe I can see it because I was there for so long. He's not a whole man, and I'm worried he might take you down with him."

"Yeah, I know what you mean. He's been pretty clear that he will never love again, never fully share himself with another. Part of me sees the futility of it all, but Bond, it's ... it's also different with him."

"How so?"

I didn't answer right away. To explain something that felt ethereal seemed practically impossible. How could I explain it to another when I really didn't understand it myself? "For one, everything feels so intense, and I don't just mean the sex, but wow in that department. For a man who doesn't want to feel, he seems to feel everything too much. He surrounds me. I feel him. That sounds stupid, but I do."

"Not stupid." He pulled me close and hugged me to him, his head above mine. "You're already in trouble."

"Yes..." I love Bond for many reasons, but none more than that he knew me better than anyone else did and he never judged me.

"I'll be here for you."

"Thank you." I snuggled in tighter against him and then kissed him goodnight.

His breathing quickly evened out as I lay awake. I wondered if Tate was in bed. I thought of his hands as I drifted off to sleep.

CHAPTER EIGHT

Stay with Me

by Sam Smith

B ond left to go back to Red's house where he lived part-
time, and I headed home for a quick shower and a
change before my women's group. I packed a bag of clothes
so I had something comfortable change into after work.

Once at the Bread Building, I made it to our meeting
room just before group started.

"Before we begin, I need to let you know there will be
no meeting next week. I'll be out of town next Sunday.
Who would like to start today?" Ann asked.

We all stared at each other until I noticed most of them
looking at me. "What?" I demanded, throwing up my hands.

"I think they're interested to hear about the man you
mentioned last week."

"Soap opera a' la Judy?" I mumbled.

"You can consider it interest."

"Yeah, we're interested all right," Charmaine said,
leaning forward toward me.

"What do you want to know?"

"Did you fuck him?" Charmaine blatantly asked.

"Yes."

Three of the women gasped, and two covered their
mouths.

I shook my head and rolled my eyes.

"Care to elaborate?" Suzie asked.

Then I just blurted it all out, mostly because I wanted

to shock Charmaine. "It was good, no great, and then he abruptly took off. He's broken, emotionally unavailable, and the hottest man I've ever been with. Complete and utter trouble but well, you know me, a magnet for the emotionally retarded. He wants me. He made me Post-It notes to add to my collection of affirmations. I can't share them all, but one says, 'Blue is everyone's favorite color.' That's my nickname."

"So a romantic, emotional retard," Suzie crooned, practically swooning.

"I think he might have been perfect for me, if I'd found him before he got broken. Anyway, I saw him again last night and will see him again tonight."

"Is this the best choice for you, Judy?" Ann asked with no judgment in her expression.

"The absolute worst, so far as I can tell."

The women in the group shared a collective laugh, except for Ann.

"It's not too late to change your mind," she said. "One of the goals of therapy is to make different choices for you, to find strategies to support taking better care of yourself."

"Obviously, she's not there yet," Charmaine said.

I pursed my lips and narrowed my eyes in her direction.

She held up her hands, palms out. "I'm nowhere near close myself. I took off my assistant's head just yesterday."

"What does he want from you?" Toby asked me. She rarely spoke up in group at all.

"He says friendship and sex."

"So, like Mitchell?" she asked, shifting her knees in my direction. The group knew Bond by his given name.

"Not exactly. Well actually, exactly how it used to be with Mitchell before he shared his past." Bond's fiancé died in a car crash, and he did prison time because he had been driving the car.

I continued, "Yes. There is one huge difference, though."

"What's that?" Toby asked.

"Mitchell and I have been friends for years, and we love each other in our own way. Tate? I don't know him, and he has no intention of letting me in."

"Judy, what do you hope to get out of spending time with Tate?" Ann asked.

"Heartbreak and devastation." I looked around at the women with mouths agape. "I'm sort of kidding. I mean, I am. I hope he decides to lower his fortress of protection and lets me know him, maybe even love him."

"Why him?"

"Probably because he's unavailable. I clearly see what I'm doing, but how the hell can I change it when my body leads me astray? I guess I'll have to settle for really amazing sex until I meet Mr. Right, or Mr. Wrong morphs into Right."

"I'd like to advise you that you still have a choice," Ann stated.

"Come on, Ann. Even I'm on Judy's side this time," Charmaine piped in. "Maybe you've been with your husband too long to remember what it's like out there. It's not like there's a line of healthy men to choose from. Are we supposed to remain alone and celibate waiting for Mr. Perfect?"

"Wow," I whispered.

"Yeah, I know. Shocking, right?" Charmaine agreed.

"Very and thanks."

She nodded.

"If we spend the time working on ourselves, setting our standards at the appropriate levels, then a healthier match will present itself," Ann lectured.

"Sorry, no, I'm with Judy and Charmaine on this one,"

Suzie said. "I'm not saying it's impossible, just not as easy as you make it seem. Being alone in life sucks the big one."

I chuckled to myself thinking, *And oh, he has a big one!*

"Since you sound determined to move ahead with Tate, I task you with establishing boundaries for yourself so that the relationship isn't completely on his terms."

"That sounds wise. I'll have to think about that before heading over to his place after work tonight. Thanks for listening and for your support," I said to the group.

I had extra zip in my steps at work later that evening. I had reworked the first chapter and applied Tate's suggestions to chapter two before going in. As I cleared a table and laid down a check, I combed my brain for boundaries as Ann had suggested. The only one I came up with so far was no sleepovers. For me, there was something very intimate about waking up next to a person in the morning. Until recently, Bond and I had never done it. Because of our tight friendship, it worked and hadn't changed things.

After cleaning my section and side station, I checked out with the night manager and headed to my car. That night the driver's side door seemed to be possessed. *I do solemnly promise that I am going to call Tate's guy and get this sucker fixed.* I plugged Tate's address into my phone's GPS and followed the instructions. The closer I got to Fort Lauderdale beach, the more confused I became. Did he come from money? A professor at a local college could not afford a house on Fort Lauderdale beach. I relaxed just slightly when I pulled into the driveway of a smallish home on the beach.

He met me at the door of my car and opened it for me.

"I'm calling tomorrow."

"Good." He held out his hand and lifted me to my feet.

"You live on the beach?"

"It's a rental."

I gazed up at him, questions bouncing around in my head. I held them in.

"Thank you," he said, taking the bag of clothes from me and leading me around the car to the side door of the house.

"For what?" I asked, taking in his sharp features. The planes of his clean-shaven face looked stern as ever, but his mouth looked more relaxed. I couldn't help imagining his full lips on mine again.

"For not asking."

"Oh."

Inside the house, I scanned the furnishings. "Love the dark wood floors. It's great."

"It came furnished."

"Kudos to the owner then."

"The place is great except for—"

"Holy shit! Check out this view. I'd live right out here." I walked out onto the deck. The beach, ocean, and horizon spread out below.

"I spend a lot of time out here: planning my classes, marking papers, reading for pleasure, having coffee in the morning, etcetera."

I wondered if he'd ever had sex out there, but then I remembered he hadn't had sex in over three years before meeting me.

"I see where your mind's going, Blue."

"Oh yeah?"

"Has anyone ever told you, you have eyes the color of the ocean?"

I paused before responding, not sure if the truth fit the

moment. I went with, "That's how I got my nickname."

"Bond." He figured it out anyway.

"Yes."

"That man is going to be the bane of my existence."

"That's rather dramatic, don't you think. I have to contend with your past, and you have to do the same."

"He's not in the past."

"Neither is your past in the past. It lives in your present. Besides, Bond is the exact buffer we need. You don't want me falling for you, and Bond will provide me some balance."

"I still don't like it."

"Good."

"Good?"

"Yep, totally great really. I shouldn't have to be the only one to suffer."

"Oh, you will suffer plenty tonight."

His words torpedoed my clit. My breathing accelerated as we stared at each other.

"Let's get you showered first. I wish we could shower together, but the bathroom is the worst feature of the house. It's definitely not made for two."

The tiny bathroom was completely white: the tile, walls, toilet, sink, and even the shower curtain.

"What's with the two mirrors?" I asked, pointing to the two framed mirrors hanging on the wall, one over the sink and the other over the toilet.

"I have no idea. Here's a towel," he said, handing it to me and placing my bag on the closed toilet seat.

"Thanks."

Once he left me alone in the bathroom, I pulled back the curtain and set the temperature to warm. I stripped off my clothes, wondering if I should dress again or just don my robe. I used my own shampoo, conditioner, and soap. After finishing, I lifted his soap to my nose. Lemon, wood, earthy, and something else I couldn't discern. It definitely was part of his unique smell and being at his place, I understood why he smelled of the ocean breeze.

I dried off and wrapped myself in my robe, hung the towel up on the hook on the wall by the door, and threw my bag and dirty clothes into the corner. "I hope wearing my robe isn't too presumptuous," I said as I approached

"Not at all. Come here." He held his arms out for me and I stepped into his embrace, his lips gently kissing mine. He maneuvered us over to the plush, white couch and positioned me on his lap, my legs draped over his thighs. His teeth caught my bottom lip and then he increased the pressure of our kiss. His tongue slid alongside mine, at first leisurely, and then ardently.

When we parted, I whispered, "You taste so good."

"I was thinking the same thing." His eyes were dancing and affectionate. "Would you like something to eat or drink before we get started?"

"I'm good. I ate at work. I feel anxious to get started."

He laughed. "Okay. If anything I do is too much, just say red."

"Why does hearing you say that turn me on? At least part of it anyway. Let's not use Red's name and choose another word? Geronimo?"

"Very funny, silly girl. It turns you on because you're a very naughty, kinky woman and you need to be used appropriately."

"Appropriately, huh?"

"Let me show you." He untied the sash and slipped my robe off my shoulders. He led me to the bedroom that had a king-size, blond wood, sleigh bed against the back wall.

The dim light shrouded the brown walls in shadow. He set me on my back in the center of the bed and shed his jeans and shirt, revealing an astonishing portrait of masculinity.

I never imagined being so drawn to a man who towered over me and yet, when he wrapped me in his arms, I never wanted to leave. My body trembled, waiting for what he would do to me.

"Put your arms above your head," he ordered, lifting a piece of rope from the nightstand. He wrapped my wrists together and tied it off at the base of the headboard. His large, firm hands ran down my arms, neck, and stomach, following the curve of my hip. They didn't soothe me but instead, awoke every nerve ending on the surface. "Spread your legs wide."

When he lifted another piece of rope, I uttered, "Uh ... Tate?"

"Yes, darlin'?"

"Please don't lie on—"

"I have other plans for you. Relax." He ran his hand down the center of my chest, across my stomach to my left leg. Then he rendered me helpless, tying my ankles to the bottom corners of the bed.

I tried to regulate my breathing but failed as I started to pant. My adrenaline fired, causing my nipples to harden into tight peaks and sending moisture to my pussy.

"I love it, you're nipples are ready for me." His warm mouth descended over my right bud, suckling and yanking on it, his teeth grazing back and forth. He kept at it until I tried to move away from him, the sensation so intense. The ropes allowed me no such escape. His mouth moved to the other side as his blessed hands began exploring my body. They modeled my flesh, leaving their heat behind. He avoided the one spot that needed the most attention.

I groaned heavily, lifting my pelvis, praying for a single touch on my clit.

"You're a very naughty girl." He ran a finger through my wetness and continued, "Not only do you let strange men tie you up, but it makes you so wet, you drip onto the bed." He stalked around to the other side and asked, "What should I do with you?"

My body vibrated and shook with anticipation.

His back faced me, and I saw a flash of light reflected off the dresser mirror. When he turned around, I gasped. He held a lit, long-stem candle and his incredible phallus jutted out toward me.

I shook my head back and forth, and he nodded in response. He sat on the edge of the bed and kissed me, taunting me further by making me wait. His taste infiltrated me, inciting deep arousal while melting my resistance. I had never experienced wax, and the idea stirred and scared me.

"So beautiful," he murmured. The first drop of wax fell between my breasts.

"Ohhh!" I called out. It stung momentarily and then faded into raw heat. My eyes widened.

"I knew you'd like it." He tilted the candle so another drop fell on my right breast. Then he created a circle around my areola and I knew where he was headed.

I wiggled, "I don't think—"

"Exactly, don't think. Trust me and just feel." The hot wax landed directly on my nipple, but he didn't stop until it was fully covered.

"Holy fuck!" I cried, pulling on the rope that held my arms above my head.

"Let's see how you really feel about this." His fingers strummed against my labia, dipping into my entrance. Parting his fingers, the gossamer veil of wetness spread between his fingers. Then he sucked on them, moaning. "So good." He stalked back to the top of the bed and said, "Should I stop?"

I shook my head "no."

"I didn't think so. However, I need to hear it. Tell me what you want, tell me what you are."

So aroused, I wasn't sure I could get the words out. "I ... I ... please more wax."

"And what are you, Blue?"

"I'm a libidinous woman ... that needs..."

"Nice word. Come on dirty, lustful, Blue, tell me what you need."

I took a deep breath and forced the words out. "I need you to use me ... fuck me ... make me cum so hard I can't see straight."

"Good girl," he praised, pouring the wax across my other breast, covering the hardened peak.

I tugged against the restraints, groaning in sexual torment.

Then he trailed the wax down my soft stomach and filled my bellybutton.

"Oh, oh, oh, that's intense."

"Just wait," he said.

"No, no, no," I uttered. But that didn't stop him. My spread legs left my pussy completely vulnerable.

"Not yet." He set the candle in a holder on the dresser. On the bed, between my legs, he fingered my sopping wet pussy and spread the moisture over my clit. "I'm going to cover this clit soon, too, but first I need to get it really big and swollen. He circled my arousal, slowly teasing.

My head thrashed back and forth, the stimulation rousing.

"Before I let you cum, you need to tell me your dirtiest fantasy."

"That's not fair!" I whined.

"I don't have to be fair, my sexy vixen. *You* are tied to *my* bed."

I tried to think of something that wouldn't be mortifying: Double penetration, be a voyeur at a sex club, anal sex, being cropped in front of an audience. They were all too personal.

"Oh to be in your mind, I can see you sorting through the options. Why don't you tell me all of them? That way I can fulfill each one."

"Come on, Tate!"

"Is this what you want?" He applied pressure on my clit and then removed his hand. "Just spit it out, and I'll continue to fondle you."

"Ummm..." I decided on anal sex, since his cock would never fit. I thought the other ideas might put him off. "Anal sex."

He lay next to my side, resumed the massage, and asked, "Have you done that with Bond?"

"No," I moaned, his touch bringing me closer to the edge.

"Have you ever done it?" His free hand lightly floated over my belly and thighs, heightening the climb.

"No."

"That's good."

"I'm not ... doing ... doing it with you. With that," I forced out, tilting my head in the direction of his hard heat lying against my thigh.

"Of course you will. Not tonight, but soon." He increased the tempo and pressure of his fingers. "You're close."

"Mmmhmm," I murmured. "Ohhh, very. Please!"

"Okay, naughty girl, but the payment comes next."

"Holy hell, I'm cumming!" My body bucked against

the restraints, the contractions thrumming my core.

"Let it go, Blue."

I screamed out my release, my body arching up, my orgasm saturating Tate's hand and then I collapsed.

He shifted up and kissed me gently. "You're incredible." He held me as I floated back to reality and then asked, "Do you need some water?"

"Please. Was I loud? My throat feels like I yelled."

"Very." He bestowed a slight smile upon me and left the room. When he came back, he tilted my head and fed me water.

"Thank you."

"How do you feel?" he asked after he took the candle out of its holder once again.

"Is that a trick question?"

"No, I'm checking in."

"Euphoric and nervous."

"Exactly what I was going for. Ready?" he asked, only he didn't wait for an answer. He spread my labia and filled my folds with wax. Then he covered my mound with the hot lava and drizzled it over my clit.

"Oh god, oh fuck, please!" My body shook of its own accord.

"Please what?" he whispered.

"I don't know!"

"Yes, you do. Tell me."

"Please fuck me. Hard. I need you inside me."

"Yes, you do, just not yet."

My hearted drummed in my ears as I wondered what came next.

He poured more wax over my nipples, the previous layer keeping the intense heat from my sensitive bits. Next, he untied my arms and massaged my shoulders.

"Oh, that feels good," I breathed out. I felt relaxed for about a minute, until he untied my legs.

"Stand at the end of the bed in front of the mirror, legs wide and hands behind your neck, elbows out."

He followed me over and after I got in position, he placed his hand behind my head and kissed me deeply, his tongue tangling with mine. He sufficiently stole my breath, my common sense leaking out with it. "Remember *Geronimo* if it gets to be too much." Then he rummaged in a drawer in front of me and pulled out a flogger, but nothing like the ones Bond used.

The black leather held by Tate looked mean, each strand of the whip was braided with a knot on the tip, instead of broad strips of soft leather.

"Naughty girls must be punished," he stated, his dark brown eyes penetrating mine.

"I'm scared," I whispered.

"You're in control."

I nodded.

He circled behind me and struck me a few times on the back. "See, that's not so bad." Once in front of me again, he directed, "Keep your eyes on me the whole time."

"Okay." My heart pounded in my chest, my breathing erratic. I so wanted to please him but before he started on my front, I folded in my elbows in fear.

"A punishment for a punishment ill received will be far worse. Stand up straight and push those gorgeous globes out for me."

I complied, struggling to stay still.

The first strike on my right breast forced the breath out of me. "Holy shit!"

"Do you want me to stop?"

"No."

"Good." The whip knocked off the wax around my right areola, strike after strike.

The impact to my nipple caused my juices to drip down my thighs. The acute sensation rode my threshold of tolerance. "Ahhh," I yelled out. I could feel my pulse pounding in my throat as I struggled to remain standing.

"You're the sexiest woman I've ever seen, Blue. Your submission is so very hard to resist."

I logged both of his comments for later as I grappled with all the feelings eddying around in my mind and body.

"Ready for more?"

"Yesss," I hissed.

Then his whip struck my left breast repeatedly, removing all the wax that had hardened there. He reached between my legs to scoop up my cum and then fed it to me. I dipped my tongue into his palm and lapped at it. Gathering more, he rubbed the wetness across my nipples and then licked it off. He murmured against my boob, then gave me a steamy kiss, sharing my taste on our lips.

"I have to be inside you now." He quickly rid my pussy of the rest of the wax and drew my torso over the dresser. I heard him rip open a condom. "I'm going to fuck you from behind, hard."

His steely cock slid in about halfway with his first thrust. As wet as I was, my body still had to relearn that I could accommodate his length and girth. Through the reflection in the mirror, his eyes locked on mine, claiming me.

Do not fall in love, do not fall in love, echoed in my head as I grunted each time the head of his cock hit my cervix and forced my hips against the dresser.

I had convinced myself that no other man could handle my dark needs, and with each moment I spent with Tate, I found out I was wrong.

Don't fall in love!
Don't fall in love!

A master of self-deception and denial, I believed I could avoid love's trap.

Tate's body heat covered my back, his hands tugging on my nipples. His left arm trailed down to my pussy and found my sweet spot. "You're going to cum with me," he growled as all the ridges of his phallus exquisitely stretched my insides. He took long strokes, in and out of me, slamming his cock in fast and drawing back out slowly.

Our voices resounded off the mirror in front of us.

His hands mastered me yet again and I cried out with him, his orgasm quickly following.

Breathing heavily, we remained connected as we both struggled to recover.

"Are you still hard?"

"I am," he said, the heat of his words rippling against my throat.

"You came, right?"

"I can barely stand from it."

"But you're still hard?" I asked, astonished.

"It happens sometimes when I've been hard for a while."

"Can you cum again?"

"Yes." He tilted his head up and gazed at me through the mirror.

"Wow. That's a mighty fine feature. God granted you the goods in that department."

He shrugged. "If you believe in that sort of thing."

"I believe in your cock."

He smiled over my shoulder. "Are you hungry now?"

"I am. As long as you promise that I can play with your cock before I go."

"You're spending the night."

"I'm not."

He stood up, his cock slipping out of my body. "I thought you said you had tomorrow off."

I walked out through the living room, and he followed me to the bathroom.

He tossed the condom in the trash and loomed over me, leaning against the doorjamb.

With the towel from my shower, I dried my sopping pussy and thighs, and brushed at the remaining wax on my chest.

I left the bathroom, retrieved my robe, and tied the sash. "No sleepovers. There will probably be other stipulations to this ... this thing between us, but I haven't figured them out yet." I stood my ground with my hands on my hips.

"I'll change your mind."

"Doubtful and definitely not tonight. This can't all be on your terms."

"It's not."

"It's not, because I won't allow it to be. Otherwise, you'll chew me up and spit me out. I won't have it."

His stern expression was back, and I couldn't fathom what it meant. After a moment, he said, "I have no intention of doing that. Come here." He held his arms out to me.

I let him wrap me up in his energy. A sigh escaped me as I settled against his chest.

He smoothed my hair and rested his chin on my head. "Sooo ... food?"

"Anything desserty?"

"I have a slice of chocolate torte."

"Just one slice? Okay, I'm willing to share it." I laughed.

That granted me a slight chuckle. "Outside?" he asked.

"That would be great."

"Grab the torte, and I'll throw on a robe."

125

"Deal." I padded, barefoot, into the kitchen on the dark, shiny, wood floor. The cabinets were beige and the backsplash had small square tiles in various shades of brown. I loved the dark, granite countertops. One of those fancy coffee-making machines sat on the counter. I opened the stainless steel refrigerator and took in the contents. He clearly ate out a lot. There were various takeout containers. Once I located the torte, I searched around for forks and filled two glasses with water. I sat in one of the white beach chairs out on the deck, placing the dessert container, forks, and glasses on the table between the chairs.

"You eat out a lot," I said when Tate sauntered outside wearing a navy robe that came down past his knees, loosely tied, leaving his defined chest exposed. "Do you eat alone?"

He ignored my question and stabbed the torte with a fork, holding out the bite toward me.

The torte tasted great, but his lack of response to my question left a sour taste in my mouth. I took a sip of water and held the glass in my lap.

"You'll get used to it."

I knew what he meant. "Doubtful," I said. Just a few minutes before I felt so connected to him and now, we were back to the fortress of steel.

He brushed the hair away from the side of my face and looped it behind my ear. "Just give it time."

Time, I knew for sure, was not on my side. I listened to the waves of the ocean cresting on the shore, trying to let it settle me.

He took a bite of the dessert and then fed me another. "How was that for you?"

Shaking off my disappointment, I said, "Good."

"Just good?" In a quick maneuver, he moved the table

from between us and dragged my chair next to his. He took my left leg and draped it over his.

"Very good?" I said with a shrug.

"Are you going to punish me?" he asked as he ran the tip of his finger up my inner thigh. That one finger had more power over me than my entire self-respect. My lips parted and a moan escaped.

"If you really want to know what it was like for me, share something and I'll do the same."

"That's not the deal." His forehead creased, but he continued to touch me, moving under the hem of my robe.

My body's constant betrayal flabbergasted me as it blushed in need. Trying not to give in to the power of his hands, I said, "I guess you'll have to ask me ... next time you have ... ahhh ... me tied down."

He sighed. "I sometimes eat with friends, other times I call in takeout."

"Was that so hard? Will I meet your friends?"

"No. Now answer my question." His fingers had migrated to the juncture between my leg and my radiant core.

I stroked the hair on his forearm and then looked up. "Better than I imagined it could be."

"Better than with Bond?" His fingers crawled across my mound and played in my ever-growing wetness.

"Ohhh ... I'm not sure how to answer that."

"Truthfully." He forced two fingers past my labia.

"I can't think," I groaned. I held his forearm as he drove into me, his thumb shimmying over my clit. "My orgasms ... best, so good."

"But?"

"And ... so exciting. New. Unexpected, but..."

"But?"

"So close. Oh, Tate, yes ... so fast ... fierce ... so, so good."

He stopped moving and said, "Not yet."

I pouted.

"And Bond?"

"He knows me better than anyone, even better than Cat."

He resumed his manipulations and brought me right up to the edge again. "I want to know you."

"No." I closed my eyes and rode the tide of my arousal.

"Yes." He inserted a third finger.

"Ohhh ... don't stop," I cried. But he did stop. I pulled away, covered myself, and propped my feet up on the railing. "Not until you're willing to risk yourself. You can't possibly expect me to lay myself out for you to pick over and then discard once you've had your fill."

"I'm not a vulture."

"What are you, Tate? You can't expect more from me than you're willing to give."

He looked away toward the ocean, and I did the same.

Part of me screamed, *Go get dressed and leave*. My pussy, however, wanted her satisfaction. It throbbed, waiting for relief. I took matters into my own hands, literally. Before Tate could stop me, I opened his robe and firmly grasped his still-hard cock. My two small hands did not cover the length of him, so I took the head and the remaining shaft in my mouth. The first order of business was to get him to let go of his need for condoms. Tasting the remnants of latex on his skin instead of my own juices reminded me too much of being with Bond. I popped my head up and said, "I'll trade sharing a bit of myself if you give up the condoms."

"That's a very bad idea," he said, pushing my head back down. "That feels amazing."

I worked my saliva down with my hands and reveled in the feel of him. "Your cock would taste and smell so much better. Like you, instead of a condom."

"I'll think about it."

My mind leapt and prematurely high-fived itself. *Progress!*

Reaching for me, he pulled me onto his lap. "So you want to try anal sex. I'll share a secret, so do I." He kissed my temple and absently played with my nipple.

"You haven't before?" I squirmed in his lap from his touch.

"No." He shifted me to his right leg and wrapped his arm around my waist, his left hand touching me again.

"Hmmm. That's not at all surprising, given your size."

His fingers slid inside. "Let's just say I've never met a woman like you before."

"Oh, Tate, that feels so good, but can we drop the bullshit and just play?"

"Excuse me?"

"I doubt you just bought that whip and who knows what else resides in that drawer of yours."

"I didn't just buy that whip."

"Obviously. You're too good with it."

"Thank you, I think."

I opened the top of my robe and tweaked my nipples between my fingers.

Tate's eyes dilated. "There's no one else like you, Blue."

There's no one else like you, Blue, stored for later use in my self-torture. As I scanned his physique, he opened his robe, pushing it to the sides. I heard the tear of a condom wrapper and watched him roll the latex down his shaft.

His hands took over, shifting me to face the beach. He lowered me down onto his cock, my back pressed against his chest.

Once fully seated atop of him, I groaned. "So good," I whispered into the ocean breeze.

One of his strong arms held me under my breasts while his other hand rolled my clit between his fingers. He rode me hard, up and down.

It didn't take long for my orgasm to fire after all of the foreplay and teasing. "Ohhh," I cried out.

His hand covered my mouth as my release continued to contract around his engorged cock.

I giggled through his fingers and then lay spent against him as he rolled his hips underneath me and reached his own climax.

We stayed like that, relaxing in the breeze, listening to the ocean. Then he moved me off his lap and stood, the navy robe hanging from his shoulders. I wrapped mine around me and sat back down as he headed inside.

He strolled back out with the robe tied tightly around him, and leaned against the sidewall. "So how'd it go with Bond last night?"

Ah, and another boundary rears its head. Ann would be so proud. "From here forward, talking about Bond is off limits."

"That's not going to work for me," he said, crossing his arms over his chest.

"It's going to have to."

"Are you going to talk about us with him?"

"Number one, we are not an 'us' and two, definitely. You can limit a lot with us, but not with whom I share."

"I can if it's about me."

I rolled my eyes. "You won't give me any details about you, so I don't know anything about you to tell."

"So what is there to say?"

"Unless you've lived under a rock—quite frankly as

rocks go, this place is stellar—and have never had a friend, I'm certain you know what there is to discuss. I didn't go into detail about our sex or anything like that, although the girls know about your cock."

His mouth dropped open, and he appeared stunned.

"Not my doing, you can thank Cat for that."

He shook his head and said, "I don't think I want to know."

"Trust me, you don't."

"I want to see you tomorrow." He stood up straight.

The boundaries were starting to pile up. "I don't think that's a good idea. Besides, I sometimes see Bond on Mondays. Let's meet up at Red's on Wednesday. Does that work?"

"That's three days away."

"Good counting skills." I felt proud of myself, three whole boundaries and counting.

Before I knew what was happening, he pulled me out of my seat and held me on the deck railing, my feet off the ground. He ground his body and mouth against mine, holding me prisoner.

Jerking his head back, he said, "I can't wait three days. Just stay tonight, and I'll see you tomorrow."

"No," I insisted, trying to get out of the hold he had on me, even though his aggression totally reignited a need in me.

"Tuesday."

"Okay, okay. Put me down."

He lowered me to the deck. "Or tomorrow would be better. You have the whole day off."

I walked back through the house and to the bathroom. As Tate watched, I changed into shorts and a T-shirt. It would be so easy for me to give in and spend the whole day with him. Locking eyes with him, I already knew I wanted more. More than he would ever give to me.

Say yes! My body cried.

"No. It'll be late, but I can see you on Tuesday after my shift at Tap 42."

"Okay."

I threw my dirty work clothes and robe into my bag and zipped it up.

He walked me to the side door and kissed me gently. "Thank you for tonight. I promise, it'll get easier."

"That's not a promise you can make," I mumbled as I made my way to my car.

CHAPTER NINE

Black and Blue

by Miike Snow

All day Monday, I fought with myself about calling Tate. Even after two back-to-back step aerobics classes, I still felt antsy. I tried to write and edit, but I couldn't focus. The sex, what he said and didn't say, it all just swirled around like a tide pool in my head.

For someone who refused to open up, he sure seemed to want a full-on relationship. Maybe it was just sex. He had years to make up for, and I needed to remember that. Oh, the sex. It pissed me off that I felt so much when he could go on feeling nothing. His stupid, fucking hands and energy touched more than my body and yet, that was all I was, a body. The very situation I had struggled to avoid for years.

Part of me hoped Bond would call so I could lose myself in him for a few hours and yet, I wasn't sure I could do it. Just as I thought about reaching out to him, he texted me.

> **Bond:** Can I see you?
> **Me:** Come here?
> **Bond:** Sure. Should I pick up food along the way?
> **Me:** Please!
> **Bond:** See you soon.

I changed the sheets on my bed and jammed my overflowing laundry into the closet, forcing the door closed. *Laundry as soon as Bond leaves!* Knowing Bond's routine, he wouldn't be staying long. He'd be back at Red's by dinnertime.

Bond strolled in without knocking, placing a white paper bag on the table. "I got us some burgers and fries." All in black, with his long, dark hair down, tight jeans, and a fitted T, I had a hard time not comparing him to Tate. He walked off to the bathroom and when he came back into the kitchen, he sat casually, legs spread open.

"I'm starving, thanks." I hadn't eaten anything since my oatmeal before working out. "Something to drink?"

"What've you got?"

I opened the fridge and said, "Margarita in a bottle, Dos Equis from the last time you were here, OJ, which may or may not still be good, and water."

"Dos Equis."

I opened the beer and poured me some water. "How are things going with Jacqs and Red?" I asked as I joined him at the table.

He swallowed his bite of burger. "Same. Jacqs insists all is grand, but I get the feeling Red's ready for me to move on, as if it's a given he gets her in the end."

"Bond?" I touched his arm.

"Yes, love?"

"We all do."

He raised an eyebrow. "I guess we'll see."

"You're not mad at me, are you?"

"You know I'm not. I count on you to cut through the bullshit." He dipped some fries in ketchup and tossed them in his mouth. "And Tate. Have you seen him since Saturday?"

I blushed uncontrollably.

"That good, huh?"

"Worse."

"Cute Post-It on the mirror," he said, one eyebrow raised. "What are you going to do?" He took another bite of his burger, watching my expression.

"I'm trying to take Ann's advice. She said I need to establish my own boundaries."

"And have you?"

I took a sip of water. "Some. He's very pushy, though."

"Care to share?" He put his burger down and leaned back.

"You'll laugh."

He wiped his hands on a napkin and said, "Tell me anyway."

"No sleepovers."

"That's not funny, that's smart. What else?"

I sighed. "He wanted to see me today, and I said no."

"So you are making him wait? That's also very good. More?"

"I told him questions about you are off limits." I expected Bond to laugh, but he didn't.

He tilted his head and scrunched his eyebrows. "Why?"

"Because he's constantly asking about you, and why should I share my personal life when he doesn't."

He brushed his hand over his long hair and seemed to be thinking. "So he's possessive. Is he dating anyone else?"

"No."

"You're both in trouble." He sat forward and continued eating his lunch.

"What does that mean?"

He placed the beer bottle back on the table. "He wants you for himself on his terms—"

"Yes, he's been very upfront about that," I said, nodding.

"If he wasn't at all invested, Blue, he wouldn't give a rat's ass about me."

"What are you saying?"

"Like I said, you're both in trouble."

"That makes me feel better." I laughed.

135

"I get it. Equal suffering."

"That's what I love about you, Bond. You get me."

"We're two peas in a far-out pod."

"Oh my god, that's funny coming from you. You must have gotten that from Jacqs. Sometimes I wish we, you and me, could just fall in love with each other."

He touched my hand. "It would make things easier, wouldn't it?"

"Yeah," I said, staring into his light brown eyes. Sometimes life seemed so unfair.

"In the meantime, I kind of like this turn of events." He helped himself to another beer from the fridge.

"What do you mean?"

"You distract me from Jacqs, and now I get to distract you from Tate. It's more equal."

"Yeah, I guess that's true. Will you do me a favor?"

"Sure, anything," he said, sitting back down.

"Get to know Tate."

"I shouldn't have said 'anything.' If he won't let you in, what are the chances?"

"I need to know your opinion. It matters to me. You're like the big brother I wish I had."

"He already has an issue with me. I don't see it happening. But fuck, I'll try. For you. I'll talk to Red. He has a better shot, Stay too."

"Good idea. Thank you." I hopped onto his lap, wrapped my arms around his neck, and kissed him.

"Are you done eating?" he asked when we broke apart.

"For now."

Bond carried me to the bedroom and granted me two wonderful hours of distraction from Tate. I did tackle the laundry and actually dusted after he left.

CHAPTER TEN

Ride

by Somo

On Tuesday, I ran home between my lunch shift at The Chart House and the night shift at Tap 42. I showered, pulled my hair back in a ponytail with my long bangs hanging past my eyebrows, lined my eyes, and dressed, choosing a sheer, sexy bra and matching thong.

The Tap 42's bar didn't fill up like it did on Saturday nights. I had way too much time to think, and I didn't like it one bit. By around 8:00 p.m. the distraction himself showed. I felt him before he rounded the corner.

"I couldn't wait," Tate said as he took a seat at the bar, empty seats on either side of him, his expression as serious as ever.

"You shouldn't say stuff like that," I admonished, flipping a coaster in front of him.

"Another rule?"

"What will it be?" I pulled a frosty mug from the freezer and held it up.

"You, under me as soon as possible."

I glanced up and our eyes locked. "You're incorrigible."

"My pants have been tight all day."

"Stop it!"

"What?" he said, shrugging as if he didn't know he was tormenting me. By his stare, I could tell he knew exactly what he was doing.

I turned my back to him and pulled the newest IPA.

Setting it in front of him, I asked, "Could you come to Red's a bit late tomorrow?"

The corners of his mouth turned down even more. "Why?"

"So I can have some time with my girlfriends before you get there."

"And boyfriends. Who's the guy over there?" he asked, flipping his head to the left.

I saw Stuart angled against the wall that led into the kitchen.

"My boss. He's the bar manager, why?"

"He's watching you just like he was the other night."

"So?" I rested my arms on the bar top.

Tate wrapped his fingers around my forearm. "Have you—"

"No. I haven't and wouldn't. I learned that lesson a while ago."

"Which was?"

"Judy," Stuart called. "Can you come here?"

"Sure." On my way over to him, I wiped the bar and cleared a glass a few seats down from Tate. "What's up?"

"I thought you said he was no one." Usual upbeat Stuart didn't seem so upbeat anymore.

"He wasn't at the time. He's since come back around."

"Be careful," he warned.

"Why would you say that?"

Stuart glanced from Tate to me. "He looks so serious. He hasn't smiled once since he sat down."

"Yeah, that's how he is. He's not big on smiles."

"We could have fun, Judy. It wouldn't have to be serious."

"My dance card is all filled. Please don't take this personally. I like working here and don't want to lose this job."

"Rejection is always personal. However, I won't let it

138

affect us working together."

I hoped he meant it. I passed by Tate and checked on my other customers. After placing an order for food, I stepped back in front of him.

"What was that about?" he asked.

"What you might guess."

"Jesus, Blue." He practically glared at me.

"I assure you, I didn't ask for it." I cleared his beer mug away and filled a new one, setting it in front of him.

"Is it always like this?"

"More often than I would like," I said with a shrug.

"Way more than I'm comfortable with."

"I don't know what to say. Why does it bother you?" I filled a glass full of ice and water for myself.

He didn't answer.

I crashed smack into his wall of steel. Trying to shift the mood, I asked, "Are you hungry?"

"Very." The flare of his eyes told me food wasn't on his agenda, eating me for dinner was.

"I sometimes think we should avoid talking altogether. It's a mine field."

"I don't want to talk." He reached across the bar for my hand. "When does your shift end?"

Not soon enough, I thought.

As if he read my thoughts, he said, "Definitely not soon enough."

"A couple of hours. I don't see Stuart letting me off early. Definitely not while you're sitting here."

"You should look for another place to work."

My mouth dropped open. "Dude, back off. I'm serious. You don't get to keep me out of your life and control mine."

He pursed his lips and brushed his hair out of his face.

"You're right, I'm sorry." After breathing out heavily, he asked, "Do you get a break?"

"Yeah, I have thirty minutes coming to me."

"Come outside with me."

I glanced in Stuart's direction and looked back at Tate. "Give me a few minutes." I grabbed the plastic ice bin and went to the kitchen. I filled it and then noticed that I had food up. Leaving the ice in the back, I picked up the appetizer and delivered it to the guy at the end of the bar. Catching Tate's eye, I smiled as I passed by him again. Back in the kitchen, I found Stuart. "Can I go on break as soon as I dump the ice?" I lifted the bin and waited for him to respond.

He looked to be searching for a reason to say no. Apparently, he couldn't find one. "Okay." Grabbing the other side of the ice bin to help me carry it, he followed me out to the bar and we poured the ice into the receptacle.

Once Stuart moved away, I said, "I'll meet you out front."

"Let me pay—"

"Don't worry about it."

Tate had his hands in the pockets of his relaxed-fit jeans as he leaned against his motorcycle. "Let's go for a ride."

"I only have a few minutes."

"I'll have you back in time. I brought an extra helmet for you." He handed me a glossy, black, half helmet with a striking graphic of purple and blue feathers.

"Wow, it's pretty."

"It's yours."

"Mine?" I pulled it over my head and Tate tightened the strap under my chin.

"Very cute," he said, touching my nose. He slipped on his full helmet and straddled his red Harley.

I climbed on behind him, wrapping my arms around his waist. "Where are we going?"

"For a ride." He pulled out onto Andrews Avenue and then turned onto AIA following the bridge.

I called out in excitement. I had never been on a motorcycle and laughed over the thrill of it. It felt like we were going really fast, water passing on either side of us. The power of the bike, the vibration, my arms around Tate's waist, my cheek pressed against his back all turned me on. When we were across the water, he made a U-turn and took me back to the parking lot of Tap 42. Once he stopped, I hopped off the bike.

Unbuckling the helmet, I said, "That was so much fun, but it was way too short."

"You look gorgeous with your cheeks all red and your eyes sparkling," he said, his eyes smiling at me.

"Thank you." I stood on tiptoe so I could kiss him.

He swept me up in his arms, his kiss full of passion.

"I wish I didn't have to go back inside," I murmured against his lips.

"You have no idea."

"Sure I do. Are you coming back in?"

"No, I don't think I could keep my hands off you, bar be damned."

"Okay." I pulled his mouth down to mine and kissed him softly goodbye. As I walked away, I said over my shoulder, "I love my helmet. Thank you." I thought I saw a slight smile as I headed back into the bar.

The next two hours dragged on like ten. Stuart kept eyeing me as if he wanted to say something, but thankfully, he kept it to himself. Just before the end of my shift, I ordered and ate a half order of grilled chicken avocado salad. I boxed the other half to go and then texted Tate.

Me: I'm almost out of here. My place?

Although Tap 42 was located closer to Tate's house, I didn't want to be tempted to spend the night after a long day of work. I figured it would be easier to kick him out of my place when I got too tired.

I cashed out with Stuart, paying for Tate's drinks too, and said, "Goodnight."

"Be safe," he said.

Safe? That occupation had fled my DNA. Safety wasn't in the cards. I still hadn't heard back from Tate by the time I drove home. I heard my phone chime as I pulled into my apartment complex. I found Tate waiting for me on the steps to my place. "Been waiting long?"

"Way too long, but I've only been here a few minutes."

He didn't get up, so I sat next to him on the step and rested my hand on his thigh.

He smoothed his hand over my head and tugged at the tie keeping my hair up. "How'd it go?"

I shook my head once my hair was set free. "Endless. It was a slow night, and waiting to see you again made it painfully so."

"Your boss?"

"He was fine."

"I want to lock you up like Rapunzel," he confided, shifting my legs over his lap and drawing me close.

"For someone who doesn't want a real relationship, you're very possessive," I said, touching his face, his stubbly cheek.

"I agree," he admitted.

Tracing his full lips, I asked, "What are you going to do about it?"

He kissed the tip of my finger and then pushed aside

my collar, kissing his way up my neck. His dangerous hands wove their magic against my back, inciting a riot within me. Then his lips found mine and I melted against him. His tongue leisurely explored my mouth, one hand resting on my lower back and the other holding my neck. "Let's go inside," he whispered when he pulled his mouth away. He stood and held out his hands for me, lifting me to my feet.

As I fumbled with my keys and unlocked the door, his body pressed against mine. I felt his breath in my hair. Once inside, I asked, "Do you need anything?"

"Just you." He took my hand and led me to the bedroom, turning on the light and dimming it. We faced each other and I unbuttoned his shirt, pausing so he could lift my shirt over my head. He kissed along my collarbone, lowering my bra strap. As my large breast spilled out, he lifted it to his mouth and swirled his tongue around the nipple before sucking it into his mouth. I arched into him, loving the attention. His other hand found the button on my jeans, and my hands found his and unzipped his pants, pushing them down. We paused in our play and kicked our jeans away.

"Very sexy," he said, fingering the V in the front of my black, lacy bra. He pivoted me to the side and fondled my ass, the matching lacy thong showing between my butt cheeks. "It's hard for me to decide which side of you is my favorite." He turned me back around. "I have to go with front because of that mouth of yours." His lips came down on my mine as his hands explored all of my exposed flesh, branding me with his touch. He lowered the other strap of the bra, freeing my left breast. "So beautiful," he murmured as he twisted and tugged both nipples until they were completely aroused.

Then Tate's hands trailed down my narrow waist, his

thumbs looping the sides of my thong, drawing it down my thighs. His mouth followed his hands, breathing against my mound. "I love that you keep your lips smooth but have a path on your mound." His tongue shot out and I kicked away my panties, spreading my legs for him as I unhooked my bra and tossed it aside. He groaned against me, wrapping his arms around my buttocks. His mouth pressed into me, his tongue seeking my sweet spot.

I held his head against my pussy. "Wonderful..." I uttered. My legs shook when his fingers played at my entrance along with the stroking of his tongue.

He brought me oh so close and said, "I want you to cum with my cock inside you."

"I want that, too."

He climbed onto the bed and knelt in the center of it, holding his hand out to me. He drew me against him, sitting me on his lap, my legs on either side of him. As he adjusted himself under me, I lifted up and slid down on his naked cock.

"Oh god," I cried. "You forgot—"

"I didn't."

"That's so ... oh Tate." And then, I couldn't speak.

His mouth kissed my breasts and tugged on my nipples. Then his incredible hands cupped my ass and tilted my hips so my clit ground into him. He shifted his legs out in front of him and I wrapped my legs around his back. The deepened penetration drove me insane. His cock hit all the right spots as we aggressed together.

His mouth sought mine, and neither of us closed our eyes. The taste of him roused and liquefied me as if we were one fused being.

My hands touched his back and shoulders, settling on his face. Our lips hovered close as we both moaned aloud.

"I want you to cum first," he growled, slowing his pace. "It feels too good." He shifted our position again, moving us to the side of the bed, where he sat with his right leg on the ground. He placed me on my back, draping my legs over his thighs, pulling me onto his cock. His hands held my sides as he rocked in, back and forth. The trail of his hands caressed my breasts as he continued his incursion. Then his fingers found my center, and I knew it wouldn't take me much longer.

His intense stare mystified me and yet, I could not look away, trapped in the strength of the moment. As he took me over the edge, every bit of me opened up, and he flew into my heart and soul before we both exploded out together in a confounding climax. Wave after wave of release, he continued to permeate my soul until I couldn't take it anymore.

"Please go," I said, still breathing heavy and trying to catch my breath. Tears hovered at the surface, and I refused to cry in front of him.

"What? Why?" he asked, lifting me in a tight embrace, his cock still inside me.

"You can't make love to me like that and not give me your heart while you're busy stealing mine."

"Shhh," he whispered, kissing my temple and gazing down at me. Pulling out of me, he spooned me against him, placing his warm palm on my chest between my breasts. "It's going to be okay."

Only I knew it wasn't as my tears silently spilled down my cheeks.

"Blue, it's okay," he whispered. "It was intense for me too."

I turned to face him, tears staining my cheeks. "Please go. I need to get some sleep before tomorrow."

"I don't want to leave you like this."

"Then tell me something about you."

"I can't." He moved to get up, the anchor of his past pulling us both down.

"Or won't," I said as he picked up his clothes and left the room.

I finally heard the front door shut, and I let the deep grief spill out. I would never be more than a body to anyone. Doomed to spend my life as someone's plaything or holding place. I damned my body again as I often had.

Why did stupid men like Stuart think that it's appealing to be offered causal sex? Why did stupid women like me keep accepting less than we deserve?

I wailed out my pain, all the bad memories weaving my noose of misery. When I came up for air, I thought of calling Bond, but I didn't dare bother the sanctified trio. Instead, I cried myself to sleep.

CHAPTER ELEVEN

I've Told You Now

by Sam Smith

In the morning, I found a note from Tate. It simply read:

I'm sorry, Blue.

"Yeah, well, so am I." I crumbled up the note and threw it in the trash. "I'm sorry you're damaged goods." I also mentally threw away all the little tidbits I had saved from what he had said. That boy needed to keep his cock and his hands to himself. *He probably won't show up at Red's anyway.*

I trudged through my shift at The Chart House, sorting through every moment with Tate, beating myself up over it all.

Back at the apartment, I showered and stood in front of my closet, trying to decide what to wear. I hadn't bought anything new in a while and decided I needed to visit Lainie's Bella Boutique soon to rectify that.

I wanted to look hot just in case Tate showed, mostly to torment him. Shifting a bunch of hangers to the right, I looked at the skimpier summer dresses I owned. Most were too dressy for the occasion. I finally decided on the sleeveless, white, chiffon dress, with a swirly, black decal covering the front. It had a short hem that became longer in the back. It didn't show cleavage, but it was flirty nonetheless. Coupled with sandals, it read causal.

After lining my eyes and gathering my belongings, I

arrived at Red's early. As I had hoped, only Bond was in residence.

When I walked into the living room, Bond whistled. "Very nice." He swooped me in his arms and kissed me hard.

I rested my head against his chest and sighed. "I almost called you late last night."

He tilted my head up. "Is everything okay? You should have called."

"I didn't want to bother you."

"Don't, Blue. You can always call. Sit," he ordered, pointing to the couch facing the back of the house. "What happened?"

I didn't speak right away and searched my mind for the right words.

"Just say it."

"It was too good and I made him leave and then I cried. I know I'm being stupid, but I can't help it."

"Is he coming tonight?"

I shrugged. "I don't know. I invited him before all of that and told him to come late. He wasn't thrilled with that part."

"I bet. Why did you tell him to come late?"

"So I could chat with the girls, which is what I said."

"He didn't believe you."

I shook my head.

"I wouldn't have, either. He thinks you want him here late so you can spend time with me."

I nodded.

"This should be interesting."

"If he comes."

"Oh, he'll come. No doubt about it. Do you have anything on under that dress?" His hand reached along my thigh.

"No." I laughed, swatting his hand away.

"You ladies are all the same. Love to torture us men."

I chuckled again. "There might be some truth to that."

Bond pulled me close and kissed me, his hand sneaking back under my skirt.

I reveled in the opportunity not to think about Tate. That is until we heard the front door open.

"Fuck," he sighed out.

I quickly fixed my dress and moved to the opposite end of the couch.

"Hey guys," Jacqs said as she rounded the corner and she and Red deposited bags on the counter.

I stood up and we hugged. Then I moved over to Red so Jacqs and Bond could have some time alone.

"Looking good," Red said, giving me a big bear hug.

"Thanks." I followed him into the kitchen and watched him unpack the groceries.

"Should I take this to mean Tate will be stopping by?"

"I guess we shall see."

"Trouble in paradise already?"

"If by paradise you meant rocky terrain along a cliff, then I'll answer in the affirmative."

Red gave a deep belly laugh.

"What's so funny?" Jacqs asked as she entered the kitchen and helped Red put the food away.

"Blue's metaphorical spin on words. You should be a writer."

I stuck my tongue out at him. "Speaking of which, Tate gave me feedback on my first chapter, and I've been reworking my novel. I plan to share some soon."

"That's exciting. I'm between books and could use something new to read. Honey, do you mind if I take Blue out back and leave the food to you?" Jacqs asked Red.

"Go, enjoy."

She rose up on tiptoes and kissed Red's cheek.

Grabbing my hand, she led me outside to the swinging loveseat. "So tell me all of it," she said as she took her place next to me.

"I think we should wait for the others so I don't have to repeat myself." I pulled the bottom of my dress down and crossed my legs.

"Okay, but just tell me, is his cock really thicker than Red's and longer than Bond's?"

I broke out in hysterical laughter. "Yes."

"I wonder if it would fit in me."

"I'm not sharing this one," I shot out, the laughter gone completely.

"I'm sorry, Blue, I didn't mean I ... that was a stupid thing for me to say."

I took a deep breath, trying to quell the simmering jealousy. "No, it's okay. I get the fascination."

"Is he nice?"

"He's ... hmmm, I don't think I would call him nice. He's distant but attentive, a rather odd mix of things that..."

"That?"

"Hey!" Cat called out, Lainie by her side. They grabbed two wrought iron chairs and placed them facing us.

"Is Sam here yet?" Jacqs asked.

"She should be here any minute," Lainie said as she sat down. "She left Bella's early so she could get here on time. We all want the lowdown. Is he coming tonight?"

"Wait for me!" Sam waved and carried over another chair.

"Drinks, ladies?" Bond asked, hanging his head out the French doors.

"Water for me," Sam said.

"I'll take whatever non-beer drink you have," I said. "Thanks."

"Same," Lainie said.

"Me too," Jacqs said.

"Beer for me," Cat said. "So spill it."

"I just asked her if Tate was nice and she said, 'not really,'" Jacqs relayed, sitting back and bringing her legs up on the couch.

"That could be good if you mean during sex," Lainie said with a wink.

I chuckled.

"So tell us. First, is he coming by tonight?" Sam asked.

I paused and smiled at Bond as he handed us our drinks. Jacqs touched his thigh and whispered her thanks. He smiled down at her and then winked at me.

Once he was out of earshot, I filled the girls in on everything.

"Based on his age, I'd guess he's been through a horrible divorce," Sam said. "Did he really say it had been over three years since he's had sex? Lucky you!"

"I think you should go for it," Cat said.

"And be damned my heart?"

"I'm with Cat," Lainie said.

"I think you should be careful," Sam said. "Your therapist is smart. You have to keep up your own walls or Tate—"

"Or Tate will what," he interrupted, staring straight at me. He took us all by surprise.

Over Tate's shoulder, I glared at Bond who mouthed, "I'm sorry." I stood up and went to Tate. "Let's go for a walk." I took his hand and led him to the far edge of the dock. "I wasn't sure you were coming."

He glowered at me, his jaw clinching.

I gently touched his cheek and saw the surprise in his eyes, yet the frown on his face remained unchanged.

Then he surprised me by holding both of my arms

behind my back and yanking me tightly against him. He ravished my mouth with a grunt, sparking an intense need in me.

Feeling the wetness on my labia, I wished I had chosen to wear panties. *Two pairs.*

"I want to take you away from here," he said, staring down at me.

"If you need to leave, then go. I'm staying. This is my favorite day of the week because I get to see my friends. I didn't get a chance to check in with them. They were too interested in you."

"What did you say?" he asked, absently playing with the ends of my hair.

"You don't want to know. Why don't you have a drink with the guys?"

"Will you come home with me tonight?" His fingers trailed up to my neck and massaged.

"Why?"

"Because I want you in my bed. Spend the night with me." His eyes pleaded with me.

"Do you know what it feels like to walk down the plank, knowing you're heading to your own demise?"

"Blue..."

"Do you? That's what this feels like, my final steps to the gallows."

"I'm very familiar with it."

I scanned his face, believing him. "And if I ask you to leave me alone?"

"I can't."

"Because you have a lot of sex to make up for?"

He tilted his head. His eyes looked so sad.

"Okay. Just grant me time with my friends."

The girls still huddled around the couch swing,

probably chatting about Tate and me. I sat back down and lifted my drink. "So, what's the verdict?"

"He's ridiculously hot," Cat said, smiling.

Sam nodded frantically in agreement.

"Stay and I want to invite you both over Friday night. He'll cook," Lainie said.

"I don't know how much longer I can take it."

"Which part? The big cock?" Cat asked.

They all laughed and I shook my head. Looking up, I saw Tate watching me. I flashed him a thumbs up. Bond had an odd expression on his face.

Bringing my attention back to the girls, I said, "His cock I can stand for just about forever. However, the rest of it? He's like a man handing out candy, leading me along to a very dangerous place."

"Heartbreak," Sam said. "I'm an expert."

"Sometimes you just have to take the leap of faith," Lainie said.

Jacqs nodded her head in agreement.

"Let's just hope I don't land on the jagged edges below. Enough about me, please! What's new with all of you?"

Lainie said, "I've been spending more time with Stay's grandmother and I just love her. I wish I could set her up with my father. My mother told me the other day, when she picked up the phone while I was chatting with my dad, that she would be very surprised if Stay goes through with the wedding. My father actually yelled at her and told her to get off the fucking phone. That was a first. Edith and I have been checking out wedding dresses and florists. It's been so fun. It's like having a real mom."

"I'm so happy for you, Lainie. For Stay, too," I said and meant it.

A huge laugh erupted amongst the guys. Tate had a

genuine smile on his face. I wished he would smile like that with me.

"We're all happy for you, Lainie," Sam said. "I was thinking about moving into Lainie's old condo, but my mother insists she doesn't want me or Sarah to leave, and it would mean a lot more driving back and forth to drop Sarah off. She's convinced me, so I'm staying put. Also, Sarah started preschool two days a week and loves it."

"Any men on the horizon?" Cat asked. She raised an eyebrow. "Or women?"

"I'm not ready yet. Between working, Sarah, and school, my life is happy and full. Soon though."

"I've got nothing new to share," Jacqs said, standing up. "I want to go check on the boys."

"Me either. Other than a trip Kev and I are planning to Connecticut to see his family. We are thinking of going for Thanksgiving."

"That's great," I said, watching Jacqs approach the men standing by the door. Stay caught my eye and tilted his head toward the house.

"Anyone else want another drink?" I asked, rising to my feet and straightening the bottom of my dress.

"All good," Sam said. Cat concurred.

"Yeah, when you come back out," Lainie said. "Thanks." She handed me her empty hard apple cider bottle.

I scooted past the group by the door and avoided catching Tate's eye. In the kitchen, I found Stay waiting for me. "So, should I run fast in the other direction?"

Stayman was the most intuitive of the group, and I trusted his opinion completely. "That's hard to answer at this point. There's a hole the size of the Grand Canyon inside his chest. On the one hand, he keeps himself separate, but his need is tremendous. He does have a great sense of humor, though."

"Really? I've not seen that side of him at all. He's so serious most of the time."

"That's self-protection, Blue. I'm sure it's hard for him to keep it up around you."

I burst out laughing. "Quite the contrary."

Stay looked confused until he played it back in his mind. He laughed with me. "That was funny. You know what I meant." He winked.

"Yeah, but do you like him? Do you think there's any chance he'll fit in here? Should I even bother?"

"He and Bond don't get on, but that's to be expected."

"How do you mean?"

"Let's not do the dance, okay? I love you girl, but you and Bond? How long now? Since before that drunken night, I'm guessing."

"Does Lainie know?"

He shook his head. "No."

"Bond said he would tell the group if I wanted, but I don't. I probably would have before, but now—"

"But now you're falling in love with someone else."

"Is it that obvious?" I felt Tate's stare from outside, but I didn't turn around to meet it.

"To me it is. Want some advice?"

"Please, yes."

"Be true to yourself and be honest. Love is always a risk and sometimes it rips you to the core, but sometimes..." He glanced outside at Lainie and then looked back at me. "Sometimes it becomes the air you breathe, and I want that for you. We all do, even Bond."

"I know. Bond's been great. He's keeping me sane."

"Plus, we'll be here to catch you if Tate doesn't."

I stepped forward into Stay's embrace. He rocked me

back and forth and kissed the top of my head.

"You're the best," I said, tilting my face up.

Tate came in and Stay stepped away from me to leave.

"Lainie wants another drink," I said, touching Stay's arm.

"Gotcha," he said, getting one out of the fridge and popping the cap.

"Thank you," I said as he passed by.

"Anytime."

"I like him," Tate said after Stay shut the French doors behind him.

"Me too."

"Did you and he—

"No."

"Good," he breathed out. "Can I steal you away now?"

"Let me say hi to Kev and say my goodbyes and then, yes." I reached my hand up and said, "You're smiling." I traced his lips.

"You have a good group of friends. Even Bond isn't so bad. I promise I'll like him much more once you're done with him."

"I don't know what to say."

He gave me a quick kiss. "I'll get Kevin for you and say my goodbyes."

Kev in his typical skinny jeans and sleeveless shirt joined me on the couch where I sat, watching our group of friends outside.

"Care to weigh in?" I asked.

"I keep telling Cat to butt out, but she never listens to me."

"What do you think of him?" I watched Tate outside talking with Red.

"He sort of reminds me of Red when he used to be gruff with Jacqs, keeping her at a distance. Really, it doesn't matter what I think, just what you think."

"Yeah, I know."

"We all want you to be happy and in love. I know that's why Cat's always meddling."

I leaned against Kev, and he wrapped his arm around me.

"He's a striking mountain of a man."

I laughed. "That he is."

"Cat mentioned something about a double date. Let's do something fun."

"She's too much. I'm going to say my goodbyes. Tate wants—"

"Understood."

I hugged Kev and made a beeline to the girls.

"Don't have too much fun," Cat said as we hugged goodbye.

Sam said, "Be careful and trust your gut."

"See you Friday," Lainie said.

Jacqs stood with Red, Bond, Stay, and Tate towering around her.

"Ready?" Tate asked as I approached.

"Yeah."

"Thanks for having me," Tate said to Red.

I hugged Bond goodbye and he whispered, "Call me if you need me. Anytime."

CHAPTER TWELVE

Ghost N Stuff (Nero Remix)

by DEADMAU5

I followed Tate to his house as promised, noticing a red Jeep Cherokee parked out front.

"You like red," I said after he opened my car door and I got out. "Kind of funny. The Native American with a Jeep Cherokee."

"We prefer American Indian, and I'm not Cherokee."

"Lighten up, dude. I saw you laughing with the guys, so I know you have it in you."

He wrapped his arm around my waist as we walked to the door. "My mind is focused on being *in* you."

After unlocking the door, he pulled me just inside the entryway, across the dark wood floors toward the living room. Not taking the time to shut the door, he took the hem of my dress and lifted it over my head, leaving me in just my bra. His hands stroked all of my available flesh, his lips trailing up my neck. With my ass in his palms, he asked, "You strutted around Red's with no panties? Oh, you naughty girl." As if making up his mind, he took me by the wrist and pulled me over his lap, along the length of the couch. His hands continued their dance over my calves, thighs, and onto my rounded rump. "I bet Bond knew. Didn't he?" His large palm spanked across my ass.

"Ohhh," I moaned.

Then he spanked my bottom repeatedly. The heat of my punishment shot to my clit and nipples, causing me to gasp. "I don't strut."

"Are you going to answer me about Bond knowing?" he asked when he paused.

"Never!"

"Naughty *and* rebellious."

The spanking resumed, my butt flaring red from the pain and pleasure. Then his hand soothed my buttocks and delved between my legs, touching my wet entrance.

I turned over on his lap and said, "Fuck me. Hard. Take me from behind."

"I want to see your face." He lifted me over his shoulder like a sack of potatoes, easily carried me as he kicked the outside door closed, moved through the archway to the bedroom, and deposited me on his bed.

I laughed. "You should probably grab a towel or two." I took off my bra as he shucked his clothes. When he stepped out of the room, I flipped over onto my front in the center of the bed.

"What're you doing?" he asked when he returned.

Wagging my ass in the air, I said, "I think that should be obvious."

He laughed and easily flipped me over. "But I want to kiss you."

"Then kiss me first, but fuck me from behind."

"I know what you're doing." He sat on the bed next to me.

"Good, then we're on the same page."

"We're doing it my way, Blue. Do I need to spank you again? Apparently, it wasn't hard enough. And if you recall, it was you who wanted to lose the condoms."

I can always shut my eyes.

"No," he said as if he could read my mind.

I pushed him over, onto his back and crawled my way down his body. His cock twitched against my cheek when I breathed in his masculine scent. "So much better without the condom," I murmured next to his testicles. My tongue flowed up the length of his shaft, my mouth covering his wide-brimmed head. "Yummy," I said, memorizing his smell.

"Come here." He pulled my hips over his face. "You have the perfect pussy. Your clit wants me already, poking out and swollen." His finger petted my outer lips and my hardened nub as I struggled to focus on his cock. He dipped his fingers inside and then trailed them to my ass. "Your little red bud is calling to me. Does Bond play with your ass?"

"My mouth is full," I mumbled, groaning over the sensation. "Can't ... answer."

"Do you play with your own ass? Toys?" he asked as he worked his finger in deeper.

"Mmmhmm." I took his cock in as far as it would go, drew back, and then suckled the tip, fondling his balls with my free hand.

"You're the naughtiest woman I've ever known."

Propping myself up, I said, "You must have led a very sheltered life."

"Will you show me sometime?"

"Maybe."

He swung me around so we faced each other, lying side by side. "Maybe?" Aggressively, he devoured my lips, pulling my thigh over his leg and penetrating my pussy. He started fingering my ass again, causing me to cry out.

"Towel," I managed to say.

We worked together to shift one underneath me and resumed our play.

"I want in there," he demanded, thrusting his finger deep in my ass as he circled his pelvis against me.

My gush sloshed between us. "We—oh that's so

good—have to work up to that. Toys ... first."

He paused and said, "Let's get dressed and go to your place."

I laughed and saw him smile. Then I wiped that smile off his face when I bit his full lower lip and kissed him roughly. All the sensations eddied like a tide pool building up to a tsunami. I closed my eyes and my heart and allowed my body dominion.

He stopped moving and ordered, "Look at me."

I shook my head back and forth.

With his free hand, he grasped my jaw.

My eyes flew open.

"I want you here with me."

"Please don't."

"I need you here with me, Blue. Please." He slowly continued our fuck, morphing it again into lovemaking. Our mouths hovered close, our breath comingling.

He kissed my cheeks, his eyes locked on mine. "Stay with me." He removed his finger from my ass and used his other hand on my clit. We slowly moved together, his breath my breath.

We rode the edge of forever, losing ourselves in each other. He rolled his hips into me, mirroring the motion with his fingers on my clit. I held his face in my right palm and his waist in my left, rocking into his lashing. We roughly kissed with our eyes open until I soared outside of myself and screamed out my climax. Tumbling down in freefall, my eyes locked on Tate's as he yelled out, "Bluuue!" and filled me with his energy and cum.

He kissed my forehead, eyelids, cheeks, and softly nuzzled my mouth. "That was beyond..." he whispered.

I snuggled against his chest, burying my head in tight, struggling to keep it together. Fear shrouded around me and in his arms, I clambered to fight off my demons.

"You're shaking. What is it?"

"I'll never be good enough."

"Baby, you already are. More than good enough. Shhh. I'm here."

"For how long?"

"I can't answer that. No one can, really. If I've realized anything in life it's this: nothing and no one can be counted on."

"I can count on my friends."

"Well then, you're luckier than most. I'm here now, and I'm not going anywhere."

Lying in his arms, surrounded by his energy, I thought, *How can your heart break as you're falling in love?* It had to be self-torture in the extreme. Why was I so mean to myself?

"Stop it, Blue. I can hear the gears grinding."

"You're too nice to me. You need to cut it out."

"You know that's not going to happen. Like I've said, give it time."

Time was my enemy, sitting on my shoulder, doubled over in hysterics, lazily kicking his leg. When did time ever make anything better? Not during my lifetime. My father and brother were still out of my life. And good riddance. Neither ever deemed it important to apologize or make amends for treating me like a body they could use for closing a deal or sharing with a friend. Those memories never became easier to bear. I sighed out heavily.

Tate lifted my shoulders so he could see my face. "Tell me, Blue."

"I can't."

"Come on, sure you can. I'm a great listener, and I won't judge you."

"Only if you share something, too. Anything."

He sat up against the headboard, pulling me up with

him. As if it pained him, he said, "I once had a group of friends like you do."

"Your motorcycle friends?"

"No."

I wanted to ask what happened, but I assumed that would cause him to shut down. Instead, I asked, "How long were you all friends?"

"Years. Since high school."

I wondered where they were now. Choosing my words carefully, I asked, "Was your wife one of them?"

The crease in his forehead deepened. "Yes."

In my head, I started calculating. Forty-three-years-old minus sixteen years for the approximate age when they met, minus another three for the past years of no sex, equals twenty-four years. *Holy shit!*

"It's your turn to share," he said.

"Just two more questions and you can ask me anything you want." I couldn't allow the window of opportunity to shut before I knew a few more things.

"Get it over with, please."

"This isn't the dentist."

"Feels just about like it."

I held my breath and then asked, "Was your wife your first?"

"Yes."

"How many lovers have you had?"

"Like you, none."

Uh huh.

"Lovers, four. One-night stands? Every night for about six months straight."

"That's a lot." I would bet my left boob that the six-month fuck-a-thon took place just before his long stretch of abstinence.

"Four lovers before me or three."

"You're number four."

"Hmm, okay."

He brushed the hair away from the right side of my face and looped it behind my ear. "Who hurt you so badly? Left you feeling you aren't the most amazing, gorgeous, kind creature that walks the earth?"

I put some distance between Tate and me and sat cross-legged. "There's a long list."

"Bond?" He rested his hand on my thigh, and I liked having it there.

"No, not Bond. I'm not saying it's always been peachy keen with him and it hasn't hurt sometimes, but that was more circumstance than intent."

"Your parents?"

"Yes, definitely."

"Do you have brothers and sisters?"

"One. Matt and my father aren't in my life."

"Who else?"

"Why?" I had an odd sensation in my gut. Like he planned to track them all down and make them pay. I liked it.

"Tell me."

"My brother's best friend. I thought I loved him."

"How old were you?"

"Fifteen."

Tate's face lit up in anger, and I knew he knew. "He took your virginity, missionary." It wasn't a question.

"Yes."

"And your brother?"

"He watched and egged him on."

"I'll kill them both," he growled, the heat crawling up his neck, making his ears red.

"You sound like Bond."

"He knows?" he practically roared.

"Yes. He's the only one."

"That doesn't make me feel the least bit better."

"Minus the sex, Bond is the big brother I wished I had. Be jealous if you must, but he's helped me cope with the shit in my life. He's helped me to not hate my body so much."

"Hate this body?" He drew me closer. "It's meant to be worshipped. You're a goddess and if I ever see your brother, he will reap extreme pain."

I smiled. "It was a long time ago. He was a kid, too."

"There is no statute of limitations on retaliation for permanently hurting the people I care about."

"You care about me?"

He cares about me.

He cares about me.

He cares about me, tagged to the beginning of a new list, to mull over later.

He cares about me!

"Of course I do. I like you a lot and if you let me, I'll exorcise all your demons."

"That'll take some doing. Anyway, Matt's at the bottom of the list."

"He's on the bottom? How long is the list?"

"Way too long."

"What did your father do?"

"It's what he tried to do. He tried to force me to have dinner with one of his clients. He wanted me to flirt and I quote, 'Maybe more.'" I wrapped my arms around myself. "Apparently, my assholic brother told him I wasn't a virgin."

"How old were you?" Tate looked furious.

"We should stop talking about this," I said, reaching for his hand.

"Fuck no. Did your mother know?"

"After the fact. My parents were already separated."

"What about your mother? You said, 'parents.'"

"Skeevy boyfriends. She never believed me."

"Did they—"

"No, they tried, though. Lots of inappropriate groping when she wasn't looking. I had a lock on my bedroom door and used it."

"Jesus Christ, Blue. I'm so sorry."

"Life sucks. I learned that a long time ago. My friends are really my family. My only real connection to my biology is my aunt on my mother's side. Sometimes that has to be enough. For me, it is. I've spent so much time wishing I had a different body, that people wouldn't notice me, that I could be a wallflower. My breasts got big so young. Having grown men hit on me when I was still in elementary school started my body hatred, and my family didn't help." Tears that I'd kept at bay during our conversation finally rebelled.

I continued, "In high school, I got asked out a lot, but they didn't want to know me, they just wanted me under them. I never had sex with any of them, but that never stopped them from saying I did. I was the slut of my high school, and I hadn't slept with a single guy. Not one, unless you count my brother's friend."

Tate held me in his big, strong arms as I cried what I hoped would be the very last tears over my past.

Even in that moment, the irony wasn't lost on me. I laid my past at his feet, the very thing he was unwilling to do with me, for me.

He stroked my hair down my back. His care and attention felt a lot like love, and my heart broke open and apart some more.

Once my tears stopped, we softly kissed. "Thank you," I uttered.

"Thank you for letting me. Would you like to go for a swim?"

"Oh, yes," I said excitedly, sitting up. "Oh, but I don't have a bathing suit."

He smiled a big, warm, genuine smile. "You don't need one at night."

I decided then and there, my new life occupation was to see that smile again. "Let's!" I used the bathroom and found Tate waiting for me with a robe held out. His short green and beige striped robe dwarfed me. He wore a longer navy robe.

"Damn, you look cute." He tied my sash tight and rolled up the sleeves. After retrieving fresh towels from the bathroom, he led me out onto the deck and down the wooden stairs to the beach.

I loved the feel of the warm sand in my toes and the sea breeze floating through my hair, but Tate's hand in mine was the best part.

The half-moon rose above the horizon, lighting the beach. Tate tossed the towels on the sand, and we disrobed. He scooped up my hand again, and we ran into the ocean. We high-stepped it until we were deep enough to lower ourselves into the water.

"This feels wonderful," I said, lying back and looking at the stars.

"Will you spend the night?"

I looked up into his eyes. "I don't think that's a good idea."

"Do you have to work in the morning?"

"No."

"Neither do I."

I battled with myself. Was there anything left of me to save? I scanned his face, wishing, hoping, praying that tonight meant progress and he would open up more. "Okay," I said, giving in.

He whooped, jumping up and splashing down, covering me in salt water.

I laughed in joy.

He seemed younger than I had ever seen him. The tension in his jaw and forehead disappeared.

I jumped at him, taking him by surprise.

He rolled me over, dunking us both under the surf.

I came up giggling and scanned his new expression. The corners of my mouth fell.

His lips crushed over mine.

I wrapped my legs around him, pulling him in as tightly as he held me. I felt his desperation and understood it. I vowed I would fall for him for as long as he let me. My hands wove into his wet hair as we bobbed in the water, our lips locked in an endless kiss.

I'm falling.

I'm falling.

I'm falling.

And you care about me.

After we parted, he said, "Any chance you could get a whole weekend off?"

"It would take some planning. Why?"

"I thought we could take the Harley up the coast and go for that long drive."

"Listen to you, you like me more than you let on," I said, splashing him.

"Blue, don't." All the stern tension returned to his face. The sound of his voice crushed my newfound joy.

I stood up in the water dejectedly. "It's called flirting."

I trumped up the sand to the towels. "I'm having a hard time keeping up with your mood swings."

"I'm sorry," he said when he joined me on shore.

"Yeah, yeah. Everyone's sorry. I'm sorry, too. I'm sorry for thinking I could relax around you and just be myself."

"I'm an idiot. That's how I want you to be, be yourself. Please forgive me." He spread out the robes over the sand and we sat down.

"I don't think you really do. I don't want to argue. I just feel like I have to censor myself around you. Like I can't enjoy our time too much, or it'll send you running away again."

He squeezed out the excess water from his hair and looked out over the horizon.

I sat waiting to see if the Tate rollercoaster would spin, turn, or flip me upside down.

Leaning back on his hands, he tilted his head my way. "I think if we both understand the limitations of our ... friendship, then we can just enjoy it."

"What you mean is if *I* understand the limitations of this ... whatever is between us ... then *you* can just enjoy it."

He flashed a brief smile. "Yes."

"Done," I said, lying through my teeth.

"Are you sure?"

"Yeah, but I'm going to sleep at home tonight. I think it's better for both of us." I moved to get up.

Translation: It was better for me.

"Okay," he said.

Back in our robes, he took my hand and led me to the house.

CHAPTER THIRTEEN

Am I Wrong?

by Nico & Vinz

Tate and I agreed to meet up at Stayman's condo on Friday night. He planned go over ahead of me and have dinner with Stay and Lainie, and I'd meet up with them after my shift. I put out feelers to see if I could get my shifts covered for the following weekend at The Chart House and Tap 42. I would have to wait and see.

On my way to The Chart House Friday evening, I received a text. Once I parked behind the restaurant, I checked my message.

> **Bond:** Can I see you tonight after I get off work?
> **Me:** Have plans.
> **Bond:** Come after.
> **Me:** Promised not to double book.
> **Bond:** Hmmm. Tomorrow night might be harder.
> **Me:** Why?
> **Bond:** Long story.
> **Me:** Please don't tell me this has something to do with Rory.
> **Bond:** Okay, I won't.
> **Me:** Fuck, dude. Will you ever learn?
> **Bond:** Probably not. It actually might help if you come by.
> **Me:** How does the saying go? Not my circus, not my monkey?

Bond: Very funny, Blue. I could use a friend.
Me: Damn you. Okay. Have you slept with her?
Bond: No.
Me: Keep it that way.
Bond: Love you.
Me: Love you too. See you tomorrow.

I knew Rory wouldn't give up. Young love could be so invincible and stupid. Fuck, at any age love was like that. I was still like that. Not that I would tell Tate how I felt, but the "love" thing or maybe it was its tricky cousin, obsession, ran roughshod over me. My mind was steeped in the thick, sticky poison of Tate. His hands, his scent, his cock, his broken heart, bewitched me with its incessant brew.

Some moments, I could just float in the bliss that comes with love. *So it will end*, I thought. *No big deal.* Not all love lasted forever. Then in other moments, fear twisted in my gut, making me unsure I would recover from the loss. No other man had pervaded every inch of my soul like Tate and in such a short time.

Being kind to me in the process became impossible when the fear flooded in. At those moments, I became the flagellant, metaphorically flogging myself within an inch of my life. If I hurt myself first, he couldn't hurt me worse. How fucked up was that? Plenty!

Two moments stuck with me the most: he cares about me and "don't, Blue." They played like a broken record in my head. I had convinced myself that progress was made. He did share about himself, if even briefly. His wife was his first, and he'd known her since high school. He was no longer a part of their group of friends, so something major had severed all those connections. Was it her doing or his?

On autopilot, I made it through my shift and changed

my clothes in the bathroom of the restaurant to jeans and a fitted top before heading over to Stay's place. I parked in a guest spot next to the nine-story, multi-level, modern condominium with blue-tinted windows and balcony railings. After taking the elevator to the seventh floor, I knocked on their door.

Lainie let me in and took the flowers I brought for her. "Thanks, they're gorgeous," she said and then reminded me to take off my shoes by the front door. She left the flowers on the kitchen counter and led me through the main space of the condo, which had cream-colored walls and big, square, beige, speckled tiles covering the floor. A four-piece set of comfortable looking, plush, dark brown couches sat around a large, square coffee table. Shelving filled with books lined the right wall. On the left sat a four-top glass table. She brought me out to a large balcony with a view of the water below.

"Stay and Tate are in his office. He's showing Tate his latest project. He's working with a guy that's trying to couple dating and gaming into one site. The graphics are very cool."

"I'll have to check it out later. You look incredible, Lane. Love sure does agree with you."

Dressed in flowing, beige crepe pants and a matching top, she looked statuesque and sophisticated. She seemed softer and more relaxed. "Thank you. Life is really good these days."

"I'm very happy for you. So, what do you think of him?" I asked, resting on the wall of the balcony, scanning the view of the Intracoastal Waterway, boats, and other condominiums.

"Tate? Not sure yet. Stay really likes him, and he seems nice enough. Maybe it's because of my time with

172

Mason, but there is a part of him that's distant. I recognize it. It's very hard to have half of a connection, and I wouldn't wish that for you." Before Lainie fell in love with Stayman, she was involved with a married man.

"Yeah, no shit. Do you think he's different with the guys?"

"I imagine he's different with anyone who's not you. I saw him watching you at Red's. He has this intense stare and it's usually focused on you, whether you're looking back or not."

I took a seat next to her.

"It's too late, isn't it?" she asked.

"Way."

"He's devastatingly handsome. He must be hard to resist." She gave me a knowing smile.

"It's completely impossible. Can your heart fall in love and break at the same time?"

"Oh, Blue. I was hoping he might be your Stay and not your Mason. It's really the worst kind of love. You can feel so up, like you're floating around the sun and then within seconds, you come crashing into the earth's surface."

"That about sums it up."

"Sums what up?" Stay asked, joining us on the balcony with Tate in tow. Stay wore his usual jeans and a plaid shirt with the sleeves rolled to the top of his forearms. His golden-brown hair had grown in since he started dating Lainie.

"You have a bad habit of sneaking up on people," Lainie said with affection in her smile.

"Only you, love. Are you hungry, Blue?" Stay leaned on the railing, facing us.

"I ate something at work," I said, still avoiding Tate's gaze.

"Blue," Tate said. "Can I steal you for a few minutes?"

Once our eyes connected, I felt the familiar pull on my heart and other places. "Sure."

"You can use the guest room," Lainie said, showing us the way.

A murphy bed remained closed against the wall, and we sat on the blue couch.

Tate seemed calm. "It's good to see you."

My translation: He missed me. Of course, my translation software was about as good as Google's.

"It's good to see you too. Are you having a good time?" I asked, not knowing what to do with my hands. Usually we would be touching each other, but for some reason he hadn't initiated it.

"It's been ... nice. Better now that you're here."

My translation: He likes to be with me better than anyone else.

I smiled. "Why are you sitting all the way over there?" There were only mere inches between us, but the gap felt like a crater.

"If I start, I'm not sure I could stop, and I'd hate to leave a bad impression on your friends, let alone a mess."

My translation: He can't control himself with me.

My smile grew and I felt the car on the rollercoaster riding up through the clouds. I climbed up on his lap. "I need a kiss."

"It's too early for us to leave, and you know what happens once we start."

"Too late," I said, feeling down the inside of his thigh.

"Don't make it worse," he admonished, but his eyes shone mischief.

"Kiss me, Tate."

"If I have to," he said, suppressing a smile. And then he did, full of passion and unrestrained heat.

While attempting to catch my breath, I said against his lips, "Your kiss should be registered as a lethal weapon, rendering all women incapacitated by the mere touch of your lips."

He burst out in laughter, and my heart soared. I memorized his face, taking a mind picture to mull over later. I thought of Claire in the movie *Elizabethtown*, shooting pretend pics with her fingers. I had captured one of Tate laughing.

"You, Blue. Thank you for that. I haven't laughed that hard in a while."

"Happy to be of service."

"Speaking of servicing, what's your schedule tomorrow?"

"Nice double entendre. Uh ... I'm working at Tap 42, night shift, but..."

"Bond," he said, moving me off his lap.

I touched his arm and thankfully, he didn't pull away. "He wanted to see me tonight, later, and I said no."

"Will you have sex with him?"

I took in Tate's sad eyes. "I don't know."

"It's not a given?"

"No. The night after you and I met at the beach, Bond and I just talked."

"Did you spend the night with him?" His hand covered mine, which I took as a good sign.

"Yes, I did."

"In his arms?" His hand fell away.

Not good. "Yes."

"What if I say I don't want you to?"

"Sex or sleeping together?" The tenor of the conversation unsettled my stomach.

"Both. Especially sleeping together."

"Why?" *Why, oh why, can't relationships be easy for me?*

"Because you won't spend the night with me."

Sitting next to Tate, for once I had no clear comeback or direction to head. I opted for a question, "Do you know why I haven't spent the night?"

"Yes, but you said you understood the parameters and what I can offer."

"Either we're fuck friends or we're more."

"More."

My eyes widened and I gasped.

More.

More.

More... What a fucking dangerous word.

"Blue, I ... nothing has changed. I won't fall in love with you. We won't move in together, although sleepovers are very welcome. We won't get married and have children together. We can have now, for however long that lasts. I don't want to share you with Bond."

I stood up, paced away, and faced him. "That's not up for you to decide. What are you offering in return? Why should I stop?"

He shifted forward on the couch. "I'm offering as much of me as I have to share. I know it's a paltry offering, but I believe if we can get past this one step, we can have a lot of fun together. And when the right man comes along, I'll step aside."

I stared at Tate, my emotions pervading me: fear, anger, sadness, need, desperate need. That same need I'd felt coming from him. Could I somehow get what I wanted without sacrificing my self-worth? *Doubtful.* "I'll think about it," I finally said. "I'm seeing Bond tomorrow night regardless. I've made plans, and I intend to keep them. I can't spend the night tonight or by definition, tomorrow night will be double booking." I wrapped my arms around myself, trying to protect my heart.

"I'll make an exception if you spend the night. We'll consider it a carryover."

"How convenient." I bit my bottom lip and looked away.

"I need more time with you, Blue. Here's my last plea." He stood up and stepped over to me. He pulled my lip free of my teeth and tilted my head up. "You're not in a situation with long-term potential with anyone else, right? Is there someone I don't know about?"

"No."

"Use me until that happens," he said, lowering his mouth to mine. His kiss spoke of yearning, the deep down kind. His very kiss willed me to give it a shot, to let him in, even if he wouldn't be doing so in return.

Then all my rationalizing began: I've managed okay with Bond, I can manage Tate, too. *I can do this!*

"Okay," I whispered.

"Okay?" he hummed against my neck. He kissed and tickled there.

I pushed him away. "We should get out there."

"Yeah, I guess we should."

We walked out of the guest room holding hands. Lainie pulled me away and said, "What happened? He looks, I won't go as far as saying happy, but not so serious."

"I said I would give it a real shot, whatever that means," I whispered. "Understanding that it's temporary and all of that."

"He's staring at you now."

"I can feel it."

"You can? Be careful, Blue. You can always call me. Stay, too."

"I know and thank you. Let's hope I don't have to take either of you up on it."

177

"Definitely."

"Stay, why don't you show me your new animation project," I said, looping my arm with his.

His office contained three distinct spaces. On the right was a large, wooden desk with a hutch. The back left corner held an altar with a Buddha effigy in the lotus position, candles, various stones, and a mat laying in front of it. The last area had two guitars, a keyboard, and a stereo system. We sat in front of his desk as he moved through screenshots.

"I wish I was out there, hearing what Lainie is saying to Tate."

"I bet. How are you doing?" Stay asked, scrolling through animated images.

"It changes minute by minute. Right now, I'm good. He wants us to have a full-on relationship with no option to move forward."

"So temporary?"

"Wait, slide back one. So, will the gamers meet here for coffee?" The screenshot showed a swanky coffee shop with small circular tables out front.

"Exactly. They can virtually order drinks, hang out, and chat."

"Cool. Will they be able to search by city for dates?"

"That's what the programmers tell me."

"Impressive."

"Thanks. Tate's an interesting man."

"How so?"

"Did you know he used to own a big construction company? They did a lot of the residential subdivisions out west."

I rubbed my forehead and said, "No. He told me he's a professor at FAU."

"That's just been the last few years."

I tried to wrap my head around what Stay had shared and how it fit with what I already knew. "What else?"

"His partner bought out his half of the company."

Taking my eyes from the screen, I looked at Stay. "Did he say anything else about his past?"

"No."

I stood up and smoothed my jeans. "Thanks for telling me. Shall we rejoin them?"

"Sure."

We all played Three Thirteen, a rummy card game, which was a lot of fun. I enjoyed seeing a more relaxed side of Tate, and it was nice not to be the third wheel.

Outside of Lainie's and Stay's place, we waited for the elevator.

"Your place or mine?" Tate asked, swinging my hand in his.

"Your place is closer, but I don't have a change of clothes with me."

"Good thing you won't be needing any clothes."

I laughed. "Okay. Did you have a good time?" I asked as we entered the elevator.

"I'm not much of a game person, but it was fun. Stay's an interesting chap."

"A chap?"

"Kind of fits him, no?"

"Yeah, it does. He told me you used to own a construction business."

Ignoring my comment, he said, "Lainie is worried for you."

"Oh? What did she say?"

We stepped out of the elevator, and he walked me to my car. Fighting with the door, he said, "I thought you were getting this fixed."

"I have an appointment to drop it off on Monday. I haven't sorted out how I'll get around until—"

"The Cherokee is at your disposal. You can leave your car at my place, and I'll take care of it."

"That's not necessary. I can see if Bon—"

"Part of being a couple is helping each other out."

What?

Wait?

A couple?

"Okay," I said, standing a few inches off the ground.

"Better yet, let's leave your car here and I'll have it brought to Rick's garage. Grab whatever you need out of it."

"Okay," I said, *a couple, a couple, a couple*, dancing in my head. *I might grow to like this.* I grabbed my bag with a hidden surprise inside. "So what did Lainie say?"

By the Harley, Tate handed me my helmet and placed my bag in the sidesaddle. "She said you were worth far more than something casual and that you were—how did she put it— generous and people easily take advantage of that."

"She said that!"

"I thought it was sweet. She's looking out for you."

"I'm not generous."

"Come here," he said, taking the helmet. He placed it on my head and buckled the strap. "You're very generous." He bent my head back and brushed his warm lips against mine. After swinging his leg over the side of the bike, he held it steady for me to climb on behind him. Off we went into the warm night.

CHAPTER FOURTEEN

Closer

by Nine Inch Nails

O nce inside Tate's house, I took the car key off my keychain and gave it to him.

"What's in the bag," he asked, placing it on the table.

I blushed crimson. "That's for later."

"Let me see," he said, untying the closure. He pulled out the six-inch glass dildo I kept in a thick sock. "Damn, woman." He held my hand to the front of his jeans. "I'm rock hard."

I glanced up at him, the heat of his expression stealing my breath. "Oh ... I."

"Don't be embarrassed, you naughty girl. I'm so turned on I think my cock might rip through these jeans."

My breath released and I stepped forward. "There's a simple solution for that." Popping the buttons on his 501 jeans, I freed his beautiful cock.

He lifted me up and sat me on the edge of the table. His hands cupped my face, and his lips found the pulse in my neck. He kissed up the side of my throat to my mouth. His taste had become my new addiction. Our tongues collided, and I gasped when he sucked on mine. Then my top was pulled over my head and my bra unclasped, falling to join my top on the floor. He kicked off his pants and stripped off his shirt. "You're still too dressed," he groaned.

I hopped off the table and quickly shed my jeans.

He set me back on the table and resumed his attack on my mouth.

My hands got lost in his hair as my legs wrapped around his ass.

"Your kisses drive me crazy," he grunted.

"I know what you mean." I smiled against his mouth. "They're lethal."

"I'm battling myself right now."

I reclined back onto my palms. "Oh? Do tell."

He rolled his hips against me and yanked me in tightly. "I want to slide into your warmth, and I also want to watch you play for me."

"First things first." I aimed his cock at my entrance and slid him in. "Holy hell, I don't think I'll ever get used to that. There's so much of you."

"A few more strokes and I'll be all the way home."

Home. Yes home!

Grasping my ass, he rented me forward, and my body opened for him. Then his hands sculpted me, molding my body against his. They were in my hair, smoothing down my neck, caressing the flesh of my back.

"So good," I moaned. His delicious scent surrounded me, all male. My hands did a dance of their own, shaping along his spine around his broad, coppery back.

"Lie back for me," he said, lowering my torso down to the table. Then his blessed hands stroked up my hips and stomach, waltzing around my breasts. He taunted my nipples, twisting and pinching them between his fingers. My back arched over the attention. All the while, he drew out slowly and forcefully thrust back in, his eyes locked on mine.

"Let's quit ... our jobs ... oh, yes ... and run away. We—Christ!—could do this all day ... every day," I cried.

Then his thumb migrated to my clit, and I could no longer speak. Only wild animal sounds unwittingly shot out of me.

"Holy hell, Tate ... ohhh now!"

"I'm chasing you!"

My body convulsed, arching and contracting, as Tate ruled my clit and plowed into me. I gushed and squirted all over us, finally melting into the tabletop. My lungs rose and fell, my breath coming out in pants. I shook my head back and forth.

His hand stopped the motion, holding my chin. I opened my eyes and could have sworn I saw love in his. It might have been lust, but it felt like way more.

Me too.

"Don't move," he said. "I'll get us towels."

Where would I go? I floated in bliss, contemplating his sexual prowess and attention.

He gently dried me off.

"Thank you," I mumbled.

He drew me up and wrapped his arms around me. "Are you hungry?"

"I could use a snack," I said, hugging him back.

"There's a robe hanging in the bathroom for you."

I smiled and hopped off the table. In the bathroom, I found a matching green and beige robe, only smaller than the one I wore Wednesday night. I loved it! The sleeves were still a bit long, though.

Ambling into the kitchen, Tate turned to me. "Adorable." He rolled the sleeves for me.

"You don't play fair," I pouted.

He wore the matching robe while fixing us a plate of nachos. He tilted his head and said, "I plan to spend money on you."

"Is the money from selling the construction business?"

"Yes, and no more questions about that." He didn't

seem angry or upset, and that was a relief.

"Okay. You know, you don't have to buy me things. That's my mother's gig."

"How do you mean?" He put the plate in the oven to melt the cheese and turned to face me.

"She has always looked for a man with money to take care of her. I don't think she even likes some of them, and she would quickly drop one for another. I vowed never to be like that."

"You're nothing like that, Blue. Let me spoil you."

"Well … if you must," I said, holding back my smile.

"Come here." He brought me into his arms, and we held each other.

I planned to store the memory. Us standing in the kitchen in matching robes, my head against his chest, my heart falling harder and faster each second.

He pulled the plate out of the oven with a mitt and rested it on the stove. "Would you like a drink? Margarita?"

"Sure."

He gathered a pale ale, a Cayman Jack margarita, napkins, and the plate of nachos.

I followed him outside to the deck where we sat down. "Another beautiful night," I said.

"Yes it is." He handed me my drink and set the nachos between us. "Tell me more about your childhood."

I scrunched my nose and pursed my lips. "Will you share about yours? Before whatever happened, happened?"

"Okay."

I jumped internally, doing a twirl. I ate a couple of chicken nachos and sipped my drink. "Okay. So, there was a definite dividing line in my childhood. Almost like my parents wore a costume of domesticity until the day they split. Then they seemed like two entirely different people from the ones I thought I knew."

"How old were you?"

"Nine or ten. I was in fourth grade. My brother changed, too. He became sullen and angry. At first, it wasn't so bad. I liked going to my dad's every other weekend. He spent more time with me than he ever had. However, after about the first year or two, he spent all his time in his room. My brother and I watched TV or played games. Other than eating together, I didn't see my dad. Plus, his new girlfriend wasn't a nice woman, and I never felt comfortable there after she moved in. I didn't want to go there anymore, but my mother forced me. She wanted time alone with her latest wallet. That's what I called them anyway."

"You said your brother lived with your father?"

I closed my eyes, enjoying the ocean breeze circling around. "Yeah. He came to my mother's on the odd weekends until..." I opened my eyes to Tate's soft expression.

"Right. Did you still go to your father's place after that?"

I swallowed some more of the margarita. "My mother forced me a few more times. That's about time the whole shit storm happened with my Dad. Haven't seen either since. Your turn."

He looked out over the ocean and responded. "I spent my early childhood on the Rosebud reservation in South Dakota. My father was an anthropologist doing his dissertation on the American Indian and met my mother there. He was enamored with the culture, the positives of it anyway. The tradition and history. The realities of living on the reservation became too much for him, and we moved to South Florida when I was eleven."

"Are they still married?"

"They're divorced, but still together." He took a slug of

the beer and continued, "They can't live without each other, although they try for stretches of time. The older they get, the less of a struggle it seems to be."

"Do they live here?"

"No, they're back in South Dakota."

We sat quietly eating and drinking, my mind whirling around all the new information.

I wiped my mouth with a napkin and asked, "What were you like as a kid?"

"Free. I missed the open land, moving here. The reservation had a much more fluid idea of structure and time. It was important to my father that I excel in school, so I did. For my mother, school meant very little. She values art, tradition, and self-exploration above all else."

"So your parents' cultures never really blended."

"No."

I pulled my legs up in the chair and shifted my body toward him. "Who are you more like?"

"That's an interesting question. Would you like another drink?" He stood and gathered the empty plate and our drinks.

"Sure." I wrapped my arms around my legs and rocked in my seat. I could make out the big dipper in the sky. *Had I pushed too much?*

He handed over my drink and answered my question, "I used to be much more like my mother. Over the last few years, I think I'm more like my father. They're like a feather and a rock."

"I see." I wanted to say and ask so much more, but I refrained. We clicked our bottles together and sat listening to the waves and the wind. I wished I could crawl into his mind and listen to all of his thoughts.

"Are you tired?" Tate asked, pulling my chair closer to him.

I laughed. "No." I turned up my drink and finished the contents.

"Let's go inside then," he said, holding his hand out for mine.

He left our bottles on the dining table and grabbed my bag and a towel, leading me to the bedroom.

"I'm nervous," I uttered, holding onto the edges of my robe.

"Don't be. Just pretend I'm not here but make sure to maintain eye contact," he said with a full smile.

I playfully put my hands on my hips. "You must realize those two things are contrary."

"You're procrastinating." He opened my bag, finding the small oil bottle and retrieving the glass dildo.

Lifting the towel, I folded it in half and spread it near the bottom of the bed. I caught Tate's expression and shot another mental picture. He appeared lustful and young, the corners of his lips slightly pulled up. His eyes looked wild and dilated.

He untied my sash and gently herded me toward the bed.

"Impatient much?"

"You have no idea."

I positioned my lower body over the towel and lay back onto the bed. Just his gaze on me ramped up my heartbeat. The surface of my skin felt flush and alive. Before I even began, my nipples tightened to peaks and heat surrounded my clit.

"So beautiful," he whispered, his stare absolute.

Without looking away, I reached down for the oil and positioned it by my hip. I fanned my hair out behind me and brushed my bangs out of my eyes. Then I trailed my fingers down my neck and chest, cupping my full breasts in my hands, lightly jiggling them for show.

He grunted, his hand wrapping around his hard cock.

"Damn, that looks good," I hummed, taking another mental shot.

"Exactly what I was thinking." He slowly ran his fingers up and down his shaft.

So hot!

I pulled and tugged on my nipples, feeling the wetness gather in my folds. Then I raised my breast to my mouth and sucked on my nipple.

"Holy fucking shit. You're killing me here."

"Now you're flinging the 'holys.' Come here and suck the other side."

He climbed on the bed beside me, licked his lips, and lowered his mouth to my nipple. We both sucked, his hands getting in on the action until I couldn't take it anymore.

"Okay, okay. Go back there." I waved to the end of the bed. "Otherwise I'll just jump you and forgo the show."

"We have plenty of time for that." He stood back at the foot of the bed and watched me crawl my fingers down my stomach, stopping to play with the light smattering of hair leading to my honey pot. "Jesus," he hissed.

With my knees spread wide and up, I splayed my lips apart, exposing my clit. With our eyes locked, I teased my arousal, circling my hips in time. My other hand dipped into my juices and spread them down over my anus.

His eyes flamed with desire.

I felt certain I would never tire of that look. "No one has ever looked at me like that," I confessed, pausing in my play.

"I've never been so turned on in my life. Have you done this before?"

"Tons of times, but never for an audience."

"Praise the Great Spirit and the ancestors."

I clicked the top of the oil bottle and coated my fingers,

rubbing them around my ass. I dipped my finger inside, spreading the oil around.

"Blue," he groaned. He had a stranglehold on his cock.

As much as I avoided men his size, I had to admit, I'd never laid eyes on a better looking man: his smooth, cut coppery chest, abs, and the V. Other than his sad eyes and cock, the V was his finest feature.

"Don't stop," he pleaded.

Our gaze reconnected, and I worked a finger into my ass past the second knuckle. A little gush trickled out and I blushed. "This might be very wet."

"Good. I want to see you work another finger in there."

I swirled the first finger around, pushing at the sides and then inserted a second.

"I wish I could be kissing you right now, but I don't want to miss a thing."

I loosened the area, sliding my fingers in and out, pulling at the sides of my entrance. "Can you hand me the glass?"

He slipped off the sock and handed it to me. "It's very cold."

"I know. It makes it even more stimulating."

"Damn." A pearl of precum crested the tip of his cock.

"Bring that over to me," I beckoned.

He straddled my face and I licked and suckled the tip of his cock, savoring his taste. He then stepped back off the bed as I poured oil over the dildo. "Do the ribs in the glass feel good?" he asked.

"Amazing."

"Fuck! Show me."

I giggled at him.

The slightly curved, glass phallus had an etched head at the top, spiral ribs along the shaft, and a flared end to hold onto. Wiping my hand off on the towel, I held the invader and perched it at the edge of my hole. I pushed gently, working the cold tip inside. "Holy shit, that's intense!"

"I think I might spontaneously cum. *You are* so fucking sexy."

Watching the landscape of his face, all the tension gone, I reveled in my ability to reach him, even if only sexually. In and out, I worked the phallus, my other hand tapping my clit. Then the waterworks started. I gushed like a mini fountain, the stream endless.

"How much longer?" he groaned.

"That depends."

"On?"

"Do you want me to cum with the glass in my ass or you?"

"Blue, my very naughty girl?"

"Yes, love."

"Me."

I pulled out the glass and handed him the oil. "Please go slowly, and you might want to grab the other towel."

We placed another folded towel under my hips, then he dragged the towels and me to the edge of the mattress. So excited, I watched him oil up his cock, and had to remind myself to breathe. "Please go slow. You're longer and thicker than the toy."

"Okay." He pushed against my bud, but it took a few times until the head popped in.

"Wait, wait, wait!" I cried. "Holy fuck, oh my god! Give me a second." My heart pounded erratically, my nipples stiffened, and my pussy flushed. "Okay, okay, easy now."

"You're so tight. I've never felt anything remotely..." He hitched his hips forward, sliding farther inside and stretching me with his girth.

I struggled to settle my breathing, the sensations so fucking acute.

"Ready?" he asked.

"Okay..."

"Stay with me." His eyes lassoed mine. About half of his cock slid in and out of me. "I had no idea," he groaned. "It won't take me much longer."

"Ohhh ... me either." I massaged around my clit, my fingers playing in my gush until my orgasm spasmed and the real waterworks began. My gush morphed into a massive squirt-a-thon, lubricating and opening my ass even more. "Taaate!"

"Jesus, I'm going deeper," Tate grunted and then growled. "Fuck, I'm cumming, Blue."

The warm cum of his orgasm filled my ass, his ejaculation firing repeatedly. Then he collapsed on top of me.

So blissed out from my orgasm, I didn't even mind. My hand absently played with his hair and ran up and down his spine. Several minutes passed as we drifted in our mutual release.

He slowly stirred and pulled out of me. "I'm going to go clean up," he muttered, without making eye contact.

I used the towels under me to wipe up and wrapped the gifted robe around me. After getting a glass of water from the kitchen, I went out on the deck, wishing I had a cigarette. I was never a smoker, but there were a few times in life that called for one. Really, I just wanted something to do with my hands. Fear hovered at the edges. It seemed as soon as we drew closer to one another, the backup would start. He didn't look at me when he left the room, so I had no idea which Tate I would be contending with.

He joined me outside, standing by the railing, and immediately said, "You've never done that for Bond?" Possessive Tate had apparently shown up.

"You already asked me that." I pulled my legs in and

draped the robe over them.

"Tell me again." He crossed his arms over his chest.

"No. Only you. I've never masturbated for anyone other than during sex, and that's not the same thing."

"Good." He breathed out a big sigh and then sat down in the chair next to mine.

"I know I'm breaking my own rule, but why does Bond bother you so much?"

"I don't like sharing."

His wife cheated on him. That must be it. I wanted to know what happened after he came, but I was scared to ask. He'd been so much more forthcoming, I was scared to do anything to cause him to go dark again.

"You're so transparent, Blue."

"Am I?" I yanked my robe tighter around me.

"Come here." He opened his arms out to me, and I climbed onto his lap. He held me to his chest and spoke into my hair, "You are amazing and that just before, you were so open and fearless. I've never cum so hard in my life."

"Me, fearless? I'm a walking scaredy-cat."

"Trust me. You're incredible." He lifted my head and kissed me.

The potion of his lips wiped away my insecurities, if only momentarily. I lost myself in his arms and any hope of escaping clean. My heart no longer belonged to me.

"Are you ready for bed?" he asked, scanning my face.

"I'm getting there. Do you have an extra tooth brush?"

"I do." He lifted me off his lap and took my hand.

The bathroom seemed very small with both of us in it. I sat on the covered toilet and brushed my teeth while he stood over the sink.

"Do you always brush your teeth with your eyes closed?" he asked me after he rinsed his mouth.

"I didn't realize I was," I said, holding the toothbrush away from my mouth.

"It's very cute."

I rinsed my mouth and said, "I need to pee."

"So pee."

"Excuse me?" I blinked my eyes rapidly.

"Have you never peed in front of a lover?"

"No. I grew up making sure the doors were locked."

"Right. Well, this is different."

"You first then."

"Okay." He stepped around me. "You can help."

I furrowed my brow and scrunched my nose. Then I smiled. "That could be fun." I stood behind him, looking around his broad frame and clasping his cock in my hand.

"Gently," he said with a chuckle.

"Oops, sorry." I aimed for the toilet and felt the pee come out, first in a trickle, then a torrent. I moved his cock around, drawing my initials.

He laughed.

"Do I shake it when you're done?"

"I'll do that," he said, taking over for me. He stroked up and down a few times and then closed his robe. "Your turn." He lowered the seat back down.

"I don't think I can pee with an audience."

"Try."

I bit on the inside of my lower lip and then decided to try. I couldn't fathom why it mattered to him, but it seemed to. Moving the bottom of my robe to the side, I sat down, leaning over my legs.

Tate loomed over me, waiting.

I peered up. "I don't think—" Then a small stream started, and I let go.

"See, that wasn't so hard."

I wiped myself, stood, and flushed the toilet.

Tate turned on the water and we washed our hands together, sharing the soap and sudsing each other's hands. It was an intimate, romantic moment.

Who would have thought? *Not me.*

"Are you a spooner?" he asked as we entered the bedroom. He folded the towels from our play and tossed them in the laundry basket in the closet.

As I took off my robe, I said, "I tend to move a lot during the night, but I enjoy being held. Which side is yours?" Glancing up, I took in his odd expression.

His lips were clamped shut. "I sleep in the middle."

Oops, I thought. He hadn't thought it through. Either he sleeps on his old side, the side he slept with his wife or he sleeps on her side. *Not good.* "Should I go?"

"No definitely not. Which side do you sleep on?"

"If you're facing my bed, then the left side."

"And with Bond?"

"On the right." I held my breath, waiting for his response.

"You take the left then."

I breathed out a sigh of relief and climbed into my side of the bed.

He scooted up against my back and kissed my recent tattoo. His warmth surrounded me, and I couldn't help noticing the difference between Tate and Bond. Tate's larger frame covered me from head to toe. I liked it. A lot.

He quickly drifted off, breathing deeply, puffing out into my hair.

I ran through the snapshots in my head and felt hopeful. His heart might be broken, even shattered, but I believed it was on the mend.

CHAPTER FIFTEEN

Nicest Thing

by Kate Nash

The sun shining into the bedroom woke me. I stretched up my arms and opened my eyes.

Tate, leaning on his elbow, lay watching me. "Good morning, beautiful."

I blinked my eyes a few times and rubbed the bridge of my nose. "How long have you been awake?"

"For a while."

"Watching me?"

"And listening."

I scooted to a sitting position against the headboard, pulling the sheet up to cover me. "What did I say?" *Please, no, please, no.*

"You sounded like you were having a lot of fun. Moaning and grunting and grinding your hips."

"Oh my god," I said, covering my mouth. At least it wasn't as bad as it could have been. I could have said, "I love Tate," or worse, "Bond, oh Bond."

"It was adorable." He tugged my hand away from my mouth. "Are you hungry?"

"Let's take a walk on the beach first?"

"Coffee, then walk?"

"Deal." Carrying the robe with me, I went to the bathroom and freshened up. I ambled to the kitchen, the smell of fresh ground coffee filling my senses.

"How do you like your coffee?" Tate asked, packing

coffee into a metal scoop.

"Like coffee ice cream."

"Seriously?" He looked offended.

"You drink it black? Seriously. Lots of cream and sugar. I don't drink it often, but when I do..."

He used his fancy machine, creating coffee shots. "Gotcha. Not black for me, although I do drink it that way if I run out of half-and-half."

"Is my coffee drinking a deal breaker?"

He laughed. "No." He held out a mug for me. "Sugar's in the canister on the counter on the other side of the stove. Cream in the fridge."

"Thanks." I fixed my coffee and had a sip. "Yum."

He poured half-and-half into his mug, and we settled outside on the deck.

I squinted into the sunshine. "This is the way to start off a morning. I'm very glad I stayed."

"So am I."

I glanced over at Tate and believed him. It seemed to mean something to him, and that warmed my heart.

"What time do you need to be at work?" he asked.

"Four-thirty," I said, holding the coffee mug in my hands.

"Can I stop by?"

I shrugged. "I'm going over to Bond's after I get off work."

"I'll drive you," he said, his expression serious.

"Very funny."

"Why are you going?"

I rested my head against the back of the chair and tilted my body toward him. "It's personal. He needs some support."

"In the middle of the night, on a Saturday night? Doesn't he work until really late?"

"He wanted me to come over last night, if you recall.

196

I'm not sure what you want me to say."

"Tell me you're not going to have sex with him or sleep over there. Come to my house after you're done."

I looked out over the ocean. "I..." *I won't have sex with Bond*, I thought and kept it to myself. I couldn't possibly. My heart would revolt. If I gave up this last part though, all my boundaries would be gone. It would solely be on Tate's terms. *Fuck!*

"Blue, I want you here with me. Look at me."

My eyes started to fill and I looked up, trying to blink the tears away. "You're trying to take away my last..."

"Your last what?" He totally startled me when he jerked my chair around so I faced him.

I brought my feet up on the seat and wrapped my arms around my legs.

His hand circled around my foot.

"I'm not sure I'm cut out for this sort of thing," I mumbled.

He let go of my foot. "The sort of *thing* you're already doing with Bond?"

"It's not the same thing. It doesn't feel the same."

"I don't want it to." The stern set of his lips indented his cheekbones.

"I wish I could read your expressions. What do you want?"

"I want *you*, Blue. Please say you will come back here tonight."

I took a deep breath and exhaled. "Okay."

"Excellent. Let me take you out to lunch."

"I'll have to wear what I wore last night."

"Let's get dressed," he said, standing up. His robe fell open, and I could see his erection.

"You're hard."

"I have been since this morning, watching you."

"And this conversation?"

"No."

"Wow." I knelt down in front of him and brought his cock to my lips. "Precum too. Hmmm." Staring up, I said, "Does jousting with me turn you on?"

"No, just having you close."

Just having me close!

"Double wow." I breathed in the masculine heat coming off his cock and balls. It was so heady, I felt high on his scent. I closed my mouth over his head, losing myself in the taste and feel of him. Glancing up, I watched him tug on his own nipples. *Damn!*

He pushed my robe off my shoulders, and it gave me an idea.

I worked both of my hands up and down his shaft and followed the motion with my mouth. "Let me know when you're close," I muttered.

"Not far. Oh, there ... you go. Close," he moaned, burying his hands in my hair and schooling my mouth around his cock.

I let him have control as I continued to run one hand along his length and fondled his tight, scrunched balls.

"Oh, just like that. Oh, faster. Yeah!" He bobbed my head up and down on him and then grunted, "Now!"

I took the first shot of his ejaculate in my mouth and then let his orgasm spray across my chest and nipples.

"Goddamn," he said, collapsing back on the railing.

With my hands, I spread his cum all around my breasts, rubbing it into my skin.

"Jesus, woman, what are you doing?" He brushed his hair back from his face while struggling to catch his breath.

"Wearing you to lunch." I peered up and jumped for

joy over his expression.

Ruddy lust riddled his features. "I'm hard again."

"I see that. It's hard to miss."

"I want to fuck you, hard, right now, but more so, I want to sit in a restaurant knowing my cum is covering your beautiful nipples and breasts. Let's get dressed."

We strolled inside and rinsed out our mugs in the kitchen sink. I gathered up my clothes and followed Tate to the bedroom. I slipped into my panties and matching, sheer bra. After donning my jeans, I reached down for my shirt.

"Wear one of my shirts," he said, opening the closet door.

"Dude, you're like twice my size."

"I need to see some cleavage. No point in taking you out with my cum all over you and not be able to see where you rubbed it in." He rummaged in a drawer and pulled out a white V-neck T-shirt. "Lift your arms." He lowered the shirt over my head and the V dipped beyond the edge of my bra. In his hands, he gathered the white cotton, yanking it down slightly in the back. Then he tied a knot at my hip. "Damn hot," he said, walking me over to the dresser mirror.

I swallowed hard. The outline of my bra showed through the shirt and the V left nothing to the imagination. "I don't usually go out like this."

"Good. Only with me."

"You won't get mad if men—"

"Let them. You're mine."

Holy hell! His!

In relaxed-fit jeans and a green T, he took my hand and we left in the Jeep Cherokee.

My head spun around his words. I had a hard time not jumping way forward, knowing all the other stuff he had said: no love, no lifetime. In an effort to shut myself up, I asked, "Where are we going?"

"Do you like sushi?"

"Love it."

He drove from A1A to Las Olas Boulevard and parked in front of Sushi Rock Cafe. "It doesn't look like much from the outside, but the food's great." We occupied the last empty table, Tate sitting cattycorner to me. As we waited to order, he said, "Was this one of your fantasies?" He tickled his finger down my cleavage.

I squirmed. "It wasn't on the list but damn, it's making me hot, just sitting here and smelling you on me."

"It was spontaneous?"

"Completely."

He captured my hand between his, surrounding me in his energy. "You're truly one of a kind, kiddo. Tell me another fantasy, so I can fulfill it."

"What about yours?"

"You've more than eradicated my top one. However, we'll need to do it several more times in various positions. I'd love to watch you straddle me and work me into your ass. Toy first. Shit," he said, looking down into his lap.

"Precum?"

"I think so." He placed his napkin over his lap. "So tell me."

The server approached, staring straight down my cleavage. He deposited our glasses of water and took our order of three sushi rolls and an appetizer of sashimi, without looking up.

When he stepped away, I said, "I don't want you to get mad at me."

"Why would I get mad at you? The waiter?"

"No, just my fantasies."

"Spit it out."

"I have three more: double penetration, which we

200

could never do together, being a voyeur at a sex club, and the other one is way too embarrassing to share."

"You're right about double penetration. I would never want to share you."

"That's not what I meant and it could be done with a toy. The point is, there's no room down there with you inside me."

He threw his head back and laughed heartily. His laughter filled my heart. "Spit out the last one, Blue."

I huffed and said, "I'd like to be cropped and/or whipped in front of an audience, then maybe fucked as they watch."

He gasped and I figured I'd gone too far.

Fuck!

I scrutinized his face, trying to interpret what the set of his jaw and his pinched-in eyebrows meant. I was at a loss.

His breathing increased noticeably as I held mine. He brought my hand to his thigh and aggressively kissed me. His mouth on mine rapidly accelerated the craving between us until I broke it off.

"You're not mad?" I asked, trying to clear my fuzzy mind.

"I'm a lot of things, but mad isn't one of them. You're the most baffling and beautiful woman I've ever met."

"Thank you." My face burned over his compliment.

He forced air out. "I want to get out of here."

"We'll eat quickly."

Just in time, the server delivered our food. This time the waiter tried to catch my eye, but I ignored him.

Tate pulled out his wallet and waved his credit card in front of his face. "Please bring me the check."

I poured soy sauce into the little dish provided and piled wasabi and ginger onto a slice of the rainbow roll. Before tossing it in my mouth, I said, "Are you going to explain your reaction, or am I left to guess?" His eyes lit on my face, and I wanted to touch his cheek. But I refrained. "Tell me."

"It's my new favorite fantasy."

I chuckled. "You had me scared."

Another odd expression crossed over his face. His smile faded as he rubbed the back of his neck.

If I had to guess, I would call it fear. *Wow*.

We ate quickly and headed back to his place in silence. When I couldn't take the quiet anymore, I turned on the radio and sang *Your Body Is A Wonderland* with John Mayer.

He finally broke the standstill and said, "This is your song, Blue. You, not just your body, are a wonderland which I plan to thoroughly explore."

"Care to talk about what happened in the restaurant?"

"Not in the least." He pulled into the driveway and hit the remote to open the garage door.

We sat, watching it go up.

"Okey-dokey. Are you still okay with me using the Jeep?" I asked, releasing my seatbelt.

"Yes. Are you taking off?"

"I am. I just need to gather my stuff." I opened the car door and climbed out.

"Are you coming back here later?" he asked as he opened the hatch. He grabbed out a gym bag and tossed it into the garage.

"I will." My anxieties ricocheted all over the place as we entered his home. I hung my new robe in the bathroom and gathered my toy, oil, and shirt from his bedroom. I hadn't left yet, but I missed him already. "Can I have a kiss?"

"Of course." He swept me up in his arms and kissed me gently. "I'll see you later."

"Okay," I said and left in a vortex of mixed emotions.

CHAPTER SIXTEEN

Latch

by Disclosure ft. Sam Smith (DJ Premier Remix)

It felt odd as hell to be driving Tate's Jeep to work. It seemed like such a relationship/couple thing to do, but I stoically pushed those thoughts away. His ongoing confliction plagued the rollercoaster ride and kidding myself otherwise was impossible. Maybe I was growing up. Doubtful, but I liked the idea anyway. Surrounded by his smell, I wished I could bottle his scent.

The bar at Tap 42 filled up early with a large party of twenty-somethings, mostly guys. Stuart and I split the bar down the middle since we were the only two currently on the clock.

"Fuck," he said as he scooted behind me.

I knew exactly what he meant. They were an unruly bunch. I threw down more coasters and said, "What will it be?"

"You, definitely you," said the skinny, young guy in a pink dress shirt.

"O ... M ... G!" I mocked in a high voice. In my normal voice, I said, "That's the first time I've heard that one. Order please."

"You're a feisty one," his redheaded friend said. "I bet you could take us both on."

Their silent friend nodded in agreement.

I rolled my eyes. "If you don't order quickly, I'm moving down the line."

"Four shots of tequila with the works. Three for us and

one for you."

"Well or top shelf?"

"Top shelf," he replied to my chest.

I rang them up and poured out 1800 tequila into three shot glasses on top of the bar, placing a saltshaker and lime wedges on napkins in front of them. Then I covered the spout with my finger and pretended to pour myself a shot under the bar. I filled it with water and shot it back quickly.

Before taking another order, I quickly ran into the kitchen, ostensibly to retrieve a food order but also to place a text.

> **Me:** If you want to come by, now would be fabulous. If, and only if, you can keep your fists in your pockets. There's a gaggle of young guys and somehow your LARGE looming presence might give them pause. Stuart has his hands full on the other side of the bar.
>
> **Tate:** On my way.

Please, oh please, don't let me regret this.

I delivered two orders of calamari to Stuart's side and an order of chicken wings and crab and tuna rolls to mine. "Your turn," I said, frisbeeing the coasters to the next three people down the row.

Pink shirt, waving his hand, called out, "Can we get another shot and some food?"

"Give me a sec," I shouted back.

"I'll take a strawberry margarita," said the cute girl with the pixie haircut.

"Scotch neat," said a young guy with a blue dress shirt and a navy tie.

I almost broke out laughing but contained myself.

The last guy at the end of the bar ordered a beer and pork sliders.

I rang up the orders, mixed and poured the drinks, and delivered them. Back in front of pinkie, I filled their shot glasses and laid out more limes. "What would you like to eat?"

The redhead said, "Honey, you, all day long. I'm great with my tongue. All the girls say so."

Before I had a chance to respond, Tate pushed between the two guys and leaned in. I hopped up on my palms and met him halfway across the bar. His hand cupped the back of my head and he kissed me hard. Once we broke apart, I licked my lips and smiled.

"Sorry lads, she's unavailable. Slide down for me." He retrieved one of the stools from the tall circular tables and sat down at the bar.

"Thank you," I mouthed.

He winked at me.

"Since you won't be eating me for dinner, what can I get you?"

Redhead frowned and said, "Is he your boyfriend?"

I glanced at Tate and back at the boy. "He's my lover."

"He's a big dude."

"Yep, he is. Food?"

"Beef sliders and the spinach dip and chips."

"Great. Tate?"

He lifted the menu off the bar and said, "The mussels and a beer."

"Have a shot with us," redhead said.

Tate shrugged and I laughed. I poured another shot and placed a lime wedge and a saltshaker in front of him.

I rang up the new orders and headed into the kitchen to retrieve more food.

In thirty minutes time, two more bartenders showed up

for work. With more time on my hands, I wiped down the bar, cleaned glasses, and filled up the ice, finally settling in front of Tate.

"Need anything else?"

"No, I'm good." He circled the top of his glass with his finger. "Those boys were very entertaining. The one with red hair will come back. He's convinced he can seduce you."

I laughed and reached for Tate's hand. "Listen, thanks for coming."

"Anytime. Can I steal you away for a couple of minutes?"

"I'll check in with Stuart." I found him in the kitchen, and he waved me off.

Back behind the bar, I said, "See you outside." I left through the rear of the restaurant.

Tate looked so sexy sitting on the edge of his bike. The summer wind played in his hair as his deep-mahogany eyes reeled me in. "I enjoyed watching you work," he said, holding his arms open.

I stepped into his embrace. "Oh, you smell so good."

"You smell like food."

"Yeah, sorry about that." After a warm hug, I asked, "Are we good?"

"We're great. What time do you think you'll be over later?" he asked, twirling my ponytail around his finger.

"I have no idea. Late."

"What're you doing between the end of your shift and meeting up with Bond?" He tugged my hair and my body responded.

"You?"

"That's the best answer you could have said. Your place?" His eyes danced with delight.

"Yeah. That gives us the most time, don't you think?

My place being closer to Bond's?"

He stood and lifted me onto the Harley's seat. "I'm getting addicted to this," he said before he lowered his mouth to mine. His sultry kiss triggered a base need in me I found difficult to contend with. I wanted to climb inside of him and swim in his passion. His soft lips' caress parted my own. Our tongues sparked against each other, causing an ardent pulse between my thighs.

"I have to get back in a minute," I said, resting the top of my head against his chest.

He massaged my shoulders, working his hand along my neck.

"Oh, that feels so good."

He lifted my head and kissed my forehead. "Let me know when you're out of here."

I hugged him to me as he easily lifted me off the bike and deposited me on the asphalt. "See you soon."

Back inside, I got into the flow of customers again. Once Tap 42 started to die down for the night, Stuart came over to me.

"The dude was here again."

"Yeah, I asked him to come by, hoping he would settle down some of the guys that were here earlier."

"You could have asked me."

"You had your hands full. Listen, did Sheila say she would cover my shift next Saturday? I can pick up the following Monday night if you need me to."

He nodded.

"Excellent! Thanks so much!"

"You can clock out. Sheila's closing with me tonight."

Something told me she was going to get the same pitch from Stuart. "Good luck," I said.

I hopped into the Cherokee and booted up my phone.

Me: Heading home.
Tate: Meet you there.

We pulled into the apartment complex at the same time, my heart thumping in my chest, wondering what would happen next and how Tate would deal with me leaving to go see Bond.

"Shower first," I said as I opened the door with Tate's hands already touching me everywhere. "What's in the bag?"

"Supplies," he said as he unpacked the contents. He placed a six-pack of Henry Weinhard's Woodland Pass IPA and more margaritas in the fridge, and left a bottle of Hershey's syrup and whipped cream on the kitchen table. "I plan to make you very sticky." With a quick smile, he stalked over to the bathroom. He hung his head out and said, "You have a tub."

"I do, but it's not big enough for two, or in our case, two and a half."

He chuckled. "Very funny, you. Nice Post-It front and center. Let's play first and bathe you afterward for your *date* with Bond." He walked out with a couple towels under his arm.

"It's not a—Opfff!"

He scooped me in his arms and then dipped me so I could grab the chocolate and whipped cream. Depositing me at the edge of the bed, he began stripping off my clothes. "Watching those boys lusting after you turned me on," he said, unbuttoning my shirt.

"But not when Stuart was watching me? Why?" I reached behind me and unclasped my bra.

He pulled it forward and let it fall, cupping my breasts. "You called me in for protection, so I knew you couldn't possibly be interested in them. You're in your thirties, right?" He tugged and twisted my nipples.

"Thirty-one. So?" I arched into his touch.

"Wow, I didn't realize there's twelve years between us, not that you look a day over twenty-five. I guess I just didn't think about it."

"Is it a problem?" I lifted my hips when he unbuttoned my jeans and slid them down my thighs.

"Not for me."

"Good."

"Stuart's attractive and a *man*. Those kids tonight were babies. You should have heard some of the things they were saying."

"I'm not sure I care to."

He pushed me onto my back, my legs still dangling off the bed and then took off his dress shirt and jeans.

I fondled his erection, loving that he was always hard for me.

"Oh, you should hear," he said as he trailed his fingers up my inner thigh, "the boys on the other side of me wanted to know if your breasts were real. We were all hard watching you move around. It made me feel young again." His palm skirted my mound and brushed across my belly. "They wanted to know if you were a good lover. I told them so, so."

I sat up and slapped his thigh. "You did no such thing. What did you really say?"

Holding my face in his hands, he said, "That you were beyond imagination, way beyond their boyhood dreams."

"Ohhh, that's so much better."

He pulled out my hair tie, and draped my hair across my shoulders. As he ran his fingers through my auburn bangs, he said, "The redheaded kid said that he was man enough to handle you and has the goods to satisfy."

"Did you guys whip it out and compare tools?" I asked, sliding my hand along his shaft.

Tate shook through a held in laugh. "I didn't want to discourage his ambitions in life, but I did clearly state you were off limits."

I uncapped the whipped cream and dispensed a ring of the fluffy cream over the head of his cock. With my mouth open, I used the tip of my tongue to lick at the sweetness, slowly revealing his hot flesh underneath. I lowered down over his shaft and tried to take in as much of him as I could.

He held my head as I bobbed up and down. "That feels incredible, but don't make me cum just yet."

"Okay." I dropped back onto my elbows.

He scanned me up and down. "I want to tie you up again, but that'll have to wait until tomorrow when we're back at my place. When do you work?"

"Not until the dinner shift. My women's group was cancelled for this week."

He ripped the plastic protection off the top of the syrup and popped up the cap. "Praise the Great Spirit. I need to have you at my mercy again."

"I already am," I said, swallowing hard over my disclosure. "I'm sorry, I—"

"Shhh," he said, sitting down next to me. He circled my right areola with the whipped cream and covered my nipple with the chocolate. "The best sundae ever." He lowered his mouth, licking and sucking me clean. He lustfully nibbled on my nipple.

"Ohhh," I sighed.

He treated the other side, tugging and jerking on my left nipple. Then he made a line with the whipped cream, down my chest, filling my navel, and crossing my mound. The stimulating cold along with his attention had me shaking with piercing desire. He straddled my waist and leaned over, kissing and licking his way down my body. His fingers found my wetness as he rose back up and kissed me with his cream-covered mouth. "Put some chocolate on your lips."

I grasped the Hershey's and painted my lips. Some dripped down my chin.

His fingers plunged deeper as his wicked thumb strummed my clit. He kissed and licked his way up my chin and then bit and savored the chocolate off my lips.

"I need you inside me," I moaned. "Please."

"I want to try a different position. I think you might be able to cum this way."

"Okay," I said, sitting up.

He lay down on his back in the middle of the bed, situating a towel underneath him. "Climb on top of me, covering my body with yours, lying down with your legs straight."

I draped my body over Tate, my legs between his, and lifted my hips, angling him home.

"Yesss," he hissed. He had to bend up for his mouth to reach my lips.

I held his head as he used my hips to shift my body up and down over his cock.

"Is it hitting the right spot?" he mumbled into my mouth.

"Oh my god, yes! I've never done it this way before."

He rammed into me and said, "Good. Kiss me again."

Back and forth, I slid against the ridge of his pelvic bone, my clit sparking against the friction on each pass. The length of his cock filled me and his girth stimulated my G-spot. But the best part of all was his mouth on mine, his kiss, his taste, breathing in his exhale. His dark eyes held mine, and I never felt more connected to another in my whole life.

He broke away from another steamy kiss and scorched

me with his eyes. "Tell me you won't let Bond touch you," he pleaded.

"Tate, I..." *I'm falling in love with you.* "Only you."

He grunted and then plundered my mouth, making my lips swollen with his fervor.

"Ohhh, I'm getting close," I groaned.

He stopped moving his hips and said, "Wait for it."

"Oh hell!" I felt dizzy with desire, my heart pounding frantically for release.

"Do you think you would ever trust me enough to flip you over? I think you would cum that way too."

"I don't know," I said, touching his cheek. *Maybe one day, if you ever love me back.*

He circled his hips under me and resumed riding me up and down over his body. "Cum for me, Blue. Eyes on me the whole time."

"Tate, ohhh, please, I don't know if I can take— Holy fucking hell!" Every cell in my body contracted, trapping the air in my lungs. My feet flexed, toes curled, and then a scream tore out of me, "Ahhh, Tate, ahhh!" My body convulsed on top of him and around his cock.

"Blue, yesss!" he yelled, finding his own fulfillment. He jerked into me several times and then melted into the bed. His hand smoothed down my head, holding me with his other arm.

I breathed against his neck, floating in the afterglow. My pussy continued to spasm around him.

"Intense aftershocks," he whispered. "I can feel them."

"Mmmhmm."

"Should we have a drink before your bath?"

"I don't want to move yet."

He chuckled, rocking us up and down on the bed with his laughter. "Okay." He wrapped both arms around me and pulled me in tight.

I felt his breath in my hair and surrounded by his energy, I never wanted to move. I sighed and kissed his neck.

"We don't have much more time," he said, peering down at me.

"Okay, okay." Pushing myself up on his chest, his cock slipped out of me, his cum dripping down. Using the other towel, I dried him and myself off. "You're soft this time."

"The orgasm was incredible."

I smiled. "Do you want a beer?"

"Sure. I'll run the bath."

"Okay." I kissed him and left the room. Wrapping my arms around myself, I stood with the fridge open, staring at the contents but not seeing them. I still felt discombobulated from the intense orgasm and our forged connection. I couldn't fathom letting him go, and I prayed I would never have to. Some things you never recover from, and I felt certain I would never recover from the loss of Tate.

"Coming?" he called to me from the bathroom.

"Yeah, coming." I drank a glass of water and then opened a beer and a margarita. After traipsing to the bathroom, I handed Tate his drink and took a sip of my own.

"Step in," he said, holding out his hand to help lower me down.

"Oh, it feels so good. I haven't taken a bath in years."

Sitting on the rim of the tub, he said, "Can you hand me the soap? Thanks." He lathered up the bar and started on my shoulders and neck, massaging as he washed my skin.

"Ohhh," I moaned.

He ran his soapy hands down my arms and then under them. "Scoot forward."

I did and he stepped into the tub behind me. "What are you doing?"

"It'll be easier for me to clean your front if I'm sitting behind you."

"I don't think you'll—" I guffawed.

He inserted himself under me, lifting me onto his lap and legs. The bathwater spilled over the side of the tub. "I'll clean that up after we're done."

Sandwiched between his heat and the warm water, I sighed. "You're spoiling me."

"That's the plan."

So many responses whipped through my head, and I discarded them all. He clearly planned to make me fall and being so far gone already, I knew the battle was lost. What he hadn't counted on was that I planned to persuade him to fall back.

His hands floated over and between my breasts, then down my stomach. He shifted his legs under me. "When we go away together, we must stay in a place with a big tub. This is ridiculous." His comment didn't keep him from cleaning my private bits, which caused me to blush.

I flipped over and hung my arms around his neck. "I'm going to drain the tub and start the shower."

"I get to wash your hair."

"Okay." I stood between his legs and pulled him up to me. We both almost slipped, but he caught us by bracing his arm against the wall and holding me up with the other. "Thank you. That gave my stomach a whirl."

"Mine too. For a second I thought we were both going down and not the fun kind."

I chuckled. "Right." I backed into the flow of the shower and wet my hair.

Sensuously, he worked the shampoo in, making sure to keep the suds out of my eyes. "Have I told you how much I love your silky auburn hair?"

"No and thank you. I have the same hair color as my mother's sister, Helena. In middle school, I dyed it jet black because I hated it. Now I love it."

"It's the perfect match to your sultry blue eyes." He led me back into the shower stream and rinsed my hair.

"You sure are full of compliments tonight."

"Just to be more forthcoming with my thoughts."

Yay!

"It was great to watch the boys admire you without feeling jealous. I got to see you in a new light." After he rinsed off, he turned off the shower.

We stepped out and dried off.

"I'd loan you a robe but—" I laughed so hard I couldn't finish the sentence.

He laughed with me as he used our towels to dry the bathroom floor.

Back in the bedroom, I dressed in a pair of black jeans and a sleeveless top and Tate redressed in the clothes he wore over. Checking the clock on my nightstand, I saw that it was close to the time I needed to leave.

When we walked out into the living room, Tate said, "Do you mind if I finish my beer before I take off?"

I shrugged. "That's fine. Just lock the door behind you. Please don't be mad at me."

He hugged me. "If you keep your promise, I'll be okay."

I gathered my keys and wallet. "Why don't you crash here, and I'll come here after we're done?"

"I won't sleep waiting for you."

"Tate..."

"Do what you need to do. Just keep your promise. I'd be happy to drop you off and pick you up."

"No, that's fine. I'll meet you at your place later."

CHAPTER SEVENTEEN

Clarity

by Zedd

I pulled in the parking lot at the Crobar and texted Bond.

> **Me:** I'm here.
> **Bond:** Come in and see me.
> **Me:** Okay.

I yanked on the heavy club door just as someone was pushing out. "Oops, sorry," I said, stepping out of their way.

Inside, the lights flashed across the dance floor and *Gooey* by Glass Animals thumped against the walls. Even at that late hour, there were still plenty of people gathered around the central bar. I waved to Frank and headed to the deejay booth.

Bond smiled as I approached and gathered me up in a bear hug. "Thanks, Blue. You're the best."

Stepping back I said, "Is she still here?"

"Yeah, she's working the bar in the front room."

"What can I do? What happened?"

"Hang on a second." Bond paced away and said something to a young, gangly guy. The guy nodded and walked over to me, Bond following behind.

"Clint, Blue, Blue, Clint. He's going to cover for me for a few songs."

"Hey," I said as Bond grabbed my arm, pulling me along with him.

Outside the club, he said, "Can we hang in your car? I need a break from the noise."

"Sure." I clicked the remote to unlock Tate's Jeep.

"What's this?" Bond asked.

"It's Tate's. I'm just borrowing it. I finally gave in and am getting the door fixed on my pile of junk." I climbed in and so did Bond, his brow furrowed.

"What?"

"So things are progressing." His hand reached out and caressed my neck.

I shrugged and rested back into his palm. "I guess. They're definitely progressing on my end. He's sharing more of himself with me, but the edge always feels so close."

"You're not staying over tonight, are you?"

"I'm sorry, Bond, I'm not. I don't think I can have sex with both—"

He seemed a little lost and his eyes looked sad. "I get it."

"I'm not abandoning you." I reached across the console and touched his thigh. "Tell me what's going on."

"Rory cornered me the other day and told me all about the soulmate thing. Not that I buy into that shit but if I did, my soulmate would be Jacqs."

For once, his words of praise for Jacqs over me didn't stab my heart. "I understand. So?"

"So she threw herself at me in the back of the club and I ... well, you know I'm not one for tons of self-control, so I kissed her back. She surprised me."

"That's it? I mean I'm not saying that's a good idea or anything, but nothing else happened?"

"No. I took her by the shoulders and pulled her off me. I said I was sorry and that it wasn't going to happen again."

I turned in my seat toward Bond and brought my knees up. "What aren't you telling me?"

"I can't stop thinking about her. She doesn't make it easy, either. She rivals me as a flirt and if I don't give her attention, she flirts with someone else in front of me. She insists she'll stop doing it once I change my mind. She told me she wants me to have her body to use as I like. She says she needs a big, strong man to dominate her. She wants to be my slut." He shifted in his seat to face me.

"She even said she was up for a threesome with you and me. She says she'll take whatever she can get. There's so many reasons why it couldn't work. She's too young, we work together, although she said she would quit if that were the reason. Plus, there's you and Jacqs, and I'm getting too old to juggle so many relationships."

"Holy fuck, dude, now you're the one in serious trouble."

He rubbed his forehead and said, "I know."

"Sounds like, at the very least, you and she are sexually compatible. More than Jacqs?"

"Yeah," he said, glancing up.

"I don't know what's going to happen with Tate but for now, I've promised him no sleepovers and no sex."

"Wow. Is that a good idea?"

I looked down at my hands, fiddling with the hem of my shirt. "No, it's the worst idea in the history of the world, but the truth is..." I paused and glanced up. "I only want him now."

"You're in love."

I nodded. "I wish I could be a buffer for you in this case, but I can't. Maybe you should give Rory a shot. Maybe she can help you get over Jacqs."

"And you."

"Seriously?" I said in disbelief.

"The last few months together, we've grown so close.

Of course, it's a loss. In some ways, I'm closer to you than Jacqs. We tell each other everything."

"Damn," I said, tears spilling down my cheeks.

"I didn't mean to make you cry." He opened his arms to me, and I climbed over the console into his lap. He kissed me, and I let him. Then he held me as I cried.

Once my tears had run their course, with a shuddered breath I asked, "What are you going to do?"

He wiped my cheeks. "I need to talk to Jacqs before I do anything. This situation will be different."

"Ouch." That time it hurt. My raw heart ached.

"Jesus, Blue. I'm so sorry."

"At least it's happening to us at the same time, right?"

"I'm going to miss this." He hugged me tightly.

"Me too."

CHAPTER EIGHTEEN

One And Only

by Adele

I drove back to my place in a daze. Inside, I gathered a set of my work clothes for The Chart House, a bathing suit, and my overnight cosmetic bag. In the bathroom, I noticed a new Post-It note in the center of the mirror. It read: *Spend all your free time with a half-breed American Indian with a bad attitude.* I laughed out loud but then felt fear spiral out from my gut. The image of a wicked spider luring me into a web to be swallowed up later reared its ugly head. I gave myself a dirty look above the note and headed out.

When I arrived at Tate's, I knocked on his door and waited. Once the door swung open, I dropped my bag and threw myself at him.

"What is it? Did Bond hurt you? You look like you've been crying."

"No, yes, I mean, not like you think. Can we go sit on the beach and talk?"

"Of course." My hand firmly in his, he carried my bag into the living room and dropped it on our way out to the deck. He led me down the stairs onto the beach. I kicked off my sandals and followed him closer to the water. He hugged me tightly before we lowered down onto the sand. "So tell me what happened." In the moonlight, I could see the firm set of his jaw and the tension around his eyes.

"What I'm going to share has to—"

"I would never betray your trust."

I believed him. Facing him, I hugged my knees in front of me. "There's a young woman working at Bond's club who believes she's his soulmate. I met her there a week or two ago. She actually asked for my help in getting Bond's attention." I shook my head at the memory. "Anyway, she's definitely gotten his attention."

"So you're upset and jealous?" His frown deepened. "Did you kiss him?"

"Please don't be mad. He did kiss me and I kissed him back, once, and then he held me as I cried."

"You were crying because it's over between you and Bond?" he whispered, not quite sounding like himself.

"Yes and no. Before he told me about her, Rory, I told him about me. About us... How I couldn't possibly continue to have—" I cut off my words, frightened they would send Tate running away.

"Finish what you were going to say."

"No."

"Yes," he said, gripping my upper arms and drawing me closer.

I closed my eyes and shook my head.

"I want to hear it. Look at me."

My eyes watered as I hooked into his gaze. "I only want you and couldn't possibly have sex with him or anyone else."

He breathed out heavily, leaving me waiting for the consequences of my confession. "How did he hurt you?"

"I was crying because Bond and I were saying goodbye to what we've had together *and* because of you and me. At some point, I'm going to need more, and you won't give it to me. It feels like that moment is careening forward, and I can't do anything about it."

"Shhh. I'm right here."

For how long? "Bond said he needed to let Jacqs know about Rory."

"That's what hurt?"

I nodded. "Yeah."

"That's understandable." He looked out over the horizon and then back at me. "I'm not happy that you kissed Bond."

"I don't know what to say. I love Bond. I always will, but he doesn't have my heart." Holding Tate's gaze, my heart beat wildly.

"Okay, good. Come here."

I moved onto his lap, and he embraced me to his chest.

"No more kissing," he whispered into my hair.

"I'll miss your soft, full lips and your wicked tongue," I said with a playful frown.

He peered down at me with smiling eyes and licked his lips. His fingers wove into my hair as he angled my mouth to his.

I lost myself in his arms as his lips possessed me.

His kisses were tender but adamant. He broke away from my mouth and kissed my eyes and my forehead. "Are you tired?"

"I'm exhausted."

"Let's get you to bed."

The next day I awoke alone in Tate's bed. I brought his pillow to my face and breathed in. There was nothing better than his smell. I stood, stretching up to elongate my back and rolled my neck from side to side. Padding naked through the house, I saw Tate, sitting in his robe, on the deck.

He waved me over.

I sat on his lap and covered my mouth. "I haven't

brushed my teeth yet."

He hardened underneath me. "Do you want coffee? Are you hungry?"

"No."

"Good. Go get freshened up. I need to take you again, hard."

I hopped up and said, "Yes, Sir." Excited, I shuffled off to the bathroom.

Back in the bedroom, Tate stood naked, his cock fully engaged. Two coils of white, cotton rope and a long, red scarf lay on the bed. "Turn around and cross your wrists up behind you." My heart ricocheted in my chest as soon as he covered my eyes with the scarf, knotting it at the back of my head. Then he used the long ends of the red material to secure my wrists behind me, my elbows bent, my wrists crisscrossed.

"I'm trembling," I said. "I've never been blindfolded before."

"Trust me and keep breathing."

"Okay, okay," I panted, trying to regulate my air intake. Arousal and fear caused my pussy to crimson and my nipples to strain for his touch.

"How does that feel?"

"Uh ... okay. I can't see anything."

"Good. Now step back and sit on the bed." He lifted my right foot and wrapped the rope around my ankle a few times, securing it with a knot. He did the same thing to the other leg. "Now scoot back and bring your heels to your thighs."

I couldn't use my hands to help, so I had to wiggle my butt to move me farther up on the bed. Then I felt Tate circle the rope attached to my ankles around each thigh, fastening my legs open wide. Heat pulsed in my pussy, and I could feel my rigid clit. I felt vulnerable to the extreme.

"Easy. I need you to take slow, even breaths." His hands roamed my body, teasing around my juicy flesh and my nipples but never quite touching them.

"Your submission is so beautiful, but I miss watching the arousal play across your face. Especially while you're panting. So sexy."

I felt the bed dip behind me and then my hands were freed and my eyes uncovered.

He retied my wrists up again with my elbows out, and then moved in front of me. His hands cupped my face as he stared down at me. "So lovely. See how hard your nipples are, and I haven't even touched them. Yearning, craving my touch. And your pussy is leaking onto my bed, so sweet. I *need* to taste you." He pushed me onto my back and spread my knees wide. "Look at this clit of yours, so swollen and excited," he said, pulling back the hood and sucking it into his mouth.

I rocked on my arms behind me, trying to move away from the ferocity of his attention.

"You can't escape me now. I've thought about this all morning as you moaned and groaned in your sleep."

Can one blush when their heart's already racing mach-a-million?

He stepped away, the heat of his mouth leaving my pussy. With his back to me, he opened the top drawer of his dresser and retrieved an odd-looking set of nipple clamps. They looked like tweezers with black, rubber ends. He lifted me up to a sitting position and said, "These will work on your large nipples, and I'm so curious to test your tolerance. Do you see this metal ring? The closer I push it toward the end, the tighter it gets." He slid the first on and I thought, *Heh, not bad.* After he attached the other one, he shifted the rolling bars up and my eyes watered.

"Holy Jesus Mother Murphy! I'm .... ahhh ... I'm..." My body shook from the extreme sensation, and I couldn't get away from it.

"Shhh." He held my head and soothed down my back. "That's a good girl." His fingers leisurely brushed over my clit. "I'm going to fuck you so hard in a minute, but first I need to punish your nipples some more."

I peered up, shaking my head rapidly.

"Are you saying no?" He pulled back the hood, exposing my clit, and then spanked it. "Do you remember the safeword?"

"Yesss."

"Then use it," he said, twisting the right tweezer clamp, "or behave. Shall I continue?"

"Use me."

He raised one eyebrow and said, "I will. Here we go." He tightened the clamps more and continued massaging my clit.

Fire spit out from my nipples and raged through my body.

"Breathe, baby. So sexy." He used the back of his hand to stroke the flesh of my breast. "I'm going to get you really close to cumming and then I'm going to spank your clit to orgasm."

My arousal hit an all-time peak from his words and manipulations. I so wanted to please him and myself.

"Do you know what happens to naughty girls?" he said, dipping down into my wetness, spreading it around my clit and tapping the tip.

"They ... ohhh ... get used ... punished by a—sweet Jesus—a big hulkin', half-breed ... American Indian. If, ohhh, if they're lucky."

"Excellent answer," he said, laughing. He kissed me hard, causing me to fall back onto my arms tied behind me.

With his fingers, he tightened the clamps even more and then with his right palm, he pushed down on my mound and exposed my clit.

Before he spanked even once, I mumbled, "Oh god, oh god, oh god, oh god."

Then he spanked my clit over and over and said, "Cum for me, baby."

"Ahhh," I cried out.

"Do it, I need to be inside you."

Panting and screaming, sure my heart never beat so intensely, I squirted as my climax detonated. Like a bomb imploding within, my body convulsed with each wave of release. I struggled to maintain eye contact as the contractions raped my core.

"I've never seen anything like that," he whispered in awe.

I wanted to say I had never felt anything remotely like it, but I couldn't speak. While still floating in the rapture of my orgasm, I felt him roll me forward and climb onto the bed behind me.

In my ear, he whispered, "I'm going to take you now and pound into you until I cum so hard I can't see straight." Using my tied arms for leverage, he thrust deeply on the first stroke. Then as promised, he rammed into me again and again. "It won't take me long."

So turned on, I gushed and squirted throughout the luscious assault.

"Now, Blue!" He bit down on my shoulder and jackhammered through his orgasm, which seemed longer than ever before. He fell to the side, sweating and panting. "Give me a sec. Sweet Jesus. That was..." he pulled on the knot that kept my hands secured behind my back. Once released, I rolled over and collapsed to the side. He pulled my back against him and breathed against my neck.

After a few minutes, I murmured, "I need help."

He curled around me and untied my feet from my thighs. "I..."

"Yes?"

"I'll be right back," he ended up saying, but I wondered if he felt more like me. Was he about to say that he loved me?

I love you.

When he came back, he brought a washcloth for me. "We need to strip the bed. I forgot a towel and we made a mess." His eyes smiled at me.

I relaxed.

Together we remade the bed, and Tate laughed when he heard my stomach growl.

"I'm starving," I said, slipping into the terrycloth robe.

"Eggs, bacon, toast?"

"Yum!"

He took my hand and said, "Thank you."

"For?"

"For trusting me."

"It was incredibly intense. I don't think I've ever cum so hard in my life." I laughed. "My lady bits are still vibrating and twitching."

"Lady bits?" he said with a deep laugh. Then his face became serious. "Yeah, intense is a good word. It was for me, too."

Out on the deck, I chowed down on breakfast. "God this is good. I never take the time to cook breakfast for myself."

"What do you usually eat?"

"Instant oatmeal. It's easy and quick."

"Easy and quick isn't always the best way to go."

Was there some double entendre I was supposed to

understand with that remark? He was definitely not quick and easy in the love department. "Did you mean it when you said you have never cum so hard?"

"You betcha." He grinned. "Do I have Bond to thank for exploring your depraved ways?"

"A question for a question." I sipped my coffee and placed it on the table between us.

"About sex only."

"Okay. Yes. Bond is the only other man I've let tie me up and discipline me."

"So he's into that sort of thing."

I chuckled. "Oh yeah. He's got a lot of restraints, whips, and toys. I get the impression that most of my guy friends are a bit kinky. Not sure about Kev, but Lainie has been hinting about Stay."

"And Red?"

"He's into Shibari, Japanese rope art, but other than a light spanking, he's not. At least he wasn't with me. I know that Bond and Red have shared Jacqs together, so I guess he's kinky in that way. My turn. So the stuff in the secret drawer? Ever use that sort of thing on your wife?"

He shifted uncomfortably in his seat. "No."

"So the string of one night stands?"

"The nipple clamps I bought for you, but yes."

"Let me get this straight," I said, turning in my seat to face him. "You pick up women and they let you, someone they don't know at all, tie them up and whip them?"

"You didn't know me that well..."

"True, but you didn't tie me up that first night and Cat's known you for a while and wow, they really just go home with you and let you do whatever?"

"There was usually alcohol involved."

"Right," I said, shaking my head in disbelief. "It must

be because you are so formidable and good looking. It rattles their brains."

"I thought I wasn't at all your type."

"Yeah ... well..." I blushed. "When did you start having interest in bondage and discipline?"

"Always."

"But—"

"Enough questions."

"Okay, okay," I said, holding my hands up in defeat.

We cleaned up the kitchen together as I drifted on a domesticated high. I felt more and more like part of a couple with the man who was adamant he would never be part of a long-term partnership. We had a rhythm together, and not just a sexual one. Even knowing there were parts of him I could never reach, he wove more into my heart and soul every day.

As if a radio that could pick up my brainwaves, he asked, "So, relationships before Bond?"

"Nothing worth writing home about. Sexually, I didn't feel comfortable. I rarely came with them. They didn't care, and mostly neither did I. I enjoyed the physical connection. Serge, my boss at a previous job, made me cum. On the one hand, we had to keep our relationship secret at work. Otherwise, he wanted to wear me like a piece of jewelry. We lived two different lives. I won't lie, the sneaking around was fun. Stealing away to his office so I could blow him, then return to serving my tables, turned me on."

"Was he married?" Tate asked, his lips tight.

"No, I would never. When Jacqs and Bond were officially dating, I never had sex with Bond."

"Good." His expression softened. "So how was it outside of the restaurant with Serge?"

"He bought me very revealing clothes to wear and I

tried to get on board with it, but I never felt safe with him. He liked to play games."

"What kind of games?" He dried his hands on a dishtowel and rested against the edge of the counter.

"He liked for me to go to a bar, all slutted out. I'd throw on very tight, low-slung jeans, sheer, plunging blouses, and high pumps. I mean slutty. I would sit at the bar and wait for men to approach."

"Which I'm sure they did," Tate said, crossing his arms over his chest.

"Yes, and I let them buy me drinks and flirt, knowing that Serge sat watching a few stools down."

"I think I get the picture. So, after a while he would swoop in, which I'm certain the men weren't happy about."

"Yeah." I nodded. "There were a few fights, and I hated it. He was pretty much a dick, so when I caught him in the office with another girl from the restaurant, I quit."

"How long ago was that?" he asked, rubbing his chin with the palm of his hand.

"Not long. A few months. Don't worry, I got tested. I was completely stressed out until the results came back."

Tate's face clouded over. "You thought he was being monogamous?"

"Yes. Yeah I know, but to be honest, I was relieved. Not that I got to skip over the devastating rejection that comes with realizing the person you care about doesn't give a shit about you, but I needed a way out and he opened the door."

"And then you and Bond resumed—"

"Yes, he helped me get over it."

Tate's brows furrowed and he asked, "Do you and Bond go bareback?"

"You mean, did we?"

That earned me a huge smile. "Did?"

"Never. I believe Jacqs is his only exception."

"Hmmm. And Serge?"

"No, but he broke a condom or two."

"Why me?"

I knew what he was asking. "Two reasons, really. You said you hadn't had sex in over three years, and I believed you. I figured the STD risk was low. And, smelling the condom on you reminded me of Bond, and I didn't want to think about him while we were together. Honestly, I didn't think you were going to change your mind. Then once I felt your cock in me, I never wanted to go back."

He took one giant step and closed the gap between us. His strong arms lifted me onto the counter and we wrapped our arms around each other, my legs crossed over his ass. Our kiss ignited like a brush fire morphing into a full-scale inferno, scorching the land. He tore his mouth from mine. "I think I heard your phone."

"Huh? Oh?" I rested my head on his chest, trying to recover from his ravishment.

"Shouldn't you check it?" He peered down at me.

"Yeah," I said, reluctantly jumping down from the counter.

Tate followed me into the bedroom where I retrieved my phone from my overnight bag.

"Shit!"

"Who is it?"

"My mother. She texted an SOS and I have three missed calls from her."

"Do you want space?"

"No, but let's go out back. I bet the reception is better there."

"Okay."

I called my mother, settled myself on Tate's lap, his arms holding me tightly.

"Where have you been?" my mother's voice sounded frantic.

"What's happened?"

"Helena. She won't make it through the night."

"Will she let me see her?" I covered my mouth with my hand, trying to keep from breaking down.

"She's asking for you."

"Text me the hospital address. I need to shower and then I'll head over." I shut off the phone and saw Tate intently watching me. "It's my aunt. She's been battling cancer and—"

"I'll drive."

CHAPTER NINETEEN

Skipping Stone

by Amos Lee

Tate and I took quick showers and since I only had my work clothes for later, I dressed in my black pants and The Chart House long-sleeved, gray shirt.

"You should call work and tell them you can't make it," he said as we climbed into the Jeep to head to the hospital. I threw my bag on the back seat.

"Yeah." I called Stan and he said he would get one of the day servers to cover my dinner shift. He also said I had the following weekend off but in that moment, it was hard to care.

"Tell me about your aunt," Tate said as he pulled onto A1A.

"She was the bright spot in my otherwise dark childhood. She and I connected in a way I never did with my mom or dad. Kindred spirits, she always said. Such a free spirit, I idolized the way she floated through life. Courageous and just the opposite of me."

"Don't sell yourself short, kiddo. The brave push forward in spite of their fear, not because of the lack of it."

I wondered if Tate would ever be brave again. *Please*, I thought. I watched his profile as he navigated the streets, grateful to have him with me.

He took my hand in his and squeezed it.

At the hospital, we took the elevator to the oncology ward and found my mother and Daniel sitting in the waiting room. My mom stood up and embraced me as Daniel shook Tate's hand. For the first time I could see my mother's age. No makeup filled the lines, and her red-rimmed eyes bespoke her pain.

"I'm so sorry, Mom," I said, touching her arm.

"Go on back and I'll wait here with—"

"Tate," he said, extending his hand.

"Jude never mentioned dating anyone."

"It's relatively new." I glanced from one to the other. "Be normal please," I said to her.

She waved me away.

Daniel walked me to Helena's room and said, "I don't want to step on any toes. Just know I'm here to help you and your mom in any way you need."

"Thank you, Daniel, that's very nice."

He opened the door for me, and I waited as a nurse stepped out. Inside the room, I approached Helena's bed. All the vibrancy in my aunt had vanished. All that remained was a shell of her former self. My tears spilled as she held her hand out to me and I grasped it, sitting on the edge of the bed next to her.

"Hey, Love Bug," she said in a gravelly voice.

"Hey, Mama Butterfly." I struggled to force down a sob.

"My wings no longer work here, but I'm set to fly away on the next phase of my journey." She smiled but then grimaced.

"Should I get the nurse?"

"No," she said, holding up her morphine pump. "I want to talk to you first. Tell me what's happened. Your energy is so different. A man?"

"Yes."

"And you're in love. I haven't seen you in love since—" Her forehead creased, and she breathed out slowly.

"We don't need to talk about me. Please."

"That's exactly what we need to do. This is the last time we can have girl talk, and it's what I want most."

I sobbed and said, "Okay."

"Is he handsome?"

"Ridiculously so."

"I can tell you're clearly smitten. Does he love you too?"

"No, Auntie H, and he won't."

"You're the most lovable person on the planet. Of course he'll love you."

I shook my head. "Something really bad happened to him. He won't share what it is, but I think his wife cheated on him. He's no longer in touch with any of their friends, and he's still grieving."

"Is he here with you?"

I nodded. "Yes."

"Send him in."

"No."

"Who's dying here? It means I get what I want. Get him."

I forced out a breath. "Okay." I waved down the hall at Tate, and he came to the room. "Helena, this is Tate."

"Leave us for a few minutes," she said to me.

"But," I said, throwing up my hands. "Fine." I stepped outside of the room and waited.

Minutes slowly ticked by until the door opened. Tate brushed his hair away from his face. "She wants you."

I brought his mouth to mine for a quick kiss, ignoring his knotted brow. *What the fuck did she say?*

Once back inside, Helena said, "He's in love with you honey, but that's part of the problem. It's scaring the shit out of him."

"He said that?"

"No, I felt it. There's more than an affair in the mix.

The betrayal goes deeper." She patted the bed beside her.

"What do I do?" I asked, sitting close.

"Love him. That's all you can do."

"I am. It's too late to stop. Do you like him?"

"In another life, I think we'd have been great friends. He's a free spirit too. It's just buried right now."

"Yeah."

"His sexual energy is *intense*. I'm so happy for you."

I laughed at her and blushed. Only she could get away with saying such things. "What am I going to do without you?"

"Try to be friends with your mother. She'll need you even more now. Daniel seems to be good for her. Hopefully, this one will stick."

"Yeah. Helena, how can I ever thank you for being there for me over the years. Giving me a place to crash between apartments, to just holding me when I needed a shoulder."

"Love Bug, I love you like I had you myself." She rested her hand on my thigh. "It's time for you to become the butterfly and chase all your dreams. I'll be watching over you."

I lay across her and cried. She, the woman who helped me survive my childhood was leaving me. I always thought of her spoiling my children when I had them someday.

"Give your mom a chance and just remember, I'll love you until the end of time." A wave of pain crossed her face, and she depressed the morphine pump. "I'm going to rest for a bit," she said, closing her eyes.

I hugged her gently, kissed her cheek, and left the room. Down the hall, I trudged, straight into Tate's arms.

"I'm here," he said as he comforted me.

My tears burst forward with renewed vigor, my heart

breaking. Why did it seem that the ones who had life sorted out, were the ones to leave too early?

Tate rocked me on his lap, his chin on my head, his hand resting reassuringly on my back.

After my tears sated, I glanced up.

"Some arrangements need to be made," he said. "Helena wants to be cremated and Daniel is looking into it right now."

"She hasn't died yet!" I said way too loudly as I turned to face my mother.

"Honey, there's not much time left."

Just then Daniel came back and took a seat next to my mother, resting his hand on her back.

"Why did you wait so long to call me?" I felt crushed to my core.

"It's what she wanted," she said apologetically.

"You shouldn't have waited!" I said, taking my anger out on her.

"Easy, love," Tate said, lifting me to my feet.

I looked from him to my mother and saw the devastation in her eyes, mirroring mine. I hugged her, and we cried together.

"Excuse me," a male nurse said.

We all looked up and knew.

Daniel stood up and followed the nurse to arrange the transport of the body.

"I'm so sorry for your loss," Tate said to my mother.

I knew my aunt had been sick, but she had fought through it before, so I just assumed she would again. Beating myself up, which I was the master at, I berated myself for not pushing harder to see her, to spend time with her, to take care of her. She meant the world to me, and I let her down.

"Stop it, Blue," Tate whispered, wrapping me in his

embrace. "Only meeting her once, I could tell she lived her life on her terms and no one else's. She waited for you to come so she could say goodbye before departing. Stop second-guessing yourself. Just like in life, she managed her death how she wanted."

I peered up, tears clouding my vision. "Thank you for being here."

"There's no other place I'd rather be."

I choked on my sob and laughed, "Uh huh."

"Well, other than having you tied up underneath me, that is," he whispered into my ear.

I cupped his face and brought his lips to mine.

Daniel rejoined us and said, "If you want to see her before she is moved..."

"No, thank you," I said, holding onto Tate's hand.

"I'd like to go back and see her," my mother said. "You kids go, and I'll let you know the arrangements."

"Okay." I hugged her tightly and thanked Daniel over her shoulder.

I didn't mean to, but I slammed the door of the Jeep hard. "Can you drop me off at my apartment?"

"Your car won't be ready until mid-week. Why don't we go to my place?" Tate drove out of the hospital parking lot.

"No ... I. Listen, you've been great, but I can't keep taking advantage of your generosity."

"What are you doing, Blue?" He glanced at me and then back at the road.

"I just can't right now. I'm too vulnerable and you taking care of me... I just can't."

"I want to."

Tears filled my eyes, and I tried to blink them away. "That's not the relationship we have, Tate. It's not the one you want."

"I'm telling you that I want to be here, with you. Let me."

"That's what my friends are for. I'll call—"

"I don't expect you to have sex with me, Blue. I'll drive you home if that's where you want to be and then I'll go by my place to get some things and stop by the store to get whatever you need."

I wept and shouted, "Stop being so nice to me!"

He parked the Jeep on the side of the road and got out. Opening my door, he pulled me into the backseat with him as I cried some more. Once I settled down again, he said, "No more arguing with me, Blue. Should we go by your apartment and get your things or go by my place?"

"Okay," I shuddered. "I'd rather be by the beach."

"Good." He drove me to my place and waited in the car for me.

I emptied my overnight bag and repacked it with a few different clothing options, the bathing suit, a vibrator, nightclothes, and my cosmetic bag. I also packed up my laptop computer in my backpack. In the kitchen, I gathered the beer, margaritas, and turkey deli. I poured the orange juice down the drain, lifted the garbage bag from the can, and tied it.

Deciding to try to make one trip, I swung my backpack onto my shoulders and put the strap of the overnight across my chest. In one hand, I carried the groceries and in the other, the garbage. I placed the trash down on the landing and locked the apartment door.

Tate saw me trying to navigate the stairs with all my bags and jumped out of the car to help me. He swung the overnight bag over my head and took the garbage from me. "Where does this go?"

"Around the corner in the dumpster," I said, pointing to

the far side of the building. I climbed into the car and waited for him.

He then placed the rest of my belongings in the back seat. "That's a lot of stuff."

I didn't care for his expression. "Never mind. I didn't think this was a good idea." I clicked the seatbelt to let myself out.

He grasped my arm and simply said, "No."

"Then stop it. I'm not moving in. I brought my computer because I thought I might write. It makes me feel better to get lost in a story."

"I called your friends," he said as he started the Jeep.

"You did what?" My mouth dropped open.

He headed north on I-95. "I thought you would want them around. I invited them to my place later."

"Jesus, Tate. Did you ever consider asking me?"

"Did I fuck up? I'm sorry. I wanted to help make you feel better."

My phone vibrated, and I swiped the screen.

> **Bond:** Stay told me what happened. Can I come by Tate's?
>
> **Me:** Yes. Thank you for asking.

"Who?" Tate asked.

"Bond. He was checking to see if it was *okay* for him to come by."

"I get your point." He seemed to be grinding his teeth.

Was it my displeasure or Bond coming over? I didn't know. "Good. You *will* be nice to him."

"Hey, I'm sorry for overstepping." He took my hand and kissed the back of it.

"Really, it's not you, I mean part of it is you, but

mostly I'm just so sad." I sank back against the passenger seat and stared out the window at the King Palms swaying in the breeze. "Who's coming?"

"I think everyone but Sam. Her mother has a reading group tonight. Jacqs was having brunch with Lainie when I called Stay. He said they planned to come and Jacqs was going to call Red."

"You've never met Doug aka Dawg. He comes and goes."

"Have you—"

"Yeah, once. He's the king of the one-night stands, and I didn't want any more than that. It was really an angry fuck and it served its purpose."

"Angry at Bond?"

"Yeah."

"Recently?" he said, making a right turn off the highway.

"No, a few years ago."

"Your group is rather incestuous."

"Just some of us." I nodded. "I think I'm the worst of the group." I laughed.

"It's good to see you smile."

"Thanks for not letting me crawl into a ball in the middle of my bed."

"You're welcome. Do you have pen and paper in your backpack?"

I reached behind my seat and grabbed a Post-It pad and pen.

He smiled. "Those sure come in handy."

"I'm rather fond of the new one in the middle of my mirror. So..."

"Shopping list for food and drinks for us and your friends."

"Okay."

CHAPTER TWENTY

Where Is The Heart

by Alex Clare

Tate left me alone in his house, and part of me wanted to rifle through his drawers to learn more about him, but I refrained. Instead, I sat on the deck and appreciated the view, taking in the cloudless blue sky. On reflection, I was grateful that my friends would be coming. Letting Tate take care of me had its own pitfalls. Maybe he realized the same thing and therefore, invited the gang over.

I thought I heard a knock, so I went back inside the house. I pulled the curtain on the side window and saw Bond standing there. Unlocking the door, I let him in.

"I'm so sorry," he said, sweeping me up in his embrace. "Did you know it was so close? You never mentioned it."

"I didn't. Helena didn't tell me. I mean I knew she wasn't well, but she pulled through it last time."

"They say the second time battling cancer is worse." He looked around the house and said, "Nice digs." Stepping in farther, he took in the view. "Sweet place."

"Let's sit outside." I took my seat on the deck. "I need to text Tate."

Me: Bond is here.

My stomach tightened waiting for Tate's reply. "So did anything happen after I left last night?"

Bond sat next to me. "Blue, I'm here for you, we don't need to talk about me."

"I'm certain that Tate invited you all to distract me. So distract me."

"I thought that was off-limits," he said, raising an eyebrow.

My phone vibrated.

> **Tate:** I told Stayman five o'clock.
>
> **Me:** Maybe it got lost in translation.
>
> **Tate:** I'm not happy.
>
> **Me:** Do you trust me?
>
> **Tate:** That's not the point.

"You're scowling," Bond said. "Who's that?"

I looked up. "Tate."

"About me?"

"Yes. He says you were invited to come at five."

"Yeah, Stay said that, but I have to work tonight. I asked if I could come, and you said yes."

"You're right, I did."

> **Me:** He has to work later. He asked to come by, and I said yes. We're out on the deck talking. Should I ask him to leave?
>
> **Tate:** No.
>
> **Me:** Stop frowning. I can feel it through the phone. I already told you we aren't having sex anymore. That I won't kiss him again. Please be safe and don't rush back.
>
> **Tate:** Grrr.
>
> **Me:** Are you at the store?
>
> **Tate:** Yes.

Me: Do you want to call me so you can talk to him?
Tate: No. Do me a favor.
Me: Okay.
Tate: Go in the bedroom and take a sexy picture for me. Text it to me.
Me: Okay.

My clit twitched over the suggestion and I hopped up. "I'm going to change out of my work clothes. I'll be right back."

"Are we good?" Bond asked.

"Yeah."

Once in Tate's bedroom, I stripped off the black pants and long-sleeved gray shirt. I rummaged through my bag and grabbed the vibrator. I wouldn't send a pic of my pussy or boobs but I did want to send something provocative. His suggestion set my pulse racing, and I so appreciated being able to focus on the task. Also, I wanted to make him feel more secure but with a bit of added torture. I laughed at myself.

In my blue lace matching panties and bra, I climbed on the bed and spread my legs. Pulling my panties to the side, I rested my purple vibrator against my clit. It sufficiently covered my pussy. With my camera in hand, I tried to angle it so he could see most of my body. It wasn't easy to accomplish. After taking nine shots, I finally got a decent one. I sent it off to Tate and hurriedly dressed in jean shorts and a purple T-shirt.

A knock on the bedroom door startled me. "Are you okay in there?" Bond asked.

"Yeah, fine, just another minute." I rejoined him on the back deck. "So what happened last night?"

"Rory saw us leave the club together. She wasn't happy."

Bond leaned forward, his forearms resting on his thighs.

"When do you plan to talk to Jacqs?"

"I'm not sure yet. I'm still on the fence about what to do. Blue, I'm sorry for hurting you last night. If we could go back, I'd want to be open about us from the beginning. I thought it's what we both wanted."

My phone vibrated, but I ignored it. "It was, Bond. I guess I just didn't realize how much it was hurting me. I so appreciate your willingness to tell them. Now, it's a moot point."

"Yeah," he said, touching my thigh. "I miss you already."

"Me too." I climbed into his lap and we hugged each other. Tears spilled out as the loss of Helena seemed to compound my loss of Bond. Although the situation was never ideal, I felt safe with him. Tate, on the other hand, left my heart in peril. My thoughts were interrupted when I glanced up to see Tate standing over us. I scurried off Bond's lap and went to him.

"Beer?" Tate asked Bond.

"Sure, thanks. Great place you have."

I followed Tate to the kitchen. "Did you like the picture?"

"Yes, much better than the one I caught coming in." In a completely different tone, he said, "You packed a vibrator."

I knew he must be hard and looked down to see. With my fingers, I traced the impression. Then my eyes locked with his. "For us. I'll give you a hint. Sex is the perfect distraction."

"Had I known, I'd never have invited—"

I didn't let him finish. I touched his cheek and brought his mouth to mine.

He lifted me up on the bit of counter not covered with grocery bags and riveted my mouth to his.

After a steamy, sultry kiss, I said, "I will never cheat

on you, Tate. Not ever."

He searched my face. "I believe you."

I forced out a breath I hadn't realized I'd been holding in. *Thank you!* Breaking eye contact, I scanned the kitchen. "That's a lot of stuff."

"I figured your friends will be eating dinner here."

I hopped off the counter and started unpacking the groceries.

Tate fished out two Dos Equis and opened them. "I'm going to have a beer with Bond."

"Is that a good idea?" My breath caught in my throat.

Staring at my expression, he said, "Trust doesn't come easily for me. It probably never will again. There are a few things I need to say to Bond, and I promise to hear him out."

"Okay. Let me know when it's safe to come out."

He kissed me hard and fast and then walked away.

Helena, if you're around, please watch over those two. Part of me wished I could hear what they were saying. The rest of me figured it might hurt to know. I unpacked the groceries and threw away some of the take-out boxes to make room in the refrigerator. I left out the spinach dip mix, spinach, sour cream, mayo, scallions, watercress, and the veggies I assumed were for the dip.

As I mixed the ingredients together, I heard a loud laugh and some of the tension in my shoulders relaxed. Checking the time on the stove, there was still an hour until the others would start to arrive. I covered the dip and put it in the fridge and then started cutting up the vegetables.

"Blue!" Tate called.

With dishtowel in hand, I hung my head out the back sliding door. "Yeah?"

"Bond and I have an idea we'd like to pass by you."

My stomach dropped and I frowned. *This cannot be*

246

good. "Oh?" I asked, stepping out onto the deck.

"Tate thought a threesome might—"

My heart stopped beating, and I wanted to perish on the spot and join Helena on the other side.

"Wait Blue, I..." Bond started to stand up.

I looked from Tate to Bond. "Nice job to both of you for making me feel like a piece of ass." I dropped the towel and ran down the stairs to the beach. My legs propelled me forward, my heart left on the deck by their feet. I ran south, wondering how long it would take me to make it back to my place. *No keys.* I stopped, leaned over, hands on my knees, trying to catch my breath. I had my phone but who to call?

Only Stay knew Bond and I had been fucking, and putting him in the position of keeping more from Lainie wasn't fair.

I cried, completely convinced I would never be more than a piece of ass to anyone. I, Judy, Jude, Blue, didn't count for shit. Just my stupid fucking boobs and ass did. My best friend and my lover wanted to bond by using me. They could all go to hell. I needed to leave. I planned to call a cab as soon as I could summon the courage to head back.

Tate came upon me as I cried, sitting in the sand. "I thought you would—"

"Would what?" I used my hand to shield my eyes from the sun as I squinted up at the man I thought I loved. "You aren't who I thought you were. I'm going home. Tell Bond to call the group." I struggled to stand up in the sand and Tate made to steady me. "Don't!" I cried.

"Blue, please listen to me. It was stupid. Bond even said so but I pushed, saying it would fix things."

"Why?"

"I ... I got..."

"What?" I yelled, wrapping my arms around myself.

The wind blew his hair into his face, and he brushed it out of his eyes. "I got scared, jealous. You clearly love Bond, and I can see he loves you too."

"So making me feel like one of your one-night stands makes you feel better?"

"No." He glanced down at the surf. When he looked back up at me, I saw tears in his eyes. "I never wanted to make you feel like that."

"Well, you have, and we're done. You told me a while ago that I deserve more and you're right. I deserve a lot more. I have a lot to give, but I have to stop giving myself away to the wrong men. You've hurt me so deeply. I can't believe I was so wrong about a person. I know something horrible happened to you and for that I made allowances, but no longer."

"Blue, please. Just hear me out and then leave if you want to."

I shielded my face and looked at him again. The anguish on his face, tears in his eyes, tugged at my resolve before he had spoken one word.

"I'm sorry for not trusting you. I've been lied to by the people I trusted the most, over and over again, for years. It's hard for me to believe anything anyone says. You've been honest and open about everything, including your relationship with Bond." He dropped his shoulders and wiped the tears from his cheeks.

"This is the very reason I'll never fully share my life with another. It's not because I don't trust you. I no longer trust myself. When your intuition fails you repeatedly, you realize that you have zero self-protection in life. I've consciously built up my walls and have no intention of lowering them. I know that makes me far less appealing, but I also believe we can be good for each other." He held his palms out to me.

"I never thought I would laugh again or enjoy the touch of a woman. You've given that back to me."

"I'm so glad to be of service," I said sarcastically.

"I didn't mean it like that. It's you, Blue. You're the most incredible person I've ever met. I wish I had met you before... Please give me the chance to make it up to you."

Just then, a black and gold butterfly fluttered between us and I watched it float away on the wind. *Helena?* Then I recalled her words. *He's in love with you honey, but that's part of the problem. It's scaring the shit out of him.* She said I should risk loving him. "I don't know." I shook my head.

"Please just think about it. Your friends will be here soon. Give me another chance."

I didn't know if I could, but I also didn't want to be alone. "I'll think about it. I might have one of my friends drive me home tonight."

"I understand. Bond's waiting to talk to you. He said he needs to take off to get ready for work."

We walked back to Tate's house, me in front of him. I ascended the stairs and found Bond.

"I'll go inside," Tate said as he passed us.

"Well," I said to Bond, crossing my arms in front of me.

"I told him it was a stupid idea. That we'd already decided to shift our relationship back to friendship. He seemed convinced that you would want it. I stupidly thought I was helping."

"Men can be so fucking dumb."

"Yeah, we can. And often," he said with a chuckle. "I want you to know that I told Tate that I'd always love you. That I will always have your back. That I will beat the shit out of him if he ever hurts you."

"Too late for that."

Bond tilted his head. "He's running scared. I think there's a decent guy in there somewhere. Some of us are a real work in progress."

"Are you saying you like him?"

"I wouldn't go quite that far, but I think he might be okay. Walk me out."

I took his hand and led him to the front door, not looking into the kitchen as we passed it.

We hugged tightly and he said, "You can reach me at any time, Blue. Please call or text."

"Thanks, Bond." I opened the door and watched him leave. With my back against the closed door, I tried to organize my thoughts. I knew if Helena were around, she would tell me to put myself first. *Let this moment be about what you need and stop putting everyone else first.*

I entered the kitchen and said, "I need a drink and an orgasm."

CHAPTER TWENTY-ONE

Dark Side Of Me

by Coheed and Cambria

At first, Tate seemed shocked by my proclamation. He opened the fridge, retrieved a margarita and a beer and popped the caps. "We don't have much time," he said as we both looked at the clock on the stove that read 4:30 p.m.

"Hopefully, they'll run late. Come," I said, downing half my drink and then tugging on his hand.

In his bedroom, I slipped off my shorts and panties and handed him the vibrator. Then I drizzled a bit of oil over my clit.

"Jesus, Blue." His eyes flared with lust. "Let me kiss you first."

"No, there isn't time." I didn't add, *I don't want you to.* But I didn't want him to. I wanted the release without all the other complications my heart and head threw into the mix. I also didn't mind if Tate were left with a straining hard-on. I liked the idea of him suffering.

"I see what you're doing," he said, and I felt sure he did too.

I pinched my nipples through my shirt and bra as he lowered the vibrator to my pussy.

He circled around my labia, grazed my clit, side-stepping my swollen bundle of nerves. Then he pressed down on my mound, causing my arousal to poke out farther. Teasing me mercilessly, my pelvis followed his movements in hopes that he would flick across my sweet spot. The tip of the vibrator finally rolled over my most sensitive place.

"Yesss," I hissed, knowing it wouldn't take me long to trip over to the land of fantastic. My hips gyrated of their own accord. I continued to tweak my nipples until my back arched into my orgasm. "Oh, yesss!" I shot past myself, and my thoughts, to the very place I wanted to be, hovering outside of me.

"I think I heard the door," he grunted.

I waved him away, and kept my eyes closed as he shut the bedroom door behind him. I lingered in the afterglow, not wanting to move.

When I heard voices outside the door, I forced myself up into a sitting position and worked to get my bearings. Back in my panties and shorts, I brushed my hair, and straightened my top. I tipped my drink back and polished off the contents, wanting another.

I stopped at the entrance to the living room, watching Lainie and Stay talk to Tate.

"Here she is," Lainie said, pulling me along to the kitchen. She took the empty bottle from my hand and replaced it with a fresh one. She opened a hard apple cider for herself. "Let's go outside." She moved me forward with her hands on my shoulders.

We sat down on the steps leading to the beach.

"Stellar view," she said, scanning the beach and horizon. She looked back at me. "Bond called Stay just before we got here. He gave him the impression that things are rocky between you and Tate." She took a sip of her drink and then set the bottle down beside her.

I knew Bond meant well but, *fuck*, dude.

"Tate and his rollercoaster moods are the least of my concern right now. How do I wrap my mind around never seeing my aunt again? She was my failsafe in life."

"Like my dad is for me. I can't even imagine. I don't think you ever really get over something like that. I do hope you find someone who can be there for you. Like Tate, maybe?"

She looked so hopeful, I felt bad letting her down. "Yeah, no, I don't see that happening." I slugged some of my margarita and felt light-headed. I needed to eat something.

"Well, you have us, and we'll always be here for you. I think you might be wrong about Tate. If Bond can let go of his past, I'm certain Tate can as well. Plus, you two have that thing."

"Dare I ask?" I turned and leaned back against the post.

"Rip-roaring chemistry. The kind of legends." She smiled broadly.

"When did you become the romantic?" I rolled the bottle in my hands and took another drink.

"Let's just say that Stayman has made me much more aware of energy, and it's hard to miss the sex wafting in the air." She touched my leg and then said, "This place is great. Have you been in the ocean?"

"Once, the other night. I should go back inside and finish cutting the veggies and put the other food out."

"Okay, I'll help."

Tate stopped me on our way to the kitchen. "Are we okay?"

"Can we deal with us later?"

His expression darkened. "Sure thing." Right words, wrong tone. "Stay and I are going to grab more chairs from the garage."

"Good idea. I'm going to get the cheese sticks and wings into the oven and finish the crudité." I knew I was being mean, but I couldn't help it. How would he have felt had I been the one to suggest the threesome?

"You were cold," Lainie said, sidling up next to me.

I turned on the oven and continued cutting up the celery. "I can't worry about him right now. I mean—"

"He invited us all into his home for you. He's trying to—"

"Lane, you know I love you, but there are things—"

"I know more than you think, something to do with Bond being here. I'll take your word for it, but here is some unsolicited advice: if you already know you're going to forgive him, do it sooner rather than later. You need him right now, and he needs your reassurance."

I paused in utter frustration. "I really think I'm capable of deciding what I need."

"Yep, not hard if you pay attention. Trust me on this."

I felt my tears threatening to surface. "I'm angry."

"At who?"

"Helena for leaving for me, and Tate for being such an idiot."

"It's easier for you to be mad at him."

"Yes." I felt wetness on my cheek.

"Go, I'll finish the vegetables. What's going in the oven?"

"Breaded cheese sticks and wings in the freezer. Eighteen minutes for the cheese, longer for the wings."

She touched my shoulder. "I've got it covered. Send Stay to me, and I'll listen for the door."

"I love you, Lane."

"You too, girlfriend, now get."

The cotton clouds in the sky had turned a soft magenta, enhancing the blue that reflected from the ocean.

"Stay, Lainie needs you in the kitchen."

"Okay." He kissed me on the cheek and gave my arm a squeeze.

I waited for Stay to go inside the house. "Did you tell

him?" I asked, peering up at Tate.

"I think he put two and two together. He's rather intuitive." Tate rubbed the side of his face.

"Yeah, annoyingly so at times." I sighed. "Lainie says if I plan to forgive you, I should do it now."

"Do you?"

"Tell me something. What would you have done, felt even, if I had suggested the threesome to you?"

"I would've been furious, jealous, doubting that I could have a ... a..."

"It's called a relationship," I snapped, but then backed off. "No matter how dysfunctional." *He can't even say the fucking word.* "Maybe you should have considered how *you* would've reacted before you suggested the threesome. Have I ever given you an indication that I'd be open to something like that?"

"No, Blue, you haven't." He looked away. "Seeing you like that, on Bond's lap, him holding you, it triggered—" Even in profile, I could see the memory was unpleasant to him. "It was too much. Then I tried to diminish my reaction by making it about sex." When his eyes reconnected with mine, I read an apology in them.

"Fuck," I said and dropped my head. I waited, not to punish him, but to be certain of myself. "Okay, but let's be clear. Until we tell the other differently, we are monogamous. I know *relationship* is a dirty word to you, but hopefully you can live with monogamy."

"I don't want to share you."

"Oh? Then what? You were lashing out?"

"Yes. Seeing you made me see red. Not Red, I mean."

I cracked a smile. "Got it."

"I promise it won't happen again."

"See that it doesn't. I don't think I could forgive you

again if you make me feel like I don't matter to you, like you did today." I held out my hand to him and he scooped me up, perching me on the wooden railing.

"Thank you. I don't deserve you," he murmured against my mouth. He kissed me gently and then started to deepen the kiss.

"Get a room," Cat said, walking out back with Kev in tow. She whistled. "Nice view. We should all go swimming later."

I hopped down and locked into Tate's gaze, reaffirming our connection. "I'm going to check in with Lane and Stay."

He touched my bottom lip and smiled.

I quickly hugged Cat and Kev and headed inside toward the kitchen. Jacqs and Red intercepted me.

We embraced. Jacqs went out back, and Red pulled me into the living room.

"Bond wanted me to check in on you. It wasn't his idea."

"I think I'd feel better if Bond did a better job of keeping his lips zipped."

"He's very worried. He had to take off when you're grieving and on top of that, he upset you. And I understand you both have parted company in other ways."

"So much for things being kept a secret." I fished my phone out of my pocket and texted Bond.

> **Me:** I'm doing okay, and I'm not upset with you. How long has Red known?
> **Bond:** Since the toothbrush incident.
> **Me:** I see.
> **Bond:** Don't be mad. I want to see you tomorrow.
> **Me:** I'm not sure if there will be a service or anything.

Bond: You're not working, right?

Me: Yeah. I'll be in touch.

Bond: I'd be there if I could.

Me: It's probably better that you aren't at this point.

Bond: Love you, Blue.

Me: Love you too.

I peered up at Red and asked, "Did you tell Jacqs?"

"No, because her preference is not to know. I'm glad it was you. In many ways, I think you helped him heal more than Jacqs and I put together."

I drew my head back. "Really?"

"You've let him be him and—"

"And he did the same for me."

"Exactly." He glanced outside and then said, "I'm very sorry for your loss. I remember meeting her years ago. She was a force."

I smiled. "Yes, she sure was that."

"Tate's watching you. He reminds me of myself."

"He's more like a mix between you and Bond."

"I can see that. Listen, Blue, we're all here for you, however you need us. I'd like to go to her memorial if there is one. I know Bond wants to be there too."

I hugged Red tightly, my eyes brimming with tears. "Thank you." I might be a mess when it came to romance but damn, I hit the mother lode on friends.

He slipped his arm around my waist and led me forward. We parted in opposite directions.

In the kitchen, I found Stay and Jacqs. "Where's Lainie?"

"She abandoned ship," Stay said, smiling.

"We've got it covered," Jacqs said. "Are you hanging

in there?"

"Yeah." I grabbed another drink from the fridge. "Thanks for helping and for coming."

"Of course," Stay said, holding out a bowl of chips to me.

I tossed a couple in my mouth and took the bowl from him. "I'll bring this outside." Passing the dining table, I walked out onto the deck.

Tate took the chips from me and situated me on his lap.

I felt split in two. Part of me watched my friends interacting. I made sure to smile at the right times and laugh at their jokes. It was nice to have them there and yet, I felt consumed with deep dread. Grief was there as well. Helena's death, however, felt like a harbinger of worse things to come. What I really wanted was to be sitting on the sand, listening to the waves crash on the shore.

My heart still stung over Tate's behavior. Even though I sat in his lap, I didn't feel his energy surrounding me like before. I wasn't sure if I had closed off from him, or if he felt tentative. Maybe it was the alcohol. I had already consumed three margaritas and planned to drink another. I ate a couple of cheese sticks when Jacqs passed them around but otherwise hadn't eaten much all day.

Watching my coupled friends interact, I felt envious. Me, I was on borrowed time, but they had found their partners in life. Red just adored Jacqs who clearly loved him back. Lainie and Stay had softened each other. They seemed so open and radiantly happy. Even Cat with her defensive ways, the love between her and Kev was palpable. And then there was me, the forever bookmark, a holding place for someone else.

I didn't rate a happily ever after or even a shot to get there. My body and my heart led me astray each and every time and those attracted back never seemed capable of more. Ann would say I attract what I feel about myself and what I'm capable of. I'm capable of great love, so why did I keep finding less than I deserved?

The one person in the world who made me feel special was gone forever. I didn't get the chance to help her through the end. She didn't even have the decency to let me know she was dying. She definitely didn't leave me feeling special to her.

I abruptly stood. "Someone get me another drink and let's go for a swim." I glanced up and read concern on Tate's features. I wanted to smack the look off his face.

He raised his hands up and stepped back. Apparently, he could read the intention on my face. "I'll go get towels," he said.

I walked inside after him, tripping over the lip of the sliding door, quickly righting myself.

"Blue," Tate said, reaching out to me.

"Don't," I slurred, shuffling to the kitchen.

Red followed behind me and said, "I think we should go. We can swim another time."

My face grew hot, and I spun to face him. "You, too?" I pushed against his big broad chest.

He stood still, letting me poke at him.

"She didn't tell me she was dying," I cried. "Who does that? I never rank more than half. Not to you." I shoved him again. "Not Bond." My fists banged his chest. "Not Tate. Definitely not my parents and now, not even Helena."

"Blue, we don't feel that way about you. Helena—" Red stopped and glanced over my shoulder.

"Baby," Tate said, placing his hands on my shoulders from behind me.

I turned around with my fists at my sides. "No!" I shouted. "You don't want me. No one does. Just leave me the fuck alone."

Tate lifted me off the ground and carried me to his bedroom as I squirmed to get out of his grip.

"What the fuck do you think you're doing?" I shouted when he put me down.

"Baby, please listen to me."

"Stop calling me baby!" Tears joined my anger, and I brushed them away with the back of my hands.

He held his palms out in front of him. "I'm so sorry you're hurting. Please let me help you."

"No one can help me. Nobody wants me. Just leave me alone." I collapsed on his bed and let out a gut-wrenching sob. I have no idea how long I cried, but Tate gave me the space to do so.

"Blue?" I heard through the door.

"Bond?"

"Yeah, it's me. Can I come in?"

I opened the door and let him take me in his arms, my tears renewed. "What are you ... doing here?"

"Tate called me. He said to get here if I could. I told work I had a family emergency and got here as soon as possible."

I shuddered out a breath. "Did the rest of them leave?"

"Yes," he said, brushing my hair away from my face.

"I was mean."

"It's okay, Blue. You're hurting. Red said to call him anytime you need a punching bag."

I groaned.

"We all want to help."

My stomach grumbled, and I abruptly stepped back from him. "I think I'm going to be sick." I ran across the living room to the bathroom. I couldn't miss the slump of Tate's shoulders as I passed him on the couch. In the bathroom, up came the drinks and the little bit of food I had eaten. Thankfully, I made it to the toilet in time. I rinsed my mouth and brushed my teeth twice.

When I walked out, Tate still sat on the couch. I went to him and took his hand in mine. "I'm so sorry."

He lifted me onto his lap and sighed into my hair. "No, I'm sorry. I wish I could do this day over for you."

"I can't believe you called Bond."

"You needed him."

I tilted my head up and lightly kissed him.

He tightened his grip around me, and I sank against him. We sat like that, clinging to one another.

Bond came in. "Should I go?"

"No," Tate said. "Are you hungry? Blue needs to eat something. Breakfast?"

"Yeah, that would be great," I replied.

"I can always eat," Bond said.

To say I was mortified by my behavior would be a gross understatement. I took the worst of it out on Red, and according to Bond, he was up for more. I don't know what I did in life to deserve my friends but thankfully, they hadn't given up on me.

We sat outside, chowing down on eggs, leftover chicken wings, and toast.

"Daniel called me," Tate said, wiping his mouth with a napkin.

"What did he say?" I asked, placing my fork down on my plate.

"Helena didn't want any type of religious ceremony, so they're holding the ashes until after the reading of her will."

"There's a will?" I asked. "She never seemed much into possession, so that seems odd. However, having control after death seems just like her."

"Yeah, and you're in it. The reading of the will is on Tuesday at nine in the morning. Daniel said he would text you the address."

"I'm having a hard time wrapping my mind around it," I said, rubbing the back of my neck.

"I bet," Bond said, moving his chair away from the table. "Thanks Tate. That hit the spot."

"Thanks for coming by," Tate said.

"Anytime for Blue. I'm going to head out now."

"I'll walk you out," I said, standing up and taking his hand.

By the door, Bond hugged me to him. "Call or text me tomorrow. I need to know you're okay. Red said you could stay with us if you don't feel like being alone and don't want to stay here."

"I feel horrible for hitting him."

"Don't. He can take it and you know him, he likes feeling useful."

I squeezed Bond tightly and kissed his cheek. "I'll never forget you coming to me. Thank you."

"Like I said, anytime for you, Blue. Be nice to him," he said, tossing his head in Tate's direction.

"Yeah, yeah." I waved goodbye and closed the door. I pushed off the door and walked back through the house to the deck out back.

CHAPTER TWENTY-TWO

Upside Down

by Goldford

Tate came in from the deck, carrying our plates. "A storm is blowing in."

I followed him to the kitchen. "Seems fitting."

"Stop beating yourself up, Blue." He opened up the dishwasher and loaded our plates.

"Do you work tomorrow?" I asked, slumped over the counter.

"I have two classes tomorrow. Not until the afternoon."

"Do you want me to stay?"

He nodded. "I understand if you want to be alone."

"I don't want to be alone." I sounded depressed, even to myself. "I shouldn't drink when I'm so upset. I know better." I filled up a glass of water and drained it.

"We all do, but sometimes we make bad decisions, even knowing they aren't good ones."

"Yeah," I said, scanning him up and down.

"I didn't mean you dating me."

"Uh huh."

"Come here." He flipped me over his shoulder and spanked my ass, then carried me to the bedroom and deposited me on the bed. "Are you ready for sleep?"

I shook my head.

"Do you want to watch a movie?"

I shook my head again and crooked my pointer finger, calling him over.

"Are you sure?" he asked, kicking off his shoes.

"Ah huh."

"Is your stomach okay?" He unbuttoned his shirt and tossed it to the side.

"Tate?"

"Yeah?" He kicked off his jeans.

"Shut up and come. Now."

"Yes, ma'am!" He dove onto the bed next to me. His hands were everywhere at once, stripping off my clothes, running them over my naked body.

"Ohhh, that feels so good."

His mouth found mine, taking me on a journey of sensation, his heart on the tip of his tongue, coaxing mine there too. The kisses traveled from hard and fast to soft and slow, the passion of emotion always present. As he pressed me to him, I melted against his body, his hands molding the flesh of my back. He then buried them in my hair.

My heart opened to him again, freeing the tears that hovered close.

He held my face away from him, scanning my features.

If I were a betting woman, I would say I saw love reflected in his eyes, the tilt of his head, and the firm set of his mouth.

Okay, Helena, I'm going to go for it.

Tate, I love you, too.

He shifted me onto my back at the edge of the bed, with my legs up in the air, his eye contact absolute. Kneeling, he held my legs against his chest as I felt the head of his cock tease my entrance. "You're so wet," he moaned.

"It's that wicked mouth of yours."

"You like my kisses?" He trailed his pre-cum along my labia and then pressed the tip against my clit.

"Ah huh," I grunted as he dipped the head of his shaft

into my entrance. I hitched my hips forward.

"Not yet," he admonished, backing out. "Do you know why I like this position?"

"The better to torture me?"

He laughed heartily. "No, but that's definitely a perk. For one, I can watch your face easily. I love when your eyes cloud with your arousal and desperation." He dipped back in and circled his hips. "Plus, I can easily reach you." With his big, warm hands, he grazed across my mound, followed the curve of my waist, and cupped both breasts. Squeezing my nipples, he continued to roll his hips, pushing more of his length into me.

"Yesss. More!"

He withdrew and ran his hands up my neck, cupping my face. Leaning forward between my legs, he bit his way up my throat, suckling it, marking me. "And I can commandeer your lips, too," he murmured and then devoured my mouth with fervor.

Once we broke apart, he sat up and held my legs against him, running his hands over my ankles, down my shins, between my thighs, seeking my swollen clit. "But most importantly—" He thrust into me deeply, causing me to cry out. "—I can make you cum with me firmly inside you." His fingers brushed back and forth across my clit, the heat of his attention causing me to writhe against him.

My nipples tightened even more as the rush of desire raced over and through my body. Tate and I were perfect just like this, his attention unequivocal. I lost myself in his eyes, expressing all my feelings to him in my gaze. "Ohhh, Tate, just like that."

"You're so close. I feel your sexy pussy clutching and pulling on my shaft."

"Holy fuck, holy fuck, holy yesss," tumbled out as the

fierce orgasm rippled inward and then exploded like a supernova lighting up the sky.

"Damn that was hot," he mumbled, slowly resuming his incursion.

I spread my legs out around him and pulled him forward on top of me.

"Wait, Blue," he said, holding himself up beside me. "I don't think this—"

"Please don't think. I want you to." I drew his mouth to mine and felt him lower his body weight onto me. I panicked, trying to breathe through it.

He stroked slowly in and out of me.

I tried to enjoy it, but I couldn't. "Fuck!" I struggled to get out from under him.

"It's okay, shhh," he whispered, lifting his body weight onto his arms.

"I'm sorry, I wanted to." Tears dripped off the side of my face.

"Don't be," he rolled off me and held me in his arms. "Thank you for trying. No one has ever given themselves to me like you just did, and we both knew it was a risk. I'll never forget it."

"Thank you for understanding."

"Let me do something for you."

"Shouldn't I be taking care of him?" I asked, pointing down between us.

"He can wait."

"What do you have in mind?"

"Let's get ready for bed and you can ask me anything you want that doesn't have to do with my marriage or divorce."

I sat up and smiled. "Anything?"

He chuckled and said, "Yes."

I hopped up and spun around.

He's letting me in. My mind and heart high-fived each other.

"You're cute," he said, standing up next to me.

I peered up at him and pulled him along with me to the bathroom. I had an easier time peeing with him in the room. We both washed up and brushed our teeth.

In bed, we climbed under the covers and lay on our sides, facing each other.

"Can I ask you something first?" he asked as he played with my bangs.

"Sure." I touched his five o'clock shadow and licked my swollen lower lip, knowing how it got that way.

"That tongue of yours is quite distracting."

"Sorry," I said, rubbing my lips together. "Ask."

He draped his arm over my waist. "Why did you let me try to take you that way, after everything that happened today?"

"Are you sure you want to hear the answer? I don't want to push you away. I need you, Tate."

"I promise."

I inhaled a deep breath and took the chance. "You were there with me, open, our energies ... I'm not sure of the right words."

Love, love, love!

"Do you always forgive so easily?" He tugged me closer.

"It's a tremendous flaw."

"You haven't forgiven your brother or father."

"That's because they haven't asked me to."

"Oh." He nodded as if he understood. "Thank you for trusting me. What happened for you?"

"It seemed okay for a second, but then overwhelming fear flooded in and I couldn't breathe. We'll try again another day."

"Are you sure?

When you're ready to love me.

"Yes," I said to us both. I rolled away to take in his expression. He seemed calm. "Are you ready for my turn?"

"Fire away."

"How long were you in the construction business?"

He seemed to be calculating and said, "Cal and I worked construction during the summers for his dad, starting in the tenth grade. His father sold us the company when I graduated from college with my Master's in English. The opportunity was hard to turn down. I had student loans up the ass and had no prospects for paying them off. He gave us incredible terms, and we were able to pay him back from the proceeds each year. Took us eight or so years to manage it, and I paid off my student loans in that time as well. We caught the building boom out west and did very well."

"Why didn't you file for Native American status? Wouldn't your schooling have been paid for?"

"Because I was young and stupid. I thought I shouldn't get a free ride."

I laughed. "That is dumb! I would've happily taken it."

"Thanks," he said, laughing with me.

"This might be a touchy one, but it fits within the boundaries. Is Cal part of the friends you are no longer in touch with?"

"Yes."

"Okay, gotcha. When did you sell the business to him?"

"Coming up on four years now."

I ran my fingers across his forehead, trying to smooth out the creases. "How long have you lived here?"

"About a year and a half. I had an apartment in downtown Ft. Lauderdale for a while. Then I moved here."

"There's no personal stuff here of yours that I can tell. Is it boxed up somewhere?"

"You sure are the curious one."

I touched his arm. "You said anything other than..."

"Yes, I did. I have a storage unit."

"I see. Do you miss the construction business?"

"Part of it. I liked getting my hands dirty and working with the guys. I went out into the field mostly, and Cal ran the business from the office. Plus, I didn't need to work out like I have to now."

"Whatever you're doing is working!"

"Very funny," he said, tickling me.

"Hey, I'm not finished." I slapped his hands away.

"Okay, okay." He held his hands up in surrender. "Give me a kiss first." His mouth took mine, melting me with his taste, rattling my brain.

Pulling away, I said, "No fair. You're trying to distract me."

"Is it working?" He kissed his way up my throat and tugged on my ear with his teeth.

"That feels good," I said. "But I'm not done. Did you want kids?"

"Yes. Move along."

Too close, I gathered. "Do you go visit your parents at all?"

He seemed relieved by the new topic of conversation. "Every couple of years. My mother and I text and Skype occasionally."

"Not your dad?"

"He's more of an in-person kind of man."

"Gotcha. How did they feel about you selling the business?" I was curious what they thought of the divorce, too, but I didn't bother to ask.

"My mother was thrilled, and my father thought I was

being stupid, short-sighted."

"Do you believe in the Native ... I mean American Indian spiritualism? Medicine men and talking to the ancestors and stuff like that?"

"Yes."

"Just yes?"

"When you live on the reservation, you see it all the time. It's normal. I lost touch with a lot of the mysticism when we moved to Florida."

"What would surprise me most about the reservation?"

"Good and evil are both represented. There are witches in our culture."

"Get the fuck out of town. Really?"

"Yep," he said, trailing his fingers along my arm.

Trying to ignore his touch, I said, "Wow, I had no idea. What's it like when you go back?"

"My mother has a slew of women trying to seduce me. She wants me to stay."

I frowned. "When are you going back?"

"No plans at the moment."

"Good."

"Damn, you're cute. Come here." He rolled me on top of him and kissed all the other questions off my tongue.

CHAPTER TWENTY-THREE

Inscape

by Stateless

I stretched into the mid-day sunlight, feeling better than I could have imagined. Touching the cold bed beside me, a chill ran down my back and I wondered how long Tate had been up. Out of bed, I rubbed my face and searched for my clothes. I gathered them together and placed them by my bag.

I saw Tate out back as I scurried to the bathroom. Once freshened up, I made my way to the deck. "Good morning," I said, leaning in for a kiss.

He gave me a brief peck. "I'm going to be leaving soon."

My gut clinched over the cold reception. *What the fuck!* "Oh, okay, I'll take off." I went back inside, my eyes watering, and found my phone.

> **Me:** Can I come over? You at Red's?
> **Bond:** Yeah. Just waking up myself. Coffee?

I smiled through the pain.

> **Me:** Yes. Be there in 15 minutes or so.

I gathered my belongings, showered quickly, and dressed. Outside again, I asked, "Can I use the Jeep or do you want to drop me off at Red's?"

"I'll drop you off and can pick you up after my classes."

"I'd appreciate the ride, but don't worry about picking me up."

"Judy," he said, reaching for my hand.

"Fuck you. I'll have Bond pick me up." I stormed through the living room and out of his house, slamming the door behind me. With my backpack slung over my back and my duffle across my chest, I stomped down his drive to the street. I heard the tires of the Jeep squealing after me.

"Get in," Tate ordered, pulling up beside me.

"Fuck you. I'm such a colossal idiot." I shook my head and kept walking.

"Blue, come on. I'll drive you to Red's." The Jeep kept rolling slowly beside me.

I stood in the road, staring at him.

The groove between his eyes, right above his nose was as deep as ever. He looked like the man I had first met. Closed, in pain, and oh so sad.

"Fine, just don't talk to me." After throwing my bags in the back, I slid into the front passenger seat, belted in, and folded my arms around myself.

He didn't say anything until he pulled off of A1A onto US1. "I haven't had a dream about Christina in a long time."

I sighed in relief. *Christina.* "That makes sense."

"How do you mean?"

"You're opening up. That shit has a way of escaping or inscaping as in your case. The unresolved past has a way of pushing out, whether we want it to or not."

He scratched his head. "Do you still dream about—"

"Occasionally. Bond woke me not long ago and I was back in that very moment, crouching against the headboard as if—"

"Damn, I'm sorry." He touched my thigh and I just stared at his hand, not feeling his energy. The fortress of steel was back.

"One of these days, you'll realize I'm not her."

"I know that," he said, driving onto Red's block.

I looked at his profile. "Unfortunately, you still don't. I think we need some time apart. We can touch base tomorrow."

"Blue, I—"

"Yeah, yeah, I know." I got out of the car and grabbed my stuff from the back of the Jeep.

CHAPTER TWENTY-FOUR

Over My Head

by The Fray

Lugging my bags, I walked up to Red's door. I knocked and waited.

After a few minutes, Bond opened the door and took my bags. "Why did you knock?"

"I figured it would be locked."

"Nope. Red and Jacqs have already taken off. Come."

I followed him into the living room and plopped down on the couch, facing the pool and the Intracoastal Waterway.

Bond brought me a cup of coffee with lots of cream and sugar. "What happened?" He sat next to me, draping his arm across my shoulders.

Letting the coffee cup warm my hands, I filled him in on the night before.

"Wow. I have to be honest, I'm sort of jealous you tried with him. You've never even let me get close."

"Really?" I turned my body to face him.

"Yeah."

"It's my turn to say wow." I fell against his side, and he embraced me.

"Do you think we were wrong about us?" he asked.

I sat up straight. "I think you were too wrapped in Jacqs for it to be anything more."

"Yeah. So messed up." He laced his fingers behind his head and leaned back.

We both watched the drizzle out back morph into

pelting rain. The palm trees bowed to the wind, the sky mirroring my mood: cloudy with a chance of thunderstorms.

"How are you feeling about Tate now?"

"He's like surfing the ocean and so far, I've been able to pull myself back on my board."

"That's an interesting analogy."

"Simile."

"Right. I always get those mixed up."

I shrugged. "Maybe I'm too empathic. I get his pain, even though I don't know all the details. Maybe, it's partly because of us. You and me."

"Huh?"

"It took you years to share your past, and I know you kept a part of you closed off for a long time."

He held me tightly. "He's in love with you, Blue. I don't know if knowing that helps."

"That's what Helena said."

"She met him?"

"Yeah. Yesterday." My eyes widened. "Holy crap, was that just yesterday? Fuck, if I didn't live a lifetime in that one day." I took a sip of my coffee and stared out the French doors. "So tell me about Rory. Anything new?"

"She's a very jealous woman."

"Oh? And?"

"She was super pissed off that I left work early to be with you..."

I lifted my head. "But you saw her last night after you left my place?"

"Yeah."

"Have you talked to Jacqs?"

"No, and nothing happened. I told Rory that I need time. You know, Blue, you and I ending has me thinking a lot."

275

"In what way?"

He sighed out and pulled his long hair away from his face. "Truthfully? The threesome with Jacqs and Red never would have worked without you and..."

"And?"

"I'm not sure I love Jacqs the same way anymore. I'm trying to sort out how much is male ego, not letting the past go, or genuine love."

"And what have you come up with?"

"I know we've missed our shot, but I'm hurting more over the loss of us than the idea of losing Jacqs."

"Holy hell, dude."

"I'm not trying to confuse you. I think we've helped each other grow up a bit."

"Yeah, I understand." And I did, but my eyes filled with tears anyway. Where was Bond and his revelations *before* I met Tate?

"I put Jacqs up on a pedestal and never totally let her in like I have with you."

Holy hell,
holy sheep shit in a bucket,
holy moly,
holy guacamole,
holy cow,
holy priests,
but mostly HOLY FUCK!

"Trying to take that in," I said, shaking my head. The words I had so longed to hear, for what felt like forever, had finally arrived and yet, I wanted them from Tate, not Bond. "So what now?" I managed to get out.

He chuckled derisively at himself. "I don't know. I mean, I do. I need to bite the bullet and talk to Jacqs. I'm not sure my heart can deal with another goodbye just yet."

"I'm sorry you're hurting but in all honesty, it's reassuring that it's hard for you too."

"Yeah, I get it. I'm sorry I didn't do a better job loving you, Blue."

"You gave me just what I needed. Don't forget that. I love you, dude."

He kissed my forehead and held onto me.

Watching the rain ripple on the surface of the pool, I thought of Red. "Red must be beside himself."

"He's ready to ask Jacqs to marry him."

"Wow. How do you think Jacqs is going to feel about what you have to say?" As bad as it sounded, I wanted to kiss Bond's pain away but refrained.

"Part of me thinks she'll be relieved, but I was her first love and those are hard to let go."

"Yeah. Dude, pull the Band-Aid off. It's better to get it over with than letting it fester."

"I know. Is that your phone?"

I fished my phone from my short's pocket and swiped the screen: three messages.

> **Unknown number:** This is Daniel. I emailed you the address to the attorney's office. Give your mom a call. She'd love to check in with you.

Instead of my mother checking in with me, she had her minion tell me to do it. I loved the woman, but she frustrated the hell out of me as well. I added Daniel to my address book and texted him back.

> **Me:** Thanks. I will soon.

I pulled up the next message.

Lainie: Hey you. Hanging in there? Sam sends her love and hopes you're okay.

Me: With Bond at Red's. Could be better, could be worse. How's the shop?

Lainie: Rocking and rolling. We have a sale going on right now.

Me: Love you, Lane. Thanks for the check in. Give my love to Sam.

Lainie: Will do. Later.

Me: Later.

I looked up to find Bond watching me. "First one was from Daniel, my mother's boyfriend. I just texted Lainie back, and I still have one from Tate. Then I have to call my mom."

"Want something to eat?"

"Sure, whatever's fine."

Bond got up and I checked my last message.

Tate: I think we're going to have to change my name to Dick.

Me: LOL! Well if we go with the meanings for Tate, "wind" suits. You sure blow hot and cold. Did you know that Tate in English means cheerful? Got that wrong. I found another American Indian meaning: A man who talks too much, or something like that. Wrong again! Plus, I actually ran into a "Dick" and lucky for you, you're nothing like him.

Tate: You looked up the meaning of my name?

Me: Yes. Keep up with me.

Tate: I'm trying. :) I won't say sorry again because I know you hate it, but can we chalk it up to a bad morning?

Me: Are you at work?

Tate: Yes.

Me: Do you have an office?

Tate: Yeah.

Me: Send me a cock shot.

Tate: No!

Me: Yes. It's your apology. Two-way street and all.

Tate: Clearly, you need to be tied up again so you know who's boss.

Me: Clearly. Now send me that pic.

I strolled into the kitchen, my mood vastly improved, and hopped up on the counter.

"Sandwiches okay?"

"Great." I dialed my mother's phone and waited for her to answer.

"Hi Jude."

"Hi Mom. How are you doing?"

"Crying on and off. My face is so puffy."

"I understand. I got Daniel's text. Is he with you?"

"Yes, he's been amazing. He's taken care of all the details."

"That's great. I'm glad you have him. I still can't wrap my head around that Helena is gone. It still seems so—"

"Unreal, like I'll wake up and it'll all have been a really bad dream."

I sighed. "Yes, exactly." I felt my phone vibrate and couldn't help but smile.

"Let's go to brunch after the meeting tomorrow, k?"

"K. See you then?"

"Yes. Daniel's going to take me to lunch now."

"Okay. Bye."

"Bye."

Bond handed me a sandwich. "That was awkward."

"Yeah, she doesn't do good phone. I'm used to it." I swiped the screen again and pulled up my text. *Holy hotness!*

Wearing dark slacks and sitting in front of a desk, Tate had taken a shot of the outline of his hard cock bulging down his thigh. The caption read, *Only for you.* I giggled and glanced up to see Bond watching.

"I guess you guys are sorting things out."

I blushed. "We're working *hard* at it." I burst out in laughter. I texted Tate back.

Me: Very hot. Now don't go to class like that.

Tate: I don't plan on it. Are you with Bond?

Me: Yes, and he's professed his undying love.

Tate: That's not even funny. Major discipline tonight. I'll be there at around 5:30 or 6:00.

Me: Is there a question in there?

Tate: I need you in my bed tonight, and I want to drive you in the morning to your meeting. Blue, will you please come back to my house when I'm done teaching?

Me: Better. I'll think about it. :P

Tate: You're killing me.

Me: I have to make you work for it, or you'll think you can be Dick whenever you want.

Tate: I put Dick away for good.

Me: As long as Mr. Cock is still mine.

Tate: All yours.

Me: There you go. That's how to woo me.

Tate: My cock wants to do more than woo.

Me: Pound nails?

Tate: Hahahaha! Shhh. You're not helping.

Me: Take this as a lesson. I could've been under your desk right now, taking care of you.
Tate: Definitely not helping and class is soon. I need a cold shower. Lesson duly noted.
Me: Good. Have a good class and please feel free to have a HARD time keeping me off your mind. :P
Tate: Twice as hard, Blue. Very, very red ass.
Me: Mmmhmm. Have to catch me first.

I clicked out of my text and took a bite of my sandwich. "Yum, thanks."

"Sure." He swallowed and said, "I'm going to talk to her tonight."

"Good luck, dude."

"Going back to Tate's?"

"Yeah, later."

After lunch, I took a nap on the couch and slept through the afternoon. I apparently needed the rest.

"Hey, Blue," Red said, shaking my shoulder.

"Oh crap. What time is it?"

"After five," he said, sitting down next to me.

"Where's Jacqs and Bond?"

"Outside talking."

I sat up. "Holy shit, really?"

"It's happening."

"I'm glad we have a few minutes. I wanted to apologize for assaulting you last night."

He faced me and held my shoulders. "There's really nothing to apologize for. You didn't hurt me, and I felt honored that you felt safe enough with me to let it out."

"You're crazy, you know that? Seriously. Thank you."

"You're welcome."

"Do you think Bond and Jacqs are ending today?"

Red rubbed his chin. "I don't know. I think it might be the first step in that direction."

"You're a patient man. Me? The in-between is driving me crazy. You would think I'd be a pro at it by now."

"Love makes it different."

"Yeah."

Bond came in and said, "Blue, Jacqs wants to talk to you."

"Me?" I asked, hopping up. "Did you—"

"No." He shook his head.

"Are you okay?" I asked, touching his arm.

"No. I'm confused. Give me a minute with Red?"

"Of course. I'm going to grab some water and head out back." *What the fuck is going on? And why did she ask for me and not Red?* I took a glass down from the cabinet and filled it with chilled water from the fridge.

Outside, I sat next to Jacqs on the glider loveseat and placed the water down on the ground beside the couch.

"Have you met Rory?" she asked, looking down at her feet. Her eyes looked red.

"Yes, I have, but probably not like you think. I was at the club one night and she was there."

She glanced up, her eyes wide. "What's she like?"

"Can I ask you something first?" I said, bringing my legs up on the cushion, wrapping my arms around my knees, mirroring Jacqs's body posture.

"Okay?" She said it like a question.

"What did you tell Bond?"

"I said I wasn't ready for us to be over." She bent her head back and squeezed her eyes shut. "I haven't told anyone about this."

"About Bond."

"No. About ... oh fuck, Blue. I might be pregnant and I'm not sure—"

I hit my forehead and shook my head. "Holy fuck! Holy hell. Jacqs, you have to tell them."

"I'm not ready, and not until I know for sure."

Stunned, I couldn't even process what she had shared. *Why, oh why, did she tell me? Me of all people?*

"You can't tell anyone."

"Fuck, Jacqs. Is that why you told Bond you're not ready?"

Her eyes filled with tears. "I was hoping it would be him to pull away, but when he told me about Rory ... I hated it. Plus, I don't understand."

"What don't you understand?" Inside the house, a movement caught my eye and I saw that Tate had arrived. I held up my pointer finger like a one.

"He says he hasn't known her for very long and isn't even sure where it will go. Over the last month or so, I felt like he was falling for someone else, but he said he hasn't known her long."

Whoosh, her words flung right over my head, circled around, and crashed right into me.

"It's you, isn't it?"

"Whoa! Can we please slow down here?" My heart thundered against my ribs, and I didn't know what the hell to say to her.

"I've seen how he's reacted to Tate. I saw him question him and how he watches you when you're with Tate."

"Jacqs, I—" I forgot how to breathe.

"I thought so. I guess I'm confused. Where do things stand now?"

My body flushed with the heat of her revelation. "I'm just dating Tate."

"Is this recent?"

I knew she meant the ending with Bond. "Yes."

"You're toothbrush girl."

I nodded.

"Fuck, girl."

"Yeah."

We stared at each other as apologies floated around in my head, but none landed on my lips.

"That had to be hard on you," she said. "I'm not sure I would have dealt with knowing, but now who knows. I guess we never will. Are you sure about Tate, because I think Bond might—"

"Bond and I love each other, Jacqs, and we've grown comfortable in our relationship, but it's not a love affair."

"If you say so."

"I do." *Holy fucking hell and motherfucking shit. I must still be in my bed in my apartment dreaming all of this in some macabre version of my world. My aunt is still alive and not a butterfly on the beach. I've never met Tate and his brand of crazy, and Bond most certainly isn't in love with me. Someone fucking wake me up and fast. I don't think I can take anymore.*

Jacqs jostled my shoulder. "Blue."

"Yeah, sorry. I zoned out for a second. So what are you going to do? You should tell Lainie. She can hold your hand while you take the test."

"I don't want anyone to know. I didn't even mean to tell you. I'll get a blood test in another week or so. Please don't say anything."

"Frankly, if we can pretend this conversation never took place, I might be able to screw my head back onto my shoulders. I think it's rolling around by the pool."

She chuckled quietly.

"Are you mad at Bond and me?"

"I just wish we all had handled it differently. I told

Bond I didn't want to know and I was mean to you the night you slept with him. That wasn't the first time though, was it?"

"No, but I never ever slept with him while you guys were officially dating. I wouldn't do that."

"I don't know about you, but this is a lot to digest."

I felt so overwhelmed with a chorus of conflicting emotions. "No kidding. Let me know if you want me to come with you to get the test."

"You would do that?"

"I'm certain Lainie will lynch me when she finds out but yeah, of course."

She surprised me when she hugged me close.

Once we broke apart, I said, "Tate's here and I need to get going, and you need to reassure Red."

"Blue?"

"Yeah?"

"Sorry about your aunt. I know you loved her like no other."

"Thanks, Jacqs." I stood, pulled down the legs of my shorts, and straightened my top. I blew out a sigh and turned to go inside. "Should I send Red out?"

"Yeah."

As soon as I walked inside, I said, "Red, she's ready for you." I turned to Tate. "Can you give me a couple of minutes with Bond?"

He nodded.

"I'll be quick." I grabbed Bond's wrist and pulled him into Red's game room. Sitting on the edge of one of the pool tables, I said, "She knows about us. I didn't tell her, but she figured it out for herself. I feel like we need to have a long conversation, but that can't happen now with Tate waiting for me. I just wanted you to know that she knows."

"Is she mad about it?"

I stood up straight and rolled my neck. "No, she doesn't seem to be."

"This is a mess."

"Fuck, yeah, it is."

"Come," he said, waving me to him. Once I stepped into his embrace, he sighed against my cheek.

I didn't know what to feel, but life just got seriously complicated, and I was right in the middle of the storm.

CHAPTER TWENTY-FIVE

Can't Pretend

by Tom Odell (at Dean Street Studios)

When Bond and I walked out of the game room, I grabbed my stuff and said to Tate, "Let me use the bathroom and then we can take off." I quickly peed and brushed my teeth. Once I came out, he led me to his Jeep, holding my hand.

"What the hell is going on?" he asked as we climbed into the car. "The energy at Red's was all kinds of weird."

"You don't even know the half of it." I rested my forehead in my palm.

"Then tell me."

"I ... I can't share everything."

He started the engine. "Can't or won't?"

"To some extent both. I promised not to disclose part of it to anyone, and my word means everything to me. The other stuff is opinion and conjecture, and I'm not sure where I stand on it."

He drove onto the street out front of Red's. "Tell me what you can."

Phew, I thought. "Thank you for understanding. Bond told Jacqs about Rory and Jacqs isn't ready to let Bond go. I'm curious as hell what she's saying to Red right now. Here's the real shocker—"

"She figured it out about you and Bond."

"Yes. How did you know?" I swiveled in my seat to face him.

"If I figured it out..."

"Right."

He made a left turn. "How did she take it?"

"Far better than I imagined."

"That's good. So the stuff you aren't sharing, is it about Jacqs?"

I searched around in my skull, or at least it felt like that, trying to find the right words.

"Just say it, Blue."

"Yes, the major portion has nothing at all to do with me."

"And the minor portion?"

"It really isn't about me either, but it involves me."

"I think I see."

I prayed he did not. As he maneuvered the Jeep through the streets, I spun in a whirlpool of confusion. Could Bond really be in love with me or was he just dealing with the loss of our intimacy? I didn't have faith that Bond knew the difference. Besides, the loss of two relationships at once would be tough on anyone.

The most bizarre part was that I didn't know how I wanted to feel about Bond being in love with me. I also couldn't get next to how I really felt. Katness, from my novel, jumped to my mind. She forever chases the man who will not love her back. Was I doing the same thing? On some level, I knew I deserved love, I just wasn't sure I believed it.

"You sure are deep in thought," Tate said when he parked the Jeep on the side of his house. "What do you want to do?"

"Since the sky has cleared, how about a swim and then some food?"

He smiled. "Perfect. Let's change into our suits, and I'll grab a couple of towels and our robes."

I dropped my bags in his bedroom and rummaged for my bikini. After changing, I watched Tate strip and don a pair of red bathing trunks. *Damn, he looks hot!*

In turn, his eyes combed my body, leaving behind the heat of his gaze as he leisurely swept from my eyes, to my parted lips, and then my chest, rising and falling with the excitement he stirred in me. They continued their sojourn down my belly to my most concentrated desire, trapped behind nylon and spandex. He glanced up and said, "I see you sizing me up, too." He ushered me against the back of his bedroom door, capturing my wrists in one hand and holding them above my head. With his knee, he forced my stance wider. "There we go." He pushed his erection against my bikini-clad pussy, his mouth hovering over mine. "Did you like the photo?"

"Mmmhmm," I murmured against his mouth.

He bit his way up my neck, across my chin, and tugged on my bottom lip. "I'll make you forget him," he growled, grinding his hips into me as he consumed my mouth and my breath. "My cock's been aching for you all day." He shucked off his shorts and shifted my bathing suit bottom to the side, plunging two fingers into my wetness.

"Oh god," I groaned.

"I'm going to take you now, because I can't wait another second." He lifted me up with one arm, his weight pinning me to the door, my wrists still held high above me.

I curled my legs around his waist as he immersed the head of his cock into my pool of wetness.

He rocked up into me, repeatedly, penetrating as deeply with his stare. "Who do you belong to?"

"You!" I cried.

He shifted me slightly and I felt his fingers scoop up some of my juices and then douse into my ass.

"Oh fuck, oh hell!" I called out, shaking from the

fierce stimulation.

"Oh yeah, there you go, ride me."

"Let me ... have ... my arms." I tugged to free them.

He released his grip on my wrists.

I clasped my hands onto his shoulders and bounced up and down on his cock and fingers.

"Kiss me," he growled.

Our lips sparked together, igniting a need so deep and vast, I didn't think it could ever be sated. He bent his knees and thrust upright again, banging against my cervix.

I welcomed the blend of pleasure and pain as his masculine scent filled my senses. His manly aggression turned me on as his fingers and cock stretched my openings.

"Oh, Tate, your cock feels so good. Fill me ... take me ... so good."

As if my words affected him, his girth and length expanded as he raced toward climax.

In his arms, his cock filling me, I felt no confusion at all. I wanted this man to open his heart to me and risk it all, just like I was doing for him. All the while, we continued to kiss and slam our bodies together in ardor and passion.

Breaking away from our kiss, Tate yelled out his release, watching me watch him cum for me.

My legs lowered to the ground as he rested his forehead against mine, struggling to catch his breath. "Can you hand me a towel?" I asked.

"No," he breathed out. He reached down between us and recovered my cum-filled pussy with the bikini bottom. "I want you to walk down to the beach with my cum between your legs."

"I can do that," I said, the idea totally keeping me hot and bothered.

He slipped back into his trunks. "Give me a sec."

I followed him into the living room and waited as he ran into the kitchen and washed his hands.

"Let's go." Hand in hand, we raced across the deck, down the steps, and out onto the beach. He threw our stuff down and led me to the water.

We walked in several steps and then dove into the surf. We broke the surface and smiled at each other.

"I love seeing you smile," I said. "Almost as much as I loved you fucking me against your bedroom door."

"That was so hot."

"Beyond."

"Come to me." He had me straddle him, my back to his chest, and his mouth next to my ear. His fingers snaked under the elastic of my suit bottom and found my sweet, very wet spot. "How does that feel?" he whispered.

"Incredible."

"Look out at the people down the beach. Do you think they know what I'm doing to you?" He increased the pressure on my clit and suckled the side of my neck.

"Oh god, I don't know."

"And you don't care." He paused in the motion of his fingers, and said, "I know Bond is having second thoughts about you. Just to be clear, Blue, I'm not sharing you."

In that moment, his possessiveness thrilled me.

"Repeat after me. I am yours."

"I am yours," I groaned as he continued the choreography of his fingers, reclaiming my clit.

I am yours.

I am yours.

I am yours.

I tilted my head back just as Tate bent his head forward and our lips locked in a torrid kiss.

"Great Spirit save me," I called out against his mouth.

I saw Tate smile again just before he swallowed my cry. My orgasm racked my body, causing ripples on the surface of the ocean surrounding us.

"We're going for two," he rumbled into my ear, not stopping the circling and flicking of his fingers. His other hand slipped into the back of my suit and his fingers pushed into my ass. He rode the crest of my first climax, pushing me over to the next wave of release.

"Ohhh, holy Jesus Mother Murphy." That time I swallowed my own scream.

Tate burst out in laughter, shaking us in the water, while I crumpled, liquefied by our sex and ever-growing love. "You say the weirdest stuff. You're a funny girl," he said, still chuckling into my neck.

I twisted around until I faced him and hugged him to me. "Thank you," I whispered.

"Always my pleasure. Look at me." His warm eyes melted me even more. "Was I right about Bond?"

"Do we have to talk about that? I'm floating in bliss and so enjoying our time together." I lay back, drifting on the water, spreading my arms out wide, my legs still hooked around Tate's waist.

He scooped up my back and brought me upright.

"Okay, okay," I said, giving in. "Bond doesn't know what he's feeling. He's grieving me and the idea of letting go of Jacqs as well."

"What did you do while I was at work?" he asked in a calm voice. He lulled me into lying on my back again and held me in the water, staring down at me.

"I talked with Bond for a bit, called my mom, texted with my lover, and mostly napped."

"Where did you nap?" he asked his voice no longer sedate.

My evil twin wanted to say, *with Bond*, but fortunately,

she kept her mouth shut. "On the couch, by myself."

"What did Bond do?"

"I have no clue. I was asleep."

"How's your mom?"

I hoped his latest question meant he had finished with the interrogation. "She's as good as can be expected."

"How are you doing?"

"Honestly, I feel like I'm in some parallel universe that I have yet to sort out, where all the rules are different."

"Interesting simile."

Score two points to Tate for getting it right. Why was I keeping score? Bond wasn't in the running anymore.

"Blue?"

"Yep," I said, running my hands through the surface of the water.

"I could be good for you."

"Doubtful."

He dunked me under the water and stepped away.

"Why the fuck did you do that?" I stood and wiped the water out of my eyes. "You're the one that doesn't want the dirty word: *Relationship*," I whispered sarcastically. "Stop playing with me." I watched the features of his face close off one by one: the warmth in his eyes a cold memory, the tension in his jaw back, and the crevice between his eyes once again deep.

He stood and crossed his arms. "I'm not playing, Blue."

"But you're not open to loving me, either. Explain to me why you would be a better choice than Bond if he truly loves me?"

"I wouldn't be."

"Fuck you!" I screamed, smacking the surface of the water. I turned away from him and trudged toward the shore.

He grabbed my upper arm and brought me face to face

with him. "You push my buttons, woman."

Woman? "How is it my fault if you won't tell me what they are?"

"It's not."

I lowered my shoulders in defeat. "I'm not good at this. I don't mean to hurt you, but you hurt me all the time with your bullshit that you won't ever love again, while you're doing everything in your power to cause me to fall in love with you. How fair is that?"

"It's not." He squeezed the water out of his hair, while his hard stare scrutinized mine.

"Can I please take the Jeep? I need some time alone."

"I'd prefer to talk this out." He walked out of the water, and I followed him to the beach.

"What is there to talk out?" I asked, taking the towel he offered me.

"I care about you," he said as he dried off.

"Groovy, and?"

"The more time we spend together, the more I care." He spread out his robe and we both sat down on it.

Watching the shoreline waves recede into the ocean, I asked, "Are we replacing the word love with care?"

"They aren't the same."

"Right, so nothing has changed."

"Everything has changed. That's the problem. Each second I trust you more, the more I'm convinced it'll kill me in the end."

Holy hell! His confession should've scared the bejesus out of me but instead, it made me love him more. "There's another option."

"What's that?"

"We fall madly in love and stay together forever."

"I don't believe in forever anymore."

"Right." I fell back on my hands and looked at the sky. "Well, hopefully you'll stop punishing yourself at some point. And hopefully for your sake, I'll still be around when you do."

"You don't know anything about it."

"Like you, I can put two and two together. Why you feel at fault for other people's betrayal makes no sense to me. So, in that regard, you're right. Trusting and loyal people can be fooled. It's the plight of anyone with an open heart. I also believe we're the ones who can love the deepest with the most passion. That's what Stay tells me anyway."

"Bullshit. Where's the evidence?"

"None whatsoever, other than the love of my friends. They're loyal to a fault. I'm flawed as hell, and they still love me."

"You're not flawed. You're wonderful."

"But you don't want wonderful."

"Of course I do. Why wouldn't I?"

"I want to ask you one question about your wife. It has zero to do with the past."

He seemed to be contemplating, so I waited. "Ask."

"Am I like Christina?"

"No, not at all."

"Maybe you should think on that for a bit. Let's go eat something." I stood up and slipped on my robe.

Tate tied my sash and then shook out his robe to dislodge the sand, gathered our towels, and took my hand in his. "As tiny as your hand is, it fits perfectly into mine."

Yes, a perfect fit, I thought but said, "I think it's a case of your hands being ginormous, not mine being small."

"Oh, you're small, my little sprite."

I smacked his shoulder and he laughed.

"What do you want for dinner?"

By the steps, we rinsed and dried off. We entered the back of the house and strolled into the kitchen.

"Are you sick of breakfast for dinner yet?" I asked, hopping up onto the counter. I hooked my foot around his thigh and drew him to me.

He leaned into me, his hands on the edge of the counter. "Nope, but it's high time I take you out for a proper meal. This week?"

"You mean like a real date?" I ran my fingers through his wet hair, smoothing it away from his face.

"That's exactly what I mean. Dress nice, good food, you and me."

"Then my answer is yes. Speaking of clothes, I need to go home tonight. I don't have anything to wear tomorrow. Plus, I'm pretty sure only the people in the will get to hear the reading of it. My mother wants us to go to brunch afterwards."

He stood up straight and said, "Are you planning to work tomorrow night?"

"Yeah, I don't want to lose my shift at Tap 42."

"Will you come back here afterward?"

I touched his arm. "Do you want me to?"

He leaned in again and said, "I want you in my bed every night."

"Those are some dangerous words, mothafucka."

Pushing off the edge and turning toward the refrigerator, he mumbled, "Don't I know it." He scrambled up eggs, sautéed spinach, tossed in cheddar cheese, and produced the perfect omelet while frying up hash browns in another pan.

I cut up a ripe cantaloupe I found in the fridge.

We sat on the deck, watching the sunset as we ate our meal, both of us lost in our own thoughts.

Once I finished, I wiped my mouth with a napkin. "That hit the spot. Thank you."

Tate glanced at me and smiled.

"How did your classes go?"

"It seems some of the female students picked up on my agitation."

I frowned. "How do you mean?"

He shrugged. "They seemed extra flirty."

"Are you trying to make me jealous?"

"Not at all. Since we've been..."

"Fucking, dating, fraternizing? Pick one, for fuck's sake."

He chuckled at me. "Fraternizing? I like that one. Women seem to be noticing me more."

"Maybe you're just now noticing them notice you."

He shook his head. "Nope, I'm sure of it."

"Maybe it's because you aren't walking around with a scowl all the time."

"Hmmm. You're probably right." His bright smile floored me.

"Wow. I could live in that smile," I said, removing his plate from his lap and replacing it with myself. "Kiss me."

And he did, over and over again.

I finally pulled away when I felt the wind whip up around us and the sky darken. "So, I'm going to head home now."

"Can I come see you at work tomorrow?"

I stood up. "Definitely."

Tate followed me into his bedroom, sat on the edge of the bed, and watched me change.

"Can I leave this here to dry?" I held up my damp bikini.

"Sure, and I'll wash our robes, too. Blue, before you go?" He held his arms out to me.

I stepped in between his legs and held his head to my chest.

"Don't give up on me."

Tears filled my eyes. I peered down at him and said, "I won't."

I love you.

I love you.

I love you.

Now don't break my heart!

Back at my apartment, it felt odd to be alone. I sorted through my mail and stacked the bills to the side. Other than rent, my student loans took the largest portion of my income.

I sat, pulled my computer onto my lap, and quickly checked my email. Then I remembered that I hadn't had my phone with me while at Tate's.

Fuck! Three calls and five text messages. I swiped the screen and listened first.

"Hi, Jude, it's Mom. Please make sure you're on time tomorrow. I wanted to warn you that Matt will be there too. Well, I guess I'm going to hang up. Daniel's going to fix brunch at the house, instead of going out. See you tomorrow." Beep.

Fucking hell in a hand basket! What the hell did Helena leave for Matt?

The next voicemail came from Samantha. "Hey, girlfriend. Just wanted to see if you're doing okay. I know you're dealing with a lot. I hope all is going well with the hunk. Call me if you need me. Love you." Beep.

I listened to the last message from Bond. "Do you want me to go with you tomorrow? I left Red's for my place and will be staying here tonight. Jacqs and Red are both pissed off. I decided to leave them alone to work it out. It's a fucking mess. I miss you. Call or text me."

The text messages were from Cat, Bond, Jacqs, Lane, and Stay.

I pulled up Jacqs's first.

> **Jacqueline:** I'm sorry for dumping that on you. I'm mad at Bond, and Red's mad at me. It's a royal clusterfuck. Can you imagine how it'll be if I am? Enough about me. Let me know if you need some support tomorrow. I'm sure it'll be a hard day. Love you.
>
> **Me:** I have so much stirring in my brain, that's one thing that is thankfully on the back burner and safe with me. I'm sure Red will calm down. I guess I'm not sure why you're mad at Bond. Because of me? Rory?

I responded collectively to Lane, Stay, and Cat.

> **Me:** I was at Red's for most of the day and spent the evening with Tate. I'm hanging in there and not looking forward to tomorrow. I'll check in after I have brunch with my mother. Love you guys!

To Bond I texted:

> **Me:** I'm back at my apartment. It's hard to sort through everything that's happened in the last few days. I think I just need to focus on getting through tomorrow. My brother's going to be there.

While I waited for Bond to respond, I sorted through the clothes in my closet. I decided two things: one, I would wear nice jeans and a blouse to the reading, and two, I needed to go to Lainie's shop for a dress for my upcoming *real* date with Tate.

My phone vibrated and I swiped the screen. Instead of receiving a text from Bond, I had one from Tate.

Tate: I miss you already.
Me: You're not allowed to say stuff like that. It might mean you CARE too much.
Tate: Come back over and let me show you.

Goddamn him. My nipples tightened and my heart twirled in my chest.

The phone vibrated again.

Bond: What the fuck, Blue? I'm coming with you. Why will he be there?
Me: I'm assuming Helena left him something. No point in coming along.

Jacqueline: I just didn't expect it to hurt so much. I know Red and I will be fine. What about you and Bond?
Me: Bond and I are good. I'll touch base with you tomorrow.

Tate: Or I can come there.
Me: That's a very sweet offer and my bed seems much larger than it used to. But I think it's good for us to take a break. My vag is kinda sore.

Bond: Of course there is. I can punch out your brother.
Me: Dude, what happened, happened 16 years ago.

Tate: This wasn't a booty call.
Me: Are you pursing those full lips of yours?
Tate: How can you tell?
Me: Text tone. So easy to read.

Bond: Doesn't make me any less interested in breaking his nose.
Me: Dude, no. I'll text you after the meeting.

Tate: Let me come and you can read my tone all night long.
Me: You make it hard to say no.
Tate: You make me hard. Period.
Me: You and your cock will have to sleep alone in your own bed tonight.
Tate: Blue?
Me: Yes, Tate.

My phone rang, so I answered it.

"Please call me tomorrow, for any reason," Tate said, his deep gravelly voice full of emotion. "I know you have your friends, but I want to be there for you. Let me."

"I will. Can you hang on for a sec?"

"Sure."

I ran to the bathroom, quickly got ready for bed, and then climbed under the covers. "Okay, I'm back."

"What were you doing?"

"Peeing without you in the bathroom and generally getting ready for bed."

He laughed. "I like knowing I'm the last voice you'll hear before going to sleep."

"I'm stressing about tomorrow."

"Why?"

I adjusted my pillow under my head. "My brother's going to be there."

"That makes sense. Not that that makes it any easier. Sorry, kiddo. Are you sure you don't want me to go with you?"

I sighed. "No, I'll be fine. I just have to get through it. I can't fathom what she's left for him or for me, either. I guess I just assumed she hadn't kept in touch with Matt."

"I wish I could be hugging you right now. One of these days we should try eating breakfast for breakfast again."

I yawned. "That sounds great. I'm going to hang up, set my alarm, and crash. Thanks for calling me."

"Sweet dreams, Blue."

"You too, Tate."

I clicked out of the call and set the alarm.

My mind flitted from Helena to Matt to Bond to my mother to Tate to Jacqs's potential pregnancy and back again. So much to deal with, the grieving process seemed to be at a standstill. I drifted off, wondering what it would be like to see Matt again. Maybe I would punch him myself.

CHAPTER TWENTY-SIX

Teardrop

by Massive Attack

I parked across the way from the attorney's office at eight-fifty. The view of the door allowed me to watch my mother and Daniel walk inside the office along with three other women I didn't recognize.

A shiny black truck pulled into the lot, and I saw my brother step out. I had never seen the man version of him before, not in person and not in pictures. He appeared tall and lean. Using the driver's side mirror, he tightened his tie and smoothed his dress shirt. He seemed uncomfortable. Whether it was the situation or the clothes, I couldn't tell.

He glanced across the way and caught me staring at him.

My heart pounded and my breath stayed lodged in my throat.

He seemed to wrestle with walking over to me or staying put.

I wouldn't make the first move.

One foot in front of the other, he quickly closed the gap between us.

I opened the door to the Jeep and hopped down.

"You look the same," he said. He didn't seem to know what to do with his hands and stood awkwardly in front of me.

"You look completely different," I said, realizing the inanity of our conversation.

He looked away and scratched the back of his neck. "Listen," he said, his eyes finding their way back to me.

Blue eyes just like mine. "I tried to get in touch with you for years, but mom wouldn't let me know your number or where you worked."

"Why?"

"I regret what happened with Chandler. I wanted to apologize and try to repair our relationship."

I didn't feel shocked. I honestly didn't feel much right then. "Have you been in touch with Helena?"

"Not for years now. No. I'm not sure why I'm here."

I had an idea why. "How's Dad?"

"Dad's the same. An unhappy dick of a man. You have two half-sisters, different moms."

Whoa! "When was the last time you saw Mom?"

"Four years ago or so. She came to my wedding. So did Helena, come to think of it."

"You're married?" I asked incredulously, my mouth wide open in shock.

"Was. It didn't stick. I'm thirty-three now, not seventeen." He stuck his hands in his pants pocket and looked down at the ground between us.

"Yeah, I know that. Sorry about your marriage."

"You?"

"No. Not sure marriage is in the cards for me. I don't seem to attract men who are interested in the long-term. Are you still in touch with Chandler?"

"I never spoke to him again after that night."

"What?" I said, with my palms out and facing him.

"I tried to get him to stop when I realized you weren't into it anymore. You seemed to be at first, but then, I don't know, something changed, and he wouldn't stop."

Was he rewriting history? "I don't remember it like that at all."

"You were hysterical while I was trying to pull him off

you. He knocked me to the ground and finished. Then I beat the shit out of him, and he left the house bleeding. I'm so sorry I ever allowed the situation to start in the first place."

I shook my head back and forth, not able to ascertain the truth.

"Kids, it's time," Mom yelled and waved from the door.

Matt turned to go.

"Wait." I touched his arm. "This makes no sense. Did you tell Dad I wasn't a virgin anymore?"

"Of course not. I was embarrassed that I let Chandler... I thought you wanted it." He stared down at his shoes.

"But you watched and—"

When he looked up, I saw tears in his eyes. "That night is the biggest regret of my life. We'd been drinking, all of us, and it seemed like a good idea at the time. I've had to live with what it did to you. What I did to you, and it caused me to lose you forever. You were the only person I loved and you were gone too."

I broke down, crying as he hugged me and I let him. "Apology accepted."

"Just like that?" He held me away from him, scanning my face.

"All you had to do was ask and mean it."

"I want us to try—"

Our mother called again, and I pushed away from him. "This is a lot for me to wrap my head around. We better get inside." I wiped my eyes on the back of my hands and tried to force my emotions under control.

Inside, we entered a wood-paneled office with five chairs around a large desk. My mother occupied one chair, and two women I didn't know occupied two others. Matt and I took our seats.

The attorney began to read:

"This is the reading of the Last Will and Testament of Helena Adams of West Palm Beach in the State of Florida, being of sound and disposing mind, memory and understanding, do hereby make, publish, and declare this my Last Will and Testament, hereby revoking any and all Wills or Codicils heretofore made by me."

I zoned out for much of the jargon, thinking about Matt and the past. I liked his version much better, but how would I ever know if it was the truth?

The attorney spoke of personal representatives and I figured the primary and substitute were the two women to the left. I didn't clue back in until I heard my name.

"I give, devise, and bequeath unto Judy Radford the sum of seventy-five thousand dollars with the hopes that she will use it to chase her dreams.

"I give, devise, and bequeath unto Matthew Radford all the contents in my garage, including the antique 1947 Harley-Davidson WL with sidecar motorcycle."

Then I zoned out again, thinking about the seventy-five thousand dollars. *Holy yay!*

Once the attorney finished reading the will, he said, "The will is still in probate, so it could take several weeks for everything to be distributed. Helena has requested there be no service and that come springtime, her ashes be used to plant a Royal Poinciana tree. Also, Helena left a letter for each of you." He passed over envelopes to us.

I stared at Jude written across the front of it and zoned out again.

My mother shook my shoulder. "I saw you talking to Matt earlier. Is it okay if I invite him to brunch?"

"Yeah," I said, standing up and following her.

"Feel free to invite Tate if you'd like."

"Where are we going?" I asked, once we got outside.

"I told you in my phone message. The house."

"Right, sorry. I'm ... I'm dealing with a lot."

"We all are."

"Right. I'll see you there in a bit." In a daze, I managed to make my way to the Jeep. I desperately did *not* want to be alone and yet, I wasn't clear whom I wanted with me. If I called in Bond, Tate wouldn't be happy. My mother invited Tate, not Bond. I felt so torn and confused. What I really wanted to do was beat on Red's chest some more. With all the recent revelations, I couldn't even process that Helena had left me a small fortune.

I hit my steering wheel with the side of my hand and cried, grieving not only the loss of Helena, but also my whole fucked up life. Eventually, the tears subsided and I woke up my phone and found two texts.

> **Bond:** Did you punch your brother for me? Just say the word and I'm there.
>
> **Tate:** Thinking of you. Hope you're hanging in there.

I decided to text them both. I knew they would see each other's names on the joint text. Truth be told, I needed them both and couldn't choose between them.

> **Me:** Can you meet me at my mom's house?
>
> **Bond:** Coming.
>
> **Tate:** On my way.

I texted them the address, started the Jeep, and pulled into traffic. On my way, I stopped at Publix to pick up a dessert. My mother had drilled it into me never to show up at someone's house empty handed. I thought about buying alcohol but then recalled my previous behavior and decided against it. By the time I made it to my mother's house, both Tate and Bond were waiting for me outside. Tate seemed to be smiling, so I let out a sigh of relief.

Bond gave me a warm hug. "How did it go?"

Then Tate scooped me up, lifting my feet off the ground. He kissed my lips and set me down. "Tell us," he said.

I leaned against Bond's car. "I talked to Matt. His version of that night is different from mine and frankly, I like his better. Still can't wrap my mind around it. He seems very regretful."

"That must feel good," Tate said.

I squinted up at him through the bright sun. "Not really. If what he says is true, I lost sixteen years with my brother, and I don't know if we'll ever get back to the friendship we once had. Before that night, he was my best friend in the world."

"Damn, Blue. With everything you're dealing with, your heart must feel torn up," Bond said, crossing his arms over his chest.

I knew in my gut he wanted me wrapped in his arms, and I also knew I wanted him to. Damn the consequences, I stepped toward him and he embraced me. He held my head as Tate made soft circles on my back.

We stayed like that as I absorbed their energy and love.

I stepped back and looked from Bond to Tate. "Thank you for being here for me. Part of me feels utterly selfish to have both of you here but right now, it's what I need."

Bond hooked his fingers with mine. "I understand."

I glanced at Tate and he seemed okay. I smiled at him. "I can go back to school."

"Oh?" Tate said.

"She left you money?" Bond asked.

"Yep. Seventy-five big ones. I'll have enough to pay off my student loans and finish my degree."

Bond whistled. "Were you surprised?"

"I'm still in shock. I had no idea she had money." I leaned into the Jeep and grabbed the dessert. "I guess we should head in. Listen guys, Matt's in there. Don't hurt him."

Bond chuckled.

For the first time in my life, I had an idea of what Jacqs might feel like, having both Red and Bond around. It's not like either of them were mine, like Red and Bond were to her, but I felt uber conscious of them both at every moment. It was reassuring and exhausting at the same time.

"Judy, can I borrow you for a minute?" Matt said as I was getting ready to leave.

"Yeah." I followed him outside.

"I ... could we spend some time together? It's doesn't have to be right away. I can see you have your hands full, and I know you were very close to Aunt Helena."

"Are you on Facebook? Maybe we can chat on there sometime."

"Yeah, great. That would be great. I'll find you on there. Thank you for ... well, you know ... listening and giving me ... a chance." He opened his arms to me, and I returned the hug.

Bond and Tate joined me outside.

"I have to take off," Tate said, touching my cheek. "I have a class starting soon."

"Thank you so much—"

"Of course. I'll see you later at Tap 42 after my second class is over." He held my face in his hands and kissed me longingly.

I let the taste and feel of him wash over me as my eyes closed. "Mmmm," I murmured.

He pulled away, shook Bond's hand, and then straddled his Harley.

I waved goodbye as he rode away.

Bond hugged me from behind. "Can I follow you to your place?"

"I'd love that," I said over my shoulder.

The storm wasn't over by any stretch, but at least the winds were dying down. I just had to wait out the rest of the rough weather until the sun and blue skies returned. My biggest obstacle was figuring out what to do next.

CHAPTER TWENTY-SEVEN

Gravity

by Sara Bareilles

Bond followed me home, and as many times as Bond had been in my apartment, it felt different this time. I threw my bag down on the table, Helena's unopened letter still inside, and sat on the couch while Bond used the bathroom.

He raised an eyebrow. "I see he changed the message on the sticky."

"Yeah. Come sit," I said, patting the couch next to me. "Have you spoken to Jacqs or Red today?"

He plunked down, legs open, arms across the back of the couch. "Yeah, they've made up. Never takes them long."

"How's Red dealing with her response to you?"

He shrugged. "He wasn't happy yesterday."

"Have you seen or talked to Rory?"

"No. I didn't tell her I was at the apartment last night. Listen Blue, I don't want to fuck anything up between you and Tate. The dude's growing on me."

"But?" I brought my knee up on the couch and faced Bond.

"I'm holding off moving forward with Rory."

I sat up straight. "Because of me?"

He nodded.

"Dude, I ... I don't know what to say. I'm in love with Tate. I don't know if he'll ever admit it or allow himself to love me back, but I'm hoping he will. He's letting me in more, and he's trusting me more. He already thinks you're having second thoughts about us—"

"I am," he said, his hand resting on my thigh.

I glanced down at his hand and back to him. "Why now? Why not a few weeks ago? Dude, you know—"

"I know you love me, Blue. I've always known. I just—"

"This is so cliché, Bond. You didn't realize until I was gone? Really, Dude. Come on. We've been doing this dance for years." I pushed his hand away and folded my arms around my bent knees.

"It was different this time around and you know it."

I angled my head to the side and asked, "How?"

"I didn't hold anything back with you. Answer me this, who knows you better than anyone else?"

"You."

"And you, me."

I sighed. "We're best friends. That doesn't make us *in* love."

His light brown eyes looked pained. "I've been an idiot. You're the one who helped me open up again."

"I'm not like Rory. I could never share you and love you fully. Not like you want. You need someone who'll allow you to be intimate with other people. I might love you, Bond, but I could never be that for you. I want someone who only wants me and no one else. I have to be enough for someone."

"You are enough for me. I can be that man if you'd let me."

I held my shaking head in my hands. "And the world tilts on its axis yet again. I love you dearly, but you're delusional. Your dick is like a homing beacon for all the hot, fresh pussy around."

"I have been loyal to you and Jacqs."

"Count them, Dude. One, two," I said, holding up my fingers. "And let's call it what it was. I was never one. I was always and forever two. Let me ask you something. If Jacqs left Red and just chose you, would you choose to be with her?"

He ran his fingers through his hair. "I don't know. I've chased her for so long, it's hard to stop."

"Clearly, you're confused. I think you're scared. I'm not sure if it's losing me or meeting Rory or what, but I don't think it's love."

He leaned back again. "But you think Tate will love you like you need?"

"Are you worried for me? I don't know. I do know had you had this revelation sooner, I'd be considering giving it a shot between us, but that would mean no more Jacqs and no more dicking around with every woman from Miami to Okeechobee."

"Fuck!" He stood up and paced away.

"Yep. So what does Jacqs want?"

Stepping back toward me, he said, "The status quo."

"So you still see each other and date Rory?"

"No. She wants me to tell Rory to fuck off. She says if Rory realized I was already involved with two women, it makes her a wicked bitch to try to worm her way in."

My brows furrowed. "She said that? That doesn't sound like Jacqs."

"She was pissed off. She wanted to know if she was toothbrush girl. When I said she wasn't, she got really pissed. She said, 'Does Rory know toothbrush girl?' When I said yes, she really lost it."

Wow! "Holy shit, Dude. How was it left?" My phone vibrated in my pocket. "One second." I headed toward the bathroom to check the text. I sat down to pee and swiped my phone. Tate had sent me another picture. *Holy mother of god!*

In the photo, Tate's hard-on lay along the zipper with the head of his cock poking out. *Damn, damn, damn.* I wanted to be with him, slowly lowering his zipper and straddling his lap.

I wiped myself off, flushed, and quickly washed my hands. I rested against the bathroom door and texted him as much:

Me: So wickedly hot. I wish I were there to unzip your jeans and ride you long and hard.

Tate: Me too. Soon. Next chance I get, I'm bringing you to work. You can sit in on my class and torment me.

Me: Holy hell, Tate. Yes! I'll sit there with you knowing your cum is leaking onto my panties.

Tate: I'm caring even more for you right this minute.

Me: I'm smiling so big, I'm certain light is shining out of my eyes. I can't wait to care more about you with your cock stretching my insides.

Tate: Give me something bad to think about. I need to go to class soon. Is Bond with you?

Me: You must be into self-torture. Yes, he's here. I'm certain we have better things to talk about.

Tate: Is he professing his love?

Me: The dude is seriously confused.

Tate: Do you want him back?

Me: No, I want you.

Tate: Good answer. You've got me.

Me: Really?

I didn't receive a response right away, so I went back into the living room.

Bond was hunched over his legs, forearms perched on his thighs. "Tate?"

"Yeah." I sat down next to him and rested my hand on his back. "So where were we?"

"That's your phone again."

I swiped my screen and saw Tate's response.

Tate: Yes, really. Tell Bond I plan to keep my promise.

"Tate says to tell you he plans to keep his promise. What does that mean?"

Bond sat up and held my hand. "That he won't hurt you."

Intense heat suffused my entire being. Tate was falling in love. I was sure of it.

He loves me!

He loves me!

He loves me!

"You really love him, don't you?" Bond asked. "I want you to be happy. I made a decision while you were in the bathroom." He seemed serious.

"Oh?" I moved my hair behind my back and focused on Bond's face.

"I'm going to spend some time alone and figure out what I really want."

"By alone you mean—"

"No sex."

"Wow! Really?"

He nodded.

"Quadruple wow. I think that's a brilliant idea."

315

"I'm not giving up on us yet, so if you change your mind..."

"I'm so proud of you, Bond. I think you're doing the exact right thing for yourself."

"Listen, I'm going to take off and stop by Red's. I need to talk to Jacqs and grab some of my stuff. When I said I plan to be alone that doesn't mean we won't—"

"Tomorrow night at Red's?"

"Yeah."

I walked him to the door and we hugged hard. It seemed like a real goodbye of sorts. "Love you."

"Love you too."

I watched him walk down the stairs to his car and shook my head. *Holy moly.* Maybe we were both growing up.

CHAPTER TWENTY-EIGHT

If I Ever Feel Better

by Phoenix

In the kitchen, I fished out Helena's letter. I held it in my hands, flipping it back and forth. Part of me wanted to read her words, and the rest of me didn't know if I could take it with all the recent revelations.

"Fuck it!" I ran my finger along the flap and pulled out the purple stationary. Helena Adams with a rainbow swirl lined the top of the first page.

Dearest Love Bug,

If you're reading this, then you know this butterfly has set sail over the horizon. Don't be mad at your mom. I wouldn't let her call you sooner.

It's been my greatest honor to have had you in my life. I never was settled enough in life or in my relationships to have children of my own, but in my heart, you were always mine. No love is greater than the love one has for their child. Our relationship fulfilled me in ways you may never understand. So, in parting, I'm going to talk to you like you're my daughter.

Value love and adventure over stability. Stability is an illusion that can crumble at the drop of a hat. Experience and love broadens your horizons and your heart, leaving more room to grow. Your love did that for me.

Take risks. Playing it safe never got anyone anywhere. Your heart will break, but it will heal, too, which brings me to the biggie.

Forgive. Forgive your father. He will never ask for it because he's so damaged, and it would never occur to him to do so. The loss of your mother forever wounded him and he never forgave, leaving him a shell of a man. I'm not telling you to welcome him into your life. Just let the hatred go.

Matt needs you just as much as your mother does. He's a good soul, that one, and is worth your forgiveness. You need him, too. I don't know if you need your mother because she has always played the role of the younger sister. Even with me, and she's the older one. Forgive her, too. We all have our limitations. She could never fully let love in, so she has always been searching to feel something she could never allow. Trust me, your dad was a pussycat compared to our folks.

I've never met a person more deserving of love than you. Let yourself have it. I'm so comforted knowing that you have a supportive group of friends. Never take them for granted. You and me, we find family where we need it.

I've left you something in the will. You will do me the biggest honor if you use it to chase your dreams. Find your bliss in life and pursue it to the ends of the earth.

Your mother has a photo of us I'd like you to have. Yes, this is my way of making sure you see her again and soon, but also, it's a picture of one of my favorite days with you.

You are forever in my heart. I'm so proud of you, Jude.

I'm sending my love on the wind to help you fly,
Mama Butterfly

My tears fell throughout the reading of the letter and once I had finished, I broke down and grieved savagely. I made my way to the couch and collapsed. My one cheerleader in life was gone and I hoped when she left, she knew I loved her just as much. I would never again see a butterfly without thinking of her. In that way, she would always be with me.

I dozed on the couch when my crying trailed off to soft sobs and breathy sighs.

The guy in the next apartment dropped something, startling me awake.

Fuck! I needed to get up, shower, and get ready for work, the last thing I wanted to do.

On the way to Tap 42, I had a vague feeling I had dreamt about Jacqs. I thought about what she must be feeling. Given advanced technology, I felt certain she was choosing to wait when she could have easily found out with a disposable test. Maybe she was trying to will her period to start.

Once inside the bar, I found Sheila on the clock, which seemed odd for a Tuesday. She looked especially cute. Her short, curly, blonde hair reminded me of the roaring 20s. She had painted her tiny mouth with coral and used smoky gray around her wide, green eyes.

"Is Stuart here too?" I asked as I checked the taps.

"Yeah, he's in the back," Sheila said, removing a plate from in front of a customer.

"Oh, I didn't see him when I was coming through." I casually retraced my steps and found Stuart talking to one of the cooks. Once he finished his conversation, he turned toward me.

"Sheila's working with us tonight?"

"Yeah, she can also cover the floor if necessary."

On a Tuesday? Keeping my thought to myself, I replied, "Okey dokey."

Back out front, Sheila and I worked together, cutting the fruit and stocking the freezer with more mugs for the night.

"What do you think of Stuart?" she asked as she quartered more limes.

"He's a fine boss. Seems fair."

She paused her knife and asked, "Have you ever—"

"No. Work and play don't mix well. That's been my experience, anyway." I scooped out some maraschino cherries from the large jar and filled the fruit container.

"Did he—"

I abhorred lying, but I also didn't want to get between a coworker and my boss. Thankfully, a distraction from the other night's party of twenty-somethings presented itself. "How did you know I'd be here tonight?" I said to Redhead.

"I didn't. Your boss wouldn't tell me which days you work. I've been here every night since Saturday."

I shook my head at him. "Tate will be here shortly, so why don't you skedaddle?"

"What the heck's a skedaddle?"

Sheila answered, "She's telling you to take off." To me she said, "I didn't know you had a boyfriend."

"I don't."

"She's mine." Tate approached, taking a stool next to Redhead. "I told you he'd be back," he said without looking at the kid.

I stood there with my mouth hanging open.

"That's a relief because I thought Stuart had a thing for you." Sheila snapped her fingers in front of my face. "Are you going to take their order?"

"Yeah." I threw down two coasters. "What'll it be?" I felt certain the shock still showed on my face because my eyes were stuck wide open, staring at Tate.

"I'll take care of the kid," Sheila whispered to me.

Completely flustered, I asked, "Did you mean it?"

Tate nodded. "Kiss me hello."

I propped myself up on my hands and met Tate in a kiss over the bar.

He gently cupped my face and held my gaze as he wooed me with his lips.

Stuart walked out from the back, so I hopped back down. "Hey," he said to Tate.

"Hey man," Tate said back.

"What can I get you?" I asked.

Tate winked. "I'll take a draft of amber ale and the mussels."

"Right," I said, scanning his face.

"What?"

"You look happy."

"I am," he said. "Got a pen?"

I went to the register, tossed him a pen, and then placed his order. Sheila handed me a frosty mug, and I filled the glass.

She leaned into me. "You okay?"

I nodded, shook my head, and then shrugged.

She chuckled and whispered, "He's enough to rattle any woman."

"Oh yeah." I grinned, then turned back around and placed his beer on the coaster in front of him.

Tate slid a square napkin in front of me. It read: *Spend all your free time with the half-breed American Indian with the big smile*.

My eyes filled and I said, "Please tell me you mean it."

"Next time we're at your place, I'll make a new Post-It." Then he pushed another napkin across and it read: *I REALLY care about you*.

"Stuart?" I said.

"Yeah?" he asked from across the bar.

"I need ten."

"Okay."

I rushed through the back of the restaurant and outside to the front. I ran straight into Tate's open arms.

"Shhh," he said as I cried against his chest.

I searched his eyes for the truth. "Are you sure, because I..."

He held my face and said, "Trust me."

I wanted to tell him the truth. Maybe I wanted to test him too. "Tate?"

"Yeah?"

"I love you."

He crushed his lips against mine, lifting me off the ground.

I wrapped my legs around him, holding him just as tight. I never wanted him to let me go.

He pressed his forehead against mine, panting. "As long as you can leave the past in the past and not have to label us. Give me time to get there. I promise I'm not going anywhere." Carrying me, he walked toward the back of the building.

I loosened my arms from around his neck. "Does that mean I'm allowed to use the dirty word?"

He laughed. "Yes. You've always had a very dirty mouth."

I raised my fist into the air. "Tate is in a relationship with Blue. Yesss."

His mouth covered mine again and this time, I felt his love more than his passion. The fierce emotion left me breathless in a different way. He placed me down by the back door. "You better get back in."

"Yeah." I went straight to the bathroom, wiped the smudged eyeliner from my eyes, and retrieved Helena's letter from my bag. A few more customers had taken a seat, and I noticed Redhead flirting with Sheila. I chuckled to myself. "Here," I said to Tate, handing him the letter. "Helena left that for me."

I took a few orders, ran some food, and pulled another amber ale for Tate. "So," I said, placing the beer down in front of him.

"Intense. Did you know your mother broke your father's heart?"

"No. I had no idea why they were fighting all the time and then they split. I don't know if Matt knows, either."

"Thank you for letting me read it." He handed the letter back to me. "I feel like I understand better. Now I know what she meant to you and what you meant to her." He stared at me with a slight smile. "I'm going to take off in a minute. Are you coming over after you're done here?"

"If that's okay. I packed a bag."

"Yep, and I think it's time for you to leave some stuff at my place."

Then I did something I had never done before and thankfully, Stuart didn't see me. I turned away from the bar, hoisted my butt onto the counter and swung my legs around. I practically threw myself at Tate.

He caught me, laughing. "Don't go getting yourself fired on my account."

"Kiss me quickly."

He gave me a hot, sweet kiss and helped me back over the bar. "How much do I owe you?"

"I got you covered."

"Text me when you're on your way." He smiled and strolled away as I watched him until he was out of sight.

I love him!

Boy, do I love him!

"What was that all about?" Sheila asked, sidling up next to me.

"Progress. That was most definitely progress."

By the time I made it to Tate's that night, the emotional exhaustion from the day had set in. He was wonderfully attentive and understanding. After a shower, he spooned me and I immediately melted into his embrace and had a peaceful night of slumber.

CHAPTER TWENTY-NINE

I Would Do Anything For You

by Foster the People

I blinked my eyes and saw Tate standing above me. "What time is it?"

"It's after ten."

"Shit. I have to get going. Are you coming to Red's tonight?"

"Yes, but I wanted to talk to you about something. Do you have time to eat?"

"Something fast. What's up?" I rolled out of bed and rummaged in my bag for my work clothes. I quickly dressed and looked up. "Are we okay?"

"I'm going to be busy most of the day tomorrow, so I was thinking we could crash at your place tonight."

"Oh yeah. Sure, that's fine. I work a double tomorrow anyway. I plan to stop by Lainie's shop and then head into work."

"Go wash up, and I'll come up with something to eat."

"The left over cantaloupe is fine, and I can have something at work later."

Tate followed me to the bathroom and leaned against the door jam.

I felt the heat of his gaze as I flushed the toilet. I washed my hands and squeezed toothpaste onto my toothbrush.

"Any chance you can stop by my office later?"

I held the toothbrush away from my mouth. "Oh, to

325

pick up the car? I'm only working the lunch shift. Does three-thirty or four work?"

"We can talk about the car later. Come by when you can. It's hard for me not to—" He ran his fingers through his hair and said, "I'll get on that breakfast."

We sat down at the inside table with coffee, toast, and cantaloupe. He surprised me by shifting me onto his lap.

"This is very dangerous," I said as he dangled a piece of cantaloupe in front of my mouth. I ate the offering and licked his fingers.

His hard cock twitched under me. "If you can, get off earlier."

I laughed. "I see what you did there."

He licked the juices from my mouth and swallowed my giggles.

When I pulled away, I took stock of his gorgeous face. I ran my fingers along the ridge of his sharp cheekbones. My smile faded. "Thank you for last night. It was exactly what I needed."

"I aim to please," he said with a cheeky grin.

"No, I'm serious. Somehow, I feel I'll get through it all when you have me wrapped up in your arms. Falling asleep with you last night? It was one of the most peaceful sleeps I've had in a long time."

"I'd do just about anything for you, Blue."

Wow! And I'd let you.

We shared a cantaloupe kiss, sweet and sexy.

I pushed off his lap. "I have to get going, or I'm going to lose my job. I'm not a wealthy woman, *yet*."

"You don't have to worry about money. You can always—"

"I think I see where you're going. I make my own way."

"It was just a thought."

I retrieved my stuff from Tate's bathroom and bedroom and came back to him. "I miss you already and I haven't stepped out the door yet."

"I know what you mean. You better leave before I make you stay."

I backed up and laughed. "Going."

Nothing remarkable happened during my lunch shift other than counting down the days, minutes, and seconds before I could give my notice. I planned to keep my job at Tap 42, but aimed never to wait tables again, if I could help it.

I got off earlier than expected, changed out of my work clothes, and made it to FAU in good time. After talking to the Help Desk, I found my way to his office. He wasn't there, but another professor was.

"He's still in class. We share this office." The man looked like the quintessential professor: graying beard and mustache, along with the rounded spectacles.

"Can you direct me to his classroom?"

He led me down the hall and outside and then pointed to the building across the quad.

"Thanks," I said as I walked away.

I slipped into a large lecture hall and sat down in the back. Tate was discussing *The Fall of the House of Usher* by Edgar Allan Poe. His black fitted, dress pants and button-down blue shirt gave him a more formidable appearance. Had he been one of my professors, I would have set out to seduce him despite his large stature. As he passionately stalked across the stage, he expounded the hidden context of the story.

Watching his sexy strut, I thought, *He's mine bitches, and you can't have him!*

I, personally, always found *The Fall of the House of Usher* to be straightforward. I couldn't help myself. I raised my hand.

Tate's eyes latched onto mine and like a warm breeze, I felt him everywhere. "Yes, miss..."

My heart pounded and I had to take a deep breath to respond. "Judy."

"Yes, Judy, go ahead."

"Given that the house essentially splits in half and crumbles at the end of the story, it seems clear to me that the house was in fact sentient and the source of all the ills of the family."

"Interesting. Why do you think that Roderick dies in the end?"

"Because he's deeply connected with his twin sister. His decline mirrors hers, but in different ways. I have heard it stated that the crack the narrator first notices is symbolic of the crack between the twins. For me, that's a stretch. As someone who writes—nothing that might be considered a classic someday, but writes—sometimes storytelling is to create a mood, a feeling without all the subterfuge most critics or academics like to read into it."

"Thank you for sharing your opinion with our class today. All opinions are encouraged." He turned his attention away from me to the rest of the class. "That's all the time we have. Please make sure to read *The Tell-Tale Heart* by next week and be prepared to compare and contrast it with *The Fall of the House of Usher*."

I kept my seat and watched Tate gather his papers off the desk in front of him. He seemed to be taking his time. Once all the students had gone, he walked up the steps toward me. I couldn't read his expression. "Are you mad at me?"

He pulled me to him and placed my hand over the zipper of his pants.

"Ohhh." I fell out laughing.

"You've been a very bad girl and need to be punished right away." He tugged me after him, and led me back across the quad to his office. The other professor was nowhere in sight. He closed and locked the door, lowering the blind over the glass inset in the doorframe.

Before I could catch up, he had my shorts unbuttoned and pulled off. He fell back into his big leather chair and ran his hands up my thighs. "Those panties are killing me." He fingered the strip of pink lace that didn't cover much.

"I think he needs to breathe," I said, unbuttoning his pants.

He shooed my hands away. "This is my fantasy and you've played right into my plans." He took my elbow and laid me across his lap, my naked ass up, with just a thin piece of material separating my rounded globes. His finger found its way under the thong and circled around my anus.

I held my head up and looked at him.

"I'm getting in there again." His wicked grin turned me on even more. "First, you need to be punished." He raised his hand and smacked my bottom several times, causing my butt cheeks to redden. "I'm just warming you up. I have a surprise for you." He righted me onto my feet and said, "Check the shelf to the left."

"Are you planning to spank me with a book?"

"No, naughty girl. School girls get special treatment."

I parted the books, until I located a small, oak spanking paddle hidden behind them.

"Has Bond ever—"

I shook my head, my nipples and pussy willing and ready. "Have you used—"

"I bought it for us."

"Good," I sighed out. "I mean, maybe. It looks like it might hurt."

"Oh, it will. Count on it." He stripped my shirt and bra

329

and then shifted some papers to the side. He had me lay my upper body across the far end of the desk. "Spread your feet as wide as the desk." He shoved my foot outside the width of the desk. "Like that. Do it with your other foot."

I felt so exposed, my body trembling in anticipation of his erotic game.

Then he tied my wrists, stretching them across the length of the desk. He lifted the far end of the desk and tossed the remainder of the rope under it, pinning me there. From under the desk, he brought the rope out and around behind me.

Shit!

He bound my feet to the sides as he tied off the rope between my legs. It left me with no play at all in my confinement. His sinful hands sculpted across my body, teasing, pulling, and pinching. "Are you ready?"

"Yesss," I panted out.

He tickled over my ass. "Do you remember when I told you that I wanted to hurt you?"

"Yes, that first night?"

"Blue, my naughty girl..."

"Do it."

He swatted me with the paddle, and it stung but quickly dissipated. "More?"

"More."

"Good girl." He struck the other side of my ass and then said, "Prepare yourself."

I shook before the next strike landed. The paddle came down hard on my thighs. "Holy fuck!"

"Breathe," he said, soothing over my stinging flesh with his warm palms. "That's four. How many do you think a naughty girl deserves for barging into my class and espousing her opinions?"

"Twenty," I forced out.

"Hmmm." He ran his fingers over my mound and then squeezed my ass. "You like living on the edge. Once I'm inside you, I'll ream you without mercy. Do you still think twenty?"

I panted and said, "Twenty-five."

"Pride before the fall, such a sad, classic case. And since you seem to like the classics so much..."

I felt the air shift just before his wooden paddle repeatedly ravished my ass and thighs. I managed to remain quiet as the pain reverberated from extreme to mild and back again, accelerating my intense need.

"That was fifteen. I'll let you recover a bit as I prepare you, but first..." He strolled to the side of me, his hard cock in his hand and fed it to me. Leisurely, he stroked in and out of my mouth, my cheek against the desk as I breathed in his delicious, masculine scent. When he moved away, I felt cold metal by the side of my hip. "I'll buy you new ones," he said as he cut my lace panties from my body.

"I liked those," I said over my shoulder.

"So did I." His fingers delved into my pussy, poking and prodding. Then he drew the wetness to my anus. He worked one finger inside me, and I gushed a bit. "Hang on," he said and walked away. "Good thing I came prepared." He placed a large square pad on the floor below me. "Now back to business." His finger stretched me and then he inserted another. The fingers of his other hand caressed my clit, flicking and nudging it, bringing me right to the brink of orgasm.

"Ohhh," I called out.

"Shhh. Do I need to find something for you to bite on?"

I heard him rummage through the top drawer of the

desk and then he said, "Open up."

He was very lucky I didn't bite down because the head of his cock traced my lips with his precum. I sucked on his cock and when he pulled back, he placed a brand new pencil in my mouth for me to bite.

"Be a good girl and keep quiet. These last ten will be the hardest and then I'm going to violate that ass of yours. Are you ready?"

I nodded my head.

He wasn't kidding. The paddle abused my ass and thighs as I grunted and groaned from each strike. My juices dripped down and although he had removed his fingers from my ass, the anticipation of what was to cum had me ready and open for him.

Then his mischievous hands combed my body, inciting a riot over the surface of my skin.

I shook as much as the bindings would allow.

"It's time," he growled. I heard him kick off his shoes and his pants drop. He came up behind me, first dousing his cock into my pussy.

I loved the feel of his warm skin against my back and his breath against my neck. I angled my head toward him, wanting to be closer to his mouth.

"Are you ready?" he whispered into my ear.

I spit out the pencil and said, "Take me."

He pulled out of my wetness and poised his cock at my red bud. The head of his cock stretched me and with a shove, finally popped inside me.

"Oh fuck, wait, wait, wait!"

He stopped moving and gave me time to acclimate.

"Okay," I moaned.

Taking his time, he worked his entire length into me, my gush spilling the whole time, sloshing between us. "I'm all the way in," he groaned quietly. He slowly stroked in and out of me as his skilled fingers dominated my swollen bundle of nerves.

Then my gushing morphed into a full-on squirt fest. "Tate, Tate, Tate, I'm going to ... ahhh!" Between the bondage, my sore, spanked butt, his massive cock lodged in my ass, and his wicked fingers, my orgasm detonated with such extreme intensity that it took all my willpower not to yell out my climax. My release spasmed around his meaty shaft, causing pain and pleasure in equal measure.

"I'm chasing you," he rumbled. He thrust even deeper and fired his warm cum into me spurt after spurt.

"Holy Christ! My heart is trying to bang its way out of my chest."

"Mine too," he sighed out, his body lying over mine.

I believed him. I could feel the pounding of his heart against my back.

"I'm going to pull out." Once he did, he untied the rope that kept my legs fastened to the desk and removed the pad from underneath me.

I slid my feet together and waited for him to untie my arms. Once free, I had trouble standing.

"Here, let me help you."

I leaned against him as he dried me off with a towel. "Your laundry bill must have gone up."

He chuckled and led me to the big, leather office chair.

"Damn that was incredible," I said as he held me in his lap.

"How's your ass?"

"Sore, but it was so worth it."

"Why did you say twenty, then twenty-five? I was shooting for ten." He kissed my forehead, holding me against his chest.

"I wanted to impress you."

"And you did, as you always do. You continue to astound me. You match me kink for kink."

I felt gleeful. "I have to keep you on your toes."

"Better to keep me on my back although this last position was hot. I did miss seeing your eyes, though."

"Yeah, me too," I said, hugging him.

"Should we clean up and head to Red's?"

"Okay. Kiss me again first."

Arriving at Red's, it became clear to me just how far Tate and I had come since last week. Tate still watched me but not with a pinched brow. He seemed to enjoy his time with the guys, and it gave me time to connect with the girls. Jacqs kept her distance, and I assumed she didn't want to talk about her disclosure.

Once everyone settled outside, Bond and I met up in the kitchen.

"How's it going?" I asked, popping a chip into my mouth.

"It's hard to sleep alone every night. It sucks. Jacqs is still in a weird space. How are things with you and Tate?" He opened the fridge and took out a beer.

"Going remarkably well. We seem to be getting closer every day. There's such a mix of feeling free and vulnerable at the same time. I hope that doesn't upset you."

"My turn to feel what I've done to you for years." He took a swig of the beer.

"I don't want you to feel that way."

"I know. We're good. We'll get through it."

Samantha came in through the French doors. "Got a minute?"

"Sure, where do you want to go?" I asked.

"Front room?"

I reached out and gave Bond's arm a squeeze and then

walked with Sam to the front of the house. I sat gingerly on the love seat portion of the sectional. "What's up?" I asked.

"First, tell me about Tate. He looks like a different man. Dare I say happy?"

"He is, and I am too. He's really helped me through the loss of my aunt. I'm sure I still have grieving to do, but it's hard to be depressed when—" I blushed.

"I'm so happy for you."

I touched her arm "Thanks, Sam. So any prospects for you?"

"I'm not really looking for anything, but this guy I knew from high school has been bringing his nephew to the same preschool where I take Sarah."

"That sounds promising. What's he like?" I shifted onto my other ass cheek, still feeling the effects of the paddle.

"That's the problem. He's utterly perfect and I'm—" She shook her head.

"You're what?"

"I've never had a healthy relationship with a man, I mean, other than our friends here."

"Yeah, I know what you mean."

She looked down at her hands and then back at me. "And I have a sordid past. How do you tell a man that you don't know who the father of your baby is?"

"If he's the right man, none of that will matter." I truly believed that.

"He deserves someone better than me."

"You're someone far better than you're giving yourself credit for. You aren't your past. You are your now. Time to let that shit go. Helena said I needed to forgive. I think you need to forgive yourself."

"Yeah, I know. That's what my mother keeps telling me. She says that I've turned a corner, and it makes no sense to keep looking back." She paused and then said, "Is Jacqs okay? I know she and Bond are in flux, but she seems off to me."

"You should check in with her. I'm sure she could use the support."

We both stood and hugged.

"I will," Sam said.

Tate and I stayed at Red's for a few hours and then headed back to my place.

"We never did anything about my car today," I said once we stepped into my place.

"I wanted to talk to you about that." He placed his duffle on the kitchen table.

"Tate, where's my car?" I folded my arms across my chest.

"It's at Rick's shop like I said. He says it needs a lot of other work, and I just thought—"

"You thought what?"

He took a step toward me. "That you could keep my Jeep and I'd get something else."

I dropped my arms. "I've had that car for a long time. It's the first one I bought for myself."

"Blue, can't you let me do this for you?"

"I don't know. I can afford to buy myself a different car if I wanted to."

"Please just think about it. I want to."

Utterly conflicted, I didn't know how I felt. "I'll think about it."

CHAPTER THIRTY

Kiss

by Ed Sheeran

Big warm hands caressed me awake on Thursday morning.

"Mmmm. Morning," I whispered, my eyes fluttering open.

Tate's lips joined his hands, their dancing rousing me.

I kissed his cheek and said, "Be right back." I peed and brushed my teeth and then hurried back to bed.

He swept me back into his arms and resumed his morning constitution of love.

For the very first time since meeting Tate, it felt like smooth sailing instead of choppy waters. The last thing I wanted to do was leave the bed and go to work. "Is there time?"

"Plenty."

He made love to me, me lying on top of him, and I fell deeper for him on every incursion. His beautiful mahogany eyes, no longer sad, held mine.

It was as if he freed the energy of love within me to ooze out of every pour. We came together in a roaring release. The intense vulnerability left me feeling a bit shy and slightly scared.

"What is it?" he asked, holding me as I trembled.

"I'm scared."

"Me too. I'll keep you safe."

I snuggled in deeper, praying that he meant it.

"Listen, baby, I think I'm going to crash at my place tonight. I'll pick you up for our date tomorrow."

I sat up in the bed. "Oh?"

"I have three classes today, papers to grade, and student conferences to go over their progress for the next two days."

"It better not be a meeting like ours."

"Damn, you're cute. Not to worry, some little pixie has captured all of my attention."

"You call these little," I said, shaking my breasts in front of him.

"You've got me there. The rest of you sure is." He laughed.

I shoved him playfully and he set me on top of him, lust and love mingled in his expression. "Your eyes. They do something to me. I love that they're no longer sad."

He kissed me as if he were falling in love and then said, "That's because of you, kiddo."

"Really?"

He kissed my nose. "Really. Unfortunately, I have to get going. I have some student conferences this morning too."

"Let's do it."

I arrived at Lainie's Bella Boutique just before they opened at ten. "Hey, you!" Lainie said as she opened the door to the back of the shop. "This is a surprise."

"Tate and I have our official first date tomorrow night, and I need a new dress."

"What kind?"

"Something summery and nice, maybe a step up from

casual. Sexy, but not too revealing."

"I have a couple of ideas. Do you want to go short or longer."

"Longer."

She walked over to a dress rack and held up three dresses.

I checked them out and pointed. "The sleeveless black dress with the tan and pale orange flowers."

"It does have a V neck, though. Try it on."

I went into the changing closet and came out to see myself in the outside mirror.

"Oh, that's definitely the right one," Sam said, strolling up to us.

"I'm not sure," I said, pulling up on the front. "What do you think of the length?"

"You definitely need a different bra or maybe no bra? The halter straps might give you enough support." Sam walked around me, checking all the angles. "With high heels, the length is perfect. I love that the hem rides up in the middle and hangs longer in the back. The sash really brings your waist in, and the coloring is perfect for your hair."

"It's no wonder she sells so much," I said to Lainie.

"So true," she said and then walked away toward a customer who had just entered the shop.

"Take off the bra," Sam said.

I stepped back into the dressing room and pulled my bra off. Back in the shop, I checked my reflection. "Do you think I'm sagging too much?"

"Not at all. It looks quite natural."

"I think I might have the perfect shoes for it. I'll take it."

"Go change," Sam said. "I'll ring you up."

After working a busy lunch and dinner shift at The Chart House, I texted Tate as soon as I got home.

> **Me:** Home and about to jump into the shower.
>
> **Tate:** Me too. I'm on my deck, trying to summon the energy. Those students were draining.
>
> **Me:** How many hit on you?
>
> **Tate:** Five.
>
> **Me:** Only five?
>
> **Tate:** Three dudes and two gals.
>
> **Me:** LMAO!
>
> **Tate:** Seriously? It was hard to focus on their papers as visions of you across my desk kept flashing through my mind. That and your red ass. Good thing I had the desk for cover.
>
> **Me:** My ass is still a bit sore. I didn't mind the reminder at work, though. It made the long day bearable.
>
> **Tate:** Why don't you give notice?
>
> **Me:** Because I have bills to pay.
>
> **Tate:** I can give you the money.
>
> **Me:** Now you want to give me money too?
>
> **Tate:** Take it for what it is.
>
> **Me:** What is it?
>
> **Tate:** Completely selfish on both counts.
>
> **Me:** Meaning the money and the car?
>
> **Tate:** Yes.
>
> **Me:** How?
>
> **Tate:** I want more time with you, and cutting out the waitressing job means we'll have it. The car is a safety issue, and because I want to spoil you.
>
> **Me:** It makes me feel like I'm my mom.
>
> **Tate:** If I thought you were using me for my

money, I never would've offered.

Me: What happens to my car?

Tate: My guy sells it.

Me: We can talk about this tomorrow night. Do you have another full day of student conferences?

Tate: Unfortunately.

Me: See you tomorrow night at 7. I'm going to shower and crash.

Tate: Me too. Sweet dreams, Blue. I'll miss having you beside me.

Me: Yeah, me too.

CHAPTER THIRTY-ONE

Human

by Christina Perri

I worked the lunch shift and then impatiently waited for my date with Tate. I reworked three more chapters in *Soul Adjacent*, did my large pile of laundry, and cleaned my apartment, all in an effort to manage my excitement. I thought of texting Tate several times during the day, but I didn't want to bother him.

Freshly showered, I applied bronze eye shadow, brown eyeliner, and smoky-red lipstick. I put my hair up in a bun with my bangs and wispy tendrils down. I slipped into my new dress, tied the sash, and slid on my taupe, closed-toe heels with a crisscross strap at the ankle.

I held my clutch and waited on the couch, my heart dancing around my chest, trying to find a rhythm. Our date symbolized Tate's willingness to move forward and mine too. I decided to take him up on his offers. Although I would have never chosen a red Jeep for myself, I had really grown to love it.

Tate, with a gorgeous bouquet of Calla Lilies, knocked on the door. He looked especially handsome in his brown slacks and textured, brown, button-down shirt with parallel black stripes, his chiseled chest peeking out from the top of the two undone buttons.

"You look incredible," he said, scanning me from head to toe. "Is that new?"

"Yes, I got it for tonight." I beamed up at him.

"I'm one lucky man." He kissed me passionately and then said, "Let's put these in water and go."

Holding my hand the whole way, he drove us to Market 17 in the Jeep.

"Wow, this is fancy," I said as we strolled into the restaurant arm in arm. "Did you see that they do dining in the dark?"

The hostess sat us at a two-top, ivory-clothed table, fully appointed with plenty of light. She handed each of us a menu. "Your server will be with you shortly."

"Thank you," I said and smiled. I glanced over the menu, salivating. "Everything looks great."

"I've never done the eating in the dark. The menu changes here every day," he said, reaching for my hand.

"Really? Do you eat here a lot?"

"No, not a lot and not recently. Would you like an appetizer?"

"I'd rather have dessert after the entree. The crispy duck leg confit sounds delicious. What are you going to order?"

"The grilled antelope filet. I've never had antelope before."

"I'd assume it tastes like venison, not that I've tried that, either."

The busboy filled our water glasses and quickly moved away.

"This is lovely," I said. "Thank you for taking me here."

"It's my pleasure." His thumb brushed over the back of my hand.

"I've been thinking about your car offer. What kind of car will you get?"

"The Mazda MX-5."

"That's a two-seater, right?"

"Yeah. I figured we could use the Jeep when we need

more room."

We? Could we actually be a we?

"What did I say?" he asked.

The server approached and Tate ordered for us both, including a bottle of wine.

"I have this weekend off," I said, changing the subject. "I forgot to mention it."

"Let's take a drive along the coast on the Harley. We can decide where to stop along the way."

"I'd love that. Can we stop by my mother's on our way out?"

"Absolutely."

Woohoo! I had never taken a vacation with a man, and I was extremely delirious about it. I tried to contain my smile.

"You can let it out, you know."

I laughed and said, "Yahoo!"

He laughed with me.

My meal was scrumptious. I tried Tate's dish but didn't care for it. He ate all of his and the rest of mine once I finished.

As the busboy cleared the table, Tate asked, "What would you like for dessert?"

"Are you sure you still have room in there? Want to split the Maple Blondie?"

"An endless pit," he said, pointing to his stomach. "The bourbon ice cream with it sounds interesting." Tate flagged the server and ordered our dessert, plus a coffee for him.

While we waited for the dessert, a very elegant woman in a black, lace-inset sheath dress sauntered over to our table. "Who's this?" she said to Tate, looking down her nose at me.

I felt completely underdressed.

The steel door closed down over Tate's features.

Before he even spoke, my stomach dropped. "No one," he said. "What do you want?"

"Clearly, she's someone to somebody."

"Not to me, she's nobody. What do you want?"

I shriveled inside myself, wishing I could fade into the wall next to me.

No one!

Nobody?

Anyone who sings that stupid nursery rhyme about sticks and stones has never lived in my shoes. Words maimed and killed.

"Are you coming to the reunion next month?" She cocked her hip seductively. "Everyone'll be in town."

"Not fucking likely." His eyes bored into her, his ears glowing red.

She checked me out again and said, "I heard you had sworn off women. Years they said, or have you reverted to picking up strays again?"

My ire raged and I forced out, "You're not going to introduce me?"

"Just stay out of this." He glared at me. To the woman he said, "Jessica, buzz off."

"You should bring your feisty, voluptuous nobody. It would sure set tongues a waggin' and make Christina stand up straighter."

"If you don't mind..."

She put her hand on her hip. "Oh, but I do. Do come. It'll be so much fun. We all miss having your fine self around. Cal can be such a stick in the mud."

"The only way I'll be at the reunion is as a ghost haunting you all."

"Does she know about Christina and Cal?"

"Shut up, Jessica. I told you she's no one."

"Huh." She paused. "Well, she's definitely not your type," she said, staring straight down my cleavage. "Do you love her? Miss Nobody?"

"You all made damn sure I'd never love anyone ever again." Tate made to stand, but the woman finally took the hint.

"I'll go. Just think about it." She caught my eye and said, "You're *nothing* like Christina." She successfully harpooned me on her departure.

"I'm sorry," Tate said, touching my arm.

"You're always sorry. It no longer has any meaning. No one? I'm no one to you? Fuck you and all your lies and bullshit."

"Blue, I hate the woman and was trying to avoid exposing you to her—"

"To her what? What you exposed me to is how you really feel about me. You're embarrassed by me. *No one?* Those words will echo in my head and heart forever. Please take me home. I want to go home."

He knelt next to me and took my tear stained face in his hands. "I didn't mean it. You have to know that. You're ... you're my..."

"What? What am I to you?"

"I can't."

I turned away and I thumbed on my phone.

> **Me:** Can you come to get me right away? If not, maybe Slay? Red? Please!
> **Bond:** Are you at the restaurant?
> **Me:** Yes. Market 17 on A1A in Fort Lauderdale.
> **Bond:** I know it. I'll be there ASAP. I'm not far. Are you okay?
> **Me:** No, not in the least.

Bond: Hang in there, Blue.

"Bond's coming to get me," I said, not making eye contact.

"I'll wait with you." He pulled out my chair as I stood.

I lifted my clutch, my tears embarrassing me. I prayed I wouldn't cross paths with the wretched woman.

Outside while we waited, he pleaded with me. "Blue, please. She took me by surprise. What I said was stupid, and I didn't mean it the way it came out. She's a vulture and..."

"And?"

"Nothing. You know you matter to me."

I glanced up through my tears. "But not enough. You hurt me deeper than you can possibly understand. I don't want to do this anymore. I have to love me more than I love you. I truly hope someday you can heal and be honest with yourself, but I'm done waiting."

Before he could respond, Bond pulled up, got out of his car, and punched Tate in the mouth. "I told you not to hurt her," he shouted and then opened the passenger side door for me.

I gasped and climbed into the car, watching Tate cup his face. His eyes connected with mine one last time, and I willed myself to look away from his devastated expression.

"Where to?"

"I don't care." I leaned against the passenger door and silently wept.

Bond rubbed my back. "Do you want to talk about it?"

I shook my head and continued to cry.

"I thought this might happen," Bond mumbled.

"Not helping."

"Sorry."

"Yeah, yeah."

CHAPTER THIRTY-TWO

Hanging On

by Active Child

I opened my eyes as soon as Bond's car came to a stop. "Why are we here?"

"I thought you might want to be around people. You said anywhere."

"Right. Do you have a tissue or a napkin in here?"

"No, just use my shirt." He untucked his T-shirt and leaned over to me.

"I'll end up getting my makeup all over it."

"Like I give a shit. I'll borrow a shirt from Red."

I looked at Bond and said, "Thank you." I dried my face the best I could on his shirt and then took a couple of shuddered, deep breaths. "After we say hi, can we go up to your room and snuggle."

"It's not really my room anymore, but I'm sure it's fine."

"Okay."

Bond opened the passenger door for me and helped me out. "They're expecting us." He held my hand as we walked through Red's house.

"I'm so sorry," Jacqs said when we approached the living room. She hugged me tightly. Then she held me away from her. "One of Lainie's?"

"Yeah."

"Come with me." Jacqs took my hand and led me upstairs to the bedroom she shared with Red. She rummaged in a drawer and passed me PJ bottoms and a T-shirt.

"Thanks."

"It's a shame that tonight wasn't fabulous because that dress is stellar."

I pulled off the dress and held it out. "Want it? It's yours. I never want to see it again." I tossed it to her.

"Seriously?"

I slipped into the PJs and T-shirt. "Seriously. Just don't wear it on a Wednesday."

"Right, of course. So what happened?"

"Come down here so she only has to say it once," Red called from downstairs.

"Are you up for it?"

I shrugged. "Is it going to be okay if I snuggle with Bond? I know things are odd with you guys and wait— Did you take the test?"

"Yes, I did, and I'm not. Instead of being overjoyed, I was actually sad."

"Sorry, Jacqs. I can imagine. And you and Bond?"

"He's still on hiatus."

As sad as I felt, I still almost chuckled. "When the most sexual person you know is celibate, it's kind of scary."

"Yeah, I know what you mean." She laughed.

"Can I use your bathroom?"

"Sure, I'll go wait with the boys."

"Hey, is it going to bug you if I—"

"Snuggle away."

"Thanks."

After scrubbing the makeup off my face and using the bathroom, I shuffled down the stairs and joined them on the large couch in front of the wide screen TV. Jacqs was sitting next to Red and Bond on the opposite end. I folded in against Bond, and he wrapped me up in his arms.

"So what happened?" Red asked. "Tate seemed excited

about the date. He told me all about Market 17."

"Yeah, the place was great."

"So?" Bond asked.

"This woman, her name was Jessica, approached our table while we were waiting for dessert."

"Past lover?" Jacqs asked. "His ex?"

"No, but she is apparently a part of his old group of friends and is clearly friends with his ex. It's what he said to her about me."

"Which was?" Jacqs asked, leaning into Red and turning to face me with her feet up on the couch.

"That I was no one and nobody and I essentially didn't matter."

"He said that?" Bond asked almost as a yell, sitting up and looking around to see my face.

"His exact words when asked who I was: 'No one.' Then she said something like she must be someone to somebody and he said: 'Not to me, she's nobody.'"

"I'm going to fucking punch him again!" Bond shouted, jumping up from the couch.

Red held out his hand and said, "Wait a minute."

"You punched him?" Jacqs asked. She seemed upset, and I had a feeling it wasn't over concern for Tate.

"After that bullshit, he deserves a hell of a lot more!"

"Sit down, Bond," Red ordered. "Do you think he meant what he said? I mean, that doesn't sound at all like Tate."

"I asked him if he planned to introduce me and he said 'no,' right in front of the woman, and glared at me."

Bond came in behind me again. "That sucks, Blue."

"Did you get the feeling that Tate liked the woman?" Red asked as he held Jacqs to his chest.

"Well, no. Loathed would be a better term. You know the term, bitch on wheels? Think bitch in very nice, expensive heels."

"Then I think you're overreacting," Red concluded.

"What!" Bond, Jacqs, and I exclaimed in unison.

"My guess is that he hasn't had to confront the situation of his ex at all. Probably has avoided all those people, who from my guess are somehow involved. Right, Blue?"

"Yes. Jessica did give me a connection in all of her rambling bullshit that I hadn't made myself."

"Red, you know I love you, but you are out of your fucking mind. Would you ever have said that about me under any circumstances?" Jacqs asked, pivoting around to face him.

"No, of course not. But, I haven't had to live through what Tate has. If I had to guess, his wife cheated on him with someone from their group of friends, for years if I was a betting man, and everyone knew it except him."

"That's truly horrible, if you're correct, but that gives him no right to treat Blue that way," Jacqs insisted. "Not ever."

"Thank you, Jacqs," I said, touching her arm. "He also said he would never love me."

"That one is definitely bullshit, Blue," Red interjected. "He already does. I'm very well aware of the affliction since I had it for years. He might not be willing to admit it or truly allow it, but it's there. No doubt."

"I have to agree with Red on that one," Jacqs said.

"I don't," Bond said. "The dude doesn't realize what he has if he could ever treat you the way he did tonight."

"Bond, you're clearly biased with your own agenda," Jacqs said.

Red patted Jacqs' back. "Blue, I think you should hear him out. Did he apologize afterward?"

"Yeah, but so what? If he can't ever love me, if he won't even introduce me, I can't do it. I'm so sick and tired of not mattering to people, I can't do it anymore. I'd rather be alone."

"You don't have to be alone," Bond whispered into my ear.

"Really, Bond? You're *not* helping," Jacqs stressed.

"The last thing I want to do is bring conflict here. Can someone please take me home?"

"I'll drive you—" Red started.

"That makes no sense," Bond interrupted. "Blue is on the way back to my place and I have to be at work soon, anyway."

"I think you and Jacqs need to talk," Red said.

"Can you give the Papa Bear crap a rest? Jacqs knows where we currently stand."

"Blue, can I talk to you alone for a minute?" Red asked.

Neither Jacqs nor Bond appeared too pleased.

I shrugged. "Sure."

When we stepped into the wood-paneled game room, Red said, "You deserve the world in my opinion, Blue. Give yourself time to sort through this before you fall back in bed with Bond."

"Why do you care if Bond and I fuck?"

"Because you're hurting." He touched my shoulder, peering down at me. "You'll regret it, and you could end up hurting Bond in the process."

"Jesus fucking Christ! When did life get so damn complicated?"

"It doesn't have to be. Let me drive you home."

I thought about it for a few moments and then said, "Fine. Let's go."

"Call me or text anytime," Bond said when he hugged me goodbye.

"I will and thanks for coming to get me."

Jacqs waved as Red and I headed to the front of the house.

We rode in silence until he pulled into my apartment complex. I saw Tate waiting on the steps for me.

"Fuck!" I took my clutch off my lap and fished out my keys.

"Do you want me to talk to him for you?"

"Thank you for the offer, but I'll handle it." I reached over the console and hugged Red. "Thanks for looking out for me."

"Always."

I hopped down from Red's SUV and took a deep breath. It did nothing whatsoever to settle me down. "What do you want?" I asked as I stepped past Tate and up the stairs.

"I wanted to make sure you made it home okay, and that you had the keys for the Jeep."

I looked down the flight of steps at the man I thought I once loved. "I don't want it. Have someone pick it up for you. Please tell your mechanic friend to call me, and I'll arrange to get my car."

"Blue, please. Tonight was a total fuckup on my part. I wasn't prepared to deal with Jessica or any of it. But that shouldn't erase—"

"Do you love me, Tate?"

He shook his head before speaking. "No, you know I can't." He intently stared at me, but I couldn't feel its effects. Apparently, my own steel shield had erected itself.

"Are you ready to tell me what the fuck happened to you?" I struggled to hold back the deluge of tears.

"I can't."

"Then leave me alone. Just leave me the fuck alone."

"Please give me the chance to make this up to you. You know how much I care about you."

"Actually, I don't. I know you enjoy fucking me, but

I'm nobody to you. You made that abundantly clear tonight. Thanks for making me feel like one of your one-night stands, *again*."

I ran up the second flight of steps and unlocked my door, closing it quickly behind me. My phone vibrated and I turned it off without looking to see who had texted me. I grabbed the gorgeous Calla Lilies and smashed them into the trash.

The next three days off from work stretched in front of me like a vast wasteland of self-torture.

CHAPTER THIRTY-THREE

Eyes On Fire

by Blue Foundation

I crumbled onto the couch in a torrent of tears, mentally beating myself up. *You know better. You* should *know better. Ann tried to warn you. What the fuck is your problem? Why can't you choose someone who can love you? Why am I not lovable?*

I opened my computer and started to write my thoughts, my eyes still blurry and burning with the tears of my pathetic rejection.

This shit keeps happening because of my relationship with my father. That's no real surprise. But listening to Tate dismiss me as nobody, carved such a deep crevice in my heart that the truth came flooding in. Every child needs to be loved. It's basic survival because if your parents love you, they'll protect you. My parents didn't love or like me, and I had to protect myself. Only I never really learned how. I thought my brother did it for me for a while and then he didn't. Not that it should've been his job!

Tate got to know the real me, which I could never share with my father, and I still wasn't good enough. He didn't protect me.

It's time for me to grow some lady balls and start protecting myself.

I ran to the bathroom, swiped the Post-It note off the

center of the mirror, and tore it into pieces. I then picked off the rest of the stickies that Tate created and tore those up as well.

I better learn to lick pussy, since I'm giving up men forever.

Back on the couch with the computer on my lap, I went on Facebook to distract myself and found a friend request from Matt. As soon as I accepted, he sent me a message.

Matthew Radford
Thanks for adding me.
Judy Radford
Hey, I have a question for you.
Matthew Radford
Okay.
Judy Radford
Did you know Mom broke Dad's heart?
Matthew Radford
Yes, they fought about it all the time.
Judy Radford
She had an affair?
Matthew Radford
She said they were emotional affairs, never physical, but Dad never believed her.
Judy Radford
Did you think Mom and Dad loved us?
Matthew Radford
I think they were too caught up in their drama to think much about us.
Judy Radford
Why didn't your marriage work?
Matthew Radford
Wow. Okay, we're going deep.

Judy Radford

My "not boyfriend" has essentially crushed me, and I'm wondering if we are wounded the same. I know it's stupid, but it just might help me.

Matthew Radford

She never put me first. I was like an afterthought after her family and friends. I knew once we had kids, I'd be in fourth place. Is that what the non-boyfriend did?

Judy Radford

No, not exactly. His past came between us. One he's unwilling to share with me and yet, it was stuck between us the whole time. Somehow, I was supposed to pretend it didn't matter. Then he tore my heart out and cut it into tiny little pieces, leaving me feeling like Dad always did. Like I don't matter. Like I'm not good enough.

Matthew Radford

We're more alike than you think. Was this Tate or Bond? I couldn't figure out whom you were with at Mom's.

Judy Radford

Tate. But Bond, too, in the past, although it's been different recently.

Matthew Radford

Sounds familiar.

Judy Radford

What have you done about it?

Matthew Radford

I got divorced. I haven't been serious with anyone else since.

Judy Radford

Great! (sarcasm) We're both sad cases.

Matthew Radford

Tate seemed like a great guy. More mature than Bond. He watched you the whole time at Mom's. Is there no hope? One of us should be happy.

Judy Radford

He won't ever love me. He made that crystal clear.

Matthew Radford

Well, Sis, I'm sorry. That's got to suck to hear.

Judy Radford

Yeah well, I only have myself to blame. He warned me from the start. Do you think there's any value in talking to Dad?

Matthew Radford

DON'T DO IT! Seriously, you'll get nothing you need from him. Trust me, he's worse than you remember him.

Judy Radford

Wow, okay. Thanks for chatting with me. I'm going to sign off and cry some more. Not really. My eyes are so red and swollen already, I don't think my tear ducts work anymore. I'm sorry you're struggling the same way as me.

Matthew Radford

Yeah, you too. Thanks for giving me another chance. I've missed you more than you know.

Judy Radford

Yeah, me too. Talk soon.

I shut down my computer and looked around my apartment. Sitting there in the quiet, I suddenly felt an all-consuming loneliness skulking about the edges of my psyche. I forced myself up, brushed my teeth, and climbed into bed before I did something stupid, like text Tate or Bond.

If I slept, it must have been in dreamful fits and starts, and after all that struggle, it didn't keep the sun from rising on Saturday morning.

CHAPTER THIRTY-FOUR

Reasons

by Earth, Wind, & Fire

The pounding on my door roused me from my stupor. "What the fuck!" I scurried out of bed and ran to the door. Yanking it open, I shouted, "What!"

"You're not answering your phone," Bond grunted as he stormed in past me, looking around.

"Oh, sorry. I turned it off last night."

"You scared the shit out of me, Blue." He hugged me to him too tightly.

I squirmed to get out of his embrace, and he let me go. "I'm fine. I'm not going to off myself or something. You know me better than that."

He held his hands up. "Okay. None of us could get through, and we were all worried."

"I'm truly sorry." I picked up my phone from the couch and turned it back on.

"Tate called Red."

"Why?" I asked, seeing all the missed calls and texts.

"I didn't ask. Can I take you to lunch?"

I thought about it for a second. "I'm not much in the mood for company, and I doubt I could eat anything anyway."

"Oh ... okay."

"Please don't take it personally. Kind of like you, I need to sort out my life and do things differently."

"Yeah, yeah, I get it." He shoved his hands in his pockets and looked down.

"Thanks for understanding."

He peered up and said, "Give me a hug and I'll take off."

When we embraced, I let myself sink in against him. We held on, rocking together. Once he stepped back, he said, "The Jeep has stuff all over its windows."

"Are you sure it's Tate's?"

"Yeah, the yellow stickies."

"What do you mean?"

"Come down and see. There must be like five hundred of those suckers on there."

I quickly changed into shorts and a T-shirt, and we hopped down the two flights of stairs. I couldn't believe my eyes. Tate's Jeep windows were covered with Post-It notes, all yellow ones. It must have taken him all night.

"There's writing on them," Bond said.

"Yeah, I see that." I stepped closer and lifted the first one off the passenger side window. It read: Reason #132 – I love the way you look at me. I pulled the next one off the side mirror and read: Reason #145 – I love knowing how your body feels next to mine. Then I peeled one off the windshield. Reason #50 – I love the way you make me feel when I'm with you. "Hey Bond, do you see a number one?"

"I'll look."

Bond and I combed the car until he shouted, "I found it."

"What does it say?"

"Come read it yourself."

"I don't know if I can."

"Be brave, Blue."

I walked around to the driver's side door and saw it hanging in the center of the window. Reason #1 – I love you. "Holy fuck." My jaw dropped.

Bond glanced down at his phone and seemed to be texting. I swiped my phone and clicked on my voicemail from Tate.

"I didn't want to do this over the phone, but I couldn't be sure you'd ever hear me out. I've been the most colossal idiot. I think I started falling in love with you the moment I saw you in the tattoo shop … and then deeper every second I've spent with you. It's not that you're nobody to me, Blue, you're everything to me and I didn't want Jessica to tromp through our relationship. I'm ready to talk and tell you everything. Call me." Beep.

"Holy hell, Bond."

"Give him a chance."

"You of all people?"

"I want your happiness more than anything else I can think of. I love you, Blue."

I wiped the tears away from my face and hugged Bond as hard as I could. "I love you, too. Forever and always. Wow, can you believe this? I better call him."

"He's on his way."

"How do you know that?"

He held up his phone. "I can text too, ya know."

"Oh... Thank you."

Bond strolled away, and my heart broke for him. I wanted him to be happy too. Then I turned back around and yanked down five stickies off the back window of the Jeep.

Reason #238 – I love the way you love me.

Reason #234 – I love how adorable you are.

Reason #233 – I love how you feel in my arms.

Reason #240 – I love how your hand fits in mine.

Reason #237 – I love your eyes.

As I continued to wait, I strolled to the driver's side door again and peeled off five more.

Reason #3 – I love how you make me smile.

Reason #7 – I love that you trust me with your body.

Reason #5 – I love your touch.

Reason #2 – I love that since the day you came into my life, everything has been better.

Reason #10 – I love how you make me laugh.

I heard Tate's motorcycle before I saw him. My ridiculous heart pounded erratically in anticipation. I couldn't allow myself to believe any of it until I saw his face. His face would tell me everything.

He parked his bike behind the Jeep and pulled off his helmet. "I love you, Blue. Please forgive me." All the stress and tension had completely left his face. He appeared younger, lighter, and far less stern.

"I love you, too." My arms formed a shield around my body that my heart certainly didn't feel. "It's so good to finally hear you say it. I'll forgive you on one condition."

"You name it."

"No more secrets."

"That's a deal."

I stepped into his outstretched arms and when he kissed me, he swept me up in a firestorm of passion and love that I prayed would consume me. I freely gave myself over to him. His kiss was gentle at first, showing me all the love he had held back, whispering to my soul all the regret for his previous actions. Then he escorted me on the journey of lust and all the hedonism he wanted to explore with me. His mouth finally left mine when a drop of rain touched our faces.

"Nooo," I cried. "Quickly!"

"Ahh, man," Tate called out as he hurriedly snatched the yellow squares from the Jeep.

We peeled off all the Post-It notes as fast as we could, stacking one on top of the other.

Once he had finished the driver's side of the car, he

said, "I'll get the windshield."

I busily worked my way across the windows of the passenger side. "Rain, hold off for another five minutes. Shit. I want them all!"

"I'm almost done here."

"Come help me with the back of the Jeep."

It had started to drizzle by the time we collected them all. I shoved mine into my shirt, and we both ran upstairs out of the rain.

I sank into the kitchen chair. "Did you sleep at all last night?" I asked, fishing the stickies out of my top.

"No, you?"

"Very little if at all." I laid them all on the table in front of me.

"Do you want to nap?" Tate asked.

"No."

"What are you thinking?" he said, standing behind me and playing with my hair.

I looked over my shoulder. "That we need to get a place with lots of mirrors for all my stickies."

Tate burst out laughing. "Damn, you're cute. Come." He scooped me into his lap. "Do you want to stay here tonight or my place?"

"Yours."

"Do you have a suitcase?"

I snuggled my face into his neck and breathed in his yummy scent. "Are we still going away?" I asked against his throat.

"Not until we get some sleep. I thought you could move some of your stuff over. All your belongings?" He laughed. "I personally don't think I'll survive another night without you."

I hugged him tightly and said, "I feel the same way but

first, you've got to tell me another hundred times that you love me, so it sinks in. Of course, I could just read all your Post-Its, which I intend to do anyway. I'd like to go back to your place, but that would mean leaving the Harley here since it's raining."

"Why don't you pack a bag for the week, and we can sort out the rest?" he asked, lifting me off his lap to stand beside him.

"Before any of that, I have to know. When will you tell me about Christina?"

"Now, or at my place, it's your choice."

"Really? Any chance you'll change your mind if I wait until we get to your place?"

He took my hand and kissed my palm. "No way." He dropped his head. "Look, when Bond drove away from the restaurant, I felt like I was dying. It was worse than when I found about Christina's affair, because I knew I had lost you, and I didn't know if I would have another chance to get you back."

I gently touched his cheek. "It doesn't look like Bond did you any damage."

"He's a lefty," he said, moving my hand to the other side of his face and enfolding his arm around my waist.

"Does it hurt?"

He smiled up at me. "I deserved it. Did you ask Bond to text me?"

I moved his hair away from his face and traced his eyebrows. "No, he did that on his own."

"He's good people."

"The best." I kissed his bruised cheek and then pulled him along with me to the bedroom. "Can you grab the larger bag from the top of the closet?"

"Sure."

I tossed a bunch of clothes on the bed, and Tate put them in the suitcase. Then I mushed my pillow in with the clothes and zipped it up. I gathered my cosmetic and overnight bags and found my wallet.

"Phone charger," Tate said.

"Right." I grabbed it from the bedroom and then packed up my laptop, and took one last look around. I put all the Post-It notes in my backpack and turned out the lights as we headed for the door.

"The rain has stopped," Tate said, helping me carry my stuff to the Jeep. "Why don't you follow me over?"

"Okay."

I turned into Tate's driveway and he had me pull into the garage and park next to his Harley.

"The skies are looking gloomy again," I said when I hopped out of the car.

"Food?" he asked, shouldering my bags.

"Please. I'm starving. Do you have maple syrup, eggs, and bread?" I shut the door behind us.

"Are you going to cook for me?" he asked, placing my bags by the couch.

"I can cook. I just don't do it often. I'll need cinnamon, too," I said as we walked into the kitchen.

"I'll man the coffee and bacon. Shouldn't you be making me work harder to get you back?"

I turned to face him and placed my hands on my hips. "Did you mean it when you said you love me and want us to live together?"

"I want us to make a life together."

"The only thing standing in the way is the truth. Let's cook and you can tell me all about it. I have no need to make you suffer. I love you, Tate, fully and completely."

He stared at me with his dark eyes, without any guile.

"You're the best thing that's ever happened to me. For the first time, ever, I'm pretty happy that Christina did what she did. I would've never known my perfect other half was out there if she hadn't screwed up."

I threw myself at him and he laughed, hugging me back.

"Food first." He stepped back, wagging his finger in my direction, and opened the refrigerator.

The afternoon light was fading away but not the new light of our relationship. We sat at the table on the deck and watched the winds leaving the coast for the open ocean.

I nibbled a piece of bacon and asked, "Did Christina know you were into kinky shit?"

"She said that's what you do with your whore … not your wife."

"Ouch."

"Yeah. Do you want to stay out here and talk or—"

I stood and stepped over to him. "I'd like to be closer to you when you tell me."

"Let's get in bed."

We carried our plates inside and left them on the dining table.

I took off my clothes and Tate did the same. We climbed under the covers and faced each other.

Tate started slowly. "I met Christina when I was a freshman in high school. Cal had a thing for her, too, but she chose me. We officially started dating our sophomore year. After graduation, we went to separate colleges and we agreed to date other people."

"You were each other's first, right?"

"Yes, well, that's what I thought, but I'm not sure anymore."

I placed my hand on his chest and said, "Sorry, go on."

"After college, we decided to marry. We didn't share

with each other much about the time we were apart."

"Did Cal go to the same college as Christina?"

"No, but he apparently visited her quite often."

"So when you married, you had no idea they had a past?"

His hand covered mine. "No idea, and he was my best man. Only, I think now that their relationship never ended."

I shook my head. "I don't get it. Why didn't she marry him?"

"I don't know. She's married to him now."

"Holy fuck. How did you find out they were cheating?"

"I forgot a bid at the office and drove back to pick it up. When I walked in to Cal's office on my way out, there she was, tied naked to his desk chair."

"Tied! Holy tyrannical bullshit! What a cunt!" I lay back staring at the ceiling, wondering how he must have felt.

"It's a good thing I can laugh about it now."

I turned to face him again. "What the hell did you do?"

"I was dumbfounded. My heart sank and I just stood there. Christina couldn't move and Cal started babbling. 'It's not ... not ... what it looks like, Tate.' I said, 'It seems like you're fucking my wife. Buy me out and I never want to hear from either of you again. Chris, I'll have your shit shipped to his house.'" I walked out and never spoke to either of them again. Cal and I severed our business ties via attorneys, and I saw Christina once more to sign our divorce papers. According to Jessica, whose mouth never stops wagging, they had been lovers since high school."

"Is that true?" I couldn't fathom that kind of deceit, but it sure explained a lot about Tate's trust issues.

"I have no idea. Kind of makes sense when I think back on different moments in the past. I was far too trusting. The worst part of it all, my gut told me something wasn't right for a long time, but she always denied it.

Called me paranoid and said shit about my heritage."

"How do you mean?"

"'You freakin' Indians think you know stuff beyond the obvious. You're just an untrusting and jealous lot.' She had me convinced I was, but that's not even the worst part."

"There's more?"

He forced out a breath and continued, "Besides all of our friends knowing what was going on behind my back and never telling me, she turned out to be pregnant. She never wanted to have kids with me."

"Wait. How do you know it wasn't yours?"

"We hadn't had sex in over a year. That was a huge part of why I was convinced she was cheating on me. She always had such a high sex drive."

I felt so sad for him. No one should have to go through such pain. "Did she have the baby?"

"Yes."

"I can't think of a 'holy' that would encapsulate all of that. Why was she so mean to you?"

"All I can figure is that she regretted her decision to marry me."

"Were you a bad husband?" I couldn't imagine it.

"No, but Cal and I were very busy the first few years, trying to expand the business and pay his father back."

"Do you think she felt neglected?"

He shrugged. "Maybe."

"Was she always a spoiled bitch?"

He appeared to be thinking over my question. "Yes."

"Jessica said I look nothing like her."

"You don't. Christina is tall, with an athletic build, blonde hair, brown eyes, and very formal. She and Cal come from money."

"Why me?" I asked.

369

"You're my favorite person in the world, Blue. You're perfect for me. If you want to know all the fine details, read all the Post-It notes."

"Right now, I just want you inside of me."

"There's no place I'd rather be." Tate's lips touched mine, and his fierce kiss opened me up in a new, profound way. His taste turned me to liquid but also set me soaring free. He gave me all of him in that kiss, where we forged an odyssey of love and forgiveness. Our mouths crushed together in fiery passion and then swayed in a slow, silent dance. Back and forth, he escorted me into the depths of his heart.

I wanted to give him something significant in return for his trust and love.

But first, he had his own ideas. "I need to taste you again."

I flopped over on my back and stretched my arms wide. "I'm yours."

"I'm going to hold you to that," he said, embracing me with his gaze. Then he shifted his body. His rigid cock taunted me mere inches from my mouth as his tongue lapped up my pussy juices.

I breathed in his smell, knowing that the man above me belonged to me. Then I ran my tongue over the head of his shaft and savored his flavor. "Mmmm," I moaned.

He shifted his ass down to the other end of the bed.

"Hey," I whined.

"Shhh, just let me." He lay between my legs as his fingers tugged on my nipples. His firm squeeze, coupled with his tongue circling my clit, sent tremors through my body. "You taste so good." He rested his head on my thigh, explored my folds with his fingers, and then he plunged inside my wetness, rubbing the ridge just inside my entrance. "There you go. You're already gushing for me."

His mouth lowered to my clit again and followed the rhythm of his hand.

My body unwittingly rocked against his manipulations, desperate for release.

Then he used my wet arousal, left my G-spot, and engulfed two fingers into my ass.

"Oh, holy hell, yesss!"

"Cum for me, baby. Get me all wet." The rough attention of his tongue against my clit, coupled with his thick fingers invading my ass, had me writhing and squirting all over his face.

"Oh, Tate! I'm cumming!"

The convulsing subsided as I melted into the bed, bliss and love surrounding me. I opened one eye and saw him staring down at me. "I'm ready."

Somehow, he knew what I meant. "Are you sure?"

"I've never been more sure of anything in my life. Please don't make me wait."

His body covered me, his eyes never leaving mine. I shifted my legs up and his formidable cock slid inside.

I panicked briefly but reminded myself that I was doing the choosing. It was my choice. "Please," I cried, grasping his ass and pulling him deeper into me.

He wrapped his arms under my shoulders and ground his full, hard cock into my pussy. His lips hovered over mine as we stared into each other's eyes.

I had never felt so vulnerable in my life.

"Thank you," he whispered against my mouth.

I swallowed the warm heat of his breath.

He took his time, savoring our connection, his exhale my inhale. His eyes showed the very same fragility I felt. "Ohhh, Blue. I want to live here forever."

Me too.

I love you.

Please hold my heart safe.

He nodded as if he heard me and kissed my lips softly, waltzing his tongue against mine in synch with his hips. "I'm right there ... lingering at the edge ... and I ... oh god ... I don't want to cum yet."

"Stay with me," I said as our bodies and hearts converged.

His all-consuming gaze intensified while his hands held my head and his mouth rocked my soul with his call of release. His eyes filled with tears along with mine as the bellow of his climax shook me to the core.

He held me as we both lingered in bliss. He shifted his weight to the side of me, both of us breathing heavily. Shaking his head, he cupped my face. "I've never."

I wiped a tear from his cheek and just nodded. I couldn't attach words to the immense emotions that hovered on the surface.

We lay quietly in each other's arms, lost in our own thoughts.

"Blue?"

I turned my head toward him. "Yeah?"

"I've never loved like this before. Thank you for hanging in there with me."

"I'm ecstatic you feel that way because I do too."

"Was it okay for you?"

"I felt panicked for a second, but it passed. I can't believe I've missed out on that position for so long. It was so intimate."

He hugged me to him. "It was for me too."

After we both recovered, Tate made room in his dresser for my clothes and I unpacked.

"If we're going to stay here, can we personalize this

place?" I asked.

"If we decide to stay here, we're going to buy the place and expand the bathroom."

I laughed in joy. "Big tub and shower? Of course, a hot tub on the deck wouldn't be bad, either."

"Brilliant idea. Should we sleep and then take that drive down the coast?"

"The sky has cleared, so let's."

He scooped me against his chest.

I sighed in contentment. Reason #1 would always be my favorite.

He loves me!
He loves me!
He loves me!

CHAPTER THIRTY-FIVE

Glitter In the Air

by Pink

Before heading up the coast on Sunday, we dropped by my mother's house.

"How are you doing?" I asked my mom, hugging her tightly. Somehow, Tate's love left me free to forgive my mother and her shortcomings. Helena's words helped, too. I was genuinely happy to see her.

"I don't think it's fully set in yet." She kissed my forehead, and I savored the gesture. "Having Daniel has made it almost bearable."

"I know what you mean," I said, glancing over at Tate who sat talking with Daniel.

"Are you in love?" she asked, holding me away by my shoulders and scanning my face.

"Like nothing I ever imagined but always hoped for."

"That makes no sense and yet, I know exactly what you mean." She laughed. "I'm so happy for you, Sugar. Do you think he's the one?"

"He's the only one."

She hugged me again. "Matt's been back around to check on me. He said you've talked. Have you forgiven him?"

"I have, and Dad too."

"And me?" she asked, her eyes brimming with tears.

"I know you did the best you could, and I do forgive you. I'd like us to be friends."

"I'd like that a lot. Maybe we can make plans and have Matt over, too."

My eyes filled as well. "Sounds good. Listen, Helena said you're holding a picture for me. I can't take it now because we're on the bike, but I'd love to see it."

"Come." She led me into the guest room, my old bedroom with the same wallpaper I'd grown up with.

Leaning against the couch was a framed, blown-up photo I'd never laid eyes on. My tears began to spill as I took in the image. I couldn't have been more than two years old. Helena and I, both wearing white cotton dresses, danced barefoot, holding hands in the grass. Our auburn hair glittered in the sunlight, and we seemed to be laughing. A white butterfly flew just beside us.

"Where was this?" I asked my mother.

"I'm not sure. She liked to take you to the park."

"Wow." My heart hurt once again over the loss. "Tate," I called.

"What's up?" he asked, dipping his head inside the door.

"Look."

"Is that you?"

"Yeah, with Helena."

He wiped a tear from my cheek, and said, "I know just where we can hang it."

"Really?"

"Definitely." He held onto me as I took in every detail of the photo.

"She really loved me."

"She really did, Sugar," my mother said.

We left her house and drove over to the Bread Building. I didn't plan to stay for the group, but I wanted to check in. Tate waited downstairs for me.

"Judy, you look great!" Suzie said as I walked in.

"Thanks, I feel great."

"She must be getting laid. She has that just fucked look," Charmaine said.

"Over and over," I said and winked at her.

"Glad someone's getting some," Suzie said.

I turned to our facilitator. "Ann, I'm taking off in a minute. I just wanted to check in with you."

"He came around," she said with a smile.

"Yes," I said, beaming back.

"Something tells me we won't be seeing you anymore."

"That's probably true. I wanted to thank you all for listening and for your support. Even you, Charmaine."

"Yeah, yeah," she said, waving me away.

"I wish the best of luck and love to all of you. Thank you, Ann."

She nodded and smiled, and I took that as my cue to leave.

"How did it go?" Tate asked as I slipped on my helmet.

"Good. Now take me for a ride!"

CHAPTER THIRTY-SIX

Happy

by Pharrell Williams

The next few days passed in a blur of love and passion. Tate and I spent every free moment together. I gave notice at The Chart House and began counting down the days until I never had to wait on a table again.

Tate and I strolled into Red's on Wednesday, and I felt the joy that comes with finally being part of a loving couple. My life was no longer just my own, and I welcomed it. While Tate and I were busy cocooning, much had happened.

"Wow, *you're* here," I said to Rory when we approached the kitchen. I looked around for Bond.

"He's out back."

"Right, okay."

"You okay?" Tate asked me.

"Stunned and mystified, but good. I'm going to go talk to Bond." I lay copies of my novel on the kitchen counter.

"I'll get us a drink and put out the stuffed mushrooms."

"Great." I practically sprinted out back. "What the fuck, Dude?" Jacqs looked quite content in Red's lap, so I sighed in relief.

"Lot's happened since you went AWOL."

"Clearly. So, are you and Jacqs—"

"Over? Yes, and she and Red are already talking about a wedding and kids. Knowing him, he'll plan some wild-ass proposal."

I clapped. "No doubt. What's up with the chippy in there?"

"We're taking it slow."

I cracked up. "I'm pretty sure you aren't set at that speed."

"Yeah, it's a daily struggle, and she doesn't make it easy. And knowing me, I'll probably cave soon."

I laughed again. "You brought her here, so that's a big deal."

"Yeah." He rubbed his neck and said, "Listen, Blue, I hope you get how happy I am for you."

"I do, and thank you, Bond. You helped me in so many ways, and I'm so lucky I get to keep you as my friend."

"Your best friend and don't you forget it," he said, pointing at me.

"I won't." I smiled. "Love you."

We hugged.

"Love you too." He lifted his head from my shoulder and uttered, "Shit."

"What?"

"Rory. I told you, she's the jealous type. I better go inside."

Then I really laughed as I watched him scurry into the house.

Tate came up behind me and folded his arm around my waist. In his other hand, he held a margarita and a beer.

I took my drink and we clinked the bottles.

"She's a piece of work, that one," he said, flipping his head in the direction of the kitchen.

"She sure is. She might just be what he needs. At any rate, she'll keep him on his toes."

He nibbled on my ear and breathed against the side of my neck.

"If you keep doing that, we won't be here for long."

"That's the idea." He lifted my hair to the side and bit the back of my neck, sucking hard. "I want to do that on your inner thighs," he whispered.

I turned in his arms. "Cut that out, you're making me wet."

"I know you're dying to talk to the girls, so do it and let's get home."

Home!

"You're pushy, but I'll make it quick." I went up on my toes and whispered, "I'm ready to let you try out the tiny crop on my clit."

"Damn you, woman," he said, smiling.

"I'll hurry."

We all gathered around the pool with our legs dangling in the water, minus Rory, who had gone to the game room with the guys.

"So spill it," Cat said, kicking water in my direction. "But first, tell me what I love to hear." She cupped her ear and cocked her head.

"You were right," I said, laughing.

"That never gets old," Cat said proudly.

"Honestly, I feel high all the time. I'm not even scared, which has to be a first. I've spent my life living in fear, mostly of my own inferiorities and yet, somehow, with him I feel like ... I ... me..." I pointed to my chest. "...was put on this planet solely for Tate. Stupid, right?" I said, my voice cracking a bit.

"Not at all," Lainie said. "I totally get what you mean. Stay is my Tate. Girlfriend, I'm so ecstatic for you."

"Yeah," Jacqs said. "I think it would've been hard for me if you ended up with Bond."

"Do they all know?" I asked.

She shrugged as if it were no big deal.

"Yes," Sam answered. "I must say, you kept it well hidden. It was really Bond who gave it away."

They all nodded in agreement.

"Well, alrighty then." I shook my head at my new reality, loving it. "I brought copies of my novel for each of you."

"No fucking way!" Jacqs called out. "I can't wait to sink my teeth into it."

"Just don't bite me too hard."

"Oh we won't!" Lainie said, rubbing her hands together. "I'm so proud of you."

"Yeah, totally," Sam said.

"Good for you," Cat said. "I'll try not to be my bitchy self."

I chuckled and said, "You do that."

"So, give us the lowdown on Rory. Rumor has it that you've already met her," Cat said.

"Know her? That's a stretch. I will say she has it bad for Bond. It's funny watching him be so baffled about what to do with her."

"Give me time and I'm sure I'll find it amusing too," Jacqs fessed.

I splashed her.

"Hey!" she said.

"Is it true about wedding bells with Red and all that? At this rate, you and Lainie will be racing to the altar."

"He hasn't officially asked me," Jacqs shared.

"Stop being preoccupied with Bond, and I'm sure it'll happen," Sam admonished.

"Yep," I said. "I'm a bit confused about why you're still holding on."

"It's more about the rejection than anything else. Lane can tell you that I've wanted him to be the one to move on and yet, it pokes all my tender parts."

"Yeah." I held up my drink. "Let's drink to finding the men who love and understand our tender parts."

"That has so many meanings," Sam said, taking a drink of her soda.

"You're next," I said to her.

I had known for quite some time that I hit the mother lode in the friendship department and for years, I just assumed that would have to be enough. I absolutely love the tattoo Cat did for me, not only because of her amazing artwork, but because it brought Tate to me. Through his love, I found a real appreciation for my body and the things he does to drive me completely insane with lust.

I scheduled another appointment with Cat and couldn't wait to surprise Tate with my new tattoo. Around the side of my foot, I'm having her tattoo in script: *Wherever the wind takes me.*

Blakely Bennett grew up in Southeast Florida and has been residing in the great Northwest for over nine years. She graduated from Nova Southeastern University with a degree in psychology, which accounts for her particular interest in crafting the personalities, struggles, and motivations of her characters. She is an avid reader of many genres of fiction, but especially enjoys erotica and romance. Writing has always been her bliss.

Blakely is married to a wonderful, loving, and supportive husband, who is also a writer, and who helps to keep her grounded. She is a mother, a communitarian, a lover of music (it is always on while she is writing thanks to Pandora), and a good friend. An advocate of love and female empowerment, she is also a facilitator for a women's group. She loves to walk and hike for exercise, and finds that, since moving to Seattle, Washington, she is now one of those crazy people who walk in the rain.

Blue Persuasion is her seventh novel and the third in the Bound by Your Love Series (*Stuck in Between* and *Bittersweet Deceit*). She is also the author of the dark erotic suspense My Body Trilogy (*My Body-His*, *My Body-His (Marcello)* and *My Body-Mine*) and the co-author of the contemporary romance, *The Demarcation of Jack*, which she wrote with her husband, Dana Bennett.

You can find Blakely on the web at:

www.blakelybennett.com

NEXT UP

The fourth novel

in the

Bound by Your Love series

The Unmistakable Bond

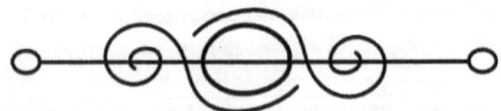